Heather Tosteson has delivered a prodigious achievement. The turmoils that shook Europe in the seventeenth century are almost matched in ferocity by the conflicts in the hearts of her characters. The great microbiologist Antoni Leeuwenhoek is partnered by his daughter Maria as he explores the teeming universe his lenses reveal. *The Philosophical Transactions of Maria Van Leeuwenhoek* is a title that conceals an unceasing tumult of passion.

This novel is entrancing and, in its own strict terms, monumental, an achievement to be acclaimed widely and enthusiastically.

Here is a masterpiece.

Fred Chappell, author of *A Shadow All of Light, Ancestors and Others, Familiars, Midquest* and the Kirkman Tetralogy

Heather Tosteson's meticulous research deeply informs and illuminates her novel of scientific and artistic discovery, professional intrigue and competition. But the beating heart of this fiction is its fascinating cast of under-sung females: daughter and narrator Maria, stepmother Cornelia, Maria—daughter of Vermeer—and others. Tosteson recreates seventeenth century Holland with authority and impressive finesse. In such capable hands, you'll relish the journey back to that time and place and most especially the language and craft that escort you there.

Kat Meads, author of *For You, Madam Lenin; 2:12 a.m.;* and *In This Season of Rage and Melancholy Such Irrevocable Acts as These*

THE PHILOSOPHICAL TRANSACTIONS

of

MARIA VAN LEEUWENHOEK
ANTONI'S DOCHTER

THE PHILOSOPHICAL TRANSACTIONS
of

Maria van Leeuwenhoek,
Antonis Dochter —

(1668-1696)

Including accounts of novel discoveries made in
Delft that bear upon the oft vexing mysteries of
sexual generation, particularly as they apply to
the fate and purpose of women

HEATHER TOSTESON

Wising Up Press

Wising Up Press
P.O. Box 2122
Decatur, GA 30031-2122
www.universaltable.org

Catalogue-in-Publication data is on file with the Library of Congress.
LCCN:2017950747
Wising Up ISBN: 978-0-9826933-8-4

TABLE OF CONTENTS

In which Maria introduces us to her father, Antoni van Leeuwenhoek, at the height of his fame; we learn how he was introduced to the microscope and through it to amazing wonders of Creation heretofore invisible; in which we also learn how Maria herself when a girl of fourteen discovered through illness and the paintings of Johannes Vermeer that there is a world of difference between the eyes of men, a truth that will shape her own philosophy as completely as her father's belief in the powers of observation shapes his.

In which Louis XIV invades Holland, the Dutch murder and devour their own Grand Pensionary and reinstate William III of Orange as Stadtholder; in which the widower Antoni van Leeuwenhoek, to the consternation of his daughter, remarries, observes the actual circulation of the blood and the structure of the globules in it, and with the help of his friend Dr. Regnier de Graaf begins his lifelong correspondence with the foremost practitioners of the New Philosophy, the learned gentlemen of the Royal Society in England; and in which Maria begins to understand what, in this time of terrible turmoil, binds mother, child, father, and country—and what her father's practice of his newfound art might mean for those who live with him.

In which Antoni van Leeuwenhoek makes the amazing discovery of animalcules smaller than the hair of a mite in rain water, well water, steeped pepper, vinegar, the spit in our mouths, and the semen of dogs and of men; in which Leeuwenhoek insists—over the doubt of Regnier de Graaf (who has himself discovered within women a nest of eggs that he believes is the source of human generation) and to the consternation of his wife Cornelia and his daughter—that it is from animalcules in the semen of men that human life begins; and in which Maria, as a woman of marriageable age, begins to ponder the implications of her father's discoveries and his theories of generation to her personally.

In which Antoni van Leeuwenhoek, already troubled by the doubts of the Gentlemen Amateurs about his discoveries, becomes more troubled by the inexplicable pregnancy of his wife Cornelia while away from him, which she insists is explained by the sufficiency of De Graaf's eggs, not her husband's animalcules, and is even more troubled by the loss of the child, whatever his origin; in which Leeuwenhoek turns his investigations to skin, bark, feathers, scales, and the scurf of the fish girl exhibited in the traveling fair to better understand the scurf that now covers most of his own body, which, if leprosy, will cause his banishment and that of his wife and daughter to the Leper House in Haarlem; and in which Maria seeks to hide from her father the truth about his newborn son and reluctantly refuses her first serious suitor in order to hide from all the truth about her father's disease.

In which Antoni van Leeuwenhoek continues his observations on generation, investigating the movement of male animalcules through the wombs of dogs and the copulation of the eel, louse, and flea; entertains many distinguished visitors including Kings and Learned and Distinguished Gentlemen; and persists in his obsession with the source of life while his wife Cornelia sickens and dies; and in which Maria, with the assistance of the burgomaster Cornelis Vallensis, takes in a rebellious young orphan girl, Grietje, to assist her and, through her own intimacy with Mr. Vallensis, comes to realize that deep within her body she holds mysteries of generation hidden from her father.

In which Antoni van Leeuwenhoek makes a discovery concerning the lice that devour the peaches in his orchard that threatens his theories of generation; in which Maria, understanding the implications of her father's newest discovery, questions how her belief in her father's discoveries and theories of generation has distorted her own choices as well as how her beliefs and choices have in turn distorted the choices of her beloved and brazen servant and ward, Grietje, for whom she is now trying to find a suitable husband; and in which Maria invites another young orphan, Aaltje, to take Grietje's place, warning her that she will, as have all the women who lived in that house, find herself ravished by the truths that her father's glasses have revealed—and by the truths that they cannot.

. . . all depends on keeping the eye steadily fixed upon the facts of nature and so receiving their images simply as they are. For God forbid that we should live out a dream of our own imagination for a pattern of the world.

Francis Bacon

We used to have a man here called Dalancé. He made microscopes and once, in a drop of water on the point of a knife, he showed me a whole oceanful of sole. There were long serpents in the vinegar. It seems to me we know both too much and too little for our happiness: enough to want to know more, but too little to do us any good.

Princess Liselotte

We therefore hope that those who investigate natural things will delve up those hitherto hidden matters deeper and deeper, so that, the truth thus having become more and more apparent to them, they may come to dislike many old errors, an object which all those who love the truth should pursue. For we cannot glorify the Lord and maker of the All more than by seeing with the greatest admiration His supreme wisdom and perfection revealed in all things, however small they may be to our naked eye, if only they have received life and growth.

Antoni van Leeuwenhoek

good order.

...Eye of the Bee, which I have take...
...g its innermost part to the Micros...
...ceives her light Just with the same...
...combs : Whence I am prone to coll...
...by art or knowledge, but only a...
...ght received in the Eye.
...le I observe indeed, as others h...
...Nose with an hole in it, out of w...
...ll draw food, thrusts its sting, w...
...ast five and twenty times less than...
...nd the head every where else very c...
...thout any ... head is ro...

I
LENS
(1696/1668-1670)

And since my thoughts were occupied mostly with the crystalline body that is the eye, I removed it from the eye and placed it before the magnifying glass. And I was greatly pleased to see through the magnifying glass, and at the same time through the crystalline body, not only the houses upside down, but I also saw people walking in the street, however small they appeared, all going with their feet upwards; nay, what is more, I could see the color of their clothes. From this sight the extreme perfection of this small crystalline body also became evident to me.
Antoni van Leeuwenhoek

I start by describing a single day in May, Aaltje, just weeks before you came to us from the orphanage, because that is a story you can see with your own eyes, bring your own intelligence to bear upon, as you soon will the specimens glued to the pins behind my father's glasses, as you will the discoveries sure to come, and the unpredictable events—wars and floods and plagues and births and deaths and unwonted excitations of the heart—that will, inevitably, sweep you up without asking and as often, without warning, let you drop. There is no doubt about it: the world transmutes us, and we it, from the day we first draw breath, perhaps even before that. None, not a one of us, is spared. We do not leave the world as we came into it. But how and why we are changed, that is given to each of us alone, woman as well as man, to decipher—and to pass on in whatever form we can. My father does so through his letters to the Gentlemen Amateurs, still written in the only languages he's mastered, his lenses and his lowly Nether-Dutch. And I do so, now, in words that last no longer than the mist on the Hippolytusbuurt, unless they are gathered, like breath, into the heart and imagination of someone hungry for them, fed as fully by what the eye can't verify as by what it can.

WE BUILD AS WE SEE
1696

"I never imagined there was so much difference between men's eyes," my father exclaimed as he pulled the sheet of paper from the engraver's hand. "Come, come, Maria. Come and look."

I closed the linen cabinet, turned and put the last of the fresh linen in Grietje's arms.

"You better hurry," she said. "Before he gets carried off. Tell him for me, Mejuffrouw, I've had enough. I'll not go hunting those fleas again. He promised he'd give them up."

"But he did—a month ago."

"So he said, but look at that poor boy." She nodded her head toward the open door of my father's study. "It's his blood those fleas are after now, not each other."

"Maria!"

"Save him, Mejuffrouw." Grietje, mounting the stairs, leaned over the stack of clean linen for a last glimpse of the young engraver. "I'd like to taste him first myself." She winked at me, but I pretended not to notice.

Grietje, at twenty, was well on her way to the spinhuis, the house of corrections for women. She was worse than the Predikant Petrus Grebius, for she took delight in what he abhorred, but they both saw lechery everywhere they looked. It floated like a mote of dust on their own eyes.

"Would you just look, Maria," my father said as soon as I entered the room. His thick white finger hammered the paper. Poor Gerrit sat with his hands between his legs. His cheeks were veined like a ripe apple, his full pouting lips were wet. His hair fell over his far cheek, shielding him from my father's eyes.

"Would you come and look at this, Maria," my father repeated.

Gerrit raised his shoulder to his ear, rubbed his cheek there like a boor warming himself on a cow's flank. Poor boy. He wasn't more than seventeen. Where Grietje saw the man, I saw the child. The falling tear glittered in the sunlight, plopped loud enough for both of us to hear on the unswept tile.

"Here, Father," I said. "Let me look."

He handed me the microscope. As always, I held my breath, hating that moment when the world opened up, we tumbled down into that mammoth land, despicable as fleas.

"What is this?"

"A louse," my father said. "A peach louse," he added quickly, "a skin it has shed."

It twinkled there on the pin, clear as glass.

My father took the brass plate from my hand. "Now look at what the boy drew."

"You told me to," Gerrit said. "'Draw what you see,' you said. And I did."

Again my father said, "I never imagined so much difference between men's eyes."

I did not share his astonishment. It seems it was the first thing I ever knew for certain. There is as much difference between the eyes of men as between the hundreds of lenses my father has ground in his lens cup.

Thinking back, I see this was something I learned, not something gulped in with my mother's milk. I was a little younger than Gerrit there. Fourteen, to be exact.

"He hasn't drawn it to scale. Don't you agree, Maria?"

My father stubbed the drawing with his finger.

"You'll ruin your own argument if you're not careful. You've already erased its leg." I took the paper from my father and stepped closer to the window. Looking out on the Hippolytusbuurt, I brought the brass plate again to my eye. The fantastic beast peered in at me, stranger than anything a man could dream. The brass plate pressed close to my cheek was warm, not from that creature's breath, rather the sudden start of blood in my own cheek.

I pulled the glass away and turned from the window. I looked again at Gerrit's drawing.

"You'll make a portrait painter yet. You've caught his idiot gape exactly."

"*Hers*," my father said crossly. "All these animals are female."

"Are you sure?"

But my father had taken the drawing from me. "It is too small. I see it four times as large."

We have been through this before with other draughtsmen. But each time my father acts as if it is willful, a matter of laziness or lack of skill. Not something Our Maker willed.

I gave the boy a piece of chalk, made a place for him at the table. "Trace what you see, in its roughest outline—like my father does," I said, handing the boy the brass plate. He held it up to his face without blinking.

"You too," I said to my father once the boy was finished.

My father, putting the glass to his eye, taking the chalk from Gerrit, noticed the boy's gleaming face, his quivering lip. My father's left cheek flinched, his left eye narrowed, once, twice, but his remorse shifted quickly to exasperation. Nothing angers my father like trying to transfer what he sees to paper. His hand ignores his eye. And my father's eye, we all know, is his fortune.

"Now compare," I said, standing back against the window, twisting a little to keep my shadow off the paper. My father stepped back; Gerrit, on his stool, slid even closer to the table.

"Can you both see clearly? To your own scale?"

Gerrit, brushing his thin blonde locks from his face, nodded. My father's periwig did not hide the flick of his cheek, the slow, magnanimous smile.

"A head and a half," I said. "And when all's said and done, it is less than a finger's breadth. And in the drawing itself, Father, he could not have been more exact."

"You're right." My father clapped the boy on his shoulder. The tic in his left cheek began again. Remorse takes my father this way. It's like a tear was boiling up under his skin.

I think Gerrit understood, for he smiled as he collected his pens and paper and chalk.

"I counted four claws on the fore-leg—and you?"

"Four, sir. They'll come out more clearly in the engraving."

"I'll mention your close sight in my letter to the Society. Let's hope that is the only fault they will find with me."

Already my father was at his cabinet, pulling out a tray, restoring the microscope. I beckoned to Gerrit and led him down the hall and down the stairs. I opened the door. The cries from the fish market echoed against the walls of the houses. They mingled with the song of the Kroonevelt's maid, who was out washing the stoop of the house next door.

"Where are you off to now?" I asked the boy.

"Oost Port," he said. "I am to do some sketches. My master too despairs of my perspective." He laughed, suddenly joyous. "Perhaps I'll catch some fen mussels in the reeds. We can watch them spin under your father's glass. Remember that, Mejuffrouw?"

"You could just lie in the grass," I said, "Rest a little. Let your flesh catch up with your bones." The boy was thin as the reeds he'd soon wade through.

"Not two weeks in the house, Mejuffrouw, and he's pining for me already," Grietje said with a laugh as she came down the stairs.

"Enough, Grietje," I said sharply. I closed the door and returned to my father's study.

"It's right here," my father said, tapping the drawer into place in the cabinet. "If anyone asks. If anyone questions me. You see?"

"Yes," I said. "Yes, father."

It's all there is to our lives now. These drawers, these hammered sheets of silver and brass that fit inside a man's open palm, these miraculous bubbles of glass.

This *ingenious* life.

Infamous, Cornelia Swalmius, my stepmother might have said. But she is dead now and mercifully silent. Besides, she was never to blame. Never. She was the first to tell you so. The eldest daughter of Predikant Johannes Swalmius of Valkenburg, she knew her rightful place in the world. She knew her duty. My father was the buccaneer.

Wouldn't she have laughed, wouldn't he laugh now to hear himself described thus. But what else do you call someone who, born only with natural gifts, makes of himself everything he possibly can. Now even the Kings of England and Elector of Brandenburg take my father seriously. I do not exaggerate. They have all come here to our town. Riding barges from 'sGravenhage with their entourages, they have dismounted on the ramparts and followed the canals until they reached our neighborhood, the Hippolytusbuurt, and our house, the Golden Head. They have all climbed up to my father's study, lifted his glasses to their eyes. Even now, as I watch him restore what he has just displayed, I feel my own chest puff like a pigeon.

Yes, I don't deny it. I swell with pride. But pride is not always a sin, it can be a kind of love. Of him. A kind of knowledge. I know exactly why my untutored father belongs among the honorable and learned company of the Royal Society.

By this time I know as well that my own life, like my fortune, is knotted inextricably with his own. Who am I? Maria Antonisdr. van Leeuwenhoek. I am in my fortieth year. A spinster, I have lived here in the Golden Head all my life. It is my fate, certainly, and, I believe, my choice.

But that is difficult to say. For we, I expect, build as we see—like my father used to say of the honey bee. He wrote, I remember, in his first letter to the learned and curious: *I find the bee receives her light just with the same shadow as we see the honeycombs; whence I am prone to collect, that the bee works not by art or knowledge, but only after the pattern of light received by the eye.*

And our lives, I wonder, do we build them the same way? Without art or knowledge, we lay brick where once we saw light?

"I could not imagine there was such a great difference in men's eyes," my father exclaims. My father sees through a bubble of glass just larger than his own pupil a world four times as large as that seen by the close-sighted boy Gerrit.

My father, at sixty-three, is surprised.

Not so the boy of seventeen who sees the secret he has used all his art and knowledge to conceal revealed at last by my father's ignorance, his clumsy hand. Which of them, I wonder, was the wiser that hour?

❦ ❦ ❦

There is a world of difference between the eyes of men. I expect this isn't the only truth my father's missed. But, like the boy Gerrit, half blind with grief, it's one of the few I happened upon young. It is what I have built *my* world upon.

I wonder what my father has assumed all these years. Our Maker in His heaven is less various in His work than my father in his studies? Surely my father believes within his glasses lies a truth the whole world can share. They provide a window on heaven. Just consider the eye of the bee. What does it reveal to us but Our Creator's purpose? For who made an eye to trap light in just such a pattern—to sieve it like sea salt from the drying pans? Our Creator, of course. And for what purpose, God only knows. My father cannot leave it there. He believes the eyes of men are as similar as their hearts, their brains. In other words, we travel together, father, mother, daughter and son, all of Amsterdam, all of Delft, out of the cold, close dark of the peasant's hut into the towns. My father believes truth is the evidence of our eyes. He believes that, like gold, once mined, drawn by sal vitriol from its ore, it will serve us all, a common currency.

I am not so sure. But I keep my doubts to myself. They would not please my father. He cherishes his art like a firstborn child, his knowledge like a fertile wife.

There are three things you must know about my father. He is a kind man. Honest. And he cannot bear to have his word questioned.

I am not inclined to. As I stand here at my bedroom window looking down at our town, I could believe we shared more than stomachs and hands, that we build these rows of houses, these walled towns with as little knowledge or art as the bee. And with just such glory to God the Maker as we give dredging the perfect honeycomb from the hollow tree.

But even when I close the shutters up here, I know that it is the construction we put on things that matters. For example, the day my stepmother Cornelia died, I saw our town take its place, upside down, on her bedroom wall—as if heaven and earth had been reversed. But I did not take this for a sign. It didn't matter whether a worm's hunger or the carpenter's clumsy hand had brought the world at last to Cornelia's feet. It was too late. She could not see to weep.

And I, my eyes awash, still saw too clearly.

Men make lenses for the same reason Our Creator made all our eyes, whale and ox, dragonfly and bee. He made them to control our perception, to monitor our faith. To help us build indescribably sweet temples, storehouses true to His own designs.

This morning the learned Predikant Petrus Grebius came with his wife to purchase cloth enough to last them both a lifetime. Or so she claims he said. I have my doubts, but like my father I have mastered no foreign tongues, certainly not the ancient ones. Since I only sold him ten ells of serge, he must not intend to greet the new century.

These, of course, are thoughts I kept to myself. Instead, I talked to them of the thread and the weave of English woolens, Leyden stuff. And their costs, of course. This was the point when Predikant Grebius rolled his eyes heavenward and began to mutter under his breath. His wife claimed he was measuring their earthly sojourn, but it appeared to me he was attempting sums. Poor man! Not to have a ledger-mind in our country is as demeaning for a woman as a man. We make little here in the Netherlands, except for butter and beer, faience and paintings. Instead, we trade. English woolens for Rhenish wine, Baltic grain for Batavian pepper. Salvation itself is the only thing we can't buy or sell. That and our callings.

"I am sorry to have missed your father." Petrus Grebius's voice rose.

His wife sniffed. I bowed my head, tightened my lips. Whatever else, she was an honest woman. Her body, round as a cheese from Edam, her face red as its rind, she had as few pretensions to beauty as she did to scientific curiosity. The Predikant, given his position in our town, felt obliged to ask about my father's investigations. But it wasn't natural to him, as it was to Benedictus Haan, the Lutheran pastor. I still recall the look on Petrus Grebius's face when he first peered through my father's glasses. You would swear Satan himself had winked at him.

"My father has been called away. Five new casks are to be filled at the apothecary's."

At this Petrus Grebius's eyes rolled heavenward again. "Rhenish?" he whispered.

I shook my head. I really didn't know. Perhaps I should have offered the Predikant a glass this morning. When my father is home, I almost always do. As a restorative—because of the horrors he's glimpsed through the glass.

"And what, may I ask, Mejuffrouw, is your father contemplating these days? The transformation of the corn wolf? The origins of the eel?" His thin lips pursed as if he were tasting something hot and bitter.

I shrugged my shoulders. "It might be the markings on the whale's eye, the salts in wine, the antipathies of sulfur and salt petre. But this serge, Frau Grebius. You will make it up yourself, or do you wish it carried to the tailor?"

"It's all the same, Mejuffrouw." The smile Frau Grebius gave me was as quick as it was crafty. "My father's a tailor. And since he's come to live with us, he has nothing to keep his hands occupied."

"He keeps busy enough lifting mugs," muttered her husband.

"His eyes aren't what they were, but that's not what's sending him to the tavern. It's grief over my mother's passing. That and my sister going too soon before, she who was to make his home for him after my mother had gone."

I folded the cloth over again, tied it up with twine. Poor woman. Her entire life was spent in perpetual honor of the dead—the dead in body, the dead in spirit, languages dead to the ear. I would not change my place for hers.

"Grietje," I called. "Come and help Frau Grebius carry these cloths."

But Grietje didn't reply, and I had to excuse myself to go and fetch her. She was sweeping the front stoop for the fourth time that morning. It was only an excuse for making conversation with Kroonevelt's apprentice. I scolded her roundly and made her run up for her cloak. She did so, laughing.

I knew I should have my father talk to Petrus Grebius. If we didn't marry the child off quickly, we would have only ourselves to blame. I knew then what I do now—but I did nothing. Perhaps the truth would have slipped through my fingers anyway, whether I had grasped at it or not.

We see only what we wish.

Looking at Grietje, my father saw a white mob cap, a rough red woolen bodice, a hand hovering over the hearth, scooping coals into the bed warmer. Looking at Grietje, Gerrit saw a hint of white throat, a line of white above the sun-burned forearm, a flash of white ankle, a face as smooth and daring as a stone cliff. Kroonevelt's apprentice saw—Judith, or Bathsheba. Even Petrus Grebius, unable to sleep remembering her lilting stride across the market square, might rise in the middle of the night and, lighting his lamp, reread the story of Susannah and the Elders.

And I? What did I see?

A model for Johannes Reynierszoon. Don't laugh. In my poor swaggering orphan, yes, I did see my friend Maria Vermeer posing before the glass, I did see her mother, Catharina Bolnes, weighing our souls. Or perhaps I felt if someone, anyone, could see her so, it would be her salvation. *In this world.* In the world she will go to, just as in the world behind my father's glasses, there is only mystery and revelation. There is no chance. There is no change.

Even on this earth, I didn't want to change the child. I wanted to preserve her. Just where she was then. Skin that gleamed like pearl, tidy white teeth frothed with morning milk. I wanted to preserve those quick eyes, the rapid twist of her head, the ready laugh. I wanted to keep her perfect skin from being branded.

Mr. Vallensis meant the best when he sent her here five years ago from the weeshuis, the orphanage. How was he to know, how was I, that the steady ant-like stream of men from morning to night would transform our orphan into a butterfly, something dying just to be seen as beautiful for a single day?

There is nothing more useless in this house than a woman insisting on her youth, her beauty. My father is enraptured with the world beyond his glasses. It is futile to intrude. I have accepted that. But sometimes I saw on Grietje's face the despair I saw so often on the face of my stepmother Cornelia. It may be the same look Mevrouw Grebius's father glimpses on his daughter's face when she leaves the Predikant's study.

Man makes his lenses as he does his thoughts—to refine his world, to give it luster, beauty. It's such a simple truth. We see only what we want to see. *We see only what we want.*

I wanted Grietje's youth.

My father wanted the fat flea she slapped from the household sheets at his command. Should she leave, he would want the same of me, or any other woman.

And Johannes? Although he died before Grietje was born, he would see in her what he wanted of all women, a mirror of his own still soul. Or that is what even now I choose to believe, what I choose to see.

Johannes Reynierszoon was much in my thoughts that day. Perhaps it was a presentiment of my next visitor, the one who followed Grietje back into the house, draped in black, footsteps light as a ghost or an angel.

She waited in the front room while Grietje came to me.

"And who have you brought with you, child?"

"I don't know, Mejuffrouw. She followed me back across the square. At first I thought she knocked a Lazarus rattle, but then upon the bridge she uncovered her face, she spoke to me. She asked for you, Mejuffrouw."

"You mean my father, Grietje."

"No. She asked for Maria Antoni's daughter. I didn't dare forbid her entrance. That knocking within her cloths, it gives me the shakes, Mejuffrouw. Perhaps she's not one of us, Mejuffrouw. Perhaps she's—"

"Show her in."

"Leave us alone, Grietje," I said when the woman, crossing the threshold, raised her head. As Grietje closed the door, I stepped forward.

Stretching out her hands, the other woman did the same.

"Maria van Leeuwenhoek!"

"Maria Vermeer! What brings you here?"

"Such a *long* time." The eyes were just as quick and mischievous as in her youth, the gesture with which she tossed the hood of her cloak to her shoulders just as imperious.

"You haven't changed," I said.

"My dear." She stroked my hand. I blushed. For it was not a mob cap she wore now, but a nun's veil. And the knocking that frightened Grietje was no leper's license, rather the clatter of a crucifix against a rosary.

"What brings you here? I thought you moved south, to Antwerp."

And so she had, but she had returned for her niece Catharina's marriage. It was for this purpose she had come to me as well. She wished to contribute to her niece's dower. She had come to me because she knew even with her vows of poverty, I was heavily in her debt. It was time, certainly, that I paid up.

And I would have, if it were humanly possible. But what price, I ask you, can you place on a child's soul?

"Elizabeth's daughter? I haven't met her."

"There are eight more to follow."

"And your brother Ignatius?"

"He lives in Gouda now. Near my uncle Willem."

Who, I wondered, attended the other? Willem Bolnes, Maria and Ignatius' uncle, had been as different from his sister, their mother Catharina Bolnes, as if they had shared neither mother nor father. It was Catharina's mother's age that made Willem as simple as he was stubborn. Or so I heard the midwife mutter when she brought Ignatius, puny, wailing, red, into the studio at the Mechelen, the tavern the Vermeers ran on the market square.

A scene from our childhood came to me then, vivid and unearthly as a dream. If I should have asked Maria, I don't think she would have remembered what I did, the figures of my father and Dr. de Graaf in the tavern room. She would have remembered the hole she scraped between the roots of the medlar tree to bury her mother's afterbirth. She would remember the bowl of caudle she ladled out in the tavern to renew her mother's strength. She would remember bathing the infant's cold arms, thinner and more brittle than kindling wood.

"Five ells," Maria said softly. "I'd like five ells of red silk."

"Red?"

And then she asked me the question I knew from the moment I saw her at the doorway she would ask. She lifted her head and peered directly into my eyes as into a reflecting glass.

"Do you remember, Maria, the painting my father made of you in that big red hat?"

"Yes," I said immediately. "Do you know what happened to it?"

"I was going to ask the same."

"And the one of you," I said. "Lifting the necklace to the glass. What happened to it?"

"Sold," she said. "They are all sold. Your father saw to that."

"*Red* silk," I said. I surveyed the bolts of serge, bombazine, chintz. "Grietje," I called, walking over to the door. "Come assist my memory."

I noticed the tilt of Sister Maria's head.

"No," I said, shaking my own. "It's not like it was then."

After my illness, Maria had been the only one I had told of the lapses, the way time tumbled, the way a thought erased itself as I watched. It was she who reminded me again and again of my very name. She who provided the hat to mask my shame at my short, sparse hair. She who held the mirror so that I might see myself as the world saw me.

I would see the pearl earring she had pinned to my ear knock against my neck. I would hold my breath, waiting for the sensation to echo in that vast, startling space that was my name. Maria. Maria van Leeuwenhoek. Antoni's daughter.

"And Willem?" I asked. "What has happened to him?"

That day in the Mechelen, even as we waited for Maria's mother to give birth, as we watched her father set up his easel, as Maria polished the mirror domed like a loaf of bread, I watched Willem, alone in the tavern with the maidservant. Every time he swaggered across the floor, swaggered back, it's true, I envied him. However slow he might be, the hand that tapped the beer barrel, the leather sole that slapped across the tile belonged to him as surely as that stubborn thirst. Willem was no stranger to himself.

"Willem?" Maria asked with a wide smile that showed her missing teeth. "He lived with my mother, over near the Moles Poort for eight years. When my mother knew her time was running to a close here, she prayed to the Virgin for guidance—and what do you think the Blessed Mother suggested?"

"You called, Mejuffrouw?" Grietje said from the door, refusing to approach closer.

"Red silk," I said. "Sister Maria is contributing to her niece's dower."

"For Uncle Willem, my mother contributed the bride," Maria Vermeer continued. "She and two of my sisters. The woman they chose they thought too old—for children or for grief. But Willem has furnished her with both. Three children she's brought into the world—and not one of them more capable than their mother of speech."

"Dumb?" Grietje shuddered.

The bell on the church rung the hour.

"*Red* silk," I said. "Help me, Grietje. When Mevrouw Bleyswijck was here, didn't she choose a red lining for her cloak?"

"Under that black serge, Mejuffrouw, fire! Her husband, when he noticed, wouldn't hear of it. It's all put back."

Along with the red silk, I provided Maria with blue velvet, yellow damask. She tested every bolt under her hands. I brought out my glass so she could see for herself the even cut of the blue threads, the niceness of the red weave. Each time her hands touched the cloth, they touched the cross, the string of carved beads. Her hands were as raw with work as they had been when she was fourteen. She rubbed the backs of them across the bolts. I saw how she hesitated over a bolt of blue velvet. I added it to the silk.

It was her occupation at the convent, she told me, to mend their habits, their altar cloths. She had, to begin with, embroidered the priests' vestments, but it had been decided by the Mother Superior that it distracted Maria from her devotions. "All the color," she said, "the threads of silver and gold. It was a glory unbecoming to our order." So now she mended their coarse black worsted with coarse black thread. When she looked up, only the crucifix called her eyes. Stitching ell after ell of worsted, her thoughts gathered to themselves, like a diamond waiting for light. She lifted the rosary. "It's all there is, Maria," she said. "It is everything."

This was the look, then, revealed to herself when she stood, dressed in her mother's coat, bound with her mother's borrowed jewels? Had it escaped her father? Had he understood her at all?

I nodded. I looked down at the heaped cloth, as brilliant and simple as the stones her father once ground for pigment.

"Grietje," I said, "help me wrap these for Sister Maria."

"And when do you return?" I asked her as we walked together to the door. My scissors and glass clattered from my belt, keeping company with the ringing of her chains.

"To Antwerp?"

"Yes," I said, although that was not what I had meant. But I know, of course, that our history cannot reverse itself like the tides.

"Within the week. I leave Delft within the hour. I will be going to 'sGravenhage. Johannes is there with the Jesuits. There are only five of us left. And Uncle Willem. Who would have thought, out of so many, we are the ones God would choose to leave behind."

Maria's mother bore eleven children, my mother five. My father is contested now because he claims Our Creator is as profligate of human life as he is that of trees and fleas. But even he can't explain why it is I and not my three brothers Philips, my sister Margriete, who lived beyond my second year.

"Not for long perhaps," I said, touching my own cheek.

"You, Maria! You will live as long as your father."

I smiled, opened the door, stepped out on the stoop. It didn't matter. Unlike Maria, I no longer believed I had anywhere to go. At forty, my life, like my person, was as clear and as compassed as the fine leaded panes set in every window in our house. I squinted against the sun, the rare blue sky.

"Packages directed to you by name at the convent—"

"Will be returned," she said. She touched her worn black cloak, pulled the string tighter around her face, hiding the bright wimple.

I embraced her, there, on the Hippolytusbuurt, for everyone to see. It was my eyes the wind whipped into tear. "Forgive us," I whispered. "Forgive him."

She stepped back, swinging the stringed package like a basket. "Remember, I am Christ's bride. I have no earthly ties anymore. I have chosen my poverty. I bear no grudges." She brought the finery up to her chest. Already the materials slipped from the clumsily wrapped package. Her finger ran over the blue velvet, drew back from the red silk as if scalded. My eyes welled with tear. How had we arrived here?

"You believe me?" she asked.

"Believe? Of course," I said. "What else is left?"

The answer, of course, was everything. Everything was left. Everything was left out.

After the bells in the Nieuwe Kirke finished their song and chimed the new hour, there was a loud clattering at the door. Both Grietje and I rushed to the entry room. My father poked his head around the door of his study.

Four men stood on the stoop eyeing each other like wary dogs. One wore a broad hat that shielded his face, while lace covered his hands, the hilt of his sword. Buckles concealed his shoes. Only his calves were unmistakable. A little bandied, like a rooster's, and equally red. I saw Grietje beginning to lean down to shine the silver buckles to serve as twin mirrors. I came up behind her, giving her a warning tug on her apron strings.

"We've been waiting a full five minutes," huffed a man wearing a black professor's robe, his little eyes blinking sadly behind large, slipshod spectacles. "This *is* the house of Heer van Leeuwenhoek, Antoni van Leeuwenhoek?"

"It is," I agreed. "But my father doesn't receive visitors without introductions. I apologize for this, but his time is as precious to him as goods are to a merchant." I drew a breath, straightened my apron. Already the men were pulling papers out of their coats, the linings of their capes.

"*Permettez-moi.*" The man who stepped forward had the tonsured head of a Franciscan, but his air was as worldly as a Jesuit's. "*Papenbroek, d'Antwerp, a écrivé—*" He waved his paper at me.

I don't speak French. Neither does my father. But I recognized the name, Papenbroek. I took the paper from him.

"Mejuffrouw van Leeuwenhoek?" The man who next stepped forward, dressed in our own somber blacks, spoke in, I believe, English. "Royal Society," he said. "Robert Hooke . . . Nehemiah Grew."

These names too were familiar to me as the names of the men and women on the Hippolytusbuurt.

"Leyden," said the third man, dressed too in professors' robes, speaking our own language, but with such a swishing and swilling it sounded like nothing human. "Professor Craaven." He pointed at the paper he unfolded before me; he prodded the sheet as if it were the belly of a dead man.

"Batavia," said the man dressed as colorfully as a parrot. He too spoke our Nether-Dutch. He brushed the lace from his hands with a rude, or beseeching, motion. In the palm of his hand was a round brown stone. "This is my introduction. I was told at the East India Company your father had an abiding interest in seeds from foreign lands."

"He has an abiding interest in everything," Grietje said, but she threw a quick glance over her shoulder to placate me.

"A minute," I said and went up to my father's study. "Three of them I believe you expected. The fourth looks like a pirate, but he claims he's sailed from Batavia and has brought you a curious seed."

My father nodded, but he didn't look up. He had already placed three boxes on the table. He opened the first one and stepped near the window. He stood there, a silhouette against the bright glass, waiting for me to bring the visitors in.

My father is as truthful a man as the light at noon, but he has learned to mount himself as he does his specimens, the better to be seen, the better to be understood. It doesn't always work. But my father persists. He prepares his specimens with the greatest care. He grinds each lens particularly, giving it just enough strength to reveal detail without dulling the eye with terror. Whatever he writes of, he preserves for demonstration. He defends his honor by substantiating his words. But still the men come, questioning.

"Gentlemen," he said when I showed them in. He slowly replaced a glass, then walked toward them down the length of his bench. As he approached, his robe gathered color, began to hum with its own thin warmth, a yellow pale and brave as the sun on a winter's afternoon. His brown wig brushed his shoulders jauntily, and the eyes too were quick and bright as a boy's. But the hair beneath the wig is grayer than a goat's and terribly sparse. The cheeks now fall in folds near as deep as those that once dredged the face of Constantijn Huygens, Seigneur van Zuleichem. My father is sixty-three this year, and as hale and eager as ever, as unwilling as ever to admit that between the eye and the tongue a world can topple and be supplanted. He can't convince himself otherwise. The man whose eye he sets to the same glass, who inspects the same amazing joist in God's mansion, who greets the same minute and marvelous guest in God's pasture, will, my father cannot help but believe, marvel like himself. Like my father, he will bend his knees morning and night in the deepest respect and will pray with an awe so great it still troubles the lips after all the words have been uttered.

But every time, he learns again that he is a singular man. *There is a world of difference between the eyes of men.* Each time my father learns this with the same pained clarity that the idiot discovers the fire's smart. If there is a time I would not be my father's daughter, it is after these visits. When I come into his study and see him hold the last specimen again to the light and shake his head, mutter to himself like a drunkard. It is the tenderness with which he fits the glass back into its velvet tray, the way he presses lips together in stubborn hope, picks up his pen and begins to mark down the findings of yet another day—in short, it is my father's innocence, this endless idiot pain that makes me at moments wish to deny him completely.

I know now that death will be the only end to it. My father will always admit the learned gentlemen, and they will, as like as not, be unconvinced by my father's glasses. And my father, seeing it all, smarting like any scorched animal, will, with a near idiot fixity *go on.*

"To my own satisfaction," he often writes. "I investigate until then." Satisfaction! It is an odd name for the trembling finger clasping the brass frame, the eyes blinking, blinking, trying to wash away disgrace like a splinter of glass. But that's the way it has been since those first meetings with De Graaf—and it is my father who still lives, whose fame has spread to Batavia, China, Brazil. No one talks any more of that brash and angry young doctor from Schoonhoven who scolded my father as if he were a servant for—for what? For what causes me anguish even now. The simplicity of my father's ardor, that curiosity, both stubborn and humble, that will not let him give way to any sword or robe. Year after year, my father stretches his hand out. "Look," he says. *"Look!"*

A WORLD OF DIFFERENCE
1668-1670

The day Regnier de Graaf brought Johannes Vermeer a lens for the small hole in his window shutter, set a piece of greased paper on the easel, and had Johannes take his place on his stool, the first man they saw take shape upon the paper was my father, stretching his neck, twisting his head like a turtle. On the sunny market square, my father stood apart, as if he were surrounded by an invisible moat. He opened his mouth, clapped it three times, clamped it shut. Even outside, I doubt I would have heard his voice, but within the Mechelen it was impossible. In the darkened room, accompanied by loud jesting, the clatter of crockery, the thud of wooden platters, clang of pewter, I saw my father silently jaw the sunny air.

"Here, try it here," the young doctor said, pulling the easel back from the window. "Your picture will be clearer."

Fearlessly wading the bright moat around my father, a young child approached, wavering in over-large shoes. My father's arm climbed, his hand twisted in the air like a drifting piece of paper, but it never touched the boy's hair, never cupped his head as he had done daily with my brother Philips.

"I've heard in Paris they have special chairs fitted with shades and a lens." De Graaf shifted the easel again until all that remained was a mottle of faded color. Even in the dim room, I could see his flushed cheeks. "It is possible also to fit a box with a lens and mirror, right the image and spread it out upon a sheet of glass like a drawing on a table."

Johannes, yawning, was pushing back the shutters.

"I'll show you," De Graaf said. He pulled out a sheet of paper, a stick of chalk from his pocket.

Johannes cupped his hand to one side of the shutter, prodded the lens out with his finger. He glanced down at the doctor's bowed head, listened to the rasping chalk.

"Paris," he muttered. "A chair. I never—"

"Come, come, Maria!" Catharina Bolnes, Johannes' wife, clapped her hands at the kitchen door.

Maria Vermeer and I both jumped, stumbled against each other, giggling. Johannes looked over to our corner with a frown; the young doctor glanced at us with the same attention he might bestow on a wandering dog.

"The other room," Johannes said, tossing the lens in the air, catching it quickly as De Graaf caught back his breath. "There's too much traffic on the market square."

Dutifully, we followed Johannes and De Graaf as they made their way through the tables toward the kitchen. Catharina Bolnes' face lengthened, softened, when her husband leaned down and kissed her lined brow.

"Again," Maria hissed to me. "We burned the string last week and she grew faint. He always dotes like this when he discovers she is with child. As if there were not enough mouths hungering for food in this house."

Dr. de Graaf turned and looked down at both of us. Maria pulled herself as high as she could. She looked off suddenly, her cheek flaring as if her sister Aleydis had pinched her.

My hands were cold, so I twisted them together. I didn't like this new stranger. He seemed to hear everything, look at everything with a bright challenging eye.

"Not my sewing room, Johannes," Catharina said, as the men passed through the kitchen. She put her hand around Maria's upper arm as well as my own. "Not the chapel—"

But the two men walked right through the kitchen, the sewing room, and stood chatting in the darkened chapel as if they stood on the market square. Catharina Bolnes followed them into the room, then stood aside, gazing down with a sober assessing look at the mantled table that served as an altar. In the dim room, her face shone pearl white, years younger than it had looked as she stood in the kitchen door yelling for her eldest daughter. She tilted her head, listening to the men.

"See here, see here," De Graaf said, laying his drawing on the table. "If the lens is set right here, and the mirror tilted so—"

"Maria, come here and hold this," Johannes said.

Maria Vermeer, with a quick glance at her mother, stepped forward to take the sheet of greased paper he held out to her. "Both of you," he said roughly. "And stand away from the paper."

He inserted the lens in a knothole in the shutter and pulled the shutter closed.

"But look," De Graaf protested.

"Step left," Johannes directed us. "Step back. Again."

I looked at the greased paper, puzzled.

"Ah, Papa, this should please you. Not a soul in sight," Maria said with a laugh and a shrug that made the houses on the paper ripple.

"Hold still," Johannes said sharply.

"Enough, Johannes. The girls can't stand like sticks all afternoon. Your daughter is needed for the mending."

"And you?" Johannes asked, pushing open the shutter, stopping it half ajar.

"Me?" I looked first at my friend Maria.

"Maria?" my father asked from the door. "Maria Antoni's daughter? She has her own house to attend to, her own mending basket to empty."

"Just regard this," De Graaf said again to Johannes Vermeer. He pointed to the drawing on the table. "If you take a sheet of glass—"

But it was my father who stepped forward and took his place beside the young doctor. Johannes had eyes only for his wife, as I expect she knew. She smiled when he ordered her to remain where she was. Her head tilted to one side, her eyes cast down, she stood just as she had in the dark. Her fingertips rested gently on the embroidered cloth. When Johannes finished her portrait, he hung it in the chapel room, a demonstration of his devotion to her as much as to their faith.

But this is my father's story, not Johannes Vermeer's.

At that moment, my father and De Graaf could have been anywhere on earth. The fish market. The Oude Kirke. The Stadthuis, the town hall. The Nieuwe Kirke. Or exactly where they were, in the papist chapel in Johannes Vermeer's tavern.

"But this," my father said, tapping the paper. "I just read—"

"At Leyden," De Graaf said. "I saw one demonstrated. As far as I understood—" He looked up at my father with a wide smile, which my father returned. They looked as self-satisfied as boys who had discovered a bird's nest, a honeycomb.

"Come, come." Catharina Bolnes beckoned to her daughter.

"Come, come," I wanted to cry to my father. I knew better. I made my way back alone to the Hippolytusbuurt, to the empty Golden Head.

Two hours later, my father mounted the stair. He found me, as he had wished, alone in my chamber, my hands swiftly plying the needle.

It had been slow to start, the friendship between De Graaf and my father. Like a windmill on a mild, gusty day, straining into motion, rocking with as great a groan back into place. But a year after crafting the camera obscura in the chapel at the Mechelen, De Graaf and my father had become frequent companions. It was not just my father's curiosity over the camera obscura that made De Graaf take an interest. When he saw my father and Pieter Spoors surveying the Nieuwe Kirke to determine the height of its tower, he stopped to watch. Soon he was stopping to talk to my father if they chanced to meet in the square, my father leaving his duties at the stadthuis, the young doctor returning from the home of a patient, or from his devotions at the Mechelen.

It wasn't an act of charity on the young doctor's part. My father, although schooled only in his letters and sums, was much the older man. He had a place in our town, unlike the young papist doctor from Schoonhoven. De Graaf was lonely, it was obvious. Twenty-four, unmarried, he longed to regain the comradeship he'd found at the university at Leyden, with all those learned professors and able students: Swammerdam, Steno, Sylvius de Boe, Van Horne. Long before my father's correspondence with the learned and ingenious, these names had become as familiar to him as the Delftware on our mantel. De Graaf chanted the names of his learned friends in Leyden as often as my friend Maria Vermeer chanted her rosary. With each utterance he revealed a longing equally deep and unassuaged. A papist, in our country the professor's black robe was forever forbidden him. Why didn't he move south, to Antwerp or Bruges? It was worse. There the sieges never ended. Who could think clearly—gasping in with every breath the stench of the unburied?

The young doctor was better off here in Delft. But even with our theater of anatomy, our Municipal Professor of Anatomy, 'sGravesende, our Municipal Physician, D'Aquet, the young doctor grew meager, his cheeks falling in, his voice thinning, as if here in our serene town he had slipped into an even stiller and more serene world, conversed silently, a shade among shades. Until, that is, he grew familiar with my father. And even then, at first, his talk was an incomprehensible rattle—as if a skeleton had sat up in his coffin and begun to chatter!

After the St. Odulphus fair, it was my father who fell silent as a shade—all for fear he'd lost the friendship of the doctor.

I remember so clearly. It was before my illness. Tents were set up as far off as the Oude Delft and the Doelenstraat. They cluttered the east side of the Hippolytusbuurt, the Voldersgracht, the Oude Langendijk. The bridge at the end of the Nieuwe Straat was lined on both sides with tables by eight in the morning.

My father set up his own table in the great square, as near the stadthuis as possible. Even then, it was admiration he desired, not money, or so I understood when De Graaf stood between D'Aquet and my father's table, blocking sight of my father as if he were ashamed of his friend's pretensions. I saw the look on my father's face, the desperate mottle of red and white on his neck and forehead as well as his cheek, as if his very heart were stuttering at the slight.

De Graaf had traveled with my father to the kermis in 'sGravenhage the September past. Together they had watched the glassblower. My father had voyaged to England the year before and there he had observed the drawings in Mr. Hooke's book and although he could not read the observations, the drawings were enough. His curiosity was engaged. Someone had told him that the complex design of Mr. Hooke's microscope was not necessary. It was possible to make lenses of great strength out of a single small bubble of glass if it was shaped just right. The young doctor had wandered off, but my father discussed with the glassblower how to shape a globe smaller than a tear.

My father spent the whole winter of '69 blowing bubbles of glass, imitating as best he could the instructions of the glassblower. He tested them again and again against what he could remember of those drawings. There was a world inside them unlike any he had ever dreamed. That day in June, I was as proud as my father of the magical bubbles of glass we displayed at our table on the market square.

"And what do you have here, Heer van Leeuwenhoek?" asked the Schout Francois van Santen, coming to a swaggering stop before my father's table. He blinked at the glittering beads I had helped my father arrange the night before within a box lined with black velvet.

My father straightened his back, spread his feet apart. He shrugged, shifted his weight rapidly from foot to foot, glanced behind him. My father is not one for fancy talk. "Look," he said desperately. "Just look." He picked up one of his small bubbles with such awkward force, I bit my lip, afraid he would shatter it in his eagerness.

Burgomaster Hogenhouk wove back and forth behind the Schout, his face dark as a beet from kermis beer.

"What's this, Leeuwenhoek?"

"Beads?" asked a boy my age who stood close to the burgomasters.

"No, no, look, boy," my father said, leaning down, relieved. He held the bubble between thumb and index finger. "Come closer. You'll see something here you've never seen before." The boy, with a glance at his father, at the Burgomaster Hogenhouk, at the Schout who rocked, with his eyes closed, his face tilted to the noonday sun in an expression of sweet drunken idiocy.

These, then, were the men my father had labored all the evenings of the spring to impress.

"Nothing," the boy said. "I see nothing."

"A minute," my father said with a laugh. "Maria," he snapped. "That fly there. Place it here." He twiddled his right thumb in the air. I picked up the dead fly by its wing and placed it on his finger tip. "Now," my father said to the boy. "Tell me when you see the veins on its wings."

"Aagh!" the boy screamed, leaping back, tumbling into the black coats of the burgomasters, drawing them close around him as if they were bed curtains.

I clapped my hand to my mouth. But my father stood up, rocked his head back, and fearlessly bellowed out his laughter.

"Monster," I heard the boy mutter. "He has more eyes than Argus."

"Magnifies," the boy's father said, nodding approvingly. "My brother-in-law brought me a book the other day. An Italian. Malpighi, I believe."

"Very good, Leeuwenhoek. You made these yourself?"

"Malpighi?" my father whispered.

"Could I see, Sir?" asked Pastor Petrie of the English church. He was accompanied by a young Lutheran pastor from 'sGravenhage.

"Isn't there someone else?" the Lutheran said. "An Englishman— Hooke, I believe. The book is traveling through the Princess's court in 'sGravenhage. Could I see?"

"I know of Hooke," my father said. "Malpighi?"

"Would you just observe," the Lutheran said. "A lost thread in my cloak."

"Are you certain?" my father asked. "Could the fulling just be missing?"

"What? "

My father, sure of himself again, explained. The burgomasters nodded approvingly. Although my father no longer practiced the draper's trade, he kept his membership at the Saye Hall, the guild for those who dealt with cloth. It was here my father had learned to use a lens to inspect the weave of serge or silk.

"How high did you say it was?" the Schout interrupted. "The steeple," he said, when my father looked puzzled.

"299 feet, Sir."

"A worthy man," the Schout said to the burgomasters. "Surveyor's license, and now this."

Man! My father stood there shivering with as much eagerness to please as any lost dog.

"Will you let me see, sir?" asked the glass-blower from the next booth.

But I had to answer for my father. He had just seen the look De Graaf gave him, the way the young doctor twisted his shoulder to shield his friend from the sharp gray eyes of his learned companion, the Municipal Physician, Henricus D'Aquet. Was it then I felt the first pang in my love for my father? The sky above us glowed a flat, steady blue, and the small bubbles on the tray winked like so many tiny scornful eyes. My father closed his own large ones. The glass-blower at the booth beside us dipped his pipe in a glowing cauldron. His cheeks bulged as if he were playing a single note on a horn. The globe he blew was larger than my father's head, an equal, fiery red.

"You there," my father bellowed to old Phillip Janszn., the tinker. "Let me show you—"

The Schout, the Burgomasters Meerman and Vander Lee, even my uncle Jan Molijn stopped to see my father's curiosities. Johannes Vermeer, at his daughter's urging, came out of the Mechelen and gathered at my father's table, jostling arm to arm with the baker, Van Buyten. "As if we were treading a new plowed polder," marveled a bricklayer looking at his fingertip.

But on the far side of the stadthuis portico, Dr. de Graaf had turned away from my father as if he were something less than a servant—as if he were a peasant come out of the polder, feathers still caught in his hair, dung on the toes of his shoes.

We see only what we want to see. Or is it more exact to say we only recall what both eye and mind agree upon?

I recall the flush in the young doctor's cheeks, the way his eyes narrowed, his lips thickened with disdain, how he pointed off toward the printing house, drawing Dr. D'Aquet's eye away from my father as if from a juggler, a clown.

My father recalls the glitter of the glass as the sun flicked in and out of the mass of burgers and burgomasters crowded round his table. He recalls my Uncle Molijn edging in to stand right beside the table, eyeing the guilders and stuivers massed there on the rug, woozy with envy.

I recall De Graaf and D'Aquet gathered around my friend Maria and her mother. I remember the way Maria lifted her father's painting before her as if it were a mirror. I recall the men leaning close to one another, talking in muted voices, as if they were conferring together under the echoing roof of the Anatomy Chamber. I recall the money Catharina Bolnes accepted as eagerly as any bawd. I recall Maria's smile, spit as fresh as dew on her red lips, as she wrapped the painting in paper, affixing it with a string.

I see the blonde head of Maria tipped back, I see the blackened board nailed over the sun. I see the men nod, smile. I see Maria's hands wrapping the painting, knotting the cords as swiftly as she now knots lace. I remember the envy, like a thorn crushed into the heel of my hand. Like my father, I wanted the approval of those two men dressed in black like predikants.

I blamed my father. If he had been Johannes Vermeer, a man with a craft, a man with something more to barter than his earnestness and dignity . . . if only he had persevered in his usual occupations . . .

"There you are," my cousin Antoni said, tugging at my sleeve. "Your father is asking for you. *Hurry.*"

My father wanted my quick mind for sums, my deft fingers to lift his bubbles of glass to the rheumy eyes of old men, the unblinking ones of children. Money passed hands here, just as at the Mechelen. But it wasn't the same. The townspeople bought fear from my father. I could see it in their faces as I placed the glass bead in their hands, a flicker in the eye, a small spasm in the fingers, as if they had bought the glass simply to crush it as they couldn't the knowledge writhing now through eye to mind.

"Not these?" I asked my father as he folded the last two glasses into their velvet pockets. "You'll not sell them as well?"

Memory can be as cruel as sight. I recall now the way my father's eyes shifted to the spot where, amid all the kermis throng, he had seen his friend pass.

"Not everything," he said, "has a price."

And he was right. The bag of coins I gathered up didn't. Nor the piercing thrust through my stomach when I realized what he meant. He planned quite simply to give them up now, these miraculous bubbles of glass, like eyes that had set their sights too high.

I couldn't let him.

Nor, it proved, could De Graaf. He simply wanted my father to lower his gaze, like a woman surprised at her morning bath. He wanted my father to recognize his nakedness—his ignorance.

"Come, come, Leeuwenhoek," he said, pacing my father's study the next afternoon. "Where is your dignity, man? Hawking wares like a wandering tinker, muddling knowledge and chicanery like a kermis doctor."

"Hooke," my father said with a small smile on his face. "Malpighi."

"Hooke!" De Graaf exclaimed. "Malpighi. Those are learned men, Leeuwenhoek."

"I too," my father said, tapping the book on the surveyor's art that he had read twice through before making his way to Haarlem to sit before the scholar Genesius Baan. "I too have eyes in my head. I too can read what Our Creator has written, here, in the palm of my hand, on the back of a fly, the leg of a louse. I can puzzle it through like any scripture."

"It's not child's play, Leeuwenhoek." De Graaf, with his flushed cheeks, his fair hair failing over his soiled collar, looked as young as my cousin Antoni.

"No, it's not that." A smile tipped the corners of my father's wide lips. "Come, my friend," he said, his voice as soft as if he were cajoling a small kitten or an infant child. "Just look at this, if you will." He drew a shiny brass plate not much longer than his index finger from the black velvet bag I'd stitched for him.

"What's this?" De Graaf asked, his arm swooping low across the table.

"A gift. To thank you, Sir, for your condescension and perseverance." My father turned and, with his hands knotted behind his back in a single fist, pretended to peruse the shelf of his own cabinet now devoted to curios. The bladder stone big as a baby's foot, the volume of Beverwijk, the small scissors recommended by Swammerdam for severing the waists of flies.

"But this is magnificent, Leeuwenhoek," De Graaf said. "I can see in every lens of its eye the steeple of the Nieuwe Kirke. I can see the flags waving on the kermis booths."

"Yes, yes," my father said, sidling up eagerly to his friend. "It's better than the camera obscura we set up at the Mechelen, don't you think?"

"Not a bit of it," the young man said, pulling the plate from his eyes and twisting it around to inspect the screw that held the fly's head. "But far more useful for true students of nature—like us. With what do you affix the fly's head? Would it hold the lens of a man's eye?"

My father moved away then. "I don't know," he said. He brushed his thinning hair away from his forehead, wet already with his eagerness. "A man's eye is much grander than an insect's, and besides, where would I find one?"

"At the Anatomy Chamber," De Graaf said impatiently.

"Not I," my father said.

"I've talked with 'sGravesende. An able man, he agrees, should be permitted to observe the annual dissection."

My father gaped like a small boy with pleasure.

"Wine?" I asked. I wanted him to close his mouth.

"Go on now, child. Play with your friends."

Friends? I had, as my father well knew, only the one. Eagerly I left the house. On the bridge, I met Maria's sister Aleydis and her brother Franciscus. They were buying cakes.

"Maria," I asked them. "Is she about?"

"Those glass beads you were selling," Franciscus said, "does your father have more?" Tearing his cake in half, he held out some to me.

"What for?" I asked. Suddenly angry, I waved the cake away. "They're not for children," I said, twisting on my heel. "They are for the learned."

I did not know, balanced on the arch of that small bridge, watching my father open the door to the Golden Head and usher the young doctor in that, like him, I was teetering on the brink of a terrifying ignorance.

Regnier de Graaf, when his name is mentioned these days, is never remembered as a physician, save perhaps by my father and me.

No, he is remembered as a learned gentleman, the author of treatises on the pancreas, the sexual anatomy of men and women. He is remembered as a regular correspondent of the Royal Society. He is remembered for his introduction of my father to that international company!

Remembered for a paragraph!

It is hard for us to remember now De Graaf's great and steadfast condescension to my father. It is a wonder the young man didn't give up hope. The distance between the doctor and the untutored Sheriff's Chamberlain was so vast. Perhaps he did, perhaps they both did. Certainly, I don't remember their meeting again—the offer to visit the Anatomy Chamber to the contrary—until the end of the summer. That day, so I've been told, my father, wringing his hands like an old woman, openly trailed the young papist doctor through the streets of our city.

For me. All for me.

So I've been told, and so I believe, although I recall even now almost nothing of that August. I remember the last day of July. I remember my father and Pieter Spoor, the surveyor, on opposite ends of the Hippolytusbuurt and the Voorstraat, raising their sextants to site the cross on the Oude Kirke. I remember the bells beginning to play the half hour. The handkerchief I put to my lips came back green as standing water. On my back I felt two wings furling. The market square was unbearably hot. I hurried toward the Hippolytusbuurt with my basket of endive, bread, butter but, recalling myself, turned back and walked to the fish market to finish my purchases.

A stork tipped its beak into a barrel of eel and lifted one, writhing, into the wet air. My cheeks were damp. Under my cap my hair had matted like felt. My step was as woozy and splay foot as the stork. Then, without warning, my neck stretched out in ludicrous imitation, my tongue too, in hidden tumult, twisted and writhed like the black eel in that long white throbbing throat.

I don't remember falling. I don't remember the crowd that surrounded me, or the fishmonger who held my shoulders down with her strong hands filthy with scale and blood. I don't remember my father shouldering his way through the crowd. Who had fetched him? It could have been anyone. We were no strangers in Delft. I don't remember, I wish I did, my father lifting me in his arms, cradling my head on his shoulder, carrying me across the bridge, into the house and up the stairs to my room.

For two days he tended me alone. He sent my Aunt Gryetgen away with a curse, or so said my cousin Antoni later with scandalized pleasure. "You tire the well with your chatter," my father said to his sister. "What do you think you will do to the sick?"

I think it was an excuse, that he would have said anything to get her out of the house. If I survived, he wanted no one telling tales. It wasn't the Devil entered me, but heat, a searing heat that made the body twist and shrivel like fat in a fire. But it was the numbing cold that followed which frightened him the most. That and the way in my delirium I taunted him. Hovering between life and death, I toppled the world and made of earth, heaven. It was he I grieved for, he who was lost to me, not my dead mother, not my three dead brothers Philips, my dead sister Margriete, who were all with me again.

For two days, until he thought the danger of possession over, my father tended me alone. Then he sent for my mother's sister, Maria De Mey. Chosen by my mother to serve as my godmother, my father asked her now to act as another earthly advocate. He refused to lose every single one of his five children. Then he went himself for De Graaf. The young doctor came and, with a terse word or two at my father's delay, bled from me two full, foul bowls.

"No more," my father said.

"No food," the doctor said. "Only tea. Light beer."

"Gruel," my father said as soon as he returned to the room. "And fresh milk. Every creature, to live, needs nourishment."

My aunt questioned him, but he tapped the book he carried under his arm. "I can read as well as any man."

My aunt could read too, read not only the words on the page, but the look on the young doctor's face, the tentative taps he made on my father's drooping shoulders. She made the sign of the cross over my head. She opened the Bible and began to recite.

My father pulled the Bible from her hands, slammed it against the table.

"*No*," he whispered. "*I won't be left alone.*"

And that was, I believe, the first time my father really saw me. White, wasted, as deaf to his pleas as I was blind to his tears.

According to my Aunt Maria, he gathered me to him as if I were a tiny child. Morning and night, he propped my head on his shoulder, he prised open my mouth and spooned in tea, gruel, broth. He aired and beat the feather comforters himself, carried away the chamber pot.

My Aunt Maria too would not give me up. For two weeks she sat in the bedroom, knotting lace, reciting psalms. The heat must have been nearly insufferable. My father banked the fire three times a day. He allowed no air from outside, hanging bed, window and door with curtains of serge. When the linen was changed, he wound me in blankets; he heaped the warming pan so high with coals it took two hands to lift it to the bed. The sheets must steam before he would return me to them.

What tested them most, they told me later, were not the first fits I suffered, but the one that almost destroyed us all. It took place three weeks into my illness. I had, they believed, begun to recover. At least I lay for hours still as the very pillows. I opened my eyes, frowned at the light, woke when someone approached my bed or left the room.

It was one morning when my father had just left the house to go to the stadthuis to supervise the preparation of the sheriff's chamber that I was wracked by a last fit so murderous in its strength that, gripping the bed curtains in my frenzy, I tore them from their posts. The oil lamp by my bed set them alight. It was the smoke alerted Aunt Maria when she returned to my room.

She pushed open the window. "Antoni!" she screamed. My father, pausing on the bridge, looked up but once, then rushed back into the house. By this time, my aunt had tumbled the smoldering serge into the hearth. She was slapping wildly at the scorched comforter.

My father stumbled into the room and, immediately comprehending what had happened, acted without modesty. He pushed my aunt aside, dragged me, arched and stiff as a bow, from the bed. He tore the scorched gown from me, wrapped me in his own cloak and dragged me to the safety of his own chamber. He did not leave me until he saw my tongue slip in and out of my dry mouth, my eyelids quiver, my hands, easing open, pluck angrily at the coarse wool.

De Graaf was the only one, other than my Aunt De Mey, my father allowed into our house during my illness. But it wasn't his young friend's learning my father called upon, it was his love. No, not of me. Not even of my father. He called upon the doctor's love of the human body, as acute as any monk's love of the spirit. The doctor's big moist roving eyes traveled from my falling eyelid to my slack mouth, from my fluttering chest to my crossed feet. He proclaimed his diagnosis as boldly as a priest might exorcise. It began here, he said, tapping those two broken wings hidden under my skin.

"But then the fire raged in her heart, ran through her brain like—,"

"A flame travels along a curtain hem," my father said.

My father sat in the chair beside my bed. He was dressed for the street. De Graaf too did not wear his physician's robe or his plague cloak, rather a broad hat, a worn serge coat buttoned fast. He dressed like this to encourage my father.

He moved now to the window in my room. He looked down at the canal.

"You're very lucky, Leeuwenhoek. Every year one survives in this deadly mist is a miracle. People don't have time to contract the plague—"

"For that we must sail to London," my father said with a frown.

"That, and many other things," said De Graaf. "Ah yes," he said, slapping the sides of his coat in vexation. "That reminds me. I brought you a copy of the *Philosophical Transactions*." The volume he had brought for my father was still in the pocket of his cloak, which lay downstairs by the door. Would my father fetch it? It would give him time to examine me.

Of course. Of course.

Alone with me, De Graaf came close to the bed. He leaned down and puffed into my ear, as if extinguishing a lamp. "Maria," he said softly. Then, when I didn't speak, he clapped his hands, a hollow sound, like a cork tugged from a bottle. "Girl," he barked. "Listen." He was quick to observe the tear slipping from the corner of my eye. "Child," he murmured. "Poor child."

He settled my head straight on the pillow, handling it as if it were stone. He held the candle, dripping, over the coverlet.

"Aha," he said when I closed my eyes. But it wasn't the light made my lids slip down, rather the scalding plash of wax into the hollow in my neck. It wasn't pain I felt, but relief. Now he couldn't fail to see. If not today, tomorrow. There was no reaching me.

Then De Graaf did something as unexpected as it was cruel. Blowing out the candle and putting it aside, he leaned over the bed, he slipped his hands in on both sides of the coverlet. He ran them down my sides, over my ribs. He slipped them into the hollow between my ribs neatly as two doves into a dovecot. He put one knee upon the bed, leaning over me, his ear to my mouth, his hair in my eyes, under my nose. Then, without warning, he pummeled my chest. *Aagh!* It was as if cousin Antoni had thrown a stone hard against a cow's flank. He hit again. *Aagh!* The fine gold hair stuck to my lashes like cobweb. And again. *Aagh!* I arched my back, opened my mouth wide enough to swallow an oyster or a man's ear, his entire skull. "*Aaagh!*" I screamed again. "*Stop. Stop. Stop.*" The words flew through my throat like peas through a straw.

He smiled as he raised his head and looked me in the eye. "Very good," he said. "Far better than I thought. There is much to hope for here."

Haah. Haah. As he slipped off the bed, I was the one who couldn't stop, either the sound or the tears or my hand slapping at sheets, at the pain, at the wakening.

"What is it?" my father asked from the door. He held the small volume tucked high on his chest between his ribs, just where De Graaf's fist had fallen, forcing the will out of me. "Does she worsen?"

"Not at all," De Graaf said. "It may take months. But she can lift her arm. She can hear. She can see. And she is not dumb. I do not think the fever stole her reason either."

"Of *course,*" my father said angrily. "Of course she can see. Her eyes follow me when I approach, when I leave. But what about her lungs, her heart, her stomach? Will she be strong again? Will she walk? Will she run?" My father walked across the room with his long jostling stride. He held the book clutched to his chest as if it were a box of jewels.

"It may take months," De Graaf said again, glancing at my father, then away at the window. "But there's no reason why she shouldn't talk again."

"Talk!" my father said with a laugh. "With her Aunt Gryetgen around it's impossible even for the most nimble tongue. Besides—" His large hand closed around my forehead like a damp cloth. "In this the girl resembles her mother. She's never been loose with words."

Haaah. The sound fluttered up through my throat like a butterfly rising in meadow grass, drifted silently down again.

De Graaf looked at me, winked. The pain between my ribs pulsed like my heart. I heard again that cow's bellow he'd forced from me. Like locks being forced. Doors opened. But I had no interest in returning to this world.

"Look, Maria," my father said, returning after having shown the doctor to the door, "You can make as much of this as I. It is all in English—or Latin. I cannot make out a word." He put the book down on the table beside my bed. He took a seat beside me, settled the lamp so the light from it spread like a pool of oil over his coat. "But here is something I am sure will delight you."

He shuffled in the pockets of his coat, drew out a small battered brass box. He prised it open, drew out a small brass plate. He slipped his arm around my shoulders and drew me close. "I'll hold it up for you. Tell me when you can see clearly."

Aaaagh. I heard a cow's snort of fear. My father heard pleasure.

"What's this?" my father said, his knuckle staunching the tear in my unblinkered eye. "What's this, child?"

♕ ♕ ♕

After De Graaf's examination, everyone took my silence to be willful, a choice. I expect I should thank him for that. From the first, I knew my ignorance did not lie in lung or throat or cumbersome tongue. It lay much deeper, beyond the prodding finger, the peering eye. It was my very mind that was afflicted. Like a newborn child, I saw shapes and colors, not cabinets and cloth. I heard sounds but not words. My Aunt Maria's singing meant as much to me as the shriek of the stork, the jumble of the Nieuwe Kirke bells. Like a newborn child, and not. A baby shuttled from the mother's womb wakes from her painless ignorance with a startled cry. She wakes to the sweet white warmth of her mother's breast. What I woke to was loss, and a devouring silence. Everything I learned, or recalled, reminded me of all I had once known, all that was now lost in the deepest distance, a boil of sound, picture, smell, touch, like a world in flames, like I imagine our town of Delft after the powder magazine exploded down on the Doelenstraat in the year '54.

This turmoil never left me, no matter how quiet I was, no matter how still. Lying in my bed, I relearned the shape of my own room. I relearned the shape of the window panes, the chimney mantel, my three Delft plates, my cabinet, desk, and chair. Studying my Aunt Maria as she tended me, I relearned their use. The cabinet held my linen, cloak, and second dress. The chair held Aunt Maria. The pitcher held beer. The cup held tea, the bowl, gruel. My tongue wagged, my throat clenched, I swallowed it all. What I could not remember were the words. *Table, chair, bowl, beer, chamber pot.* I could have as soon said *God, soul, witch, father, mother, Saturn or noon.* It took me over a year to anchor the sounds of our Low Dutch securely to the objects in my room, the rooms in our house, the streets in our city, the cities in our province.

For over a month, I spoke no language at all. I felt the weight of the cabinet on my tongue, I felt its door, swinging open, crash against the back of my teeth. The bed curtains brushed against my eyes, and, yes, I understood that red is clear, startling, that it is pain. I heard the blue of the sky and it was my mother's voice as she turned inside her coffin.

I was sure should my father learn of my true state he would send me off to the madhouse. His tenderness during my illness deluded me not at all. It was death my father was fighting. It was solitude. He wasn't fighting for *me.* The erasure I had become. Or so I believed then, and that belief was like a cold wind at my back forever pressing me on.

A blessing in its way. It meant that there was worse that could happen. It meant I wasn't entirely lost. It meant when Maria Vermeer put out her hand to me, I clung to it. When she whispered the name of the fragrant mound in my hands, *bread,* I repeated it over and over until the word itself was as warm and fragrant and sustaining as the grain.

Yes, it was Maria Vermeer who retaught me the names of things. But it was her father Johannes Vermeer who taught me that they were unnecessary. It was he who gave me back my freedom.

Just as De Graaf's love and attention gave my father back his own freedom. It was the energy my father put into his observations, his industry and his delight, that mattered to the young papist doctor. It was my father's clear eye and his receptive mind that led them to converse again and again in that one clumsy tongue they shared. It was De Graaf's harsh hiccupping laugh, his tumbling gestures, his knock on our door again and again that urged my father beyond his own deep shame: *I do not know. I do not know.*

While I, sitting in Johannes' studio in the Mechelen, was restored by the absence of speech, by the steady thrum of pure sound as he ground his paints, moved his easel, chair, stool, table, whistling, humming, mimicking the church bells, the wailing of his newborn son, the pots falling in the kitchen. He lived by choice in the world I had just woken into, as bald and helpless as the infant in the basket by the fire, more helpless in my way than Catharina Bolnes who still lay in their bed upstairs dangerously weakened by this last birth.

The portrait had been Maria's idea. It was the only way she could see to keep me close to her. Helping her grandmother Maria Thins run the household at the Mechelen after her mother began fasting for the birth the first of August, Maria had no time to visit me in my illness. Only in October, when I was well enough to sit downstairs, to pare fruit for Aunt Maria, slice cheese, lay the tablecloth, did Maria at last find the liberty to come to the Golden Head. I thank God she had been detained so long.

It took my friend only minutes to discover what I had successfully concealed from Aunt Maria and my father.

"Do you remember, Maria? The way you scolded the baker's wife last year when she charged me twice what she charged you? Do you remember how we *flew* across the market square? Today was the first day I have dared to go buy from her again. But she has the memory of an elephant. She asked after you again."

Maria rose from her chair and came over to my side of the room. She put her finger flat beneath my eye, trying to dam the tear. "Tell me what ails you. Your feet?" She stooped to check the coals in the foot warmer. "Are you cold, Maria? Talk. *Talk.*"

"If only you could get her to," my Aunt Maria said, passing through to the kitchen. "She just sits in that one chair, lost in her thoughts like an old woman. But at fourteen years, what does she have to look back on?"

Maria pulled her chair close to mine.

"There's no one here but me," she whispered.

"None," I said, putting my hand to my throat.

The side of my head throbbed. I lifted my hand and pressed it there to ease the pain. "None," I said again, glancing up to see if Aunt Maria should be coming back. From the kitchen came a constant, comforting din.

"I don't understand," Maria Vermeer said. She shook her head so hard her fine gold hair tumbled down from her bun, frothed out from the pointed edges of her visiting cap. She took my chin in her hand, tipping my face back.

I shook my head free. "Empty," I said, tapping at my head.

"We'll see." She patted my hand. Although she smiled, her eyes were bright with tear.

For the first time, I felt the tiniest flicker of hope, like a single flame fleeting between the bricks of peat in the hearth. I took her hand in both of mine, pulled it to my cheek.

She pulled it away quickly, as if she had touched ice. "Excuse me," she said.

She clattered into the kitchen in her red slippers. The dishes and pans kept rattling, but I could hear her voice and that of my Aunt Maria.

"I don't know what to do," my Aunt Maria said. "She's not strong enough to carry out the household tasks. Two months now I have slept in her chamber."

"For a month," Maria said. And then her voice was drowned in the din. I contemplated the street, the few leaves left on the limes shuddering in the wind. I would never have imagined, a year later, I would be sitting in the same chair, the same desperate thought running through my head. "Lost. All lost."

The same thought, but the words would tumble from my tongue. The same thought would be applied to a completely different world. It is not the difference between men's eyes that startles me, it is the difference between our minds. And even this startles me less than the changes that take place within each of us. The eyes' acumen, the whole heart's range, applied each year to different things, but the intensity of thought, the words, the flux of joy or pain is exactly the same.

Maria Vermeer suggested I come to the Mechelen every day that fall to sit for her father. She had neither the time nor the patience, she said, to serve as his model. But really she brought me to the Mechelen to preserve me from my own father's tender scrutiny. She believed time would bring me back to myself. Which it did. Time—and something else.

"Hat," Maria whispered, fitting the huge red hat on my head. While her father seated me in the chair and draped the damask at my back, she lifted a large mirror to her waist. But her father shook his head, sent her off about her tasks.

"I'll be back," she said, touching the base of my neck with her small rough hand. "Don't be afraid."

After the first day I felt no dread. Did Johannes know of my state? If he had, would it have mattered?

"Maria," he would call out and I would turn my head to watch my friend come in. "Stop," he would cry out. "Don't move. I want you still as stone."

Even now, when I look at that painting, I see Johannes, sitting as still as me, his head turned from the easel, his eyes wide and fixed as mine. I see the smile on his face, the bead of spit on his lower lip. I see his hand plying the paintbrush as precisely as a woman plies a needle.

"Here you are," Johannes said the day, a month later, when he had finished painting my face.

"Ah!" I didn't know if it was a cry of pain or triumph.

For indeed there I was. Whole.

Just like him.

Just like him, without a word to explain or defend myself when Catharina Bolnes came railing into the room.

"What's this?" she asked, pointing to the panel on the easel. "A portrait? Who would buy it, Johannes? She's a child. Not even a beauty. Her father won't pay. And what about us, Johannes? Have you given no thought to us?"

She went to the chimney where the infant lay asleep before the fire screen. She tugged the baby from the cradle. She turned and stared at Johannes, the baby's swaddlings slipping across her full white breasts like veils. Even in rage, Catharina Bolnes was beautiful. There was, I swear to you, no woman in Delft as beautiful as long as Johannes lived.

"One day out of my bed," she said, "and who am I asked to entertain? The baker. The apothecary. Not a stuiver do we have on hand—and we owe both of them." She closed her eyes, her long white face becoming suddenly, miraculously still. "We owe both of them," she crooned, "guilders and guilders and guilders."

"Johannes!" She walked across the room to where he still sat on the stool before his easel. He had never moved. His brush still waved in the air, stiffly, like a reed in the marshes. The baby pulled up high on her chest, she put out her left hand and put it on Johannes' shoulder. Balled into a fist she rocked it against Johannes' shoulder, his neck, as if she were grinding pigments.

"Look," Catharina Bolnes said in a small, cold voice.

Johannes looked at his painting. But Catharina looked at me. And I, finally, met her eyes. Again I saw her as Johannes did. Visiting the Mechelen, it was almost impossible not to see her so. In every room he'd hung her portrait. As if anyone could forget that face, more perfect than any statue. Colder than snow.

"Come here," she said to me. "Come here, child. Come and see what he has done to you."

Only Catharina Bolnes saw what he was up to. She looked at that portrait of me, and she knew. She saw immediately that the eyes he drew there were exactly like his own and that is why they could lift to meet his. Johannes never let Catharina or his daughter Maria watch him working. They could look at each other, look at their hands, look into mirrors at their own pearl white faces. But they could not look at the man at the easel.

It made him laugh, he said. It distracted him. But that wasn't true. Their scrutiny did something worse—it threw his world askew. The face then loomed larger than table, chair, cabinet or window. And that is what he feared most, losing this precious distance, this perfect perspective.

What we love about Johannes' paintings is that here we see man's love for our imperfect world is as cool and perfect as God's own love. Johannes' eye is imperturbable, steadier than any hand, more exact than any word. The people in Johannes' paintings are no more important than the floors, the walls. They fit into their houses as neatly as the diminished figure fits in the inverted image glowing on the sheet of greased paper in a darkened room. Brilliant and diminished, here is the image from the camera obscura righted and caught forever.

But it isn't quite so simple is it? Which is why Johannes made his women keep their eyes cast down. He didn't want to be bothered with the truth. Baker's bills, the mortgage on the Mechelen, the latest squabble at the St. Lucas Guild, the tattered shirts his children wore, their worn out shoes.

It was then I understood that Johannes saw what he wanted. And we, looking at those paintings, fell in love with Johannes himself, with his heart's pining for a world as still and stable as the white washed wall, the tiled floor, the half open window, the warm flapping tapestry.

I believe it was his own soul Johannes saw in me. The same willful stupidity. I sat there day after day simply *seeing* Johannes. If I thought at all, I thought *easel, stool, tile, mantel, brush, cap, hair. Hat*, I thought. *Hand.* I never thought, *portrait.* I never thought, *art.* Certainly, I never thought *debt* or *payment.* And I never thought, as Catharina looking at that portrait was convinced we both did, *love.*

"Come here, child," Catharina said to me.

Those eyes of hers that Johannes never let us see were blue as the sea on a winter morning. They made you feel as if you were drowning. Even now I can feel them washing over my face, my neck, my breasts.

"Child," she said. "Don't you have better things to do with your time than to sit here all day? Certainly my own daughter does."

When I looked at Catharina Bolnes that afternoon in the Mechelen, I saw my own mother's hand cupping the back of my brother Philips's head. I saw their feet devoured by mist. I saw my mother step toward me, lean closer, peer into my face with steady, savage eyes. "Maria," my mother said. "Leave us—leave us in peace." She leaned forward, pursed her lips. Eagerly, I stepped forward. She spit. She turned around and began to walk away, the mist swirling up around her, thick as smoke.

I have never, I swear it, suffered such loss before or after.

Turning from the easel and back, silently Johannes cleaned my several faces.

♛ ♛ ♛

Catharina sent me home that day. Maria came the next to bring me back. Johannes was born with as stubborn and fixed a will as his wife. He was master of the St. Lucas Guild that year. No man, or woman, not even his wife, would tell him when or what to paint. So another month I sat there, numb, a small peaked cap on my head, a flute in my hand. I didn't dare say no. I kept hoping, you see, that Catharina Bolnes would understand her error. Every morning, before entering Johannes" studio, I tried to appease her. I assisted Maria. I sewed for them. I swept the floor. I would have given up everything to belong there in the Mechelen, to have regained her favor.

But Catharina would have none of it. She offered the first portrait to Hendrik van Buyten the baker for security on their debt, but he wouldn't take it. Johannes took the second and hung it high on the wall in the tavern room. Someone asked if it had been done by an apprentice. Johannes laughed. At last I found my tongue.

"Home," I said. "I am going home to the Golden Head."

"Not yet," Johannes said.

But I knew my own mind now. He couldn't hold me back.

When I left the Mechelen that day in early December, I returned to the Golden Head empty-handed, but rich beyond belief, weighted beyond tolerance.

"What price do you place on a child's soul?" I wanted to ask Maria, Catharina's daughter, twenty-six years later. But in the portrait that hangs even now within my sleeping cupboard covered with a red velvet cloth, it isn't a child's soul I find mirrored there. No, it is that one terrible moment between childhood and womanhood when there was nothing but the open eye, the attuned ear, the half-open mouth.

But we see, as I learned from Johannes, what we want, and it is this construction we put on things that matters. Betrayal. Love. It defines us. It is something we cannot share with anyone—like wickedness or idiocy . . . or faith.

As I walked home from the Mechelen across the crowded market square, I knew I was alone. There was no one who could protect me now from my mother's wrath, my father's love. Propelled by my own shame, slick with my own fear, this was my second birth. I see that now. I never did before.

II
CIRCULATION
(1671-1674)

. . . yet what was most remarkable was to see the manifold small arteries, that came forth from the great one, and which were spread into several branches, and turning came into one again, and were re-united, that at last they did pour out the blood again into the great vein; this last was a sight that would amaze any eye, that was greedy of knowledge.

Antoni van Leeuwenhoek

...Globuls in the ... heavier than the Cryst... which they are carried, because ...ttle subside towards the bottom; and b... Blood is let out of the Veins, tho... ...aid Corpuscles, and many lying upon one a... ...nite themselves close together, and by this clo... ...n the Blood that is under the surface alters its ... ...mes dark-red or blackish; as I have observed ... of which I take the reason to be, (with submiss... judgments) that the Air cannot move every way ... ...e Globuls, and hits as 'twere against a close da... Touching the *Florid* red colour of the surface ... ...sed to the Air, that comes, in my opinion, ...at the *uppermost* Globuls are not press'd, and ... ...their nature, and the Globuls *subjacent* to th... ...together, by reason of which close ... ...cannot penetrate through them, ...light to, and about ...

REVERSALS IN THE GOLDEN HEAD
1671

In those numb, stealthy months of my recovery in the autumn, the space between grains of sand in the hourglass seemed to expand, as did the silences between the caroling of the Nieuwe Kirke bells, the lapses between words. The next sound was always startling, like knocking one's shin against something in the dark.

But in January as I watched the predikant's lips moving, announcing the banns for my father's marriage, his small blue eyes glancing up sightless at the tall chill windows, even I recognized the time for protest, if there had ever been one, was past. When had I had a chance? Save for the announcement to the family assembled at Aunt Gryetgen Molijn's on Christmas Day, my father never again mentioned his betrothal to me. Why had I believed it would be months, even a year until the marriage contracts were drawn?

Never once, I tell you, did my father, seated before his steaming plate at noonday, or eating the cold collation I set before him in the evening, again mention Cornelia Swalmius to me. Had I really understood aright? Surely I should ask my Aunt Gryetgen, my Aunt Maria—or even my cousin Antoni. Perhaps my father had thought better of it. Every day I scoured, I did the marketing with my friend Maria Vermeer's assistance. She made the requests whenever my tongue failed me, counted out the change I could sort only by sight. He'll see now, I'd think, sprinkling sand across the floor in huge swirling waves. See what? Somewhere in the space and time it took for the sand to spill from my hand to the floor, I forgot. My mind cleared again. Only the pattern on the floor recalled me to my task. No wonder I failed to ask.

But why didn't my father ask *me*? And why did my aunts and cousins say nothing? Were they all as frightened as my father that my wits would never return to me? Did they, any of them, reveal this fact to Cornelia? Even now, now that I have recovered completely, we never discuss the summer of my illness, the year of my recovery. Why? Not solely, I think, because it was concealed by greater events. It is more dreadful than a sword wound or the angry scar that seals it off—this unmarked loss and renewal of the mind.

But whether or not time stretched or collapsed in the months after my sickness, it returned with a sickening regularity as I sat in the cold church that Sunday morning in January listening to the banns. From then until my father escorted Cornelia Swalmius into our house, a second gold ring securely fixed on the second finger of her right hand, all I heard was the thud thud thud of my own heart, the splash splash of our hands, all of us, cousins, aunts, as we scoured the Golden Head in preparation. On my father's wedding night, it was more than time came back to me, it was more than thought.

The wedding ceremony was performed on January 25th in Pijnacker, a village near Delft, where Cornelia Swalmius' cousin Jacobus Swalmius Brand was sheriff. Predikant Bredius performed the ceremony.

I can still recall the cold clammy feel of the church wall on the back of my hand, then on my cheek as I looked aside at the assembled family. Aunt Gryetgen wore a new black skirt, even my Aunt Maria de Mey wore a new lace collar. Cornelia's youngest sister, Catharina Swalmius, wore a robe trimmed with fur. She stood to the right of the room with her sister Elisabet and her sister-in-law, the widow of their only brother, Adriaen Swalmius. My father's favorite sister, Aunt Catharina van Leeuwen, who had come from Rotterdam with her husband Claes van Leeuwen, stood at the front of the room, where I should have been if I were to be there at all.

My father and Cornelia stood before the company. Surrounded by the pale afternoon light coming through the windows, my father, in his black hat and black cloak could have been a shadow on the wall. But Cornelia Swalmius, in her shimmering gown of white and violet silk, she could have been morning mist over the river Maas. There would never be enough sun to dissipate her, and never enough there to count on.

I looked around the room again. Why couldn't my father have chosen a woman of substance? Why couldn't he have married my mother's own sister, Aunt Maria! In her clean black dress, her hands folded patiently under her white apron, she was the anchor we both longed for, wasn't she?

My father and Cornelia repeated their vows. My father slipped the gold betrothal ring from his own finger onto hers and doubled his wife's wealth. He threw a handful of coins down on the table. Under his hat, his face looked pale, transparent. I imagined suddenly I could see through it. I could see the stork settling into the bramble of straw on the nearby roof. I could see gulls from the sea wheeling in the square. I could see my father's second thoughts clogging his throat like a nutmeg.

Cornelia rose on tiptoe and turned her cheek to my father. She was looking away from us all, looking down on the registry book open on the table, at the coins my father had tumbled there to seal his vows. She took nothing for granted, this woman. Nothing except my father. But right there, he surprised her. He gathered her in his arms and lifted her right off the floor. Then, placing her on her feet again, he removed his hat, hid their faces with it from the assembled room. Everyone heard the smacking of his lips, her gasp.

Everyone laughed, clapped. They clustered round my father and his red-cheeked bride like chickens round the feed pail.

"Come, come," my father said, blushing himself, bowing his head right and left. "Everyone is welcome at the Golden Head. There is enough food to feed—"

The Molijns, I thought. The Van Leeuwens. The Van Berchs. The Uyttenbroucks. The Swalmius. The Brands. But will there be enough for me? Not, certainly, if my Cousin Antoni Molijn had been left to his own devices. But he wasn't. His mother slapped his hand when he began to fill his plate a sixth time. His father, Uncle Jan, pulled the tumbler from him and emptied out the small beer—into his own gaping mouth.

I sat between my Aunt Catharina from Rotterdam and my Aunt De Mey at the foot of the table. Dr. de Graaf had joined us for the wedding feast and was seated between Cornelia and her sister Elisabet. He looked pleased. Less so Catharina Swalmius, who sat beside my drunken Uncle Jan Molijn, or the Uyttenbrouck cousins who sat, their bright slithering silks muffled by our black wool, between my father's sisters, his brothers-in-law.

"We've done ourselves proud," my Aunt Maria whispered to me. When I looked at her in surprise, she nodded at the green boughs we had arranged over the fireplace, the wreath on the door.

"Excuse me," I said, rising so hurriedly from my seat that I tumbled wine from my glass onto my new dress.

"Never mind," I said to Aunt Catharina, who, pulling her napkin from her lap, made ready to press it out.

"Where's she off to?" I heard my cousin Antoni ask in that high voice of his that sounded like you'd caught a dog by its tail.

"Perhaps it is the excitement," I heard De Graaf say. "It is not so long since her illness."

I felt my cheeks flame. I wanted to go back and lean over the table, balancing myself with my fists, and scold them just as roundly as my Aunt Gryetgen would anyone who presumed on her authority. It was *my* house, wasn't it? Hadn't my Aunt Maria and I worked for weeks to show it at its best? There were no dusty corners, no unrubbed glass, no unpolished stairs. The linens were all washed and counted—and room made for those Cornelia would bring. And the food—how many trips to the market, how many lists did my friend Maria make out for me?

If I had gone into the kitchen for refuge, I found even less there than I did in my own mind. All the young cousins had excused themselves and tumbled now on the kitchen floor, while the two maids, laughing as loudly as the guests at table, carved more smoked meat onto a platter, ladled more stew from the pot hanging over the flames. A girl a little older than me drew two more pitchers of wine. She was my Aunt Catharina's new servant, who had come with them from Rotterdam to assist us.

You'd think they'd been waiting a decade for this—all my relatives.

"Yes, Mejuffrouw?" One of the big ruddy women by the fireplace clapped her friend's shoulder so that she should not waver.

"The cakes and breads are ready?"

"Your sweet tooth nagging you, child?" the other woman asked with a laugh. She came from the Sheriff Brand's house. She had no idea who I was.

"Listen here." I stamped my foot and raised my voice to be heard over the small children's cries and the yipping of the dog. "This is my father's house. I am Maria, Antoni's daughter. This is my—" I pulled myself up short. "Do you have the bowl of cream prepared for the wedding couple?"

"What?" Jannetge, Aunt Gryetgen's maid asked, a look of glazed incomprehension on her face.

"Don't you remember?" I said. "I asked you. I know I asked you."

"It was me, Mejuffrouw." Aunt Catharina's maid dipped her head at me as she passed with two pitchers of wine. "I put it on the window ledge to keep it cool."

I lifted the bowl from the sill and stuck my finger into the mound of thickened cream. I grimaced when the bitterly sour and salty cream touched my tongue. It was exactly as it should be. I was pleased.

"I'll carry this in myself," I said. But those young cousins, on their stomach to roll marbles in the corner of the kitchen, did not appear to hear, nor did the others making the dog dance for scraps. The two serving women were fondling their mugs of beer, laughing into each others faces. But this wasn't like Christmas, it would never happen again—how could I reprimand them?

"This is for you, Father." I slipped the bowl between my father and his bride. It was our best blue Delftsware, and the cream mounded above it round and smooth as a woman's breast.

"What is this, child?"

"Gruel," laughed Dr. de Graaf. "But it's not deserved. You've years left, Antoni. And a healthy wife to keep you company through all of them."

"I heard it was a custom in Groningen." I looked for the first time directly at my stepmother. Her small eyes were a bright blue flecked with gold. Right now the whites of them were flushed, as were her cheeks, with wine and heat.

"Taste," I said waving the spoon I'd brought out just for them. "I made it for you." I dipped the spoon into the bowl and brought it heaped to my stepmother's mouth. She glanced nervously at her dress, her white uncovered neck. She opened her mouth—and I slipped the spoon in before she could protest. Then I turned and immediately did the same for my father.

"Baagh!" My father spit the cream out onto the plate.

"Why you—" My stepmother wiped at her stinging tongue with her napkin.

But the laughter bubbled right up from the bottom of my stomach. I had to sit down on the floor, the laughter poured forth with such force.

"What has the child done?" I heard De Graaf ask.

"Child?" Cornelia snapped. "She's old enough to know better."

"She salted the cream—"

"She what?" asked my Aunt Maria from the foot of the table.

"Wickedness," Cornelia hissed, looking over her shoulder at me.

"It isn't," I said. "It's an old custom. It's supposed to show—"

"What Antoni already knows. Marriage is both bitter and sweet." My Aunt Maria De Mey leaned over me and helped me to my feet. She kept her arm around me as she addressed Cornelia.

"She meant no harm, I can assure you. But she should have warned you. She should have explained."

As if anyone can warn another of the pain of love—or of its consuming pleasure.

"I'm sure she's sorry." My Aunt Maria pinched the inside of my arm until I gasped and the tears started from my eyes.

"Father," I said. "I—"

"Here, Van Leeuwenhoek, let me have a taste of that, will you?" De Graaf leaned forward and dipped his finger in the bowl.

"Oh no," Cornelia's sister Elisabet grimaced as she watched him suck the white paste into his mouth.

"Yech," De Graaf said, but he swallowed the cream back with the help of his wine. "But I've tasted worse. Better too. There's a man here in this town who has blood that turns to milk. Add a little sal vitriol and it will set ten times firmer than this. But it is sweet to the tongue, not foul like this."

"Hendrik van Beuren, the brewer's servant, is that the one?" my father asked knowledgeably. "I wonder if I looked at this cream through my glass whether I should discover the cause of its sharpness."

"No harm in trying," De Graaf said. "You might look at this man's blood, or your own."

"You'll not bleed him, Doctor," my Uncle Molijn called, "not before his great endeavors."

"Never," De Graaf cried out, smiling broadly.

"The players have come," my cousin Magriete called.

All the women rose from the table, as did my Uncle Molijn and my Uncle Leeuwen. Cornelia's cousin the predikant came too, but he might as well not, for he spent the entire time leaning against the wall, his arms folded close over his breast like a bat. De Graaf and my father did not rise from the table until Aunt Catharina went back and took each of them by the arm. She scooped up the salt they'd spilled and tossed it over her shoulder, shaking her finger at them as if they were small boys.

"You're a naughty lass," my Uncle Molijn said, whirling me round the room. "But nothing near as bad as your own father when your grandmother married a second time. It wasn't enough to set nails in my father's chair, he spilled a tankard of beer into his lap and then claimed my father had fouled himself."

"Antoni? Antoni Phillipszoon?"

"Hush now, Jacob," my Aunt Gryetgen her husband as she passed by us dragging my cousin Antoni by his spindly arms. "That's all long and gone."

"Hmmph."

I was inclined to agree with my Uncle Molijn.

"Like father like son," my father always muttered when my Aunt Gryetgen complained of her husband. It wasn't enough that his mother had betrayed him by her marriage to a Molijn, his sister had done so as well by marrying her step-father's son.

"He never forgave my father for sending him off to his uncle in Benthuizen. He forgets he had more than a little to do with it. Don't you," he said, pulling me close to his hot chest. "Don't you forget."

"Forget what?" I said, breaking free.

There was no way that evening or the morning to follow I could forget that a new power had entered our house.

♛ ♛ ♛

The players my Uncle Claes had hired for the occasion gathered by the front door and played without pause for the next two hours.

"No spinet?" I heard Elisabet Swalmius whisper to her sister Catharina.

"No music of any kind," Catharina said with a shudder.

No music, I thought, clapping my hands and singing with all the rest. Here, in my own home? Why had I never noticed?

Cornelia now proved to be as fleet of foot as she would later prove fleet of tongue.

I watched my father, his face flaming red under his hat, his thin hair sticking to his cheek like weeds to a swimmer. He kept his eyes trained on Cornelia's feet, the square toes of her violet shoes.

As De Graaf turned me round the room, I looked beyond the blinding swirl of colored silks to my own family standing or sitting round the edges of the room. How dark and coarse their woolen dresses and trousers, how plain their white collars. How red their faces, how uncouth their speech.

But *these*, I thought, looking round at the women with their uncapped hair drawn high on their heads, the curls dangling round their ears, the long dresses scattering the sand I'd poured in such regular rolling waves across the floor, these were the daughters of predikants?

"Turn her round, Antoni," called Uncle Claes.

But my father, his arm round Cornelia's waist, stopped dead in the center of the room.

"Kiss her, Antoni," yelled my Uncle Molijn. "Get on with it."

"Yes, yes, let's sing them to their rest," cried out Aunt Catharina. "So that we can get our own," she whispered to me with a wink.

My father's sisters clustered round the couple. Cornelia, with a sudden toss of her head, a wide bold smile, drew closer to my father.

Then, clapping hands, singing at the top of their lungs, the whole crowd, men and women, girls and boys, pushed my father and Cornelia up the stairs to the marriage bed upon which Aunt Maria and I had carefully arranged my father and Cornelia's wedding shifts.

"Come," Catharina Swalmius said, giving me a little shove when I hesitated at the foot of the stairs.

"Yes, my dear," my Aunt Catharina van Leeuwen said, catching me up on the other side. "See them off. Then you can come with us to sleep at your Aunt Gryetgen's."

"Who's she going to favor," called Uncle Molijn pushing into my father's bedroom. "Who's caught the bride's eye for the last time?"

"Not you, old man," muttered Catharina Swalmius.

"All right, all right," Cornelia cried out, seating herself on the edge of the bed and drawing up her skirt to remove her garter. "But then you must all leave us in peace the rest of the night. No caterwauling under the windows."

In the light from the fire, her hair looked like wire, something bright and sharp.

"Well, now, who's the one to long for what he's lost?" asked Uncle Claes.

"Ai," moaned my cousin Antoni. "Whiter than cream it is."

"You little goat," scolded Aunt Gryetgen.

"Like father like son," I muttered.

"Hush." Aunt Catharina tapped the top of my skull loud enough to rattle my brain. "We're taking Maria with us, Antoni," she called out to my father with a merry wave of her hand.

"You'll not stay in my house?" he said to his favorite sister, turning his back to his wife, the puddle of men at her feet.

"*Tonight*, Brother? Certainly not! We're off to Gryetgen's. But we will stop by tomorrow before we catch the barge for Rotterdam."

"Maria can stay with me tomorrow," my Aunt De Mey added.

"Maria! She'll do nothing of the sort," my father exclaimed. "No child of mine will be driven out into the cold."

"Into the *cold*, Antoni? My house is as warm as your own," scolded Aunt Gryetgen.

"I'll have no child of mine driven into the arms of the Molijns," my father muttered stubbornly. As if, after my mother died, that wasn't where he'd tossed me himself.

"I'll take her then," Aunt Maria De Mey said, touching my father gently on the arm.

"No," my father said. "She'll sleep in her own bed. There's never a night in my child's life she won't find shelter under my roof."

"For God's sake, think of her, Antoni," Aunt Maria whispered.

"Who is it to be, my beauty?" crowed Uncle Molijn leering at Cornelia Swalmius as she waved her garter in the air.

"Me, me. Please me," squealed cousin Antoni.

"Maria," my father said sternly. He broke through the throng of aunts. He held my face in both his hands, then kissed me, a dreadful smacking on the lips.

"Now off with you," he muttered. "No argument. To bed."

"Yes," I said. "Yes, Father." I tucked my head down, afraid to look at anyone. I pushed my way out of the room.

"It's not right," I heard Aunt Maria De Mey say, her voice ringing like a struck glass.

"You don't understand," Aunt Catharina said. "He's remembering our mother's marriage to Jacob's father. There was never a child felt so angered and betrayed as our Antoni at eight."

"But Maria is not eight," Aunt De Mey said. "She's nearly a woman."

"And who's the lucky man?" screamed Aunt Gryetgen as I turned the corner of the stairs.

"De Graaf. De Graaf."

"Not at all," yelled out De Graaf. "It's Antoni. Antoni van Leeuwenhoek."

I closed my bedroom door.

♔ ♔ ♔

A house is never silent. Even if its only inhabitant is a mouse or a bat. The wood creaks, the chimneys sigh, the panes of glass rattle in their lead casings. But alone in my room I heard far more than that.

First there was the great clattering on the stairs as my uncles and aunts and cousins retreated from my father's room amid wild shouts and wilder laughter. The mutter and footsteps as they collected cloaks, children, servants. The sudden silence, the harsh coughing as the winter air caught in their throats when they stepped out of the Golden Head onto the Hippolytusbuurt. Then there were their footsteps echoing on the cobblestones, footsteps echoing on the bridge. The watchman calling the hour.

Then there was only the moaning of the wind in the flue, the barking of a dog. I took the bed warmer from its hook by the hearth and opened it and filled it with smoking coal. I took it to my bed and, drawing the curtains apart, slipped it between my sheets. Back and forth I pushed it. The floor creaked under my feet, the walls of the bed creaked, the steps groaned as I drew them across the floor and placed them beside the bed.

Outside a cat wailed. A dog barked repeatedly. Above my head I could hear a soft eerie sound, like a fingernail scratching silk—mice, or rats, shuttling across the floor upstairs. Or was it a bat, trapped amid the drying sheets? The barking dog seemed chained fast under my window. When I went to look out my window after I had hung the bed warmer back by the fire, I saw that the dog did indeed bark for me, or for someone else within this house.

It was the little white dog my Aunt Catharina had given my father for Christmas the year after my mother died. He'd been driven out into the yard by the maids. As if he'd seen me at my window, he stood suddenly on his hind legs and yipped wildly, then fell back on his haunches and howled.

I couldn't leave him out there to freeze in his thin, silky coat. I couldn't leave him alone. I slipped my shoes from my feet and started stealthily from my room. I shouldn't have been concerned. Just as I opened the door, a pair of cats began a deafening caterwaul, under the cover of which I raced down the stairs holding myself up by both banister and wall to lighten my tread.

Fire still smoldered in both the front room and the second room, filling the house with a dull red glow. I could see plates still scattered across the table, glasses upturned, napkins tossed upon the floor. The kitchen too was filled with deep shadow, frightful glimmerings. Outside the door, the little white dog yipped and moaned.

"Come, come," I scolded him in a whisper.

"Hungry?" I asked. But how could he be? Hadn't my young cousins from Rotterdam done nothing but make him prance and plead for scraps of meat, scrapings of fat? I went to the pot on the hearth and dipped out a bowl. I placed it down on the hearth.

But it wasn't food the dog now capered and cried for, it was human warmth. Scrabbling at my skirt as if it were earth, he dug under both skirt and petticoat. He lay flat across my stockinged feet.

"No," I hissed, lifting my skirt high. "No, no, no." I leaned down and slapped at the silky, supple body, so hot and soft it made my hands tremble. "Away with you," I said, desperately giving him a shove, first with my hand, then with the top of my foot.

Shameless, he faced me, furiously barking. "*Hush*," I moaned. "*Hush*."

I picked up my skirts and walked as quickly as I could from the kitchen. I closed the door behind me. The dog yipped twice, scratched the door, then settled down with a sigh.

The silence was terrible as I made my way back past the littered table and disheveled front room to the stairs. The soles of my feet stung from the sand slipping through the threads in my stockings.

Again, supporting my weight with both my hands I made my way quietly as I could up the stairs. As I reached the landing, I heard the sounds from my father's room. A rustling of sheets, a low sob, a long breath let out in a gasp. No matter how softly I tried to move, stair, wall, and banister all advertised my presence. My still weight was more insidious than the wind; it set the whole house jarring.

Drawing my breath, rising on my toes, I ran fast as I could up to my own room. Breathless, I pressed my door closed behind me, but not before I heard the two mingled cries, so high and sharp with sorrow I felt my own eyes smart.

This was the fate held in store for all of us? My mother, my aunts Maria, Gryetgen, and Catharina, my poor Uncle Claes, even my cousin Antoni, my friend Maria. Weeping softly, I made my way to my bed. I slipped my skirt off and climbed between the sheets.

Thought, I say, came back to me. Or was it only a memory from my early childhood? The sound of my parents in the bed above my trundle. No, not simply that. For the sound above me had been like the tumbling of pups, it had been filled with speech and laughter. "Me," I had called out in glee. "Play with Maria!" And my father had tugged me up over the edge of the bed by my wrists. I'd settled between them with a crow of laughter. Their hairs brushed my forehead like a summer mist.

But the cry I heard my father's second wedding night seemed to have no laughter in it, no joy. My poor father. But I'd had no hand in his choice, so what could I, a witless girl, do to save him from it?

Nothing. I need not tell you that. But all night I tossed in bed as if I heard flames licking the boards of the banister, the stairs, the locked door, the floorboards, the feet of my own bed.

Imagine my surprise then, when I woke to find it was my own shift and sheets that were stained. My own eyes the Devil had blackened.

At dawn I'd woken to bird song, a dull pain throbbing in my loins, gray as the fog filming the windows. It was only when I twisted in bed, I felt the damp and understood. What I felt was the deepest shame, as if I'd been a small child caught out by the reek of piss. But I was alone in my room; the only one who saw the stained shift I tugged off was me—and Cornelia, who discovered me in the kitchen an hour later pouring the second bucket from the well into the laundering pan.

"What *is* this? Laundering when the table is still covered with dirtied glasses and plates!"

I tried to nudge the soiled bundle into the corner with my foot. Cornelia's breath made a huge frosty globe in the air.

"And was it you let the dog loose in the house last night?"

"Only in the kitchen." I was pleased to follow this shift in subject. "It was so cold last night, besides, the howling kept me awake."

Then, to my surprise, Cornelia's face flamed. She put her hands to her cheeks.

"Never mind," she said. "Your father will be down within the quarter hour. We must clear the table."

"And set the kettle going for his tea. We should do that first. My father doesn't see a thing save the steaming cup until he's swallowed his fourth infusion."

"But *I* do," Cornelia said. "And I refuse to sit and break my fast among last nights dregs and crusts."

Although she pursed her lips, the expression on her face wasn't anger, rather a frightened petulance, similar to my young cousin Phillip when he was denied a second candy stick. It moved me.

"Just a minute. Let me dip these in, and then I will assist you."

"Assist—" Cornelia began, but glimpsing the gleaming irregular blotch on the sheet, she rushed forward. "What *is* this? On *my* linens."

"My mother's linen."

For the first time since rising, the claws of shame that had gripped my skull eased their hold.

"Are you still ill?" she asked, dropping the sheet so it draped the vat like a sleeper's arm. "They should have told me."

"It's the curse."

"Careless," she said with a disdainful toss of her head. "Make sure you salt the stain. And the water should be drained right into the canals. It blights everything it touches."

"Fiddle," my father said. "It's as natural as spit, or piss. If Our Maker cursed women with anything it was with birth's travail."

"I don't want to hear of it," Cornelia said, tossing her head from me to my father and then, in desperation, to the kitchen door.

"Well, let's leave Maria to her task then. I will help you with the table—and my tea."

"These must soak a day," I said. "I will set the kettle on myself, Father."

"And bring in the bread, butter, and milk," Cornelia said as she brought in a load of dishes and set them with a clang and clatter on the cupboard shelf. "Then you can clean these. I trust you don't intend to leave them too to soak until tomorrow."

When I'd brought in the bread and butter, then finally the steaming pot of tea, it was my father slapped the table at his right hand. "Now sit, child."

As I pulled back my chair, I saw his left hand rest caressingly over Cornelia's. The face she lifted to him was shy, dazzled.

I tore a piece from the loaf but left it untasted on my plate. I folded my hands in my lap and waited. Cornelia with a laugh freed her hand. She tore bread for both of them.

"What is it now?" she asked a full minute later, swallowing her tea with a little exasperated gulp.

When I didn't answer, she turned to my father. "Are you sure she isn't ill again? Did she ever fully recover?"

"Come, Daughter. Out with it."

"Grace," I said. "I don't remember a day with you that hasn't begun with it."

"Nor shall you, child. This day will be no different." But he swallowed his mouthful of bread back with a swallow of tea.

We all bowed our heads.

"Father," he said. "Forgive your son's impetuousness this morn, but it is born of his delight in both your creations, rye and women. Bless this table and this house. Bestow on me, as you did on Adam, the power to make my wife fruitful."

"That's it?"

"At *table*?" Cornelia asked, the look of happiness on her face extinguished now.

"Why not?" he answered both of us. "I expect your husband to offer the same prayer when the time comes, Maria. And what better time, Wife, to pray for fruitfulness than when we see what Our Maker daily brings forth effortlessly from our mother earth?"

"Those sheets, Maria. Perhaps you'd not mind laundering our own as well."

"She hasn't the strength yet," my father said. He pushed his plate from him. "Besides," he muttered, reaching for the tea pot, "I can't see the need."

"What?" Cornelia whispered.

But my father was already swallowing off his third cup of tea and the sweat was gathering in beads on his forehead, washing down his cheeks.

As I washed the dishes from the wedding feast, I heard my father and Cornelia, still seated at table, murmuring in lowered voices. The hum was interrupted by my father's full, bumbling laugh, by Cornelia's, sharp as scissors. Then there was silence. I drew the scrubbed dishes from the water and dried them and put them on the cupboard shelves as slowly as I could. At first I was stealthy in my work, then a bold carelessness filled me and I began singing to myself—an old lullaby my mother had sung over every child's cradle.

But although I sang until I finished the dishes, I could as well have kept my mouth sealed. When I entered the dining room to collect the breakfast dishes, Cornelia and my father were nowhere to be seen.

Upstairs I heard the door slam.

Now I can look back at my father's first ardor for his wife with amusement, but that morning and for the entire week to follow, the sound of that bedroom door slamming shut echoed through my soul.

I did everything I could to drown it out. I slammed my own door, or the front door in answer. I kicked the dog and set him to barking. I washed dishes, scoured floors, chopped vegetables. I sang, hummed the melody if I could not recall the words. I recited the alphabet as if it were a psalm. The only thing I did not do was pray. I did not want to draw God's attention to the licentious Golden Head.

If He looked, he could not have missed them. They were everywhere. In the kitchen, tasting the huidspot, on the patio, testing the strength of the frost-bitten vines, in the front room rearranging the tables and chairs, in my father's study, perusing his books of geometry. They were up in the drying room, they were opening the linen cupboard. Even if my father and his new wife stood apart, there was some force in the air between them. It made my heart stutter just to come near. But the heart's sad tolling when they were gone—to Rotterdam, or 'sGravenhage, or a walk in the meadows by the Oostpoort—that was even worse.

"How goes it at the Golden Head?" Maria Vermeer asked me, meeting me at the fish market. "Your father is satisfied with his new wife?"

How could I reply?

"It's all the same to me." I brushed my keys, making them jangle like bells. "My life hasn't changed. I still cook and clean. I am still mistress of the Golden Head."

Cornelia too those first weeks, brushing her hair before the mirror, seeing herself dissolve in my watering eyes or disappear behind my father's swooning lids, must have needed more than once to assure herself of her place and purpose.

The first few weeks it seemed she'd choose to be my father's constant companion. When they weren't talking together, or taking strolls through the town, she was trying to read the books of geometry and medicine, the accounts of sea voyages and treatises on botany that my father kept on top of the cabinet in his study. But before she knew it, all had changed. Again my father followed his old habits. He left his house daily for his tasks at the stadthuis; he met with his friend De Graaf; he visited my Aunt Catharina and Uncle Claes in Rotterdam by himself.

What had happened? I wasn't sure at the time, but now I think I know. *Then*, I thought my father's indifference was due to what he had overheard, as I had, of the conversations between Cornelia and her scornful sister Catharina. Catharina Swalmius did not visit her sister for the first two weeks. When she did come, she rapped on the door loud as a man. She brushed me aside as if I were a serving maid. When she found her sister in the front room reading one of the learned treatises my father had recommended to her, she mistook it, as I had so often with my father, for the Holy Book.

"Well, Sister. I'm pleased to see you so profitably occupied. Will you read to me?" She sat herself down without invitation in the chair on the far side of the hearth that was usually reserved for my father. I stood at the door, waiting to see if I should fetch her something to eat.

Catharina turned round in her chair and stared at me. "Well? Don't you have lessons, child?"

Catharina's face was pitted from small pox, but she carried herself with a haughty air all the same.

"Go on," Cornelia said, looking up with a blank expression, as if what she had been reading had loosened her ties on the day and hour. "Go visit with your friend Maria if you will. Just be sure to be home to dine with your father." She closed the book with a clap. "Off now," she said again.

Red-faced, cross, I went upstairs to fetch my cloak. As I came down, I heard Catharina scolding her older sister.

"It's not fitting. Just imagine what Adriaen would have said if he came home for dinner and found you sitting beside the fire reading."

"I never heard my brother volunteer a kind word for me, whatever I did," Cornelia said crossly.

"It's not as if there isn't work to be done here," Catharina said, her voice ominously soft. "No servants—"

"But the house is mine," Cornelia said. "No brother's marriage will ever evict me, no brother's death."

"You still harbor resentment, Sister?"

"How can you say that, Catharina? What more could I want than what I have? A good husband who loves and honors me—"

"A child who—"

"Bread, soap, brush—is there anything else we need?" I rattled as I passed through the room.

"Not a thing," Cornelia said with a yawn.

"You trust all the marketing to her, Sister?"

Oh, how I wanted to pinch Catharina Swalmius' fat pocked cheek!

When I returned, Cornelia was alone, stalking around and around the front room in a frenzy.

"Butter," she said, before I'd even emptied my basket. "You forgot the butter. From now on I will accompany you to the market." As she spoke, she trailed me through the house to the kitchen.

I removed my cloak. Cornelia stood with her arms crossed watching me store the day's purchases.

"Now, Maria," she said. "I want your assistance. Before your father comes home, I want to remove the plates above the mantel. I want to put in their place—"

She didn't complete her thought, just turned and marched off into the front room to await me. And when I arrived, her suggestions, her actions, were equally incomplete. She would move a chair, push it back against the wall again. "Have we no tapestries? No paintings? This room is plainer than the church."

I looked at our front room with eyes as restless and discontent as her own. Catharina Swalmius had unsettled us both.

"At the Mechelen—" I began, but at that moment Cornelia caught sight of my father crossing the bridge, and she rushed up the stairs to prepare herself—as if she were a girl of twenty and he had come courting for the first time.

When Cornelia's cousins Uyttenbrouck and Brand and her sister Elisabet came later that week, she had no book by her side, rather her mandolin. No sooner than they entered, she disparaged the furnishing of the room.

"Antoni has promised—" she said in a voice high enough to be heard over the laughter of her cousins. "Soon my own portrait—"

"Antoni! Antoni! Just listen to you!" Her cousin Susannah laughed.

"You'd think him the Prince of Orange."

"Let her enjoy it," said Susannah's mother. "It will end soon enough. Soon as we burn the cord."

"No," Cornelia said flatly. "Absolutely not."

It wasn't the cord Cornelia burned that spring—but her own monthly rags. I think she did it only once, late in April, the first time. What did she hope to accomplish? Certainly, she knelt on the kitchen hearth as ashen faced as a woman in travail.

When I called her name, she gave a cry and pushed what she held crumpled in her hand quickly under the tier of smoking peat. At first I thought it was a letter, but the flame caught so slowly, and there was no merry conflagration, just a foul smoking.

"What is it?"

When she looked at me, her face seemed sharp and cautious as a rat's.

"Nothing," she hissed. "Nothing.

"Yes, yes it is," I said, stepping forward and reaching out for the prod to pull the smoking object from the fire. I really did not understand yet. I thought perhaps it was something of my mother's.

"I had such hopes," she said. "And so did he. I woke every morning sick with hope. Just hope . . ."

"There will be another chance," I said, beginning to understand.

She just stayed there on her knees with her hands folded in her lap. Her tight yellow curls brushed her plump shoulders. Deep lines cupped her small, pouting mouth.

I picked up the poker. I was cross. Crosser than I'd ever felt. It was my own pity angered me. It may not have been a letter she was burning, but her attempt to deceive my father was no whit less than it would have been if she were engaged in a secret correspondence.

"What a stench," I said, dragging the rag out of the fire. "I hope this will be the end of it. Bury them out back if you must conceal them."

"The blood blights the ground."

"Nonsense," I said. "It's no worse than other human excrement."

"Shut up," she screamed. "Shut up. Shut up. Shut up."

It was of course pure foolishness and fear on Cornelia Swalmius' part. She could not cheat my father—of hope or despair. Certainly not of anger, or the sudden indifference he did indeed show when the truth became known to him.

It was then he began to follow his old habits—his meetings with De Graaf, his evenings alone in his study, the silence broken only by the dull rasp of glass ground in the lens cup. It was then he began to notice what a sloven his wife was.

Briefly, it seemed a triumph for me. It was me he allowed in his study to dust his books, his work table. It was me he complimented on the day's meal; me to whom he made his requests for smoked eel, fresh plaice, shrimp, roast chicken.

"Yes, Father," I said, my pride tempered by fear. What if I should forget? I did not want to tumble, like his new wife, out of all favor.

It was my father's behavior that made Cornelia turn on me.

"I am mistress of the Golden Head now," she said to me a week after I had found her scrabbling among the ashes. She put out her hand. "The keys, Maria."

I imagined biting into her plump white hand, and my face flushed with shame. "Never," I said. Then, seeing her upper lip draw back exposing her own teeth, I added, "It is up to my father. It will be resolved as *he* wishes."

"Yes, yes," my father said when she met him at the door at noontime. "If it will stop the haggling, take them, Wife. She's still a child. She doesn't need to serve us."

"Serve!" Cornelia said.

For a moment his attitude quieted us both. It was obvious what we were seeking was to be found nowhere if not there, in his hand, his eye, his kindled smile.

It was obvious it was not to be found—or so we both, for our separate reasons, dreaded.

"Are you hungry?" I asked.

"The table's prepared," Cornelia added.

"What is the news at the stadthuis?" I asked when we were seated.

"I wasn't there," my father said curtly. "Dr. de Graaf kindly permitted me to attend the demonstration at the Anatomy Chamber."

"Yes."

"It's not fitting," he said, suddenly shoving his food from him and rising from the table. At the door, he paused, turned, the napkin dripping from his hands like a woman's apron.

"Bring some milk to my study," he said. "When you have finished your own repast."

"Yes," Cornelia said.

"Yes," I said, even louder.

But he had already turned on his heels and crossed the room.

"Poor father," I said. "It is the stench of death that unmans him. It's not his mind but his stomach that refuses to attend. I remember two years ago, when he saw Dr. de Graaf spill blood from one dog to another. Then the doctor filled the second beast with milk, saying milk and blood were the same thing. But, as any fool can see, they're quite distinct. One, in fact, is deadly—"

"Do stop," Cornelia hissed. "There's no one left to listen."

When I brought my father the pitcher of milk and a glass, he was seated at his large chair by the fire. He kept rubbing his hands with his napkin, front and back.

"Would you care for a damp cloth?"

"What?" He glanced up at me blinking, then back at the cloth in his hand. There was no mark on it that I could see. His hands were as red as if he'd held them over the fire.

"No, no," he said, shaking his hands roughly from the wrist as if they were wet. "We filled the veins today with molten wax. I assisted Dr. de Graaf, and I'm afraid I scalded my hands in the process."

"Wax?" I said. "Not this?" I poured milk into the glass and handed it to my father.

My father smiled faintly, brought the glass to his lips, then pulled it away again without sipping.

"Blood and milk are no longer the same to him—the good De Graaf?" I spoke to get my father to stop staring so wildly. "Now it's blood and wax? The poor man—"

"Man?" my father snapped. "We explored no man today, girl. It was a woman died in her first birth travail."

"And the child?"

"It stopped moving two days before the pangs began. We saw it too, its mouth open, gulping at the caul as if it were air. Like a kitten drowned in a sack."

"What does the good doctor say she died of, Father?"

"When we touched her breasts the milk spilled out, bluer than the light behind my glasses."

"And there was no blood?" I said, angry at him now.

"It had set like cement in the arteries and heart."

"So now the good doctor agrees with you?"

"What? "

"In women, there can only be the one or the other. Milk. Blood."

"There is constant strife, the doctor believes, between the juices in our blood."

"But a woman's milk? Is that a peaceful substance?"

"Enough," my father said, clapping his hands briskly. "It is not a fitting subject for a girl your age. It may make you forget you suffer this by God's just decree."

"Forget?" I asked, backing toward the door. "Me?"

One day in early June, Johannes Vermeer, seeing my stepmother and me together in the market square, beckoned us over to the bench outside the Mechelen.

"So this is your stepmother, Maria."

Cornelia just lifted her sharp chin and said nothing.

"This is Heer Johannes Vermeer," I said. He is the headman of the St. Lucas Guild."

"Yes," Cornelia condescended to speak at last. "I am the wife of Heer Antoni van Leeuwenhoek."

"Ai, ai!" whispered Maria Vermeer coming up beside me and putting her arm around me. "Will you come inside?"

"Inside?" Cornelia reared back.

"Heer Boogaert does, so does the schout. My father's collection of paintings is notable."

"You haven't seen the ones I did of the child," encouraged Johannes. "Or the one of Maria, my daughter."

"Papa is using young Catharina now," Maria added. "He makes her wear leaves on her head like a statue. And papa dresses himself like the young Rembrandt."

"Rembrandt?" I asked.

"Ah yes," Cornelia nodded. "Rembrandt painted one of my relations—Predikant Henricus Swalmius."

"And I," Vermeer said grandly, "will paint a predikant's daughter."

Poor Cornelia. The bare walls of the Golden Head flashed before her. How could she refuse? She agreed to the painting Johannes had in mind all along just because she couldn't bear the idea of dressing in black with a plain white collar, the Statenbibjl held in both her hands like a small casket of jewels.

"We'll set it here," Johannes said, leading her into the second room of the Mechelen. "With the gilded leather behind you showing you to be a woman of much standing."

"And my mandolin?"

"She doesn't know my father, does she?" Maria whispered. "What will she say when she finds he spends more time on the tiles, the leather, even the mandolin than he will on her face?"

What would she say?

Nothing—or everything. Cornelia brought her sister Catharina along to the sittings, and the two of them chattered as if they were alone, speaking of my Aunt Gryetgen's jealousy, my Uncle Jan's lechery. But my true shame came when Cornelia suggested to Johannes he dress his daughter as her servant. My own friend Maria!

"A woman in her position," Cornelia said, pointing to the woman whose shoulders were just now taking shape in the armchair in the center of the canvas, "surely there would be someone there to assist her."

"My *daughter*?" asked Catharina Bolnes, coming to the door for the fourth time that morning. "She has to assist me. Why don't you include your own step-daughter." She wandered around the room, her eyes flicking back and forth fast as a whip. "Wrap this cloth around her head, and this other round her waist as an apron—she'll look as if she just trudged in from the polders."

"Mother!"

"Enough," Johannes said with a laugh. But the glance he cast at his wife was thoughtful, and he did not object when she took me by the arm and tugged me into the center of the room to stand behind Cornelia. If I'd had a knife, I think there were moments in the days to come when I would have gladly plunged it into that wad of flesh that padded Cornelia's white shoulders, would have gladly changed that piercing giggle to a squeal.

As it was, I stood where I was placed, my eyes fixed stubbornly on the far corner of the room. I wouldn't look at Johannes or Cornelia. I did my best to keep my back to Catharina Swalmius, who sat there chittering, as cruelly indifferent to my fury as her sister. There were times standing there I wished for the fever to stall the blood in my brain again, set it hard as the blood of the dead. There were times I wished I had never relearned my name—or that I could forget for good the place I now filled in the world.

Even now, I can't look at the painting without a feeling of acute shame—for both of us. That plain dim maid, that proud woman decked in yellow silk and fur, ringed with pearl. The squalor is intolerable—the squalor of both our hearts.

Cloths hang damp and twisted over the rim of a basket. The tapestry is raised in a careless swag to reveal the room within. Crumpled sheets of music litter the seat of the chair. The strings of the map hanging in the corridor dangle along the wall, seeming, at first glance, to be cracks in the wall itself. A broom, discarded slippers, bar the passage to the far room. There the mistress of the house sits on a stool in the middle of the room, a lute clasped by its frets in her left hand. In her right hand she holds a small envelope. Her head is turned to the right. A pearl earring dangles from her ear, pearls ring her plump white throat, something bright dandles from her small silk cap. All you can see are the whites of her eyes, as shiny as pearls. The look of her gaping mouth is both fearful and speculative.

She looks, I must say this, quite stupid. But the maid, hand on her hip, mending basket on the floor, looks not one whit smarter.

What news has come into that house in a letter folded twice over into a square no bigger than a woman's hand? Even now, I am sure only that its meaning would be as completely different for mistress and maid as the meaning of the portrait itself was for my stepmother and me. But I know also it made no difference that I saw shadow where Cornelia saw light, we were both groping through mists. All Cornelia and I both saw was the future, and that—no one shows us more clearly than Johannes—is the vainest delusion of all.

But no one could have convinced us. It was as pointless to try and make Cornelia doubt the reading of the fortune teller she consulted at the St. Odulphus fair. Cornelia was going to be a woman of position in the town, the fortune teller assured her. She was going to be married to a great man.

"Antoni?" her sister Catharina asked when Cornelia announced this as she took her place on the stool in the Mechelen. Silently, Johannes took his place before the easel.

"She just said husband," Cornelia said, smoothing out her yellow jacket.

"And children?" Catharina goaded her sister. "How many? Did she say?"

"She never mentioned—" Cornelia said with a snort of anger.

Well, the fortune teller may have been right, but Cornelia's understanding was always a dutiful handmaiden to her desires. When, in the fall, for example, Lord Zuleichem, the old and venerable Constantijn Huygens, came to visit my father for the first time, Cornelia never understood that it was the beginning of my father's fame. No, she was convinced that there was to be another husband in time, and, in preparation, she wanted to bring herself to the attention of the Princess Dowager's illustrious secretary.

I was no more observant. Every time I heard Cornelia say "I, I, I," *I* felt the ground open under my feet and saw my whole life, past and future, hammered like stakes into a marsh. I was sure it was to be over my body, over the body of my dead mother, Cornelia intended to fashion, and furnish, her dreams.

☙ ☙ ☙

Seigneur van Zuleichem came to the house escorted by Heer Boogaert, one of the leaders of our town and a director of our East India Company. He, like Dr. D'Aquet, kept a cabinet of curiosities. The worth of my father's lenses had newly come to the burgomaster's attention, so, when Seigneur van Zuleichem asked about lens makers (for it was here in Delft his sons had purchased years before the lenses for the telescope with which they discovered the emanations around the planet Saturn), Heer Boogaert promptly mentioned 'the worthy Van Leeuwenhoek'. But my father, so he himself told Seigneur van Zuleichem as they all stood in my father's study, crafted lenses to please himself, not to profit any man.

Heer Boogaert flushed and looked away from my father as he spoke.

Seigneur van Zuleichem laughed, and my father, his mouth first sagging in suspicion, at last joined in. "A true practitioner of your art," Seigneur van Zuleichem complimented him. "I can remember trying to suggest to Rembrandt—"

"Rembrandt?" my father asked, blinking furiously. "Malpighi I've heard mentioned. The Englishman, Robert Hooke. But Rembrandt?"

"A *painter*," blurted Cornelia. "From Amsterdam, Husband. He painted my reverend great-uncles Henricus and Elias Swalmius."

"A painter," my father said with a shrug.

"But he also let no man set a price upon his labors," Seigneur van Zuleichem said.

"Ah," my father coughed. "Would you like to inspect something through my glass? Let's see. Maria, bring me a length of that black kersey. And you, Wife," he said, when Cornelia rested her back against the wall, quite content to remain, "would you bring our visitors refreshments?"

Cornelia flushed the most perfect crimson. Oh, it made my heart turn round in my chest to see it. First her chin, then her cheeks, then her forehead. Only the hollows under her eyes remained white, as if someone had lined them with chalk.

Without looking up, I put the cloth on the table.

"Maria," Cornelia said, taking me by the upper arm, catching my flesh between her damp white fingers and giving it a painful tweak. "Come with me, let us leave the gentlemen to their conversation."

"A shopkeeper," she muttered stalking back and forth across the kitchen as I drew the small beer for the pitcher. "And treating me like a servant maid. Reprimanding me. Me! When he didn't even recognize the name of Rembrandt!"

"You didn't recognize the name of Huygens," I said. "And my father was familiar with his duties as Secretary of the Princess Dowager and also with the learned studies of his son."

"Before Heer Boogaert too!" Cornelia went on, ignoring the tray I held out to her. She put her hand to her head, checking the curls that hung in tatters before her ears. "It is just as Catharina has suggested. My life is—"

"No more onerous than this task," I said. "Will you carry the tray or shall I?"

But when we went into the front room, the men had their cloaks round their shoulders again. My father was shaking the hand of Seigneur van

Zuleichem.

"I beg your pardon, Juffrouw. I must catch the next barge to 'sGravenhage. The Dowager Princess waits for no man."

"Nor does the barge," laughed the burgomaster.

"May I come again?" Seigneur van Zuleichem asked my father.

"Any day save Tuesday when my obligations at the stadthuis will prevent me from waiting on you." My father started to make a small bow but stopped himself.

"I will remember," Seigneur van Zuleichem said. "And I will be back. The quality of your glasses, sir, is such as would honor a regular practitioner of the art."

"As long as they allow me to trace Our Maker's handiwork," my father said.

"Well, well," my father muttered, watching the two men turn the corner into the Nieuwe Straat. He scratched his head, rubbed his hands together, then went back into his study and began to replace his glasses. He polished each with a rag, then held it up to the light. "Well, well," he said again, the smile on his face simple delight.

"I've never been so shamed," Cornelia said with a gulp.

"Shamed?" asked my father.

"Look at you," she said. "Look at me. Look at us. In my oldest dress, my skirts wet. You with no hat, less hair than the Princess Dowager's servant. What report will he take back of us?"

"To whom?" I asked, stepping between her and my father. "Do you think the old man came here to please anyone but himself? Yet it is an honor, a great honor, for my father."

"This is no gentleman's house," Cornelia said, waving wildly. "There are no paintings, no maps, no silver, nothing."

"I've told you, woman," my father growled. "You're free to change things as you see fit."

Poor father! A month later he was wearing a brown wig with hair that fell a hand's width lower than his shoulders. That was the sight that had stuck in Cornelia's mind, Heer Boogaert impatiently striding back and forth on the Hippolytusbuurt waiting for Seigneur van Zuleichem, the way the black curls of his wig tossed in the gentle south wind.

My father was not the only one to suffer from Cornelia's aspirations. From the middle of September on, I had to suffer daily the scornful sight of

Johannes' painting over our mantel.

"He presented it to us," Cornelia lied to my father when he stood before it blinking curiously. Well he should blink. On every wall now, Cornelia had imposed her own features or those of her forbears. Cousins descended from the noble Uyttenbroucks smirked right and left. It was as if the Van Leeuwenhoeks had never existed—or the De Meys. My father in mild defiance borrowed his own father's portrait from my Aunt Catharina in Rotterdam

"What have you done with my sister's plate?" my Aunt Maria De Mey asked my stepmother.

"It decorates my room now," I said, gently patting my godmother's trembling hand. "Come with me and I will show you."

I didn't want to hear again what Cornelia had to say about my mother—or what my Aunt Maria might say in response.

Want? As if my desire modified a single thought or action in that house.

But I emphasize myself too much. What I have described is the natural state of children. And in those years there were, for adults as well as children, events stranger by far than the individual will. Good? Evil? Who can tell? It was simply as if the course of one's life were without warning completely changed. Like a globule in the blood, one minute you were shunted away from the heart, the next, shunted back.

The experience was not, let me assure you, at all like watching the blood tumble through the eel's tail, constrained by those tiny vessels, twisted and turned in patterns more intricate than lace. There was no pattern. There was no perspective. I recall it now as blinding tumult, in the house as well as on the market square. I can see the fear flowing around us, a terrible clear liquor. *Rampjaar.*

RAMPJAAR: WHAT TORE US APART
1672

Rampjaar . . .

There are times in one's life that are worse to remember than they were to live through. The summer of '72 was that, the whole year in fact. Even now my mind baulks when I remember the French savagery at Zwammerdam and Bodegraven. And the way we ourselves tore our own statesmen to pieces, more wicked than wolves. Was that really, as Cornelia insisted until the day she died, Our Creator's inscrutable will? I say that to remember is painful, but I don't mean we ever forget. It is like learning the depth of one's own rage—or passion—a knowledge that threads like the finest transparent vessels through every flesh fibre in the body.

When I remember the summer of '72, I remember the small events. I retreat to them now, as my father might to his glasses when frightened by illness, harassed by grief. These memories are as small, clear and shapely as the veins and arteries in a tadpole's tail, or the trees of gold sal vitriol will leave etched onto a glass plate.

First, I remember the Vermeers removing to Johannes' mother's house on the Oude Langendijk in late May.

"Antoni's daughter," Johannes called from the door of the Mechelen. His face was gray with dust. He'd been up to the drying rooms, gathering sacks of flour they would take with them to the next house. "Take a message for me to Cornelia Swalmius. There's still ten guilders owing on her portrait."

"Ten guilders?" I remembered the argument Cornelia and my father had had just the day before when Cornelia purchased yet another ten ells of silk from Adriaen Beijeren.

"It can wait," he said. "Just as long as the apothecary waits for me."

"And me?"

"What would you be owing the apothecary?"

"My portrait?"

Johannes glanced over my head. When he looked back down at me, he was smiling just as freely as ever but there was a narrowing around his eyes.

"It had slipped my mind," he said.

"I haven't very much. But I will ask my Aunt Maria to loan me what is required."

"No," he said.

I felt my eyes smart. I couldn't explain to him how alone I felt as I watched his family folding linens, stacking plates, fitting candlesticks and tooled leather, jewelry cases and worn shoes into the barrows. I couldn't explain that I felt exactly the same every morning when I went downstairs and confronted Cornelia and her sister Catharina.

I wanted someone, you see, to keep me company when I faced those two blonde heads with their quivering curls, those narrow mouths that pursed and opened like fishes, those sharp chins they cupped in their hands like daggers in cases. It was obvious to me, when I glanced over my shoulder and saw my friend Maria standing beside her mother, each of their arms folded around their waists, that already they had fitted themselves, mother and daughter, into their new life as neatly as they would fit plates upon the mantel. The same was true of Cornelia and Catharina in *my* house. Now, everywhere, the eyes that scrutinized me did so with exasperation. I was the chipped plate belonging to the last life.

"Take it, child," Johannes said. "Catharina said it was a profitless exercise. I can't say I'm of the same mind, but she's never become accustomed to it—perhaps this is the time to put it behind me."

"Your Allegory, Husband," Catharina Bolnes had come up behind us so swiftly I could still feel the wind rocking my skirts, chilling my neck. "Have you wrapped it securely?"

"See for yourself," Johannes said.

"Off with you, child," Catharina said to me.

"Not yet," Johannes interrupted. "I'd like her to run a message for me. But come now, Catharina. First we will secure the painting."

I was just leaving when Johannes waved me over to the window.

When I came to him, he handed the panel to me over the sill.

"Put it in your basket," he said. "Tell no one."

This secrecy was his greatest gift. It meant I could hang her like a mirror within my sleeping cupboard. I could face each day secure at least in the face I carried. This illusion, I believe, saved me that terrible year. For of course, ever day knowledge engraved itself on my body—no one was spared, except the girl Johannes had crafted out of ground mineral and oil upon a wooden panel.

When I remember that time, I remember the flurry of voices, mobs. Grauw and burger, burgomaster and nobles, we spun round the country, round the town, round the house, running from the French army, running from our own, running from the peasants, running from the statesmen—a ceaseless tumult, hectic as a dying man's feverish pulse. It's impossible to keep it all straight now. Even more impossible then.

Take June for example. In three weeks, the French King Louis XIV had taken all our fortresses on the Rhine. He had taken Zutpen and Betuwe. The Bishops of Munster and Cologne had invaded Overijssel. Delft was already filled with people fleeing from the nearby country houses and from 'sGravenhage, which had no ramparts. Now people began coming from Utrecht, Deventer, Zwolle. They were escaping as much from our own forces as from the approaching French, for, in their shameful retreat, our own soldiers plundered mercilessly, as if goods could purchase courage.

Goods could not even purchase peace. Look at the burgers of Utrecht. Did they not bar our Prince of Orange himself from their city? Did they not bar our own troops? Not a tree would they fell, not a house in the suburbs would they burn to give our troops some barren plain on which to gather and barter for our future with musket, cannon, charred flesh, blood. No, they thought they would barter privately, peace for the Domkerk, the burgomasters' houses, their stadthuis itself. And the burgomasters of Utrecht were not alone. None of us wanted to believe—in the war, in our own weakness, or, worse, in our own perfidy.

On the eighteenth of June, Utrecht gave herself to the Sun King, no less willingly, it seemed, than Maria van Dijn gave herself to Regnier de Graaf a week later. Except the Sun King had mistresses by the score while the young Dr. de Graaf swore before God and priest to devote himself entirely to the obedient young girl from Gouda. It was the French King's licentiousness, then, made Utrecht a whore?

We may not have wanted to believe in the troops flooding now into all the houses of Utrecht—but we could not escape the truth. Into all the cities in Holland, the Protestants surged, their precious goods in sacks, in satchels, in baskets, barrels, wagons. The barges rode a foot deeper in the water, every man and woman traveled so weighted with pewter and gold. The papists, they all whispered, it is they who barred out the Prince of Orange, they who opened the city's gates to the King and Condé, to Luxembourg and Louvois. Papists. They will do the same here in Delft.

"It is De Graaf," Cornelia whispered to her sister. "Papist. Papist."

Catharina and Cornelia went each Sunday to both the Oude Kirke and the Nieuwe Kirke to pray and to hear the latest news. But we heard what we wanted. We made enemies of our countrymen more readily than of the French. The day the French King marched into Utrecht, my stepmother and her sister exulted in the wounds endured by our own Grand Pensionary, Johannes De Witt, when he was attacked by Peter and Jacob Van der Graeff walking home from the Binnenhof. The sisters walked by the house in Delft where the assassins' father, Judge Van der Graeff, and his wife had sought refuge weeks before, fearing the French invasion, giving not a thought to the danger posed to them by their impetuous and vengeful sons. But the day the Judge's son Jacob was executed, the sisters Swalmius gave no thought to the young man, nor to his victim the Grand Pensionary, for twenty years the leader of the States of Holland, still languishing in his house in 'sGravenhage. Justice was no concern of theirs. Only might. God, they said, intended the Prince of Orange as our king—failing that our Stadtholder. He intended that young boy to have the full powers of his father, his grandfather, and his great-grandfather.

So when, on the 28th of June the riots began in Dort, and the burgers summoned the burgomasters with muskets and pikes to revoke the Eternal Edict, thus allowing the Prince of Orange to become our Stadtholder, Cornelia and Catharina cawed like crows. Wasn't this what they themselves had called for? When the riots spread to Rotterdam, they opened their Bibles and began to recite psalms of thanksgiving. My father, on the other hand, took the barge to Rotterdam and, after consultation with my Uncle Claes, returned with my Aunt Catharina and their six children.

Ah, then the French were forgotten in our house. So were the papists. No longer did Catharina and Cornelia Swalmius tell me of the dangers attending my friendship with Maria Vermeer, no longer did they detail what the French would do when she handed us over to them, no longer did they grow haughty and silent when my father mentioned his friend De Graaf, muttering the Lord's name under their breaths to ward off the very thought of him—as if that sweet red-cheeked man were the Devil himself. No, now they concentrated on the enemy within their own gates. They concentrated on my Aunt Catharina van Leeuwen and her bold defense of the Grand Pensionary De Witt and his followers.

"De Witt sold us to the French," Catharina Swalmius said.

"It is the Prince who will save us," Cornelia said. She turned her back on Aunt Catharina, settled her mending bolster on her lap. "He couldn't fail. Have you seen him, Sister? I glimpsed him twice as he passed through the town. Such a bold eye."

"A *child*," scoffed Aunt Catharina. "What you see in his eyes is vainglory."

"Vainglory," exclaimed Catharina Swalmius. "What you see there is despair—at the treachery of the Grand Pensionary. He has robbed the Prince of soldiers, of the money to pay them—he has robbed the Prince and given it all to the Ruwaard, his own brother Cornelis de Witt, given it all to the Navy. And how will the Navy save us, I ask you, from that hunch-backed demon Luxembourg? How will it save us from Condé? They both come to us by land."

"It will save us from the English," I said.

"Save us! From the English—no one can save us from them save Prince William. It is for him the English King Charles is fighting."

"Is it?" Aunt Catharina asked. "Is it not for the Sun King's gold?"

"The Prince's uncle loves him as the son of which fate has deprived him."

"I've heard fate hasn't deprived King Charles of sons. He has bastards aplenty. More than he can count or the treasury can feed."

"The Prince of Orange is the legitimate leader of Holland," Cornelia interrupted. "The predikants say so. So do the nobles."

"And your husband? What does he say?"

"*Peace*," my father bellowed from the hall. "I've heard enough babble at the stadthuis to last me a lifetime."

"Out with it," Aunt Catharina said. "What is the latest news from 'sGravenhage, Brother?"

"The Perpetual Edict has been withdrawn. The Prince is to be sworn in as Stadtholder tomorrow. With his father's powers—"

"All?" asked my aunt.

"And why not? Hasn't he proved himself?" said Catharina Swalmius.

"Certainly. He can retreat faster than his Uncle Maurice. He can flood a polder as well as the peasants." My Aunt Catharina snipped off her thread.

"De Witt still languishes," my father went on. "The churches in 'sGravenhage are preaching of the son of Van der Graeff as a second Jacob. But he never wrestled. He bent his head meekly. It was the executioner wrestled with his own broad sword. It took three strokes to kill him."

"Young idiot," Aunt Catharina said sadly. "What is to happen to us, Antoni?"

"Where are the boys?" my father asked suddenly. "Are you women so busy deciding the great affairs of state that you have no time to mind your own?"

"Calm yourself, Brother. I sent the boys out with Rickje for a walk."

"Where?" my father asked sharply.

"The Schiespoort. You know how they delight in the ships."

But my father was clapping his hat to his head and was out the door before she could ask him why. Only then, in the wounded silence, did we hear the roar of the crowd outside. It was like the rush of a flood, an endless tide.

That day, the crowd announced the passage of the English Ambassadors to 'sGravenhage. "Long live the King of England and the Prince of Orange! Down with the States!" The enemy, we all knew, was within us.

For every surge of fear, or love, there was an undertow. The peasants returned in the dead of night to drain the polders we had flooded to stop the French King's relentless progress. They couldn't bear to drown their own lands, even to keep them from the French. It wasn't only De Witt's friend Peter De Groot whose lands were threatened with salt. We were all to pay the price of our witless cowardice. Quite simply, we would never be as comfortable again. Our lands would never be as fruitful, our cattle as plentiful, our butter as sweet. And our loyalties, to each other, to the States of Holland, the States-General, to our own burgomasters would never be the simple fidelity of children to their father.

The young man who led us now was not his tall magic father, William the Silent. No, he was a boy, a boy who shuddered under the weight of the most heinous truths. He shuddered, but he did not act. He held fast. Perhaps that is why, even now that he is monarch of England, William III still returns each summer to the Brabant to lead the soldiers he has mustered from our towns in Holland, and from the Scots, the Swedes, the Germans, the Spaniards, and the Danes. Doesn't he know we could fight forever, until all the land in the world floods with blood as our polders flooded those two years? We could fight forever and the past will remain exactly as it is.

The Prince is not alone. Don't we all contribute our taxes, don't we contribute troops and munitions, did we not, just eight years ago, contribute the Prince himself to the ungrateful and treacherous English? We could give him to France, it wouldn't make a doit of difference. The past exists, grotesque, festering, in the minds of all who lived through that year. It will never be picked clean as the bones of those who died then, in battle, in riot, or by the executioner's sword.

It is not the small clean acts of the magistrates, the States of Holland, the States-General, or even the Sun King that seethe in memory. These are clean as pebbles turned by an ebbing tide. It is the mutter of the crowd, the mob, the grauw, the fluent and deadly strength of our vicious common will that threatens even now to wash away all our faith, in each other and in, I say this only in our great privacy, the intentions of Our Maker.

♕ ♕ ♕

We have found that men contain much less blood than was thought before. Even so, we are bled whenever fever threatens, and the blood, black or red, festering with bad humors, or sweet as milk, never fails to astonish us. It is more meaningful than any dream. Much less blood floods through us than was once thought, but when it flows it never fails to amaze us with its abundance.

Years before the invasion, the year De Graaf himself came to our town, one of our neighbors on the Voldersgracht wounded himself invisibly when he fell as he carried a sack of wheat over a board laid across the canal. For days he held his hurt inside him, but then, jostling himself as he sat down at the head of his table, the blood poured out from his private part like water from a fountain. Someone, his brother, or son, held him there, pinching his private part to stanch the flood, until the doctor arrived, but I can still remember looking into the front room as I passed by on my way back to the Golden Head from the house of my Aunt De Mey. Every wall, I tell you, the hangings on the bed, the floor, the wife's face, the doctor's hands, the children's hair ran with it. You would not believe how much blood a single man can contain, or how much they can spill and still live.

That summer of '72 we tested the limits of life. We learned, certainly we learned, but I don't know anyone in Holland now who can tell you what. Twenty years later, we are still puzzled by what poured, brilliant and steaming from our veins.

There was love for the young Stadtholder, William, certainly. Hatred of the French, yes. But an equal hatred for our own magistrates who taxed us, for the officers who ordered the flooding of our lands. And towards the brothers De Witt a rancor and cruelty worse, I swear it, than the Devil's. *Our* veins, I say, for there was no one in all of Holland who was not splattered by that blood, no one in whom the balance of spirits was not permanently changed.

We were, I believe, the first city to hear the news from 'sGravenhage that infamous day in August when the De Witt brothers were slaughtered by the grauw. By nightfall, the criers had gone through the town. Drinkers in the Mechelen and the Comanscoff were toasting the Prince and the new Grand Pensionary, Fagel. Those who, like my father, were sickened by the slaughter, kept to their houses. But there was as little peace in the Golden Head as there was on the streets.

"It was a long time coming," Catharina Swalmius said. Her pocked face was as flushed with excitement as if she'd sat inches away from the flame.

"I've paid a boy to try to buy one of the Ruwaard's fingers," Cornelia said. "You can look at it under your glasses, Husband. Perhaps you can reveal to all of us the cause of his villainy. I think it was pride ran in his veins, not blood."

"You *what*?" Aunt Catharina gasped. "A predikant's daughter, you should know there was only one human sacrifice sanctified by God. This is the Devil's work."

"No," I blurted. "It is ours."

"It's the grauw, the rabble," my father said.

"And the burgers, Brother. Verhoeff, the goldsmith, the militiamen.

All the Representatives to the States-General who stayed wringing their hands by the windows in the Binnenhof."

"And the Prince," we would all whisper days later. Who did nothing, absolutely nothing to wash away the country's sin. Indeed he paid the villains, years later, in sinecures if not in pieces of silver. But who among us dare judge him? It was our predikants who raised their voices in the churches the next day praising the slaughter, our brothers and fathers and cousins who performed it.

No one could hear about the murder of the De Witts and not be changed. Even when we stopped talking about it, it still festered in our thought. In the vleeshalle, the meat market, we turned away from the sides of beef, sickened. There had been no limit to the country's savagery. We had tumbled the brothers' entrails out, dismembered them, roasted their flesh. Who could forget that? Who should?

If we understood what we did to the De Witts, we would understand the nature of man, understand it differs not a whit from the Devil's—or our implacable Maker's.

I prefer to recall, if I must recall anything, the response of the Ruwaard's widow. My Aunt Catharina heard of it from her husband Claes. Reading the letter to me, she wept, and I, like the man who waved the Ruwaard's severed finger aloft, grew faint with something greater than shame—or even sin. I don't know its name. I only know it fills me now when I think of the woman riding the barge, listening as the men around her laugh, puffing smoke from their long white pipes.

The air in the boat is unbearably close. The man at the far end of the cabin waves his arm in the air.

"I've bought this for my sons and grandsons—to let them see how we in Holland preserve ourselves from the wicked traitors in our midst."

"How much?" someone asks. "How much will you take for it?"

"May I?" the woman asks, putting out her hand. She stands up, weaving slightly as the boat is drawn forward sluggishly against the ebbing tide. The man sees the gleam of silk, the glitter of the silver brooch that closes her collar. Her face is nearly invisible in the smoke. There is something in the eager tremor of her voice that frightens him as, in truth, he was frightened by the man running through the streets of 'sGravenhage who had waved the stick in his face, innocently as a boy holds out a pig's trotter to the fire.

The woman on the barge now takes the stick from him, but she does not hold it up to her eyes. She cups the finger in her palm, draws it gently from the stick. She holds it up close to her face. She breathes on it slowly, as if to cool it off. Somehow, she has drawn the attention of all on the boat. There is silence, even among the women, the young children.

"You have what you paid for," she said at last. "It is the Ruwaard's finger. I know it well. The last time I saw it, it was still on my dear husband's hand."

She raises the stick to pierce the knuckle again. Then, shaking her head, she clasps the flesh to her mouth as if she would consume what is left of that proud, boastful, and stubborn man more eagerly than any of his enemies. Or so the man says when he wakes from his swoon, the empty stick again in his hand.

"Is there no end?" he mutters. End of what? He, like all the rest of us, has no word to secure our fate. Already no one on the boat pays him any more mind than they do the Ruwaard's widow who sits stone still at the far end of the boat, her hands closed demurely over her basket, a small smile etched on her face.

News was the one thing there was never any shortage of and we fed on it as eagerly as we had once fed on smoked meats. Was it true that in Gouda, in Rotterdam, in Leyden, Delft, and Amsterdam, the burgers were again rioting, demanding the resignation of the burgomasters?

Soon we could see for ourselves. The crowds chanted outside our own stadthuis. "Down with the enemies of the Prince. Out with Boogaert! Out with Vander Dussen! Out with Vallensis!"

We all gathered on the stoop of the Golden Head. Except for my cousins Johannes and Antoni, none of us wanted to cross the bridge and go into the square. I could see Hodenpijl, even young Beijeren, the draper. There were faiencers and goldsmiths, brewers and painters, tailors and serge drapers, bakers and predikants, all chanting, screaming, waving banners, pamphlets. *"Let the Prince lead us! Leave us to the hands of the Prince!"* There was, from no one, anywhere in Holland, not even Leyden, or the English merchants in our town, any more talk of peace.

What we were pleading for was a singleness of purpose, a stifling of the natural tumult in the heart, such as we had never had before—such as we had never had a need for before. Now, in the back of every mind, the scaffold rose, the mutilated bodies of the brothers De Witt dangled like butchered cattle. We shouted louder. It was the magistrates fault, certainly. It was they

who had followed the Grand Pensionary, they who had drafted the Perpetual
Edict, they who exacted the Prince's oath never to assume the power of his
father. But now we burgers were to be for a moment masters of our own fate,
and we—not the burgomasters—intended to drop it, hotter than any coal, in
the Prince's outstretched hand. *Let the Prince decide! Leave us to the Prince!*

The burgomasters were no different. They resigned within hours;
they waited until the Prince sent the new list of the Council of Forty. They
sent their spokesman to the States of Holland to vote for the legality of this
riot. We were all only trying to save our souls, but they rushed from us as life
rushes from the severed vein.

Legality. Isn't that the power God gave Adam and all his sons? To
name the Maker's handiwork, name it again. This is government, we said,
watching the cities in all of Holland, Delft, Leyden, Amsterdam, replace
their regents at the Prince's pleasure. This is peace, we said, watching the
boats shuttle up and down the flooded polders, their cannon aimed at the
French troops in Utrecht. This is our country, we said, looking from the sea
to the flooded polder and back again. This is our city, we said, walking streets
crowded at all hours with strangers, hungry boors, burgers, burgomasters
from all the conquered provinces.

Even our own houses seemed unfamiliar to us—retaining as the
streets did only their names, their signs. The Golden Head rang day and
night with strange voices. Aunt Catharina's daughters Rickje and Grietgen
and Geertruyt slept on the third floor. Catharina Swalmius, Catharina van
Leeuwen, and I shared mine, while my cousins Johannes, Phillip, and Antoni
slept on the floor in the front room. Only my father and Cornelia recognized
the body they tumbled against in the pitchy dark. If my father recognized
anyone.

I think he took the changes that summer harder than any of us,
although he has never again mentioned them. All his life, or all the life I
can recall, he has gone daily to the stadthuis. He has prided himself on his
familiarity with the schout and the schepenen, those who administer our
town, even more than he now prides himself on his friendship with the
Learned Company. Although the burgomasters changed, there was always
forewarning. My father trusted this regular ebb and flux at the stadthuis in a
way he never trusted the changes in his private life.

So the resignations at the pleasure of the grauw, these new
appointments at the pleasure of the Prince, Boogaert's shameful retreat,

'sGravesende's cautious ascent—these challenged my father in a way it is difficult to describe. My father's position hadn't changed, but he had lost all faith in it, all pleasure. The stadthuis no longer represented stability to him, the common good. It was capricious as everything else in life—capricious! It was inscrutable and unsettling as all else that God commands.

It was the same in the house itself. I could see the same look slide over my father's face, darker than the shadow of his hat brim, as he stood on the front stoop, his hand on the door, listening to the din. Cornelia and Catharina Swalmius sat in the front room, one reading from the Bible while the other mended. Aunt Catharina van Leeuwen heard her son Johannes' lessons, while cousin Rickje and I taught her little brother Phillip his letters. Or the baby Antoni would be pulling the dog's ear, Phillip tugging a feather from the dove's tail, Agatha their maid would be scolding my cousin Rickje for helping herself to the last of the bread, Cornelia and Aunt Catharina would be squabbling over household accounts, Aunt Maria De Mey and Catharina Swalmius would be bickering over their differing positions as past and present sister-in-law.

"The vow is eternal—"

"Infernal," my father would bellow. "Stop this infernal din."

"I feel faint," Cornelia Swalmius would quaver, tottering back to her seat by the fire.

"Faint," my father would say, making his way eagerly to his wife's side.

"Idle talk, Antoni," Aunt Catharina would say, stroking young Johannes, Phillip, or Antoni's head. "Nothing ails her but the looseness of her tongue."

"Enough," my father would say, blinking with disappointment. "I'll be off to my study now."

"Study," Aunt Catharina would repeat thoughtfully. "Do you think we could make a pallet there?"

But my father would have the door closed fast before she'd closed her mouth.

♛ ♛ ♛

After the fall of Utrecht, the French army's impious burning of the Domkerk's lectern and chairs, Cornelia and Catharina Swalmius, daughters and granddaughters of predikants, became outspoken in their hatred of papists. My father and I let them speak as they needed within the house. I met Maria Vermeer in the market square. My father met De Graaf at the Anatomy Chamber. There was no point in objecting. My stepmother and her sister weren't alone in their talk.

So that morning in late November when Maria van Dijn, De Graaf's young bride, burst into our house, burst into my father's private chamber without so much as a word to Cornelia, she threw the whole household into greater uproar than I had imagined possible.

"In there," Maria van Dijn said. "What's in there, Mejuffrouw van Leeuwenhoek?" I had followed her in, protesting at her boldness, but she did not seem to hear me. She pointed to the tall cabinet in which my father stored his glasses. "There," she said again. "What does he hide in there?"

"The equipment for his art."

"Art!" She brushed her hand across her face. It was hot as August in the sealed room. "I call it lechery."

"This?" I asked, lifting a brass plate from the table. "Lechery?" I couldn't help smiling.

But Maria van Dijn did not smile back. She was only a year older than I and not much bigger than my Aunt De Mey.

"Do you *know*? Do you really know what they do in that chamber on the Doelenstraat? Do you know what he stores in there—any more than you know what he stores in his heart?"

"Who are you talking of? Surely not my father."

"They are all the same. Rummaging through those swollen stinking bodies—they're worse than any soldiers, French, German, or Dutch. Here, let me see." She pushed her way around the table and, going to the cabinet, turned the key. "Does he too have the testicles of a man blown up like leathern balls? Does he hang up the dried privates of women like rabbits' feet?"

"Oh no," I said, sickened.

"Does he keep the unborn young of rabbits and dormice swimming in jars of turpentine? Does he? Does he?"

"Please," I said, watching her stoop and tumble her hands through the sticks of glass, my father's pipes and sheets of brass. "It's not the way you think. You won't find anything there."

"Don't reason with her," Cornelia said. "Call Dr. 'sGravesende."

"Call her husband," Aunt Maria De Mey said.

"Never," Cornelia cried. "I'll have no papists here."

"Terrible, terrible," Maria van Dijn muttered, making the sign of the cross. "They cut us apart, hang our private parts up with ribbons. Hideous."

"There it is," she said, recognizing her husband's treatise on my father's shelf. She pulled the book down and spread it open on the table. "Look! *They* do. In the Anatomy Chamber, *these* are the sights they see. At first I didn't understand. But when I saw *that* picture, the one with the little man child tucked up into the pocket, or the next with the child released and asleep, still bound to its mother's cord, then I knew."

"Isn't he funny," I said. "With his tiny member, like Antoni Claeszoon."

"You think it funny, Mejuffrouw? Well let me show you." She opened the book toward the front and pointed to an engraving of what appeared to be a furred purse. "That's what the good doctor will do to you should you die tomorrow."

"Are you sure?" I asked, looking away. It wasn't disgust I felt, but bafflement. This wasn't what I'd seen at my Aunt Catharina's lying-in.

"See these monsters taking shape inside us?" she asked Cornelia, pointing to a dog-like muzzle draped with sheets.

"Evil," Cornelia said. "And to think all these months my husband has assisted him."

"Along with the physicians 'sGravesende, D'Aquet, and Vallensis. They're all learned gentlemen," I said. "Every day they do the same in Leyden, Paris, and London."

"I will show this to the priests," De Graaf's wife cried out.

"*Priests*," Cornelia said. "Have you no shame?"

"Shame? Yes, I have shame. For a week now I have walked around my house afraid to leave it. I think of my husband, I think of all the men in the world poring over these pages. I think of the flames licking their hands like dogs' tongues, licking the pages, but the pages never burn, their hands never tire, for the machines of the wicked are imperishable, just like the instruments of angels—and the dreadful curiosity of men."

"He meant no harm," I protested.

"Which one?" Cornelia asked. "Your father. Or that wicked papist doctor?"

"What does this say?" I asked, pointing to the words beside the engraving.

"It's not our Nether-Dutch," she said. "I can't make it out."

"But then my father can't either."

"He has eyes. Just like you and me," Maria van Dijn said.

"That I have." My father stood at the door to his study. None of us had heard him come in.

We women huddled together around the table. At last Aunt Catharina found her tongue.

"Dr. de Graaf's wife came to make her first morning visit. We were consulting your Bontekoe for a list of cooling foods, Brother. There is so little to be found in the markets now."

While Aunt Catharina busied herself with putting the books straight in the pile above his cabinet, Cornelia hurried off to ready my father's tea. I picked up Maria van Dijn's cloak from where she'd tossed it on the floor in her mad flurry and brought it over to her. All this time my Aunt Maria De Mey continued talking to the young woman in a low monotonous voice as if she were soothing a child. "Not a word, my dear, not a word until we leave the house." I wrapped the cloak around Maria van Dijn's frail shoulders and together my Aunt Maria and I walked her to the door.

"Pay no mind, Brother," I heard Aunt Catharina say. "It is woman's business she was bent on. And for that there's no fitter place to come these days than the Golden Head. Just look around you."

☙ ☙ ☙

In the end Aunt Maria and I escorted De Graaf's wife all the way down the Oude Langendijk to the Vermeers, and from there we sent for De Graaf. We had intended to escort the young woman all the way to Aunt Maria's house on the Oosteinde, but her strength failed her. It was funny, really. One moment she was railing. We were holding on to her with all four hands as if she might rise like a sail in a high wind. The next minute she slipped to the ground between us.

"Catharina Bolnes," I cried, waving my arms, when I saw her standing with her arms folded over her apron, calmly observing the commotion. "Come assist us if you please."

By the time De Graaf had arrived, Catharina Bolnes had recognized the signs of his wife's malady. She had even burned the string, just to be certain.

"Some kind of doctor you are," she scolded De Graaf. "Letting her march like a soldier half across town. Giving her these shocks, these scares. In her condition."

"Condition?" De Graaf's full cheeks washed red, white, red again. "Where is she?"

"I wouldn't go near—" I warned him.

"Hush, child," Catharina Bolnes said. "You don't know what you're talking about. Who has a greater right?"

When De Graaf sat on the edge of the curtained bed there were no harsh outcries from his wife, only sobs. There was no bluff scolding from the doctor, rather a mothering tenderness.

"Oh my dear," he muttered. "Oh my dear child."

"How can she?" I asked, watching the small blonde woman leaning on the doctor's arm as they returned together to their house.

"And why not?" Catharina Bolnes asked. "Isn't it her duty?"

"But that cabinet—" Maria van Dijn had blurted out the dreadful truth about her husband's occupations to Catharina Bolnes as well. In her rage, she had lost all sense of modesty.

"That cabinet has taught him how great the difference between life and death, how narrow the gap between disease and health. She must learn too. If anyone can ease the shock, it will be he."

"What did you say to her?" Aunt Maria asked with a smile. "When we brought her in here, she would have clutched the curtains together calling on the Virgin to save her should her husband even have shown his face."

"When you marry a man, you marry his trade," Catharina Bolnes said. "I am sure, however, that if there is another man in Delft who honors women as much as my husband Johannes it is the young doctor. Whatever he preserves in his cabinet, it is not proof of either hatred or disdain."

"All the same," my aunt said, shaking her head doubtfully. "These are shocking charges she's made against him."

"You'd not speak so if he'd come to you in childbed," Catharina Bolnes said looking at my elderly virgin aunt with anger as clear and cool as it was cruel.

"Perhaps not," Aunt Maria said, taking my arm. "Perhaps not. Our Creator hasn't blessed me so."

This was the first and last time I entered the new house of Catharina Bolnes. It was the memory of my Aunt Maria's face that forbade me—the way it whitened at the other woman's words. It was the thought of the man lying faint on the barge: "Is there no end?" End of what? What word could describe the tumult we were in?

Women against men, women against each other, against themselves. There was no quiet in the house, in the streets, in the country. Only with the New Year, with the enemy's ruthless and bloody invasion into the province of Holland itself did we begin to discover any unity, as women, and men, and Dutch. Only then, when we understood the savagery of the French to the living, did we understand that it had nothing to do with the damage the physicians did to the dead.

Even when the news came to us on the 27th of December that Luxembourg and his men had crossed the dike at Bodegraven, we did not quite believe it. The Prince was still with most of the army in the Brabant. Without him, no one knew what to do—it was as if the danger itself could not be felt without the young Prince's frail body there, numb as all of us with the dangerous frost, but his eyes quick with fury and pride. Even the commanders of the troops looked behind them as they retreated. Looked behind them, to right and left, but they never looked the danger squarely in the face.

Wherever our frightened forces turned, they could find no refuge. Leyden locked its gates to our own Kroonevelt. Gouda ejected our own Pain et Vin. France's Luxembourg and his ravenous horde marched across the treacherous ice that even the salt-sea inundations from Gorcum could not keep from freezing fast. In 'sGravenhage they felled trees before the city, hoping to slow the approach of the French troops to the unfortified town.

In Delft, the burgomasters again inventoried the munitions stored at the edge of town. "Thank God we'd not let them be transferred to Amsterdam," we muttered. Amsterdam might have the mint, but Delft had what few munitions were left in South Holland. "What about us?" yelled the burgomasters of Leyden to the quaking Kroonevelt. "What do we have to stave off the hunchback Luxembourg?"

In 'sGravenhage, the States-General wrung their hands. They drafted letters to the Prince, still laying siege in the south. They ordered the felling of more trees. As Luxembourg approached closer along the road to Leyden, a great silence fell. In our stadthuis in Delft our burgomasters clustered whispering about terms of surrender. Our representatives did the same before the States of Holland. In our houses, husbands and wives boxed their possessions, ready to ship them to Amsterdam, Haarlem, or Antwerp.

But again God wielded his inscrutable justice. A warm wind blew the morning of the 29th of December, the sun shone, the ice cracked. In deepest shame and anger, Luxembourg and his men turned quickly back toward Utrecht. Hadn't they intended, with the hunchback's blessing, to ravage 'sGravenhage? Hadn't they wished to desecrate the tomb of William the Silent in our own Nieuwe Kirke? Hadn't they wished to taste the mouths, the tears of the women from Gouda, Leyden, 'sGravenhage, Delft, Rotterdam and Dort? Instead the French devoured the villages of Zwammerdam and Bodegraven. Not a woman was left undefiled. Every house they saw they burned, every man, woman or child they saw run screaming from the flames they put to the sword.

It wasn't until days later when the few survivors straggled into our cities followed by hundreds of frightened boors that we began to understand the horror. It was not until the Prince marched back into Holland on the New Year that we began to feel it. Through his eyes we saw our frozen unburied countrymen with their mouths agape, our young women with their shifts thrown over their faces. It was through his ears we heard the tiny babe crying, half frozen, in the ruins of the farmhouse. It was through his hands we cradled it, through his mouth we ordered it clothed, warmed, brought, famished, to a full breast.

Like the scaffold in 'sGravenhage, which held the De Witt brothers, the ravaged village of Zwammerdam invaded our dreams. It was this that convinced us finally that the French were a greater threat to us than we were to ourselves. It was this that convinced us, bloodied hand, blind eye, that we were one body.

❀ ❀ ❀

Even now, as I try to speak of those times, of these armies flooding back and forth, I piece it together like the ambassador and learned historian Wicquefort—not like me, Maria van Leeuwenhoek, at sixteen. For, in truth, what worried me then, even in those desperate days, was quite different. I worried over my father's testy humor, I worried over Cornelia's scorn,

Catharina Swalmius' spite, and most of all I worried over my Aunt Catharina van Leeuwen's disappointment in the progress of her son Phillip under my tutelage.

Now it seems fantastical that Phillip should recall me as the one who taught him his letters, when in fact he taught me. Every day we would take paper, chalk. Together, over and over we would trace our letters, we would recite them. It was during that year I learned the true curse of my fever. It wasn't as if I couldn't form the letters as young Phillip did, it wasn't that I couldn't call out their names. But when a word formed in my mind's eye, another word entirely often formed under my hand. It was as if young Willem, looking through my father's glass, drew a hooked foot where there should have been a mouth. That is why I have had to ask Grietje to write my receipts. She knows my weakness, the clever, wicked girl, and whenever tired or baulked, she threatens to expose me. Expose—yes, it is true, even now I do not want the world to know the truth.

Back then, in our crowded, dinning house, it was not difficult to keep my secret. No one dared look too closely, for everyone had something to conceal. Young Phillip knew where the last cake had disappeared to on Christmas Day. Rickje the maid knew where the barge boy stayed the night. Cornelia Swalmius knew that the blood that slipped monthly from her body was more deadly than sal vitriol. My father, watching his wife's unchanging figure, her frightened, discontented face, knew he was to blame.

It was then my father turned, regardless of Cornelia's outcries, to the young Dr. de Graaf for aid. What was it the young doctor said to him? Whatever it was, my father began to patrol his wife's life as carefully as the Prince patrolled the icy borders of our diminished country. No more did my father come into the house and first gather his young nephew and namesake, Antoni Claeszn., in his arms. No longer did he first kiss his dear sister Catharina on the cheek. It was at Cornelia's side he set his chair, it was with his wife he took what little comfort he could in the news of the day: Luxembourg no longer sent patrols to the dikes. The winter, praise God, remained unusually clement. There was no need, he announced at last, for Catharina van Leeuwen to remain in Delft. Rotterdam was just as safe, and their house, they both agreed, was much the larger. Her husband Claes felt their absence. Yes, Aunt Catharina said, her cheeks burning, her hands folded over the shoulders of her two oldest sons.

"You can leave the boys here with me," my father said.

"There's no need," said Cornelia.

"You can visit with them in Rotterdam," my Aunt Catharina said, waving all her children to her.

They were gone the next day on the noon barge.

"At least this time I have my own house to go to," Aunt Catharina said as my father handed her her bags, then lifted the unwilling young Phillip under his arm and swung him onto the boat like a sack of meal.

"This time?"

"I feel as I did when I packed to go to Gryetgen's the day of your first wedding. I wish—," Aunt Catharina looked at me, then my father, then at her son's grimy hand gripping the edge of her jacket. She lifted her head proudly. "I wish I left you this time in such good hands, Antoni."

"I do my best, Aunt," I said softly, feeling my eyes smart with the chill wind.

"You?" they both asked. "What are you thinking of?"

"What are we all—" But my father caught himself up, stood back as the barge started off down the canal.

"Are you sure it was wise, Father?" I asked as we walked down the Oude Delft, past the East India House, as still now as it had been for months. There had been almost no trade in our town since the past May. "It was Aunt Catharina who tallied the accounts, bartered in the market."

"Peace," my father said sharply. "The doctor says my wife must have peace."

"Peace," I scoffed to my Aunt Maria De Mey a month later. "It's pieces of silk they're both after, ells of taffeta, velvet ribbons. It's strings for the mandolins, sheets of music. If they send me once more to young Beijeren I will melt with shame."

"Antoni's right. Things must change."

"But why?" I cried. "Why this way? Besides, it's not my father calling the tune is it now? It's that young doctor from Schoonhoven."

"From the look of it," Aunt Maria said with a smile, "he might have some right. Maria van Dijn should deliver this summer, and she appears far from discontent."

"Not I," Cornelia said that evening when my father made his wishes known. "I'll not watch that papist set foot in the Golden Head."

"I don't blame her," Catharina Swalmius said, closing her Bible over her finger. Her narrow gray eyes blinked, blinked again with sympathy for her sister.

"Silence, woman," my father said. "It's my wife I'm speaking to, not you."

Catharina swallowed so largely I could see her throat swell, but she kept her thoughts to herself. My father reached out boldly for his wife's arm. "It's time."

"No," Cornelia wailed, rushing from the room. "No, no, I'll not submit again."

She clattered up the stairs. My father stood at the foot of them watching her, but he made no move to follow, even when she paused at the bedroom door before banging it closed.

"When will she see reason?" he asked.

"See?" I wondered. Reason did not seem to me something to hold at arm's length and contemplate, but like the war, like the flood of our own blood or the battering of the sea, something to be blindly endured.

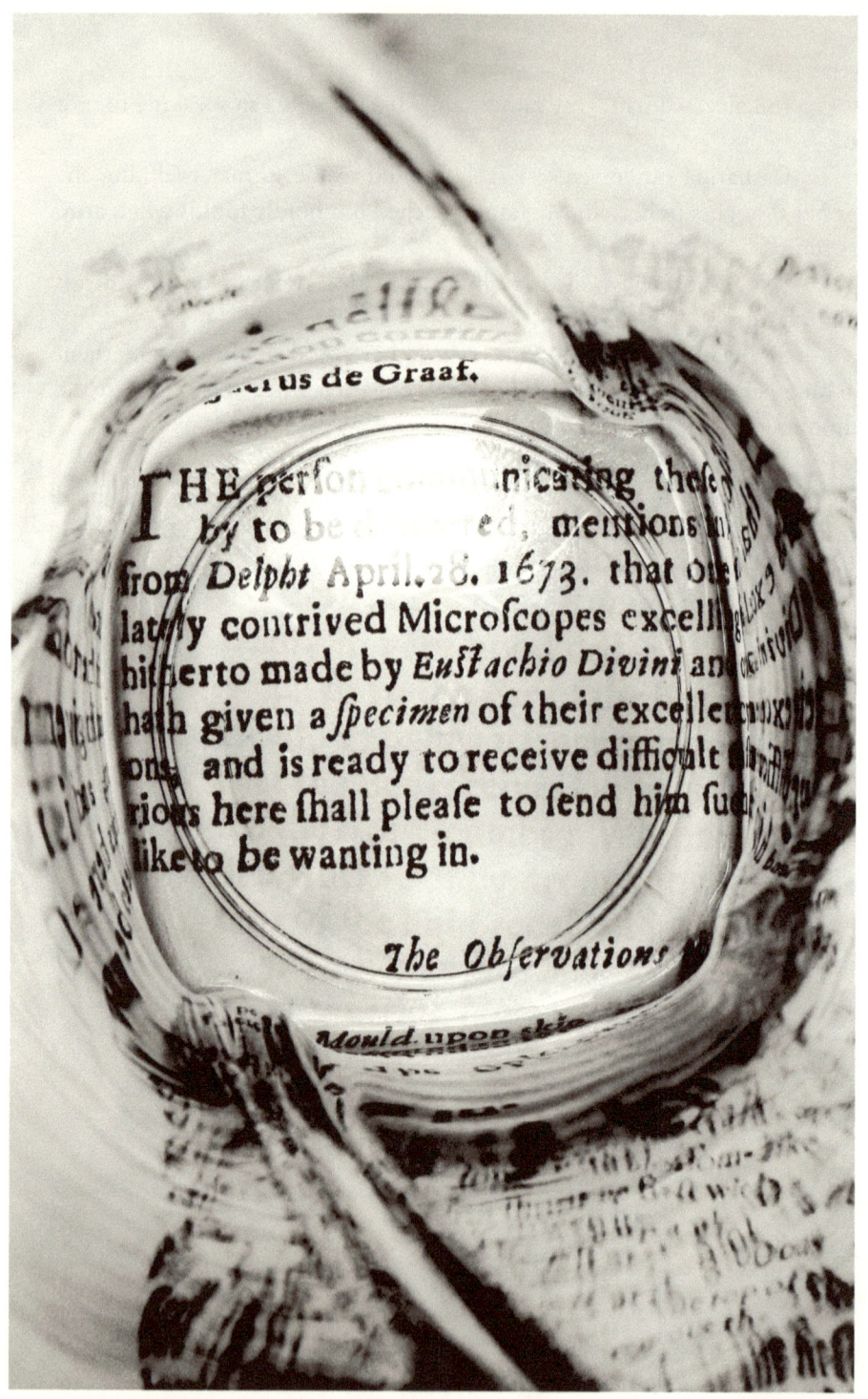

...erus de Graaf.

THE perfon communicating thefe ... by to be deſired, mentions in a ... from *Delpht* April. 28. 1673. that one ... lately contrived Microfcopes excelling ... hitherto made by *Euſtachio Divini* and ... hath given a *ſpecimen* of their excellent ... ... and is ready to receive difficult ... rious here ſhall pleaſe to ſend him ſuch ... like to be wanting in.

The Obſervations

mould, upon skin

RAMPJAAR: WHAT BROUGHT US TOGETHER
AGAIN
1673-1674

By March, when the danger of the dikes freezing fast was over for the year, we Dutch began to concern ourselves with our private fortunes again. The French invasion, it was now evident, had been stopped. The French would never again dare to cross the flooded polders dividing Utrecht and Holland. It was as if God had said to King Louis, "You can come just this far—and not a step farther."

We looked to the uncompassable sea and were reassured. We all, the learned gentlemen and merchants as well as the Prince and his soldiers, waited eagerly upon our allies for assistance. It was in this time of tentative peace, when men no longer spent their days reinforcing the city's ramparts or inventorying its store of munitions, but could not yet occupy themselves with trade for our ships did not ply the seas again with profitable regularity, that Dr. de Graaf convinced my father to write down what he'd seen through his newly invented glasses and to send it to the Royal Society in London.

My father's duties at the stadthuis were not onerous—or satisfying—enough to require his complete attention. Dr. de Graaf's practice had fallen away with the war. He and my father could meet almost daily to share their latest observations. De Graaf brought my father the book written by the Englishman, Robert Hooke, that he had seen once in England. Although Mr. Hooke's microscope was more complicated, he saw no more clearly through it than my father did through his own simpler lens. Indeed, he saw less.

"Not so," my father cried. "I see five articulations in the leg. Mr. Hooke is in error." It was a louse, I believe, they had glued to the pin behind my father's glass.

"Are you sure?"

"You're questioning me?" (Was this the last time I would hear my father laugh over this question?)

"And why not, Leeuwenhoek? Do you think they did not question me over the substance of the testicles and the epididymis? Do you think they are not questioning me now over my discovery of the true purpose of the testicles of women? Not to mention the priority of my discovery over that of Swammerdam?" De Graaf answered.

"Even so," my father said, taking out another glass and specimen to entertain his friend. "You're a man of learning, Dr. de Graaf. You are used to having your word impugned. But I, a draper, a keeper of accounts, my word is my security. Imagine, Maria," he said, glancing over his shoulder at me where I knelt by the fire adding to the blocks of peat. "Imagine young Beijeren, he'd be bankrupt in a month if his customers questioned every bill of goods he presented."

"It's not the same," De Graaf said mildly, taking the glass from my father's hand. "There is no question of dissembling. We each do the best we can, but the eye can err, an honest man can be mistaken. True knowledge is gained through the companionship of men equally attentive, equally willing to seek truth."

"And to accept censure," my father scoffed.

"Even so, Van Leeuwenhoek, even so. As long as it is rightly deserved. One can't help but be the wiser for it. Now censure undeserved—"

"I know," my father laughed. "That young man Swammerdam."

"About the organs of women, about the feeding of arteries, I agree with you—"

"With me?" my father asked, his mouth agape. "All I do is listen to you."

"But he is the man to debate this with," De Graaf said, patting the engraving of the louse in Hooke's book. "There's no one around knows more about insects than Swammerdam. And he'd believe you, Leeuwenhoek."

"And well he should," my father said. "Just bring him here and I'll let him see for himself. That's proof enough to satisfy any man."

"You can't bring the whole learned world to Delft, Van Leeuwenhoek. You must go out yourself to meet them."

So, reluctantly, my father did. Not, however, as the burgomasters of Utrecht went out to greet the invading French, willing to sell their wealth, their very souls, for safety. Neither did he go out to meet the learned company with the Sun King's pride—or young Prince William's reckless courage. No, he went out to meet the learned company exactly as he has met every other trial and delight life has held out to him.

"I can't do that, certainly," he said, pointing at the engraving in Mr. Hooke's book. "I've not been trained."

"An engraver will be able to render what you show him through your glass."

"I will ask my brother-in-law Molijn if there is some apprentice in the St. Lucas guild can assist me," my father said quickly.

"But a drawing won't suffice. You need to add your comments as well."

"What would those gentlemen be wanting with the observations of someone like me?"

"Try," De Graaf said, putting the plate down on the table, picking up his cloak.

A week later, De Graaf took my father's comments on mold, on the articulations of the leg of a louse, on the sting of the bee, and presented them with all dutiful phrases to the attention of the Royal Society. He offered my father's services to the learned gentlemen. No one reading my father's brief remarks would have known the hours he had labored over them. No one save me, for it was to me my father read each draft before he scratched it out and then, frenzied, tossed the offending sheet into the fire.

"I wish you'd just start blowing and grinding your glass again," Cornelia said to him the fourth day. "At least then Maria could be of some use around here." Cornelia looked at my father lumbering back and forth across his room, his robe loose, the sash dragging the floor, his wig askew, his hat tossed, forgotten, into the corner. "You poor, poor man," she said, and, gagging with exasperation and laughter, quickly left the room.

🐚 🐚 🐚

If my father was difficult when he tried to write the learned gentlemen in our Nether-Dutch, a language as plain and untutored as my father himself, it was as nothing to his mood in the months that followed.

Around the house he would mutter, he would speculate. He would look through his glasses again and again. He would look at Mr. Hooke's drawing, tapping the fore-leg of the louse with his big white fingertip. He would look through his glasses again, then pick up his copy of his letter to the Learned Company and read it aloud while pacing back and forth across the room, his face flaring and blanching with the words, whether he neared fire or window. "Maria," he would yell. "Be a good girl and—"

"Don't you ever get bored?" asked Catharina Swalmius, as I hurried to my father's study for the tenth time that morning.

I shook my head. If I had, I would never have told her, of course. But it was my father's passion, not its object, that enjoined me—that and his loneliness now that De Graaf was busy elsewhere. As his wife entered the time of fasting, the young doctor was never far from her side. What did the young doctor care about the structure of the sting of the bee, or about the words my father picked, one by one from his heart, with more anguish than he might pluck splinters of glass from his hand?

My father, in accordance with the doctor's advice, attended to his own wife.

"Although the Lord's will in such matters is impossible to fathom, there are women, the doctor himself told me, who were barren for more than a decade, who, then, as suddenly, conceived." He took Cornelia's arm. "Come, come," he said impatiently. "It's nearly noon. Isn't there enough to keep you women occupied within the house?"

"I'm going out," Catharina Swalmius said as soon as Cornelia and my father had retired at his request to their sleeping chamber.

"I too. I will visit my Aunt De Mey."

These afternoons were painful for each of us. Cornelia because my father would not couple with her despair and she could not couple with his hope. It was to her sister Catharina Swalmius that Cornelia turned, tearful, chattering like an angry squirrel, after my father had dressed again and left the house. Catharina, pious, aghast, listened and listened and listened, while I tried to drown it all out—my father's throes, his wife's tantrums, the sly disgust of his sister-in-law.

"Stop," De Graaf said when he came again to visit my father. My father had the doctor's treatise open on the table and was pointing at an engraving. "Childbirth is painful, child rearing a trial—it will all happen in God's good time. Why not give the woman a little relief, Van Leeuwenhoek? It's the pleasure of conjugation we must attend to—for that is Nature's reward for the pain which we can't avoid."

"Pleasure?" my father said, his face fiery as the setting sun.

"What have your wives been thinking of, keeping you ignorant?"

The answer to this was so simple, even my father, in the midst of his shame, had no trouble putting it into words.

"Me," he said. "They were thinking of me—and of the life to come."

"I'll take what I have," De Graaf said, closing his treatise with a slap, the dust clouding the pale evening air. "A woman in good health, a house in good order."

"A country at war, a government in chaos—"

"What other marvels have you discovered?" De Graaf asked, cutting my father short.

"Ahh," my father sighed. He went to his cabinet. He shuffled among the objects on the table.

"Maria," he muttered. "Have you seen—"

"The louse? I thought you'd fixed him to a pin."

"I want one alive—and hungry."

I slipped on my cloak and went over to the Oude Delft. I asked an old man I found there, who, generously, provided me with three. I carried them back to the house in a wine glass, shaking it to keep them from crawling free.

My father put one of the hungry animals to the back of his hand. He passed De Graaf the glass. Already he had set a candle upon the table.

"I like the way he stops feeding and lets the blood swirl round his mouth—like a baby musing at his mother's breast."

"Exactly," De Graaf said with a startled cough. "Exactly, Leeuwenhoek."

"Enough," Cornelia said coming into the room. "Haven't you had enough for one evening? Husband, you've been peering through those bubbles of glass since three. And what about you, Doctor? Surely your wife is longing for your company—and your expertise."

"As you must be longing for your husband's," Dr. de Graaf said, glancing quickly at my father. He gathered his cloak. My father walked him to the door. He watched the younger man walk up over the bridge, his lantern casting a weird, aged mask over the full ruddy cheeks, the smooth forehead.

"Antoni?" Cornelia said softly when at last he returned to his study. "Surely no more. I heard the Doctor himself request you put an end to these studies."

"Leave me be, woman," he said, slipping another louse onto the back of his trembling hand. He raised the glass to his eye. Cornelia turned and with a narrow smile, a glinting eye, made her way loudly into the front room. My father leaned closer over his hand. He smiled. "Take all you need," he said.

Standing outside the door, I watched my father until the hour was called. Louse and child, we each fed eagerly of what he offered us, his troubled joy, his tumultuous blood.

♛ ♛ ♛

It wasn't until June that Dr. de Graaf heard from the Royal Society. By then, my father, nearly wild with confusion, had chipped his table slamming down his hammer in frustration, had even cracked the door of his oak cabinet by closing it with extravagant force. The only thing that relieved his frenzy was the unexpected visit from that very honorable gentleman, the Prince of Orange's secretary, Seigneur van Zuleichem.

"I must tell you," the old man said, taking the glass my father offered him. "I have looked through microscopes here in Holland and in London, in Paris, Antwerp, and Amsterdam, and there's none to compare with these."

"Malpighi," my father muttered. "Hooke of the Royal Society."

"It occurs to me," Seigneur van Zuleichem said, picking up the second glass my father held out to him, "that the Royal Society might appreciate hearing from someone with your acumen, Heer Van Leeuwenhoek. I am a Fellow there, perhaps I—"

"Observe," my father said. "What we perceive as solidity in deal is really a series of tubes, like organ pipes. Those dark lines, I believe, are valves. By this means—but I keep my imaginings to myself."

"*Observation*, Van Leeuwenhoek. That is the key. How many times have I told my sons so. The eye, Van Leeuwenhoek, is the cornerstone of the new science—the eye and its extensions, the microscope and the telescope. See what my son Christiaan discovered when just a young man with the aid of the telescope: the emanations around Saturn. And you too, Heer Van Leeuwenhoek, have seen the vacuity of wood."

"But I," my father said miserably, "have had no training."

"Training? You have a mind as steady as your hand and eye. Any learned man could use such assistance, I assure you. At the Royal Society, Robert Hooke—" He put down the glass at last; he straightened his cloak.

"Why don't you confide your observations to paper, Heer van Leeuwenhoek. I will send them to the Royal Society."

"Dr. de Graaf has already done so," my father said softly. "I don't think they pleased the learned gentlemen."

"I'll add my word as well," Seigneur van Zuleichem said, putting his old, spotted hand on my father's sleeve.

"I speak and write only our Nether-Dutch," my father said.

"Oldenburg, their secretary, knows nearly as many tongues as I," said Seigneur van Zuleichem, wagging his head. "Sharpen that quill, Heer van Leeuwenhoek. Give the world the benefit of your art."

"You're not leaving us yet, Seigneur van Zuleichem," Cornelia said. She came down the stairs in a rush. She wore a pale yellow skirt, a blue bodice and fur-trimmed morning coat. She'd donned a new linen cap.

"I have business still in Delft and then I must return to 'sGravenhage."

"To the Princess Dowager's?" Cornelia asked with a sigh. "The House in the Woods . . ."

Thus, it was through Seigneur van Zuleichem that my father was introduced a second time to the Royal Society, something which embarrassed him at the moment but relieved him upon De Graaf's untimely death late that summer.

♛ ♛ ♛

I don't know which my father found more difficult to accept, the birth and death of De Graaf's son—or the doctor's own death. The child's death had driven them farther apart. For it wasn't my father De Graaf asked to help carry his son's coffin, but his landlord, another papist.

Catharina Bolnes and Maria Vermeer were, I believe, in attendance at the wake as they had been at Maria van Dijn's child-bed. Then, even they were dismissed. It was De Graaf himself who returned to his wife's childless bed day after day until the young woman recovered from fever, until she even seemed, under the loving ministrations of her husband, to recover from the grief itself.

"They say she'll not have another," Cornelia said to her sister as we all three stood in the market square watching the doting doctor assist his delicate wife through the market stalls. De Graaf carried the basket for her, while Maria Vermeer supported her other arm.

"She's none the worse for that," Catharina Swalmius said. Her pocked face flushed, the hollows darkening until they were almost blue. "The doctor still dotes on her."

"I can see," Cornelia said shortly.

"Do you need a new broom," I asked Cornelia. "This one looks well made." I tugged at the straw with all my might, but it proved tightly woven.

Catharina Swalmius tapped her sister's shoulder. A warning. "Here he comes."

My father, catching sight of us, waved his arm and crossed through the stalls to our side of the market square. But it was obvious it wasn't our company he desired.

"Maria van Dijn is well enough to walk today I see."

"With assistance."

"Ah yes, that is your friend Maria Vermeer, isn't it, Daughter? Have you greeted them?"

"Why don't you go, Father?"

"No," he said, reaching so suddenly into the air that Catharina Swalmius gave a gasp and stepped back. My father scratched his ear rapidly. "It's not the time—"

But there was no time.

De Graaf died a few weeks later the same month, just a week after my father had completed and sent his second letter to the Royal Society. He died, as did so many in our town, of small pox, not, as has since been said, due to his violent arguments with Swammerdam over their conflicting claims to the discovery of the testicles of women.

Cornelia Swalmius never forgave De Graaf his treatise on the sexual anatomy of women, even years later, when she learned what it might mean for her. Certainly she had not forgiven him the day of his funeral as she stood beside her sister at our front window watching as the doctor's grief-stricken widow, assisted by Catharina Bolnes and her daughter, passed by.

"When Antoni goes to the next world," Cornelia said with a sniff, "I'll not carry on so."

"Perhaps it was for the best she lost the child too," Catharina Swalmius said. "Who knows, living with that man, what sights she's seen, what throes of imagination she's endured. Who knows what monstrous shape her grief may have taken. No one saw that child before it went to its grave, did they?"

I don't think Catharina Swalmius had ever looked plainer to me, her full cheeks and even her forehead deeply pitted with scars. She had been, or so my stepmother said, nearly beautiful until the smallpox. Was it worth surviving? It wasn't her face but her spirit the disease had blighted—and it was in the nature of things that she infected all those who approached her with her own discontent.

"Well tell us," she said to my father when he returned from the funeral late in the evening. "Has the doctor's widow succumbed to her grief?"

Taking off his cloak, my father turned to his wife as if she were the one who had spoken.

But Cornelia's eyes suddenly sparked with tear, her mouth trembled. "Poor woman," she said. "To lose both, so close—it isn't just."

"And who are you to say what's just, Cornelia?" asked her sister, drawing a thread across her lips to sharpen it.

"It *is* a terrible loss, for man or woman to bear," my father said. "Our Creator's will is indeed inscrutable. He gives and takes life as he pleases, as you of all women should know."

My father too—for hadn't we lost my mother and my brother just so, one right after the other?

🐚 🐚 🐚

If it had been possible, my father would have recalled his second letter to the Royal Society, his daring having been buried with the young doctor.

"How will they answer me now?" he wondered. "Maria van Dijn has returned to her father's house in Gouda. Surely she has informed the great gentlemen in London of the doctor's death."

"I expect they're relieved," Cornelia said. "From what I understood, he was a contentious man."

"Not so," my father said. "He only desired to be taken at his word. I wish no more myself."

Even then my father recognized how dangerous it was to attempt a new art. As dangerous as De Witt or the Prince's rise to power. He said as much in his second letter.

I have several times been pressed by various gentlemen to put on paper what I have seen through my recently invented microscope. I have constantly

declined to do so, first because I have no style or pen to express my thoughts properly,
secondly because I have not been brought up in the languages or arts, but in trade,
and thirdly because I do not feel inclined to stand blame or refutation from others.

But, like the Grand Pensionary and the Prince, he could not resist his
calling.

I beg you and the Gentlemen under whose eyes this happens to come, to
bear in mind that my observations and opinions are only the result of my own
impulse and curiosity and that there are in this town no amateurs who, like me,
dabble in this art. Take my simple pen, my boldness, and my opinions for what
they are. They follow in no particular order.

Not so. My father's thoughts followed, as they always have, the order
of his heart. "I tell you of the pipes of deal," he wrote. "I tell you of the hunger
of the louse . . ."

He tells us still of a hungering Creation. He tells us of its nurture.

In that first year and a half of his correspondence with the Royal
Society, my father pursued his studies with great fervor. The Elector of
Brandenburg's separate peace with France, the magic ebb of the tide that
saved us from the invasion of the English fleet, the battle of Kijkduin, the
Prince's capture of the French arsenal in Naarden, Luxembourg's retreat from
Holland and Utrecht, the Peace of Westminster, the yearly summer sieges
of Maastricht, the French retreat from Overijssel and Deventer—all these
went unnoticed save as they affected the passage of mail from Rotterdam to
London.

The passage of persons, too, after the Peace of Westminster in February
of '74, came to my father's notice only because then our townspeople in their
travels to England assisted my father in his correspondence with the Royal
Society. Indeed, he noticed his sister-in-law's removal to her sister Elisabet's
house in Dort only because Catharina Swalmius carried a package of his on
the barge to Rotterdam, delivering it to Uncle Claes van Leeuwen, who in
turn delivered it to the ship's captain. Young Adriaen Beijeren, traveling to
England to purchase shipments of serge and kersey, carried letters for my
father as well, and returned with copies of the *Philosophical Transactions*. Young
Justin van Coninxbrugh carried with him on his journey to London a letter
of introduction from my father. Even Seigneur van Belois, the burgomaster

Adriaen Boogaert, was entrusted with a brass case of my father's fine glass tubes for the study of the blood. But I jump ahead of myself.

The great events of the times went unnoticed by my father because he had discovered something through his bubbles of glass as astonishing as the glasses themselves—and rather like them. The world, my father saw, was composed of globules. He perceived this truth first in the blood from his own hand. Nothing is what it seems. Our scarlet blood is really a clear liquid in which float millions upon millions of small gold globules. These globules are, my father wrote the Royal Society, 2500 times smaller than a grain of sand. It was a truth difficult to countenance, except for someone like my father who understood geometry (and knew that if the axis of one sphere is 1 and the other 20, the proportion in their magnitudes is as 1 to 8,000).

Once he had discovered the globules in blood, my father began to see globules everywhere. He saw them in the liver of a blood swollen, pletorick cow, he saw them in bile, in the white matter of the brain, in metals and our Delft clay. He saw globules in our teeth, he saw them in the flesh fibres. *"I can call them by no other name,"* he said, when the learned Secretary Oldenburg wrote him, suggesting perhaps he might be mistaken, *"I can call them by no other name than—globules!"*

My father reduced the world to what could be comprehended by a single bubble of glass ground by his own hand, and through that lens he believed he saw what bound every work of Our Creator. Certain things confused him—the florid color of blood exposed to the air—the whiteness of chalk. These were the result, he explained to the noble Mr. Boyle, of the proximity and transparence of globules. The gold globules in blood reflected light back through the first, less pressed, layer. Somewhat, I suggested, as the glory of the Prince came from the subservient mass of burgomasters, burgers, and grauw.

"What are you talking of? Off with you, child. I must collect my thoughts."

I observe the blood in this way, he wrote. *I look well to the place pricked, putting upon that point my glass-pipe, and withal squeezing my thumb to press out more blood. . . . The slenderer the pipe is, the higher will the blood rise into it. Those who do not know the cause of this will wonder at it, although I believe Mr. Boyle and Mr. Hooke must have demonstrated it satisfactorily, judging by what I can deduce from the figures in their books, which regret to say I cannot read.*

No sooner had he traced out his thought than he would call me back again. "What do you think of this, Daughter?"

I kept silent, for nothing I could have said would have satisfied him. It wasn't my company he longed for. It took only the timbre of my voice to remind him of this.

"Never mind," he would mutter, his face darkening as he dipped his quill.

Never having heard or seen the matter demonstrated, I will add my considerations on the subject. These are that all bodies on earth are heavily pressed . . .

❦ ❦ ❦

How often in the year to follow would my father wish for the company of De Graaf, the young doctor from Schoonhoven, his fresh face, his robust voice, the wild gesture with which he would reveal the latest letter from Leyden or Paris or London. *Hooke suggested—Huygens implied—Swammerdam accused—Le Boe has come over to my side—Van Horne has doubted—Willis has denied . . .*

Alone in his study, bent over the incomprehensible letters from the Secretary Mr. Oldenburg, my father's face fell in upon itself like an old man's. After he perused the letters, he would hold them close to his chest like a dying miser clutching his sack of gold. It was only when he went to his glasses, when he dipped his quill in his ink pot, that his body straightened, his gestures quickened, he smiled as if his bold young friend were again in his chamber.

If De Graaf hadn't died when he did, I wonder if my father would have dabbled so much or so long. There was something, you see, in setting his words down, in sending them off across the North Sea, that convinced my father of his own authority. Now he makes no pretenses. No one, he assures the Royal Society, loves truth more than he, no one feels a greater awe of the Creator. He knows now it isn't an art he dabbles in, but an act of translation more arduous than the scholars' translation of the gospels. It is the last text, this invisible world, and Our Maker has left it open to be read by any son of Adam with the wit, courage, patience and devotion of—my father.

I do not worry that you find it difficult to believe in these globules. I have learned in France they doubt me as well. I do not use my old method. But let me assure you I have seen the globules in blood as clearly as grains of sand on black taffeta.

My father put down his latest letter to the Royal Society. "Now Wife, Daughter, I want you to open your eyes and set them to this glass. I want you to seal your mouths, for this method of seeing must not be shared with anyone."

Watching the smile on my father's face that evening in late December when he brought both Cornelia and me into his study to instruct us in his new method of seeing, I felt his passion flood us both. I saw our skin glow, gold as those globules, in the firelight.

"You will be a famous man, Antoni. Men will come begging for your expertise. We will be rich," Cornelia cried, spinning round the room faster than blood can course a vein.

Globules, my father says now, are fed by the nutritious saps that slip through the smallest arteries and veins. Then, it was the globules themselves interested him—not what they meant, not where they went to, in the individual body, in the systems of men.

"There is no ferment," he says now, furiously slamming the door to his cabinet. "Why can't they see?"

He doesn't see, my father, the changes that have overcome him. But I do. They began, I believe, back then when he saw the globules in blood. When, looking at cotton, at tea, at birch, oak, deal, liver, brain, scale, nail, tear and milk, he saw the whole world composed of what he could only call 'globules'.

It was at that time, I believe, we all began to understand that things just as small and distinct composed a family, a city, a country. We understood this, the family, the country, by antagonism and tumult, death and dissection. We began to honor what we did not understand—the glue that bound us, globule by globule into something the mind could still recognize: mother, child, father, town, country, world, leaf and board, endive, beer, linen, lead, blood.

It was Cornelia Swalmius and I who first understood what these globules might mean to my father, and in the process we began to understand what he—and his art—meant and would mean to us. But it has been a realization as slow, painful, and baffling to us as my father's attempts to document the blood's incessant transit.

After twenty years, my father has determined to his own satisfaction, as well as that of the learned gentlemen, the true course of the blood in the wing of the bat, the wattle of a cock, in the tail of an eel, gill of a flounder. But it matters not a doit to Cornelia, fast in her tomb in the Oude Kirke, stripped of all her worldly goods. And it matters now not a whit to me whose fortunes have been changed completely time and time again by my father's discoveries.

That evening in December in 1674 was the beginning of what the world will recognize as our lives: The three of us gathered in my father's icy study, the miraculous bubbles of glass, the passion that took us up and swirled us, willing or not, through the fine transparent intricacies of Our Creator's purpose.

My father does not speak as he once did of the intricate perfection of the globules in our blood, but once he wrote: *I could often observe very clearly, where the globules that constitute a blood globule were touching together, as it then appeared to be somewhat obscure, while the round protuberance of each globule retained a clear light, so that each of the six tiny globules of blood, which had been made from an ordinary, complete globule of blood, did not look to me as if they were united to each other. This gave me greater pleasure than whatsoever else I had ever seen.*

My father does not speak of the intricacies of the individual globule because he has not seen it often enough to be absolutely certain in his own mind. But I treasure his description all the same. It is as good a description as any I've heard for the truth, that universal globule which, spun right or left, up or down, appears always the same to the inquiring eye. That perfect symmetry tempts us like death, so completely different is it from the dizzying twists and turns that comprise a woman's life—or a man's.

III
ANIMALCULES
(1675-1677)

For me this was among all the marvels that I have discovered in nature the most marvelous of all, and I must say that, for my part, no more pleasant sight has yet met my eye than this of so many thousands of living creatures in one small drop of water, all huddling and moving, but each creature having its own Motion.

Antoni van Leeuwenhoek

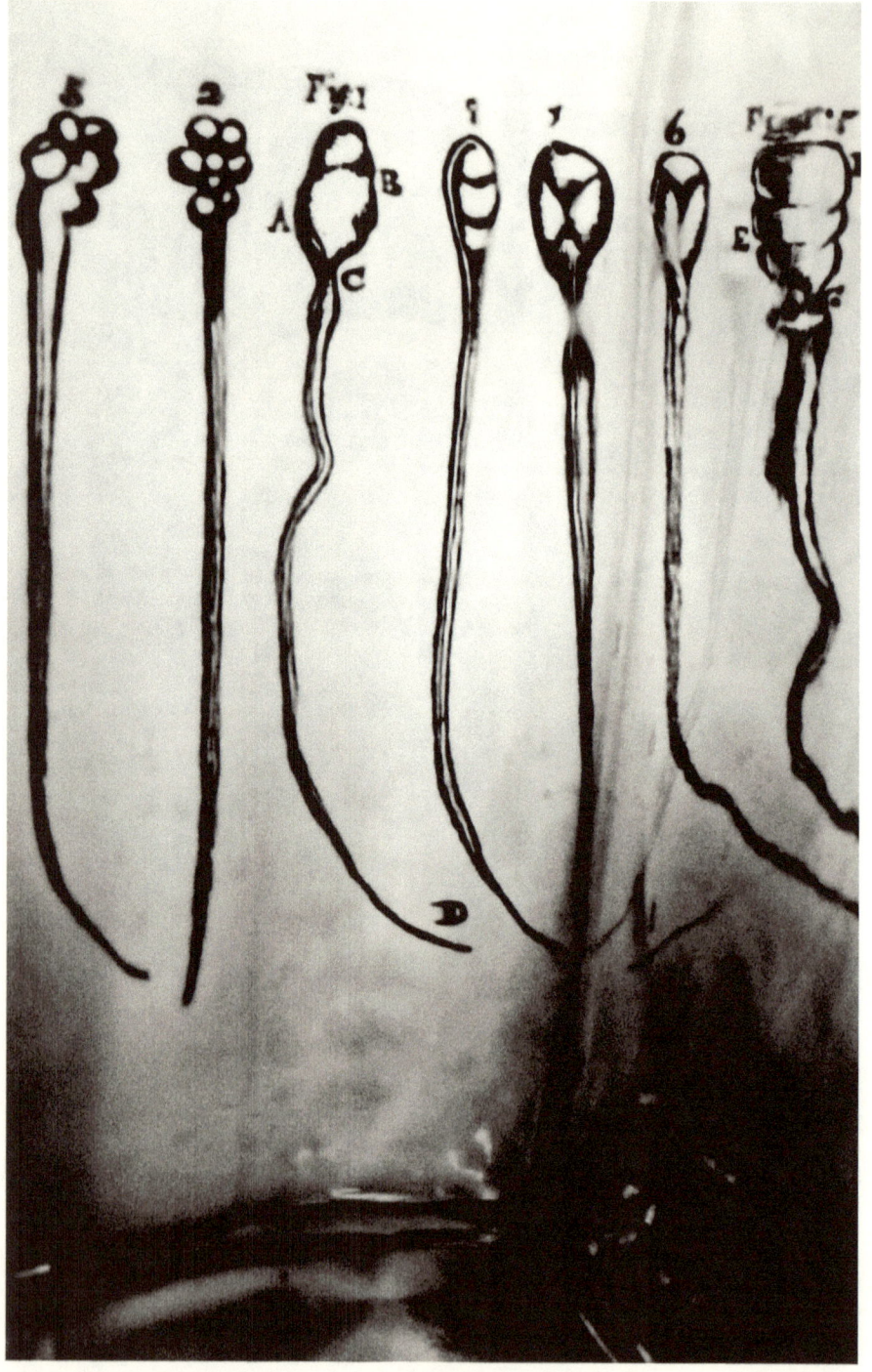

and *Snow*·water

air infused.

1675. I discover'd living cre

stood but few days in a new

This invited me to view this

ecially those little animals appea

less than those represented by

called *Water·fleas* or *Water·lice*

water with the naked eye.

by me discover'd in

consult of 5. 6

ANIMALS STRANGER THAN ANY DREAM

In 1675 my father made an amazing discovery. One that has changed forever the world for him—and me—and the Learned Society and the last three kings of England, the merchants of Rotterdam, the medical students of Leyden, the pastors of Delft, even the Landgrave of Hesse, the Elector Palatine. Even my Aunt De Mey before she died.

In rain water, well water, moat water, and writhing between steeped grains of pepper my father discovered animalcules smaller than the hair of a mite, more numerous than all the human beings born since Our Creator made Adam. Animals stranger than any dream. They have legs but no eyes. The sun shines right through them. But they are as alive as you and I. They are voracious. They are everywhere.

Take a clean Delft bowl and put it out in the courtyard when it rains—you will find them, fallen from the sky back to the earth from which they rose on the heated air like motes of dust rise in an empty attic chamber. Go to the well and draw water early on a June morning, and with each turn of the well wheel you pull toward you a multitude of God's creatures. When you scour your mouth with salt, another multitude takes refuge in the spaces between your teeth. When you rinse your mouth, you take in even more life than you have just destroyed. This happens to each of us every minute of every day—whether we know it or not.

For the knowledgeable, my father's discovery has changed our place in the world. From mite to whale is no greater a distance than that between one of these animalcules and the mite itself. Imagine that! It disturbs us as it must have disturbed our forefathers to learn the world wasn't flat. As it disturbed Seigneur van Zuleichem when young to learn that the blood returned to the heart as waves return to the shore, as it disturbed us all to learn the earth revolves around the sun no more necessary to it than the moon is to us. But I like the moon! I don't want it to fly off. It is a measure for my life more dependable, certainly, than one of Heer Huygens's new pendulum clocks.

Twenty years have passed since my father's great discovery. But it's not like a land you can sail months for, upon which you can step with a foot still rollicking with the rhythm of the sea. It's not really something you can leave. It's a truth that fixes in your mind like the shape of your mother's breast, the dent in your father's cheek when he smiles.

At least once a week my father draws water from the well or from the canal and measures a drop into a tube and fixes it behind his glass. Laughing, he will call me, the young draughtsman Gerrit, even Grietje—or Antoni. The little creatures leave my father wracked with mirth.

"Praise God," Gerrit exclaims, reluctant as my father to take his eyes from the glass long enough to sketch the whirling, writhing, squirming company. I am no different. I release the glass with a sigh. Who could tire of it?

Not I.

Not my father.

Nor young Gerrit.

Nor Christiaan Huygens.

Nor the late King Charles of England.

But Grietje has sometimes concealed a yawn behind her wet red hand. "*More* sir?"

"Where's your curiosity?"

"They scare me. I believe they're the Devil's handiwork."

"The work of the Lord."

"How can you be sure?"

"Where are your eyes, child? These are marvels."

Already, his eye again to the brass plate, my father will have lifted his face to the sky. His smile nearly tears his face apart.

Now that I think of it, perhaps that awe is as amazing as our first ignorance. When my father first gathered water and honey-dew from the Berkelse Lake, when he scrutinized water from the well, he did not know he would come to see these animalcules everywhere. In our mouths and faeces, in rain and the sap of trees. He had no idea what they would come to mean to him. No idea at all. But he never had a moment of doubt. My father saw and immediately he raised a hallelujah. I understand Grietje's fear better—

now—than my father's assurance. I understand Grietje, but I put my trust, as I always have, as much in my father's faith as in his judgement.

Before sharing his discovery with the gentlemen amateurs, my father labored an entire year over his observations of the little animalcules. He wanted to make sure that he would be believed. He wanted his observations to awe and delight the Royal Society as they had delighted us here in the Golden Head. For we had spent days—my father, my cousin Antoni Molijn, me, my Aunt Maria De Mey, even, sometimes, Cornelia—peering through the glass, wheezing with laughter, giddy with dismay.

"Who would believe this?" my Aunt De Mey asked, the summer of '75, laying the glass down on the table and looking at my father. "Animals no one in the entire world has seen before."

"There's more," my father said, rubbing his hands together, shaking them. "In water I poured over grains of pepper, I have found animalcules smaller than all I have seen before."

"No more, Antoni," my Aunt De Mey said, putting her hands flat on the table and raising herself from my father's chair. "My eyes are not what they used to be."

"You're little older than me, Maria," he said. His face was flushed. Four on a summer afternoon, he had opened both windows to air the room. We could hear the boys fishing in the canal scream out with pleasure as a fish snapped up their hook and drew taut the thread. We could hear the barrows clattering through the fish market on the far side of the canal. None of this drowned out the frightening wheezing breath of my aunt as she made her way to the door. She took my father's arm.

"Let me describe these little animals," he said, shaking her off and shuffling through the pages of his journal. "If you'll not see for yourself."

"Antoni, I *believe* you," my aunt laughed. "Why shouldn't I? When have you ever lied to me? But I am an old woman now, and I lack your patience with this world. My days here are numbered. No, no, brother. You mustn't deny me. You must take my word here. As I take yours."

My father shook his head. He was now my aunt's guardian for, only nine months after her marriage to the saddler Peter Schepens at the age of forty-eight, my aunt had been granted a separation of bed and board because of her deep and unconquerable melancholy. She lived alone again in her house on the Oost-einde, receiving as visitors myself and my father and her other guardian, Jacobus Wanne. My father had fetched her himself to see his demonstration. She had, as usual, resisted his invitation. Indeed, after her separation, my father had suggested she come live with us, but Cornelia would not hear of it. "She is no relative of yours."

My father rebuked his wife, but in the end he left her in peace. It was my aunt's own pleas convinced him, not sympathy for his wife. My aunt wished to attend to her own affairs again with, if necessary, my assistance.

"Another day, Brother," my aunt whispered.

"At such perfection in this tiny creature," my father read out in a loud voice scratchy with exasperation, "I did greatly marvel."

Silently, I gave my aunt my arm and accompanied her from my father's study across the town to the serenity of her own, the privacy of her own sleeping chamber.

That summer and fall, my Aunt De Mey took me daily down the Hippolytusbuurt to Adriaen Beijeren's shop, where again and again the young man drew up bills of sale for serge still tossing on the North Sea, for cambric the French still sequestered in ships in Calais. My aunt scrutinized each item, her eyes little more than slits. "Why so high?" she asked. "What's this?" She stabbed the sheet with her thin finger. Folding the receipt and tucking it in her pocket, she and I returned to the Oost-einde empty handed. My aunt drew out the receipts. With a sigh I seated myself at the table; I copied them out for my aunt again and again. My aunt sat beside me, her mending bolster now larger than her lap, her legs under her skirt narrower than a child's. When I handed her the receipts, she held them out as far as her clawed fingers could reach. She squinted. She put her other hand to her chest.

"The nine," she said. "It's upside down, child. You've twisted the letters in kersey. Where's your mind at?"

Shrugging, I would begin again. First I traced the letters with my fingernail, then I dipped the quill and began again. Sometimes my hand and eye acted in unison. Sometimes I wanted to toss the ink pot, break the quill. Then I looked at my Aunt De Mey. I saw her crabbed hand patiently piercing the black silk again and again, and I bit my tongue.

Daily, my Aunt De Mey balanced her own terrible accounts: the hardening around her heart, the flooding of her lungs, the breast that when brushed oozed a brackish silt.

"The seven is upside down," she said. "The three is turned around. And you spell silk—"

"I have no skill for this—I have no—"

"Choice," she said. "Until you marry, you must have something to occupy your time."

"But why not occupy myself as I have done?"

"Your father's house belongs, rightfully, to Cornelia Swalmius," she said, cutting me off with a wave of her hand. "It is she who should care for it. It is this house, child, will provide you with a dower when I die."

"You'll not die," I said. Putting my pen down with relief, I came round the table. I placed my hands on her shoulders, then drew them away, frightened by the bone jutting through the cloth.

"In time you must marry," my aunt said. She gripped my hand in both of hers. "But until then, learning a trade will be—"

"Torment."

"Duty. And more. It will give you something to share with your father—and with the young men who come to him."

"The ingenious?"

"Of course not. Young Beijeren. Young Landsvelt. Coninxbrugh."

"But my father has turned his back on trade."

"You'd be a fool to follow him, Maria."

"I don't see I have any choice, Aunt. Besides, his observations give him such delight."

"He has eyes for nothing else," she said. Her hand kneaded the dreadful knot in her chest. "Listen to me, Maria. I will die before this year is out. You must look after your own interests now. Marriage—No. Don't shake your head like that. Marriage will be your freedom as it was your mother's."

"Please," she said, tugging at my hand with terrifying strength, pulling it so close to her I could feel the fire that scorched her. "Only if you marry will you be able to claim what I wish with all my heart to give. Until then your father will manage all your affairs as he has mine this last year."

"And he has done it well," I said, tugging my hand away. "Everyone acknowledges his acumen, Aunt."

"That's not enough," she said. "He's like a boy. He's like a brother.

He has no sympathy for a woman's state. He treats it like any other."

"Is that so wrong?"

"Child," my aunt cried. Wheezing, she tried to lift the stone that suffocated her. "Listen to me. If you'll not accept my wealth, accept my wisdom. Before I leave this life, listen to me as you once did to your mother—"

I pressed my hands to my ears, cupping my skull as I had my aunt's stony breast. But nothing could deafen the breathless cry, the shattering mutter . . . my mother in the throes of love, my mother mourning my dead brother, my godmother breathless under the body of the saddler, my godmother panting, panting, under the stony weight of my own ingratitude.

"What else," I cried. "What else do we have to give him but our persons?"

"Life," my aunt whispered softly, but without hesitation. "The life to come."

♕ ♕ ♕

Often when I raise the empty lens of one of my father's glasses to the sky and see the circle of light, blue as the skin on the inside of the wrist, I think of Johannes Vermeer. The light behind my father's glass is as cool and blue and quiet as the walls of the rooms Vermeer painted. But I think Johannes would turn away with horror from what makes my father yelp with delight. That white-washed wall is crawling with life!

My father delights in this as Johannes did in the single human form frozen inside his quiet quiet rooms. There are no birds singing without the windows in Johannes' paintings, no children crying in the next room, but love floods the bodies of Johannes' women. It turns them into luminous stone. Not so the animals under my father's glass. For God made them, not any poor painter from Delft. He made them reel and writhe with His own heat. It is up to us, on the far side of the glass, to draw back our breath, bow our heads, astonished.

There are other reasons to think of Johannes when I draw a dipper from the pail of water and pour it into a wine glass for my father's observations. The year of my father's first great discovery was also the year of Vermeer's death—and of the death of my godmother. Sometimes these events tangle together like duckweed or silk thread, unless they are weighted, staked, twisted and knotted like the lace-maker's work.

Johannes Vermeer died in December of '75. I remember his funeral
at the Oude Kirke no more clearly than I do that of the Dowager Princess,
who took her place at last in the Nieuwe Kirke two weeks later. My thoughts
were filled with the illness of my dear aunt and godmother, Maria, who was
buried in the Nieuwe Kirke on January 25 of the new year. No, it was later,
October of the following year, '76, that Johannes' death, the reality of it,
came home to me.

Unlike my Aunt Maria, Johannes left this world reluctantly. He died
of fever only a week after he took to his bed. He left his wife and children
bereft of bread as well as hope. By April, Catharina Bolnes had filed for
bankruptcy. In September, the burgomasters appointed my father executor of
Vermeer's estate. Estate! Like my father, Johannes' worth was in his life itself.
As long as he lived, his hand promised more. Given time, the end of the war,
people would come again to his door asking to see the paintings displayed on
every wall, more like the Delftware on our mantels, a private treasure, than
wares to be traded, turned to profit, like the bolts in my study.

"*Paintings.*" My father bent his head again to read the paper Catharina
Bolnes had showed him.

It was a Friday afternoon early in October that Catharina came with
her daughter to consult with my father. It was the first time I had seen Maria
in months, but we only nodded at each other, standing like sentries at the
door to the room where her mother and my father conferred.

My father spoke to her downstairs, in our front room. On the
table he had laid out the papers he'd been given when he assumed his
responsibilities—the will, the inventory, the petitions for relief, the deeds to
redistribute goods between Catharina and her mother, the bills and the loans
and the promissory notes.

"*Paintings*," my father said again. "Why are they any different from
other goods, property?"

"My husband was honored as a painter," Catharina said drawing
herself up. Even with her skirt bolstered out, her black morning coat, I could
see she was wasting. "His paintings are of high value," she said, waving her
arm at all the portraits of Cornelia's people that decked our own walls. "Surely
you don't question that."

"Certainly not." My father shuffled the papers putting the bills on
top. "But their value isn't fixed, it isn't assured. It depends on the times,
the opinions of others. And we live, who can deny it, in a troubled and

disputatious time. If I had been your husband—"

"You?" Catharina Bolnes drew her cloak around her although the doors were closed.

"You know what I mean, Mevrouw Vermeer. If I had followed your husband's trade—if they had been my choices—I would have sold my wares immediately and invested my money elsewhere."

"Would a draper, sir, sell all his cloth and lend his profit at 3% to the Orphan's Chamber?"

"If he did so, he'd be well off," my father said. I held my breath. Even as he spoke I thought of the bolts of silk and serge he still kept in the fir cupboard in the study. The drawers filled with ells of satin ribbon, buttons, stitching silk.

"These are yours," he had said, two weeks before on my twentieth birthday. Turning the key in the lock he had tugged the door open. But surely my father had not saved those wares fifteen years just for me.

"It is the claim of Jannetge Stevens that truly concerns me," my father said, waving the papers he held in his other hand. "She will have to be paid. Through the sale of the paintings she has had seized by Coelenbier if not in cash."

"Never," Catharina Bolnes said. "Johannes only gave those paintings as security on the debt. They are worth far, far more than 422 guilders."

"I'm sorry, Mevrouw. The debts must be paid. That is my duty."

"I won't have them paid in this fashion."

"You have repudiated your husband's estate," my father said. "The courts have given me the responsibility for it now." Holding on to the arms of his chair, he pushed himself upright. He began to pace the room. Although I could not see her face, I was sure Catharina was crying. My father cannot sit still and look at tears. He never could.

"The courts have appointed me executor, Mevrouw, for just this reason. Good business is not something determined by the heart—"

"Or the soul," Maria muttered.

I turned to her, putting my hand on her crossed arms, but she flicked her arm as she might if annoyed by an alighting fly. She didn't lift her eyes from her mother.

"I will give everything else we have. Everything. Beds, clothes, linens. I'll sell all the paintings—all the other paintings. Not his. "

"It is not a matter of selling," my father said. "It is a matter of buying them back. They hold them now. I have arranged with Juffrouw Stevens to reduce the debt to 342 guilders. She prefers cash, but you cannot provide it. I agree, the paintings are probably worth more than that. So I will pay her out of my own pocket. This will relieve you of any further responsibility for that debt. You already owe the baker fifty guilders a year for twelve more years. When the paintings are returned, I will have them auctioned and use that money to repay myself and the other creditors."

"If you have agreed to that, you have robbed me."

"I?" My father stopped pacing then and came to the window where she now stood. He looked down at her gravely. "I? I have never robbed anyone, Mevrouw Vermeer. If I had, do you think the burgomasters would have entrusted me with this thankless task?"

"They are worth more," Catharina said. "Far more."

"In your heart and mind, I know they are. But we are dealing here with the value the world ascribes. The auction is as fair a manner of establishing their worth as any. Remember, your husband's word is also of value. He promised them as surety for the loan."

"I do not agree to this."

"The bread is eaten. The wine is drunk."

"And Johannes' body teems with worms. Life goes on. You don't need to tell me so, Heer van Leeuwenhoek. It is the pang the children and I feel in our bellies every morning. But we can endure it, if we can secure my husband's paintings again. He gave them up for us, the least we can do for him is gather them back again."

"With what?" my father asked roughly. "I can't in good conscience allow you to speculate so."

"It's all I want," she said. "All."

"I can well believe that," my father said. "But he left you more than that. He left you with her—" he pointed at Maria. "He left you with eleven children in your care. What about their dowers? Their apprenticeships? It's not enough to think only of yourself—your own grief."

Catharina Bolnes turned around and headed for the door. Then, catching sight of her daughter's face, she stopped and turned back to my father.

"I am not a foolish woman," she said. "And my children are as dear to me as your daughter is to you. It is for their sakes I want to secure their father's paintings. I am not even saying I would not sell them. But not in these days. Not until I can demand their true worth. There is no market these days except for paintings of the fleet, portraits of the burgomasters—quick—before they go the way of the De Witts. But my Johannes was a better painter than Miervelt, better than Palamedes, or Dou. Better even than Fabritius. There is no painting of his worth less than a hundred pounds of bread."

My father folded the papers and put them on the table. "The responsibility the court has given me is to find financial relief for you *and* for your creditors. I do not question the admiration you have for your husband or his talent. But art is commerce and is subject, as all trade in goods, to the wild fluctuations of the market. You would like me to hold back time, hold these paintings for twenty years in the hope their value will rise again. Your creditors too are vulnerable to these fluctuations. Can they ask *their* creditors for the same terms—twenty years of hope? They obviously do not share your faith in the markets, Mevrouw. They will accept less money, but they will not pay you more time. Remember, I have, through these actions, relieved you of years of assured debt, debt you are incapable of paying. You must give up those dreams of fortune so you can live honorably day to day."

"I *will* get them back," she said without any acknowledgement of my father's sudden pity. "With or without your help. I will apply to the burgomasters again if necessary. Come, Maria. I shall not squander the entire day in fruitless pleading."

My father opened the door for them. Bowed. I did not dare raise my head. I kept my eyes instead on my black skirt. How many years, I wondered, would we all wear mourning?

"She dared—" my father muttered as he went back into the room and gathered up the sheaf of papers. "She dared question—" But he did not finish the thought, I believe, even in his own head. He had his own cares that day.

At last after a summer of close observation, he was prepared to write to the learned gentlemen about these new amazing animalcules that thronged in even the clearest water.

❧ ❧ ❧

"*These little animals were the most wretched creatures I had ever seen,*" my father wrote of the first animalcules he observed in rain water.

These animals had two horns they moved like horse's ears. Their round body ran to a point in the back where they had a long tail, looking as thick through his glass as a spider's web to the naked eye, at the end of which was a pellet the size of one of the globules that composed their body. These tails, longer than the animal's body, helped them not at all. It was as if someone had tied a barrel to an ass's tail.

My father described their predicament more clearly than ever I could: *For when, with the pellet, they did but hit on any particles or filaments (of which there are many in water, especially if it has but stood some days), they stuck entangled in them; and then pulled their body out into an oval, and did struggle, by strangely stretching themselves, to get the tail loose; whereby their whole body then sprang back towards the pellet of the tail, and their tails then coiled up serpent-wise, after the fashion of a copper iron wire that, having been wound close about a round stick, and then taken off, kept all its windings. This motion, of stretching out and pulling together the tail, continued; and I have seen several hundred animalcules, caught fast by one another in a few filaments, lying within the compass of a coarse grain of sand.*

Wretched, yes. But I can still remember how we all laughed: my father, Cornelia, my cousin Antoni, even, the year before, my Aunt De Mey. My cousin Antoni cried with laughter, bending right over at the waist like a wicket. I laughed as loud as anyone in the room. It's now, thinking back, I want to weep. I don't see us, Cornelia, my father, my cousin Molijn. I see those creatures, without eyes, shackled as surely as we were by weights we could not see.

🐚 🐚 🐚

It's only now, on the far side of time, I see how shackled we all were. How—wretched. But is that accurate? Were we any more wretched than those first animalcules my father studied? Wretched. It's only on the far side of the glass, surely, we can give such a name to their plight. Our Maker proves as merciful to them as He was to us.

Today, I believed, dipping my quill into the ink, my hand would obey my eye. *Today*, my cousin Antoni thought as he turned to answer the barber-surgeon, my tongue will be nimble as my fingers. *Today*, Cornelia believed, a babe would anchor itself securely in her womb. *Today*, my father thought, I have made such observations the world will hold their breath, they will only nod in approbation.

What?, the men in England wrote my father. *Animalcules in pepper water? Are you sure?*

"*Sure?*" he exclaimed again and again. "Am I *sure?*"

"Maria!" he would call, twisting the screw closer to the glass. "What do you see?" he would demand.

When he called, I always came, but I never answered. What could I say? I saw animals I had no name for. Animals unlike any I'd ever seen. At times, blinking with fatigue, I saw only movement. Movement that could fill me as easily with horror as with delight. Within the pellucid flesh, green globules swirled. Outside these transparent creatures swirled splinters of salt, and even smaller animals, brighter than stars, brighter than tears on a thumbnail.

What do you see, Maria? What do you say?

More often than I saw his delight, I saw my father's pain. But I could give it a name no more easily than I could the clear animalcules under the glass. For if this was pain—and surely there could be no mistaking the grimace shuddering through my father's face as rapidly as it would through the transparent flesh of his animalcules—it was a pain he could not do without.

I was as helpless to ease it as I had been to ease the pain of my dear godmother, Maria De Mey.

Considering that nothing contributes more to the honor of God, the Creator of everything, or incites us more to the admiration of Him who alone is Goodness, Wisdom, and Power, than the exact observation of the Creation: 'for the invisible things of him from the creation of the world are clearly seen, being understood by the things that are made, even his eternal power and Godhead' (Romans I,20), the investigators of the Creation should by no means be deprived of the honor due to their unflagging labor. Now our Antoni Leeuwenhoek does not stand in the rear of those who have displayed an almost incomparable eagerness in unveiling the secrets of nature with the greatest accuracy and exactitude. This will be readily admitted by anyone who knows that Leeuwenhoek, without any

previous instruction, out of his own voluntary impulse and through indefatigable labor, has attained the highest perfection in constructing microscopes. For thanks to these microscopes he so distinctly shows the constructive parts of all natural and visible bodies, and demonstrates them so clearly before our eyes, that any one wishing to behold more after seeing this, might as well claim more light from the sun. Passing the little rods, the insects and everything else, including the minutest things he demonstrates in numerous other bodies, we mean to speak only of what he showed us in pepper water. Of this pepper water he took a quantity of approximately a milletcorn. In our presence he deftly took it up in a glass tube, approximately as thick as a horse-hair; next he divided the tube filled with pepper water into 50 parts (as may be seen in the margin) and showed us a 50th part in his microscope. Well, as eye-witnesses we affirm that we saw at least 200 living creatures in this 50th part of water; little animals which moved and swam in the water, so that we could distinctly see that they were indeed animals and by no means something else. In truth, some of these animalcules appeared to be about the size of a louse and on these little animals we could distinguish various transparent globules; for that matter, all these animalcules were transparent, not only in parts but entirely. The above mentioned Heer Antoni Leeuwenhoek asking our written attestation, we, not wishing to derogate from the truth, have justly and willingly given it to him, for which reason we have attached our usual signatures to this letter patent, as it is called.

Delft in Holland
A.D. 1677 the 18th of May
(the style of this country)

Benedictus Haan,
Lutheran Pastor of Delft
M. Henricus Cordes,
Lutheran Pastor of Den Hague

"See here, Maria!" My father waved the sheet in the air like a flag as he closed the door behind the two clergymen. "When next I write the Royal Society, I will send this patent along with it. Mr. Hooke and Mr. Boyle, my Lord Brounker, and Mr. Oldenberg won't be able to doubt me any longer."

"You turn to the clergy, Husband?" Cornelia asked him, coming to the entry room, her Bible closed over her thumb. "You think the Royal Society will be convinced by them? Why not professors from Leyden? Why not learned citizens from our own town—physicians, surgeons?"

"I will not always be bothering them," my father said with a shrug, blowing on the paper to hasten the drying of the signatures. "Besides, these animalcules mean more to the world than De Graaf's nest of eggs, they mean more than Swammerdam's anatomy of the flea. More even than Harvey's study of the circulation of the blood or Des Cartes' subtle air. They have brought us closer to the intentions of Our Maker than ever before."

"You perhaps," Cornelia said, opening her book and turning away.

"All," my father said with a snort of anger. "These men of God attest to it, Cornelia."

"Lutherans," she said with a shrug.

"You doubt their honor, Cornelia?" My poor father blushed with rage.

"Not a bit of it," she said. "It's the purpose you put it to—"

"The truth," he exclaimed. "I simply asked them to testify—"

"To what?" Cornelia asked. "That the world is more monstrous than even the mad have presumed?"

"How can you say that?" he asked. "You who have looked through my glasses more than any other woman—,'

"I deny that," Cornelia said. "The honor belongs to your daughter. Why not take *her* word, Husband?"

"They'd not believe."

"They would prefer the word of someone you have waved in off the street?"

"They came to me, Cornelia. Cordes and Haan came to me. My fame has spread."

"Ah yes," she said. "Three whole miles—to 'sGravenhage. But has it spread as far as Leyden?"

"*England*," I exclaimed. "They talk of him in England. And in France."

"Aah!" Cornelia said, twisting back and forth to fix us both, my father at his study door, me at the door to the street. "But what do they say of him?"

"For shame, woman," my father said, suddenly gentle.

"I must go," I said. "Adriaen Beijeren travels to Rotterdam this afternoon, and I have promised to ready the wares he has promised to the tailor Jan Abrahamzoon."

"I don't like it, Antoni," Cornelia said with a sob. "I don't like any of it."

I slipped out of the house, drawing the door closed behind me. My black skirt was splattered with the afternoon light that tumbled from the gutters like the rain water my father had first gathered two years before. I still wore mourning for my Aunt Maria. Cornelia had refused to put it on, as I had at the death of her sister. "She's no relation—," we had both exclaimed. "For shame, for shame," my father had said, donning each time without murmur his conventional black.

"It is easier for you," Cornelia said to him.

"Calm yourself. I have not said a word. It is your decision."

Cornelia had nodded but she hadn't smiled. There was so much, of course, that wasn't. She couldn't prevent the death that came every month, searing the inside of her thigh like fire.

"Don't carry on so," my father said. "It verges on blasphemy to rail as you do at God's will. Besides," he said, his own lip trembling, "its the tumult in your body, your anxiety and fear, that makes nature hesitant to rest there."

Twice since my aunt died, Cornelia had held us all breathless a month, two. To no avail.

Now it was our cousin Antoni Molijn, the barber-surgeon, we called to bleed her and relieve the fever she suffered right after her loss. It was fever. Her face gleamed with sweat, she tossed wildly in her bed. But I would not trust its origin. Remorse? Pride? In her dreams she cried out, but when we woke her, often she remembered nothing. Sometimes what she remembered was worse than nothing. She dreamt she had a baby, but when the midwife went to give it to my father, it turned to jelly in his hands.

"It became one of your monsters, Antoni. *One of your animalcules.*"

It was at times like that my father called for me. It was at times like that I wished desperately for my Aunt Maria. That is why I continued to see Adriaen Beijeren and assist him occasionally in his shop. I did it to keep the promise Aunt Maria never exacted from me. Cornelia thought it a scandal. My father didn't agree.

"If it pleases her, Cornelia, why not? There's no shame in learning a trade. When the time comes, she will make a good wife."

"When the time comes," Cornelia snorted. "If she continues as she does, who will have her?"

"*Silence!*" my father thundered. "Adriaen Beijeren is like a son to me. He is as honorable a man as you will find in Delft. Besides, it is at her godmother's request the child assists him."

"Child!" Cornelia protested. "Where are your eyes?"

Silly question. His eyes were where they should be—on Our Creators's amazing handiwork.

🐚 🐚 🐚

All the summer of '77 my father devoted his energies to sharing with the world this wondrous truth about the animalcules in pepper water. By the end of August, he had exacted five more attestations—exclamations, really, at the wonderful dimensions of God's creation. By then, Cornelia had convinced him to take his jar of pepper water, his glass pipes, and his glasses down to the Comanscoff, a tavern on the Oude Langendijk.

"No more of this, Husband. Morning and evening we entertain these curious gentlemen. We may as well run a tavern."

By then, everyone in Delft was full of my father's discoveries. Even Adriaen Beijeren and his friend Justin Coninxbrugh, along with their cousins and companions from Gouda and Rotterdam, when meeting my father at the Comanscoff peered as eagerly through his glasses as they would through weaker glasses to inspect the weave of serge, velvet, muslin, or India cottons. Adriaen Landsvelt lifted the glass to the light with the same cautious scrutiny he'd devote to a new shipment of Bordeaux or Rhenish wine.

First off, my father taught them all, tavern-keeper, draper, wine merchant and serge-maker, how to assess dimension. *I took 6 millet seeds*, he wrote later to the Royal Society, *and stuck them alongside one another with a little pitch. Then, with a pair of calipers, I took the width of the axes of the said millet seeds and found the distance between the points was equal to the axis of a big currant; and I remarked that the cube of 6 is 216. Now, said I, let us put an uncertain for a certain quantity . . .*

🐚 🐚 🐚

"It's a shame you did not inherit your father's head for figures," Adriaen Beijeren teased me.

"But I inherited his eyes," I said. "And this serge has not been adequately fulled. Besides, I believe it has been exposed to moths. See here— and here."

Adriaen Beijeren looked through the glass, first at the black cloth, then at the red. He put the glass down on the table, lifted the cloth nearer to the window. He peered close with his naked eye. He pushed his hat back on his head.

"Can you see it with your naked eye?" he asked me. "I can't descry the damage."

"I can," I said reluctantly. "So could my father. So probably could the tailor, used as he is to plying the needle."

"How many threads would you guess have been weakened."

"I can only attest to the six I've seen. But if I were to estimate the full length—"

Adriaen Beijeren lifted the bolt of red cloth and held it out to the light. Even from where I stood, five feet away, I could see the tears, bright as those animalcules spinning in pepper water.

"In my father's time, no one would have noticed," he said. "It's your father has accustomed us all to peering closer than ever nature intended."

"Nature?"

Adriaen Beijeren's handsome face froze.

"Closer perhaps than merchants might wish," I spoke firmly, although my heart was racing. "But it just serves to bring you closer to God's will—as my father maintains. Now that you know of the flaws in the cloth, it would be an imposition to sell the length at such profit as you intended. But is that so bad? Is it so bad to be compelled by circumstance closer and closer to truth?"

"Take this," he said, handing me the receipt I had made out for him earlier that morning. "I could no more pass this off than I could my serge. Since when does 9 plus 9 equal 81?" He shrugged. "Go home. I will close up the shop for the day."

He rose from the desk. He ran the thread through two more receipts and tacked them to the wall.

I wanted to weep. I had hoped I could keep the truth from him forever. "It's not that I have no head for figures," I said. "It's in the distance from my head to my hand that it all falls awry."

"Perhaps you have the makings of a merchant yet."

"You mean a thief," I said. I could not believe he thought I, Antoni's daughter, was lying.

"Moths," he said. "I have taken such care of my stocks. I have closed off the study to the mists that generate them."

"Surely they come from other moths, not the wind."

"So your father would have us believe."

"He is not alone in his conviction. The learned gentlemen in England believe so, as does Redi in Italy. Maggots no more come from putrefaction than moths come from mist or the East wind. They all come from eggs laid by their own kind. Only lately, my father has proved the same of fleas."

"Did he now?" Adriaen Beijeren opened the front door for me.

"He has shown that proud man Swammerdam in error."

"You'd think he'd be a little more charitable, when you think how little he himself can bear questioning."

"How can you say that? Has he ever grudged you an hour—or a guilder?"

"I am late," Adriaen exclaimed. He turned to me but the bells drowned out much of what he said. "He's been kind as a father—I want to prove—I must profit from his confidence." He touched the brim of his beaver hat, bobbed his head.

He turned and ran, heedless of his dignity, down the Koornmart. Just as he neared the corner a boy, playing with a wet piece of leather, tugged free a cobblestone. Adriaen Beijeren's toe caught in the hole. He stumbled, caught himself on one knee. He turned and grabbed for the boy, but the child escaped over the bridge. As the boy ran behind the stalls of the fish market, the cobblestone still bounced and bobbed on the end of the string, like a pellet on the tail of one of those poor animalcules my father pointed out nightly to all the tradesmen gathered at the Comanscoff.

But the boy was more agile than those wretched animalcules. We all were. We learned to live with our limitations, we learned to manipulate them as the peacock does its unwieldy train. In this particular instance, Adriaen Beijeren sold the bolts of serge at little more than cost to the orphanage. I, after much thought, reluctantly confided my difficulty to my cousin Antoni. He agreed to help me transcribe the receipts—if I would make sure to do the figuring, and to inform him who among the learned and ingenious would next come visiting the Golden Head.

The structures my father's glasses reveal are stranger than anything our naked eye perceives. Within the maggot of the flea, we don't see its adult shape writ small, any more than in man we see God. We see globules, we see sinews, we see magnified fountains, terrifying whirlpools. But we do not see our own world in miniature. In fact, when we look back at our familiar world, it doesn't seem the same at all.

It is difficult to hold fast our places in this world that stretches farther in both directions than any of our scriptures have foretold. Perhaps it is because of this my father always insisted on holding fast to his place in our city. Proudly he showed us the attestations of the medical student Gordon, of the notary public, Boogaert, of Burch, the advocate, and of Poitevin, a doctor of medicine come all the way from France. Proudly he read us the patent of Aldert Hodenpijl, the owner of the Comanscoff.

I the underwritten ALDERT HODENPIJL; dwelling in Delft do declare and attest by the troth of a man, which is equivalent to an Oath, that this day was shown to me by Sr. Anth: Leeuwenhoek a small glass pipe, hollow within and filled with liquor or water . . . & that in every part or division I saw hundreds of living creatures, some about the bigness of a louse, and some bigger, nimbly wriggling themselves with one another . . . .

My father read us the sworn word as well of the Pastor of the English Congregation, Alex Petrie:

*I underwritten, being willing to give testimony unto that whereof I was an eye-witness, do declare that having seen and read Mr. Leeuwenhoek's letter of March 23, 1677, as it is set down in the printed Philosophical Transactions, Numb. 134 p.844. I was desirous to see proof of what I found there related; and for my satisfaction, Mr. Leeuwenhoek did put a little quantity of water about the bigness of a millet-grain into a very slender glass-pipe, on which looking through his microscope, I did see a very great number of little animals moving in that water, so many that I could not possibly number them, and to my sight they seemed to exceed the number expressed in his fore-mentioned letter; and moreover, being desirous to see a proof whether these animalcula were indeed living animals, Mr. van Leeuwenhoek by adding a very small quantity of vinegar to the same water, and putting it again into the same glass-pipe, I did see those little animals in the water, but they did not move at all (being killed by the vinegar) which I beheld with admiration, that in so small a quantity of water I should see such a vast number of those little animals. Whereof, being Testis oculatus, I was willing at the desire of the ingenious Mr. van Leeuwenhoek to confirm the truth of his relation this testimony written and subscribed by me, in Delft, Aug: 20/30 1677
ALEX PETRIE, Pastor of the English congregation in Delft.*

"This should convince them," my father said. "One of their own—and a man of God."

Although my father was concerned with defending his own honor, he was equally concerned with fixing fast the shifting fortunes of all mankind.

If we now suppose, he wrote to Seigneur van Zuleichem, *that the little vessels in the little animals bear the same proportion to their bodies as those in our bodies bear to our bodies; then, in order to compare the very little vessels of the animals with the thickness of a grain of sand . . . To sum up:*

As the length of a sixth of a hair breadth is

To the length of 5400 miles,

So is one of the smallest vessels in the smallest animalcules

To the thickness of a grain of sand (80 of which put side to side cover the length of an inch).

Sir, you have here the wonders of dimension, which I imagine to exist in the secrecy of nature; and from this appears also that all we have as yet discovered is but a trifle in comparison of what lies hidden in the great treasure of nature.

Who shared this wonder? Certainly not Seigneur van Zuleichem's son Christiaan Huygens, who wrote from France that their learned men doubted my father as much as the English.

"Impossible!" my father cried. "What do they require for proof? They won't take a man's word. They won't take sworn testimony. They won't take the evidence of their senses."

My father spoke too fast and too confusedly. The learned gentlemen in Paris and London trusted their own eyes as much as my father trusted his. My father had to wait another full year before Mr. Hooke wrote to admit without any trace of chagrin the rightness of my father's observations. Read for yourself!

Having steeped then in rain water pepper wheat barley oats peas and several other grains, and having fitted up some microscopes which had lain a long while neglected, I having been by other urgent occupations diverted from making further inquiries with that instrument, I began to examine all those several liquors and though I could discover diverse very small creatures swimming up and down in every one of those steepings and even in rain itself and that they had various shapes and differing motions, yet I found none so exceedingly filled & stuffed as it were with them as was the water, in which some corns of pepper had been steeped. Of this the President and all the members present were satisfied & it seems very wonderful that there should be such an infinite number of animals in so imperceptible a quantity of matter. That these animals should be so perfectly shaped and indeed with such curious organs of motion as to be able to move nimbly, to turn, stay, accelerate & retard their progress at pleasure, & it was not less surprising to find that these were gigantick monsters in comparison of a lesser sort which almost filled the water.

It was I took that letter first to Adriaen Landsvelt, then to Pastor Petrie for translation. My father could not be bothered. For by then my father's attention was consumed by a new truth more fearsome and marvelous than all that had preceded it.

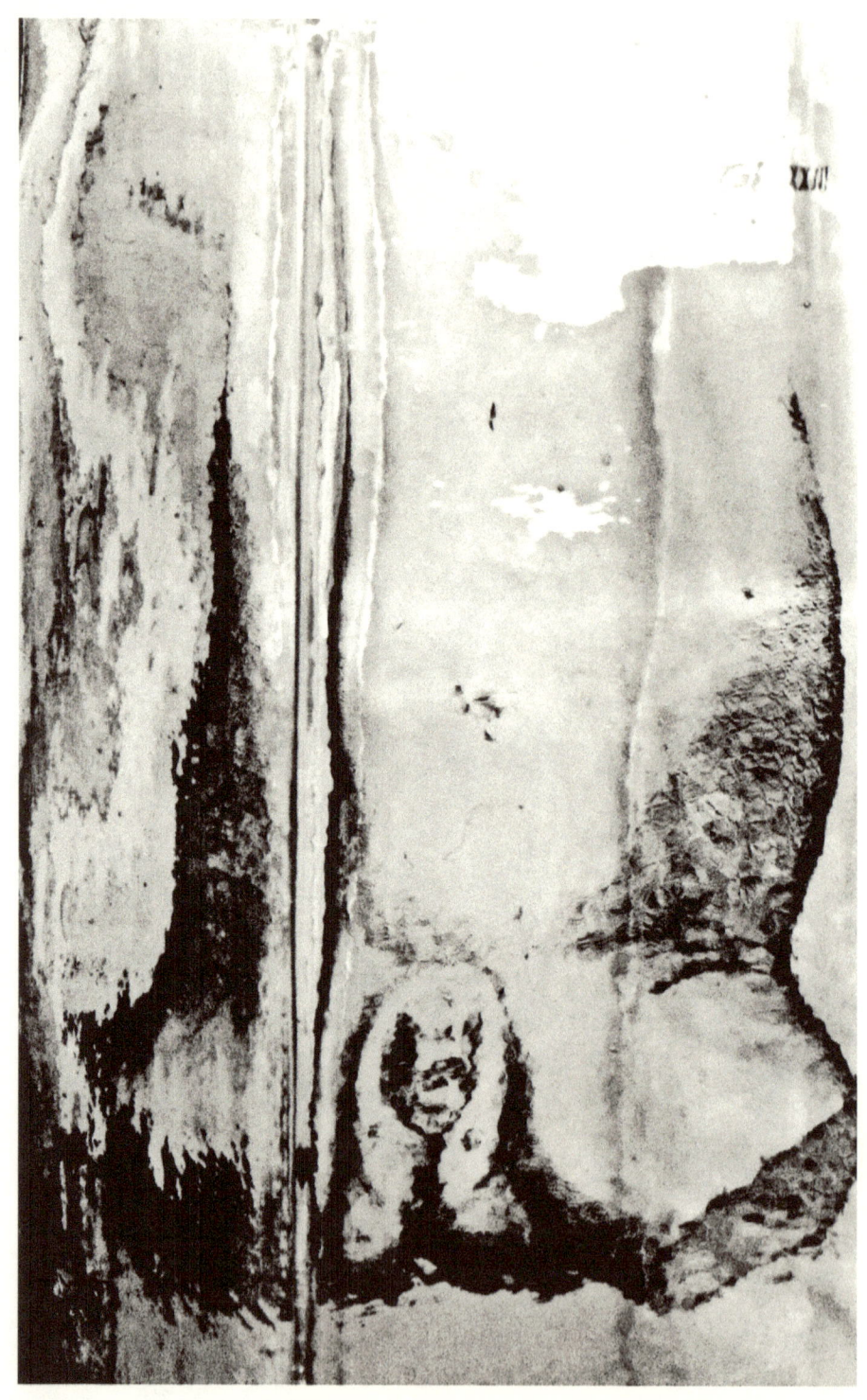

LIKE EELS IN JELLY

In the summer of '77, a medical student from Leyden came to my father with an introduction from his cousin, the renowned Professor Craaven of Leyden. He wanted to see the amazing animalcules my father had described to the Royal Society. In exchange, he told my father, he had brought a new kind of animalcule for my father to see. He pulled out from his cloak a tube like the one my father had carried to Sheviningen to collect water from the sea, He had sealed the tube, as my father did his own, with a strip of bladder.

My father took the tube with interest.

"What is it we have here? It looks thick for water. Cloudy. Saliva perhaps? Phlegm?"

The young man shook his head. He glanced over at me. I could not believe he was a student from Leyden. He dressed with the care of a burgomaster. In Leyden, so I'd been told, the students walked the streets in their night clothes.

"Well," my father said. "Let us look." He ushered the young man up to his study.

"Where's my wife?" he asked me.

"Resting. I have sent for Antoni."

My father blinked. "Could you send out to Adriaen Beijeren and ask when next he goes to Rotterdam? I have received notice from your Aunt Catharina that the parcel I was expecting from England has arrived."

But when my father looked through his small glass tube at the animalcules that Ham, the young man from Leyden, had brought with him, he thought no more of what he'd already said to the learned gentlemen. He thought only of what he was to say next. But first he had some doubts to settle in his own mind.

"Did you have him sign an attestation?" I asked at table that evening.

"Ham?"

"Beijeren?" I laughed. "Of course I meant the medical student."

"It slipped my mind. Besides, Maria, he showed me something most interesting."

"Animalcules? Isn't that what he said he had brought in the vial?"

My father stood up from the table abruptly. He dropped his napkin over his plate. He took the third plate I had set upon the table and began to dish onto it meat, raisin, carrot, from the bowl in the center of the table.

"I'll take Cornelia her meal. Antoni's been to her?"

"Yes, but he did not bleed. You might as well leave that behind. She has no appetite."

"Perhaps I can cajole her. If not, I've enough appetite for two."

"You have enough for all of us," I said, pushing my own plate away.

"Is something ailing you?" he asked, suddenly attentive.

"Nothing but lack," I said. "Of exertion. I am off to see my Aunt Molijn. She wishes to make up new dresses for my cousins."

My father was already mounting the stair.

It didn't matter what time I returned. I could not have escaped Cornelia's outrage any more than could my father.

👑 👑 👑

"Monster," she sobbed into her kerchief.

She had called me into their room as soon as my father left the house.

"Do you know what he did?"

"He brought you food. He wishes you only the best."

"Hah!" She lowered her handkerchief. The curls jittered with each snap of her jaw. "That is why, while I languish on my sick bed, he forces me to perform my conjugal obligation?"

"How else can he demonstrate his love, Cornelia?" I looked out the window. The leaves of the lime trees concealed the canal, making, with their shuddering leaves a longer and more vibrant channel. "I don't think you should—" I began, but Cornelia cut me off.

"You call it love! Do you know what he did? As soon as he was finished, he ran from the room into his study, his shirt falling over his bare legs. An hour later, an *hour* later, with no enquiry into my health, with no assistance in my sickness, he comes back to me, his face as rosy as when he pants over me. Do you know what he—"

"No," I said, opening the window to let the evening wind cool my face. "I don't want to know, Cornelia. There are things a daughter should not."

"Listen," Cornelia said, coming over to me. She put her hand on the window sill. She fanned her face. "You are old enough to be my friend. You are old enough, Maria, to suffer as I am suffering now."

"Stop," I whispered. I thought I heard my father on the stairs.

Cornelia circled the room, her back to me, as a dog might circle a pasture, hemming in the sheep. I continued to breathe in the cooling air.

"Do you know what your father did? He put his own semen into one of those glass tubes. He had the indecency to observe his own juices."

"He's already observed menstrual blood and afterbirth. Years ago. When he kept company with De Graaf."

"Do you know what he told me, Maria? His face was redder than a man wild with drink. But it wasn't shame brought the blood to his cheeks, it was excitement that burned there. It was pleasure. In his seed, he told me, laughing, he was laughing like a little boy, there are more animalcules than in the thickest pepper water. It is filled, he told me, with little wriggling animalcules that struggle through that thick phlegm like eels in jelly. Do you understand, Maria? He fills me with these. He fills me with millions of monsters, Maria. He fills me with—"

"Life," my father said a few weeks later, to both of us. "I have here proof that life begins in my loins. These animalcules are not the product of putrefaction as Ham suggested. I have never," he said, looking directly at Cornelia, "I have never lain with an unclean woman. I have never lain with any but my two wives. Barbara came to me as you did, Cornelia, chaste as she was honorable. This is not a disease, I tell you. It is a great miracle. It is one known to no one save me."

"What about Ham?" I asked. "Didn't he bring you the tube from Leyden?"

"But he did not know what it was he saw."

"Do you?" Cornelia asked. "Do you really know what you have done, to me, Antoni van Leeuwenhoek? What you will do again?"

There was a knock on the door.

"Listen," Cornelia said, getting to her feet and blocking my way to the door. "This must never go beyond the three of us. It is too shameful ever to be told."

"Nonsense," my father said. "It is a miracle, I tell you. It is what I have been waiting for my entire life. It will establish my place in this world."

"And in the world to come, Antoni?" My stepmother did not raise her voice. She didn't need to. Her words seared us all. "In the world to come, Antoni, you will burn. You will scream in torment. You will twist under the flames as I do under your kisses. Thank God I will not be there to see it."

"You take too much on yourself, Cornelia," my father said, his face white. "We none of us know, wife, who is to be God's elect. All we can do is follow our consciences. I have no choice but to share with the learned this marvelous discovery."

"You wish to destroy me, Antoni?" My stepmother took my father's arm and looked into his face. "You wish to publish our shame to all of Holland, all of Delft?"

"Shame?" my father exclaimed, prying her small hands from his sleeve. "This is proof of God's favor, woman. Why can't I get you to understand? Maria, answer the door."

When I didn't move, he shook his head. "Why can't I get you *both* to understand? "

Why couldn't he?

"Answer it," he said to me again. "For you Cornelia, I have asked this learned man to visit me. He will translate my observations into Latin. He will preserve the ignorance of your neighbors, women. Isn't that what you wish?"

I opened the door for the learned Professor Craaven, and then, while my father led him to his study, I assisted Cornelia, faint with rage, back to the living room to wait until his departure.

I think it is only fair you read for yourselves what my father, at the commencement of my twenty-second year, read to us in our common Nether-Dutch in the secrecy of his own house. It is no longer a matter of secrecy. It concerns us all, tutored and untutored, men and women, savages and kings.

Sir,

. . . I could not be easy unless I communicated to you the following marvels of nature, convinced that you will forgive the liberty I take.

After the distinguished Professor Craaven had many times honored me with a visit, he besought me, in a letter, to demonstrate some of my observations to his kinsman Mr. Ham. On the second occasion when this Mr. Ham visited me, he brought with him, in a small glass phial, the spontaneously discharged semen of a man who had lain with an unclean woman; saying that, after a very few minutes, when the matter had become so far liquefied that it could be introduced into a small glass tube he had seen living animalcules in it, judging these animalcules to possess tails, and not to remain alive after twenty-four hours. This gentleman also reported that he had noticed the animalcules were dead after the patient had taken turpentine. In the presence of Mr. Ham, I examined some of this matter which I had introduced into a glass tube, and saw some living creatures in it, but when I examined the same matter by myself after the lapse of two or three hours, I observed that they were dead. I have diverse times examined the same matter (human semen) from a healthy man not a sick man, nor spoiled by keeping for a long time and not liquefied after the lapse of some time; but immediately after ejaculation before six beats of a pulse have intervened, and I have seen so great a number of living animalcules in it, that sometimes more than a thousand were moving about in an amount of material the size of a grain of sand. I saw this vast number of animalcules not all through the semen, but only in the liquid matter adhering to the thicker part. In the thicker matter of the semen, however, the animalcules lay apparently motionless, and I conceived the reason of this to be, that the thicker matter consists of so many coherent particles that the animalcules could not move in it. These animalcules were smaller than the corpuscles which impart a red color to the blood; so that I judge a million of them would not equal in size a large grain of sand. Their bodies, which were round, were blunt in front and ran to a point behind. They were furnished with a thin tail, about five or six times as long as the body, and very transparent and with the thickness of about one twenty-fifth of the body; so that I can best liken them to a small earth-nut with a long tail. They moved forward owing to a motion of their tails like that of a snake or an eel swimming in water; but in the somewhat thicker substance they would have to lash their tails at least 8 or 10 times before they could advance a hair's breadth.

I have sometimes fancied that I could even discern different parts in the bodies of these animalcules: but since I have not always been able to do so, I will say no more. Among these animalcules there were also smaller ones, to which I can ascribe nothing but a globular form.

I remember that some three or four years ago I examined seminal fluid at the request of the late Mr. Oldenburg and that I then considered these animalcules to be globules. Yet as I felt averse from making further investigations and still more so from describing them, I did not continue my observations. What I investigate is only what, without sinfully defiling myself, remains as a residue after conjugal coitus. And if your Lordship should consider that these observations may disgust or scandalize the learned, I earnestly beg your Lordship to regard them as private and publish or destroy them as your Lordship thinks fit.

> . . .

These, Most Noble Sir, are the observations which I intended to communicate to you and the other learned philosophers. I beg your Lordship urgently to let me know the safe arrival of my letter. I remain

Your obedient servant
Antoni Leeuwenhoek

♛ ♛ ♛

"It is like a nightmare come to life," Cornelia said.

"Why must you keep repeating that?"

I was examining samples of the calico newly arrived at our East India House. The Princess Mary, Adriaen Beijeren said, had demonstrated a taste for it, and it was quickly becoming the fashion at the court. Now, he'd told me with a laugh, it might find its way into the laps of burgers—and the poor.

I held the cotton up to the window. It was sheerer than our linens and muslins, rougher than French cambric. But the color it held was as true and gaudy as the porcelain wares shipped from China. I wondered if I could convince my Aunt Molijn to purchase some for my cousins Geertruida and Margrethe.

"Why must I keep repeating that?" Cornelia mocked me. "Because it's true. It's your father has destroyed my babies. Those animalcules of his have devoured whatever life God had stored in me."

I folded the cloth. "Many women have been barren an entire decade before they conceived."

Cornelia stabbed her needle into the sheet she was hemming. My stepmother no longer longed for silk dresses, for the newest fashion in cap. She spent all my father would give her on linens.

"Why?" he had asked her.

"So when the time comes," she answered, "there will be enough for two."

What two, I had no idea. Certainly, she never indicated she would share her stores with me. She never asked me to join her in cutting napkins, seaming pillow cases, hemming sheets. To do Cornelia justice, I believe it was the tedium of the activity soothed her. When my father suggested she might take up the fine embroidery he had observed women doing at Seigneur van Zuleichem's house, she looked at him with a freezing pity.

"It's like a nightmare," she said again. "But it is in the morning when I wake that I am sick with dread. When I think of those animalcules devouring—devouring—" She hiccupped.

For me, Cornelia's fat white hand driving white stitches forever into the white expanse of linen was worse than any nightmare.

"Have you ever *seen* them, Cornelia? "

"*Seen* them? You think that would relieve this torment I am in?"

I shook my head. The only thing that would relieve Cornelia's torment was a child at her breast. Her own child. She could not abide the children of other women—even my Aunt Catharina's or her own sister Elisabet's son. The only thing that would relieve *my* torment—but I stopped right there. Even to think the thought through would break at least two commandments.

"If I had married another man," Cornelia said, drawing the needle and thread high as her chest.

"You would never find someone with more spirit than my father. "

"But I might well find one with less animalcules. I might find someone who doesn't try to deny my rightful place in God's scheme."

Poor Cornelia. She didn't, perhaps she couldn't, think things through. If she took what she deemed her rightful place in Our Creator's scheme, she was the barren Sarah, the barren Elizabeth. She was nothing without God's pity. *He* was nothing.

"Have *you* seen them, Maria? Have you been in your father's study peering through his glasses at—at his—at his *seed?*"

"No," I said, truly shocked. "How can you suggest such a thing? But I have looked at the semen of a rabbit and that of a cock. My father showed me himself. He demonstrated them to me and to my cousin Antoni."

"Antoni Molijn has told me all the learned men disagree with your father. The famous Harvey—even that wicked papist De Graaf—they both understood it was the woman who carried the power of life.

"And *death*, Cornelia. Don't you understand what you're saying?

Besides, it can't be quite so simple. Except for the Virgin Mary, there's never been a woman who conceived without a man."

"Except for Adam, there never was a man conceived outside a woman's belly," she snapped back.

"You're right. I can't make sense of it. Oh *don't*. Not again."

Cornelia dabbed at her eyes. One would think by now there were no more tears to be shed. But it was as if the very air she breathed changed into tear. As did the bread, the small beer, the tea, the pancake, even the smoked meat, the milk, and cheese. Grief did not make Cornelia waste. It grossened her terribly. She bloated with sobs, moans. She basted her entire body with nervous sweats, tears.

I collected my cloak, then took my place in my chair again. I was waiting for my cousin Geertruida Molijn, Antoni's sister. Now we took care not to leave Cornelia alone. If it did not relieve her mind, it relieved my father's. Of her moans, her tears.

"Tell me honestly, Maria. When you look at him, does he not seem a different man?"

"He alone? What grieves you, Cornelia, is the natural property of all men."

"So he would have us believe."

"Do you think the Princess Mary would speak of her husband as you do of yours?" I asked. Cornelia had, as she had always had, a fascination with the Orange Court. But with the arrival of the young Princess from England to marry our Prince of Orange, her interest had become an obsession—or had been until my father's discovery.

"Would Prince William dare to make the same claims as Antoni van Leeuwenhoek? "

"You must not lose faith. And you must try, for all our sakes, to keep your own counsel. It will help no one to spread this—" I shrugged. What was the use?

I greeted Geertruida and told her where to find Cornelia, and when to expect my father, who had gone to Rotterdam for the second time that week. Now it was to my Aunt Catharina he retreated when he needed sympathy.

"Where will you be?" my cousin asked me.

"At the market. Then visiting with the widow Beijeren. Don't mind what Cornelia says," I warned her. "Her thoughts are wandering in wonderful ways today. I believe it is this fever that confuses her. Make sure she feeds on cooling foods. Try to lull her to sleep."

I blushed as I spoke, but my cousin Geertruida believed me. Why should she not? I was Maria, Antoni's daughter. I had inherited his honesty as I had his sharp eyes, his broad brow. It was strange that my father's honesty had snarled me completely in a desperate deceit. I don't mean only with my cousin—or about Cornelia's health. Like my stepmother, I found that my father's latest discovery had changed the world for me. Years later, when my father drew the cream from between all our teeth and demonstrated to us the animalcules harbored in our mouths, I could laugh, giddy with a thought I had never uttered. It made us all equal again. We all teemed—how could I ever have doubted this?—equally with life.

But those days and months following my father's discovery I suffered more than a virgin's prudery. It is one thing to blush at the idea of a man's virile member. It is somehow a completely different discomfort to imagine what *comes* from it. And I did. I couldn't help myself. When I visited with Adriaen Beijeren under the cautious chaperonage of his old and ailing mother, when I admitted the famous Christiaan Huygens into our own house, I met these men's eyes boldly. Shamelessly you might say. The shame was in letting my eyes fall. The shame was in seeing before my mind's eye the glittering stream of eel struggling to move in that heavy phlegm dull as pewter.

The shame was in what my father told me.

The shame was in the truth.

My father believed he had satisfied himself on the matter of the animalcules in semen, but when the gentlemen of the Royal Society replied in January, they made as many objections as Cornelia. They made ones that touched my father's heart, so he picked up his glass again. He picked up his pen.

I readily accept, he wrote back, *that your Harvey and our De Graaf never found any semen in a matrix cut up immediately after conception for I state that as soon as the male semen has entered the matrix, the female must supply the necessary nutrition for the preservation of the sperm, either from the testicles (if anything issues from these) or elsewhere . . . And because we know that anxiety, fear, fright, and uneasiness will cause abortion of animals which are tied and cut in the sensitive parts, for this will cause such fright, that the sperm which has been conceived, will not only be deprived of further nutriment but that nature in its pain and anxiety will try to ease itself and expel the seeds . . . if your Harvey and our De Graaf had seen the hundredth part they would have stated as I did that it is exclusively the male semen that forms the foetus and that all the woman may contribute only serves to receive the semen and feed it.*

My father did not speak precipitously. He had, he told the learned gentlemen, seen with his own eyes on two separate occasions these testicles of women that De Graaf had claimed were the source of generation. He had examined the prints the good doctor had made.

I shall omit, he wrote, *speaking about the parts of which these so-called eggs consist. I only want to say that I was astonished how much is ascribed to these eggs.*

But was he any more astonished than Cornelia or I at what he ascribed to those little eels? How, I wonder now, did he know with such certainty as soon as he saw them that these small animals controlled his destiny?

He was not alone in his conviction, Certainly, although the Royal Society asked him to investigate further, they debated this discovery much less than his discovery of the animalcules in pepper water. The learned men believed my father so readily because they had at last come to believe in his other animalcules. They believed him because the famous Christiaan Huygens announced the same discovery in Paris in the summer of '78. It wasn't until the following December that the Royal Society saw fit to publish my father's findings. By then the young man from Rotterdam, Hartsoeker, sponsored by Christiaan Huygens, had published his observations on the sperm of the cock in the *Journal des Sçavans* in Paris. Now, twenty years later Hartsoeker dares tell the learned men of Utrecht and Amsterdam that it was he who discovered the animalcules in men. But it was not. My father has never claimed the honor. It was the medical student Ham, now a burgomaster of Arnheim, as I said before, brought the animalcules to my father's attention. But it was my father who had the courage to regard himself as an emblem of all men—who had the courage to reveal as a marvel what most men would conceal with great shame.

Within a year, my father proved that the testicles of dogs, bulls, cocks, and hares serve to store the little animalcules. He had Jan Janszoon, the porter, bring him two dogs and castrate them right out on the back stoop. He took the testicles and carried them into his study where he was able to observe within them the animalcules writhing as they did when, ejaculated from the virile member of the buck rabbit, they dripped down the doe's leg. My father was confounded at first. He thought the virile member itself spawned the animalcules, the testicles providing the sinews and vessels, the germs of the hearts, lungs, and other organs. But soon the glory of his discovery overcame him again. It was not just men and male quadrupeds, but birds and fishes, even, he has come to prove in time, the male sex of dragonflies, fleas, cockchafers, oysters and lice that generate these animalcules.

It is here we see most clearly the beautiful simplicity of Our Creator's plan. Whale and flea, man and mouse, the generative germs of all are the same shape and size. What my father has believed true of mankind, he has demonstrated throughout God's kingdom.

I do not believe it is all predestined. *We shape ourselves.* It is the care and perseverance we show in our labors that defines our faces, our figures, and our fates, within and without the womb. I know I presume. If you ask my father, he would deny what I have just said. But look at his life. Does it not demonstrate the truth of my reasonings? Look at your own life. Look at mine!

When, after visiting a month with my Aunt Catharina and her family in Rotterdam, I returned to Delft in the middle of April, something significant had changed between my father and his wife. Sometimes I see their marriage as one of those revolving animalcules in pond water, which change their shape completely depending on the impress of the water, the other animalcules, the glowing green food that fills them and surrounds them. But however difficult it is to distinguish those slow, oozy animalcules from what surrounds them, they are uniquely themselves. They have distinct boundaries, and within these boundaries the vital spirit shudders through both flesh and nerves. A marriage, I have come to believe, is very similar to those animalcules.

Following my father's momentous discovery, Cornelia turned away from my father as if he were a leper. She performed her own tasks with exhausting fidelity. She washed, she cleaned, she hemmed and mended linen for the table, linen for the bed. She scoured the floors, waxed the cupboards. In the evening, she read scriptures while my father, secreted in his study, pursued his studies. She attended church daily, thrice on Sunday. As often as not, out of pity for her, my father slept downstairs. There was pity, yes, but a little cruelty as well in this. Without him, there would be no infant to suckle at her aching breast. He needed to have her concede this. What he couldn't grasp was that without him there would not have been the need either—for the infant, for the grief.

It was left to me to admit the curious gentlemen. Cornelia was terrified our shame would spread. She didn't realize that she herself was the source of all the shame my father felt.

"*A fool.* I have married a fool. I must take it as an admonition. After your mother, Child, I should never have married again."

"Child," Cornelia scoffed, coming to the top of the stairs, her uncapped hair falling to her shoulders, stiff as straw. "Like Maria there, you should not have married at all."

"I am not a child," I said to my father.

"It is not my fault," I said to my stepmother. "Unlike you I have made no choices—no choices to pride myself on, no choices to regret."

Without another word to either of them, I gathered my cloak and left the house.

👑 👑 👑

Vinegar kills the animalcules in pepper water, as my father demonstrated to Pastor Alex Petrie. But in the absence of water, these animalcules do not always die. Some do. Some contract, rise like pyramids, then explode, like a glass globe containing grains of gunpowder. But others dry up like small seeds—and wait, for the next rain, the next snow. Even under my father's excellent glasses, you would think them particles of soil, particles of dust. Something like this happened to the marriage of my father and Cornelia.

Soon they didn't fight. They didn't even talk to one another, except to arrange the events of the day.

"I will be expecting two gentlemen at three this afternoon. I am off to the Sheriff's chamber to check that all is in order."

"I am off to the market."

"I will be visiting the Oude Kirke this Sunday."

These were both communications and warnings. When my stepmother went to the Oude Kirke, my father went to the Nieuwe Kirke. When my stepmother went to the first service, my father went to the fourth.

It was the predikants themselves greeted Cornelia. It was the burgomasters, the surgeons, the physicians, the schout who greeted my father.

I am not sure how Cornelia convinced them all to band together, but they did come in a mass in the early spring, burgomaster and physician and advocate and predikants as well, to counsel my father on the danger of his studies.

"Some gentlemen have come to see you, Husband. You will wish to speak with them alone, I am sure." The words dissolved in her mouth like spun sugar.

I followed Cornelia up the stairs to her bedchamber where we occupied ourselves with mending. When she heard my father at the door saying good-bye to the learned and honorable men of our town, she rose and seated herself at her table and began to dress her hair. But my father did not come to her. He spoke to no one for months about what had passed between him and the leaders of the church. He never even asked who had told them about his researches. They had by this time appeared in the *Philosophical Transactions* and were available to anyone fluent in the learned tongue. I think he didn't relish to know for certain what hand Cornelia had played in this visit. Maybe it really didn't matter. It wasn't with the loss of his wife's respect and affection these men had threatened him. It wasn't even with the loss of their own. It was God's name they invoked.

This time was a great trial for my father. Although it is part of our creed that we must each follow our own conscience and our own calling, it is as much a part of it that we must submit to the authority of our parents, our church, and the leaders of our earthly state. My father listened gravely to the church elders who gathered in his front room. For a month he did not enter his study. He did not walk the fields gathering samples to inspect under his glass.

Instead, he sat for hours by the fire, the Bible lying unopened on his lap. He visited the Comanscoff and discussed business with the young men of his acquaintance, Landsvelt, Coninxbrugh, Beijeren. He discussed archery with the proprietor, Hodenpijl. He discussed the troubles in England, the accusations of Oates, the escape of the Duke of York to the court at 'sGravenhage, the imprisoning, among so many others, of President Williamson of the Royal Society in the terrible Tower of London.

This was the change Cornelia had prayed for. She folded up her sheets. She herself went to the almshouse to secure a servant. She dusted off her mandolin and bought new strings. She consulted with her cousins and with the cousins Molijn about the latest fashions from Paris. Condescendingly, she came to me to place her orders. Velvet for the bodice, silk for the overskirt. Ten ells of lace. She thumbed through the work of Bontekoe to find out what to feed a man suffering, as she had diagnosed my father, from spleen. She tempted him, to no avail, with his beloved asparagus and endive. He had no appetite. His cries of *"Look! Look!"* never broke the silence. Instead there was the slow tuneless twanging of Cornelia's mandolin, the barking of the puppy she bought to console him.

But nothing, it seemed to me, would ever console him. My father's study seemed to grow darker, colder, and more vast with each day it was left curtained, shuttered, and sealed. The room grew as vast and dangerous as the mind sealed behind his huge eyes, those heavy white lids. My father turned to no one.

The world, thank heaven, came to him.

But not until he had resolved in his own mind what he must do. Like our Prince William when he assumed the English throne, I don't know that my father felt he had much choice—but that doesn't mean that he could—or even wished to—ignore the costs of his actions. He put his Bible aside. He picked up his pen.

He wrote like this to the old and learned Seigneur van Zuleichem of the amazing prodigality he had discovered in nature: *According to _____ who has speculated on the number of inhabitants of Holland, it is inhabited by 1,000,000 human beings, and if we assume that the inhabited part of the earth is as densely populated as Holland, thought it cannot well be so inhabited, the inhabited earth being*

13.385   *times larger than Holland yields*

1.000.000

13.385.000.000 human beings on earth.

The little animals in the milt number 150.000.000.000, which means more than ten animals in the milt of a cod as against one human being on the earth's surface.

I do not know, he went on, *to whom to address my researches any more. The President of the Royal Society is imprisoned in the Tower. The new Secretary, Nehemiah Grew, is a stranger to me. Would you please tell your son I have seen all of the animalcules in pepper that he has described. Your son is afraid I have not seen the long-tailed animalcules, because I speak about their motion, which he thought they did not show, though the opposite is undoubtedly true . . .* My father had seen them, stretching and collapsing, tugging desperately against their pellucid anchors. So had we all.

But it wasn't these animalcules he chose to show to the Duke of York, Prince William's father-in-law, when he came to Delft in the beginning of May. He showed him the wilder and more exhilarating struggle of those equally long-tailed animalcules in the semen of dogs.

The Duke's laughter filled us all with mirth: I, to see my father his old self (or so I thought), Cornelia to see the Duke himself in his velvet breeches, his large hat and ells of lace and ribbon, standing there in her own house, which was swept, scoured, and polished as well as any house in Holland. Her husband's honor was, obviously, her own. She pulled at her bodice, straightened her skirt. From her seat by the hearth, she nodded her head, blushed a startling crimson from her forehead to the tops of her breasts. My father too laughed to see the energy with which the Duke gripped the glass, the delight with which he announced, "I think I can even make out their tails!"

"If all learned men were like you, Heer van Leeuwenhoek," the Seigneur van Zuleichem said as he took his leave with the Duke, "if they pursued their studies with such diligence and courage—the wonders of nature would be much sooner be revealed."

My father blushed, shook his head. But when they left he hurried back to his study and continued his observations.

However, my father no longer put all his trust in learned gentlemen. When he was offered the post of wine-gauger that summer, he accepted it with great pride. He answered with pleasure the inquiries of the Loevesteiner burgomaster Velthuysen in Utrecht. Like this he referred to his trials of the spring: *My intention is not to stop my investigations in nature, but hence forward not to ask our physicians and surgeons for one thing and another. But on the other hand it is also true that I had previously resolved to stop my investigations, partly because some people have a low opinion of the labor they require, partly because those who, in my opinion, might be bent on drawing light and instruction from my discourses have been sent to dissuade me from these investigations. But when I am urged to continue my speculations by Learned Gentlemen . . . I take courage once more . . . and I am wont to say that if we only try do to good, an honorable man has done well, whatever the course of events.*

By the autumn, however, it was not only learned gentlemen who interrupted my father's investigations. His work was interrupted by Adriaen Landsvelt, the wine merchant, and by every brewer in town and every importer of Rhine wine, or Bordeaux, or French vinegar, or oil. They came to my father in his new capacity, Wine-Gauger of Delft. Those of the town ignorant of my father's studies were no longer ignorant of his abilities. They watched him measure the circumference of the barrel, plumb its depth, then, with a piece of chalk write down his calculations and within minutes, seconds sometimes, they heard my father proudly announce the official capacity of the barrel.

Cornelia too delighted in my father's new post. She now walked out with her maid Susannah. No longer was her marriage a source of mortification. "Cornelia van Leeuwenhoek Swalmius", she said loudly, "Mevrouw van Leeuwenhoek." How often in the past nine years had she wanted to deny my father's cumbersome name. No more. With the Duke of York's visit, she had relaxed her vigilance, for only after my father's appointment did she come to believe my father's observations had not exposed them both to the laughter and scorn of all Delft, all Holland. If the burgomasters could look her husband in the eye, well, so could she.

It was I who had difficulty looking my father in the eye that winter. My father and every other man I encountered. I don't believe it was shame I endured but a fiery confusion. I sometimes thought it must be like what the poor Princess of Orange felt the previous March when she discovered she had carried for nine months nothing but fat and water and a ghastly trust—in her husband, her maids in waiting, her physicians and midwives. Someone should have told her. Someone should have known.

But *who? How? What?*

Which one of them was at fault? The Princess? The Prince? Even should my father or the great Huygens take some of the Prince's seed and inspect it under the glass and discover it seething with animalcules, wasn't it equally true that the young princess would willingly nourish anything, even, poor soul, a stoup of water, the vainest hope. How could you look at that beautiful feverish face and insist she was at fault?

Were these, I ask you, fitting thoughts for a virgin of twenty-four? You need not answer. But please answer me this—how could I have avoided them? It wasn't wickedness that brought them to mind. Even if I were a simpleton, I should have inhaled them with the morning frost or mist. They were inescapable, I tell you. As inescapable as those other questions posed by my stepmother and my Aunt Catharina.

"How can you even suggest it?" I asked Cornelia.

"And why not?"

We were up in my chamber. I was knitting a pair of stockings. The white yarn mounded in my lap like snow.

"It's unnatural."

"Unnatural!" Cornelia said, "You're the one who's unnatural, Maria. You act as if you have all the time in the world."

Cornelia leaned over to warm her hands by the fire. Even in the chill air, my face and fingers burned. The hairs of the yarn scratched at my skin sharp as wires.

"He's an old man."

"No older than your father. And wealthier. He has no children, Maria. He suffers from gout and stone. He won't last long. And when he dies, it will all go to you—and to your children, should you prove fertile."

"I!"

"His first wife died in childbed. Something must have been right."

"And wrong!" Unable to contain myself, I put aside my knitting and rose to my feet. "What is it you want to prove, Cornelia?"

"Nothing," she said earnestly. Her little mouth pursed as if she were blowing me a kiss. The sky through the window was white as the yarn that had tumbled to the floor. "It would not be doing my duty if I did not suggest it."

"What does my father say?"

"Why should he say anything?" she asked. She straightened her blue silk overskirt. Her breath made stark white clouds in the pale air. "He has nothing to lose by this."

"Nothing?" The air came so slowly from my mouth it clouded the air as it would cloud a mirror. I could not see Cornelia. I could no longer hear her. Even as I slipped to the floor, I had the dreadful knowledge I would only wake again, dizzied, to other voices, the same question.

♛ ♛ ♛

"I will pose the question to your father myself, then," my Aunt Catharina said. It was early February. She had arrived at noon from Rotterdam with Johannes, Phillip, Antoni, Jacob, Geertruy, and the baby Niclaes. The boys were already out skating on the canal. My aunt and I sat in the front room by the window to observe them. February is our coldest month, the time when one gives up all hope of spring.

"If I were a child again," I said, "I would not mind it so."

"What?"

"The cold." I rubbed my hands. "Even with my felt skirt, my stockings, my fur-lined morning coat, there are mornings I cannot bear the thought of bringing my face without the sheets."

"That's what I have been saying, Maria," Aunt Catharina said with a shrug. "You need company."

"A *boy*, Aunt Catharina!"

"He is twenty-three, the same age as your father when he married."

"He has no money."

"He comes from an honest family. He has wit and enterprise. He belongs to the guild."

"An apothecary?"

"What would you rather, Niece? A draper? An auctioneer like my Claes? A surgeon, maybe, like your cousin Molijn?"

She paused and looked at me suspiciously, "You have not come to some agreement with your cousin Molijn have you?"

"With Antoni?" I asked incredulously. "Antoni Molijn?"

"You can't live here forever," said Aunt Catharina. "I know. I wanted to myself at one time."

"You?"

"I kept house for your father before he married your mother. I can recall how I sobbed when Gryetgen suggested I marry Claes van Leeuwen. He seemed such an old man to me."

"Why didn't you refuse?" I was at the window rubbing one of the panes clear with the fur cuff of my coat.

"How could I? I had no dower. He took me for my youth, my beauty. In every way, Maria," my aunt said softly, "I was the richer for it."

"And this apothecary," I said. "What would he take me for?"

Without a word my aunt rose and went to my father's study.

She knocked boldly, then entered.

"A fool," my father said to her loudly, an hour later as he called to me to come and join them. "I would be a fool to agree to this—and so would she."

"What are you thinking of, Brother?" My aunt's face was white. I had never seen her so angry in my life. "Maria is twenty-four. It is time she established a household of her own. I was seventeen when Claes and I married."

"There's a difference," my father said. "I can afford to keep her now."

"It was a good match, Antoni. Seventeen, or thirty—it would *still* have been a good match for me. As this is for Maria."

"An *apothecary's* wife?"

"Who do you think you *are*?" my aunt gasped.

My father drew his yellow morning robe around him with a smile. He waved the letter she had brought him from Rotterdam.

"I," he said, "am Antoni van Leeuwenhoek, soon to become a member of that illustrious company, the Royal Society of London."

"What?" We both gaped.

"I have it written right here. Mr. Hooke says he is eager to nominate me for membership in the august company."

I clapped my hands. I was delighted—at his honor and at what I believed to be a fortuitous change of subject.

"You will now be a member along with the famous Mr. Boyle, Mr. Nehemiah Grew, Mr. Willis and Mr. Hooke. Along with Seigneur van Zuleichem and his son!"

"It's all I have ever hoped for," my father said.

"Antoni," my aunt said, coming to take my father's hand in both hers. "I am deeply happy." She gazed up at him with eyes as large and blue and candid as his own. "For *you*. So very pleased for you. But where does this leave your daughter?"

"What do you mean?" my father said tugging his arm away.

He spread the letter flat on the table. "Read this, Catharina."

"It doesn't *answer*, Antoni. Can't you see that?"

"Can't *you* see? Everything is changed. No one will mock my labors any more. No one will challenge them."

"You'll make no fortune at it, Antoni. And fame is no sinecure you can pass on to a son-in-law. "

"Sinecure! I am no burgomaster, sister. I am simply a follower of the New Philosophy."

"And *she*?" my aunt cried, pointing at me as if I were a stranger. "She is a follower as well?"

"Certainly she will be no apothecary's wife."

"You wrong her, Antoni. Please believe me—"

At this point I left them to supervise the preparation of the afternoon tea. I didn't know the answer to my aunt's question. Was I too a follower of the New Philosophy? If she was asking whether I could ignore my father's discoveries, the answer was a resounding no. No more than I could ignore the questions with which she and Cornelia tormented me.

If indeed my father was right—and we women received life from the animalcules struggling through the thick pellucid semen of men—then life passed, like authority, money, honor, exclusively from father to son. If my father was right, it was the other man, the gout-ridden clerk in Benthuizen, or the young ribald apothecary in Rotterdam, and *their* fathers who would gain—or lose—perpetual life from this.

If my father was right, all I, a dutiful daughter, could give him was *my* life.

If my father was right.

No, I said to the gout-ridden clerk.

No, I said to the apothecary.

There was no man on earth, I believed, worth the danger to which he would expose us, father and daughter. Would you, at my age and under my circumstances, have reasoned any differently?

IV
SCURF
(1680-1683)

We certainly see many fighting on behalf of the testicles as though on behalf of their homes and their holy places but they offer such diverse explanations of how semen is confected in the testicles that one could not presume anything they say is true.

Regnier de Graaf

Mr. Francis Aston, Secretary of the Royal Society . . . wrote to tell me that my theory of animal generation through male semen is very ingenious but that I shall be contradicted by many all over the world. That is exactly what I thought for the world is prejudiced in favour of the ovary. However, I have found many learned gentlemen in our country who approve my theses. Consequently, I shall continue my observations and contemplations on this subject.

Antoni van Leeuwenhoek

all men, the *** *** *** *** without *** The *** *** ch he reiterated so often, that *** enfeebled thereby, but had no ben*** o pretended *** skill *** him so *** became such weaknd *** *** and was worse: *** that in the end, *** *** fain to beg Harlem, for a Licence to beg. I *** *** this ma*** scratch gently some of the scales *** *** his leg, whi*** I preserved in a paper, and afterward *** *** serving them I found that in many places, they were beset with small parts of dryed blood and matter. A 3d person, whom I met, was a Youth about 12 years of Age, his head was co-vered with such foul sores, that I could not stay to view it, without loathing.

A 4th person I met, was a Woman, about 30 years re, who was likewise permitted to beg; she said, th*** ease consisted in the skins scaling from her head, wh*** reamly itched, and when scratched, did very *** her, and also bled, and caused those red scab*** to uncover her head, but I was satisfi*** r being from home, and le***ing

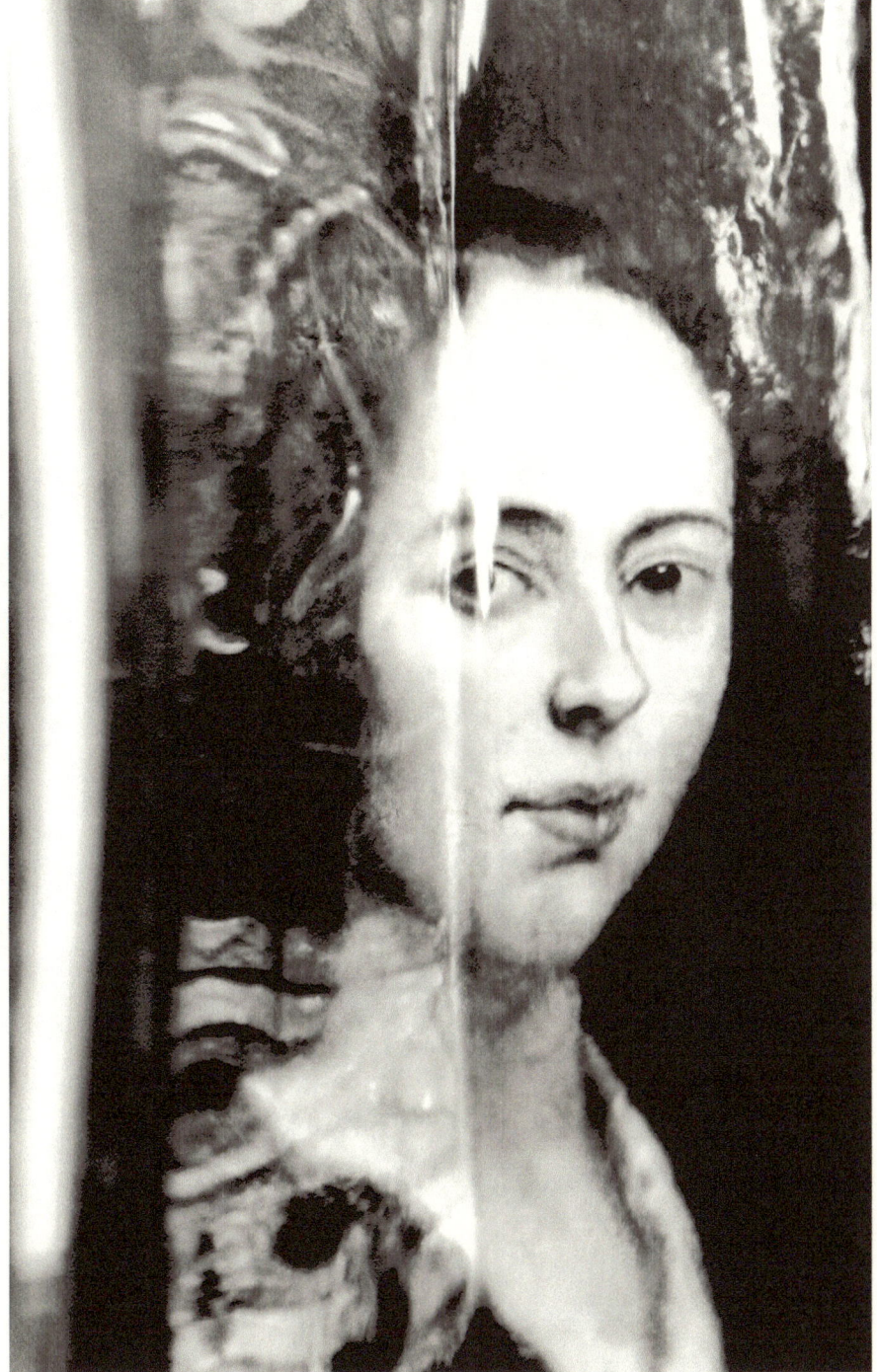

THE ITCH OF DOUBT

"It is man's duty to cultivate honor," my father wrote in February, 1680 to the Secretary of the Royal Society, Mr. Robert Hooke. "And this honor is the greatest in the world. I ask all your help in gaining it for me." My father meant membership in the Royal Society. He was touched by the man who had offered to propose him, for Mr. Hooke is as twisted in spirit as he is in body. To offer my father something like this must have racked the poor hunchback quite painfully.

All that year, both before and after my father learned of his election to the Royal Society, he pursued his observations with a wonderful vigor. He discovered animalcules in the sperm of fishes, in perch, bream, roach, and tench. He even discovered animalcules in the sperm of insects, of fleas and may-flies, grasshoppers, and dragon-flies—and he exclaimed aloud at their disproportionate size. It was as if a man had animalcules large as eels swimming in his testicles.

But my father did not restrict himself to questions of generation. He laughed with joy and went on. He studied the globules found in yeast, in blood, in wine, in water, in mother's milk, and everywhere he saw Our Creator honoured symmetry and proportion. The globules clustered like grapes in groups of six. Everywhere my father looked, he saw this was Nature's favored shape, one which, turned right or left, up or down, transmitted an identical contour to the mind.

My father's fame seemed to spread faster than rumor. Men came from Leyden, from Amsterdam, from England to meet this burger honored by the English King. Even in Paris, my cousin Antoni wrote, my father's name was on every tongue. In the square, my father bowed to the burgomasters, to the doctors 'sGravesende and D'Aquet. He opened the door for them in the stadthuis. But at his own house he had them wait for admittance. They had to give place to the Prince of Orange's secretary, Constantijn Huygens, the Seigneur van Zuleichem. They had to give way to the noble merchant from Aberdeen.

Cornelia and I shared my father's pride, his glee. I ordered new clothes for all of us. Taffeta skirts for Cornelia and me. New lace caps. A cape for my father, a new periwig from France. Cornelia weighted the table morning and night with fish from the market, fruit from the garden. She prepared to entertain the wives of the burgomasters while their husbands studied my father's glasses. The lines around her mouth grew fainter, her hair thickened, her face pinkened with relief. She even listened to my father's theories of generation with composure, picking her linen cloths with silk thread, making embroidery as fine as that made by the noble women waiting on the Princess of Orange.

I listened too, recording the day's transactions in my daybook as I did also for Heer Beijeren. It seemed much the same thing. *From* the Duke of York, one wild laugh, one generous gasp of amazement. *To* Pastor Petrie, one new observation to be translated from the English. *From* the Seigneur of Zuleichem, good words from the Academy in Paris. *To* the Seigneur of Zuleichem, new discoveries to send on to his son, Christiaan Huygens.

There was no end of visitors—and each one assured us, assured us all, of our rise in the world. It was as insidious as the rustle of our new silks.

"This is the greatest honor in the world," my father wrote the great gentlemen in England. "I will strive all my life to be worthy of it. "

He meant it. Of course he meant it. But who can blame him if the honor itself dizzied him? Like wax inside the ear, it deafened him to the rest of the world. It wasn't that my father talked of his new dignity, he demonstrated it. My father's laughter rumbled through our house from attic to cellar. At night our floors and bedsteads creaked with the joy he couldn't restrain. He decked himself daily in clean linen, settled his new periwig on his head and marched to the stadthuis as ready to usher the burgomasters into the sheriff's chamber as he would be, a few hours later, to usher them into his own house. He opened his door to all who came knocking, He propounded his theories without apologies. My father does not take censure gladly. But honors, praise? Those months immediately following his election, I would have said—certainly.

At last my father felt he belonged completely—in Delft as well as in the company of the Learned Gentlemen of London. My father had, he believed, solved the question of generation. Certainly nothing, as he even now must assure the learned Rabus from Rotterdam, arises from putrefaction. Or earwax! All life comes from procreation. From, to be more exact, the animalcules in semen.

What still amazed my father were the vast numbers of these animalcules. In the testicle of a rat, skinned and suspended in water, he'd found in just the smallest portion of the thinnest thread thousand upon thousand. To move the width of a fiber would be as great a distance for those poor eels as for a cow to cross a pasture. Imagine!

What my father couldn't imagine was how they all began. From eggs perhaps? Eggs within the testicles? But he left that to others to decide. He had seen enough, he said, to satisfy himself. My father was guilty of false modesty. Truly, he believed he had seen enough to satisfy everyone.

My father felt at rest at last, like a caterpillar settling into its warm cocoon. Poor man. He had no idea what was to happen next—any more than does the silkworm who lies sated on the mulberry leaf, the silk oozing from its lips.

The world is a contentious place. It's as true of Delft as it is of Batavia. Even within our own house, my father could not preserve the tranquility he felt he had earned. Even within the Golden Head, my father's views were open to debate. My cousin Antoni had returned from Paris looking like a courtier in his periwig and French clothes. He affected as well a Frenchman's scorn.

It wasn't he, my cousin maintained, who questioned my father. Rather the honoured Heer Christiaan Huygens, rather his learned friends. Antoni Molijn now spoke his Nether-Dutch with a French accent. When talking to my father, he kept his eyes on the ceiling rather than on the ground. He had two fine lace handkerchiefs he had his sisters launder daily. He wore a coat of flowered damask.

"The gentlemen," he said, straightening his collar, "question the origin and purpose of these animalcules. Some of them continue to doubt their existence—even with Heer Huygens and Heer Hartsoeker's observations printed in the *Journal des Sçavans.*"

Antoni straightened his lace cuffs. My father removed his new periwig and began combing it. Antoni adjusted the bow on his new shoes. They both stopped and glowered at each other like two small boys ready for fisticuffs.

"Why don't they believe me?" my father said. "Everyone else does."

"Everyone here in Delft," Antoni replied with a shrug.

"Perhaps you should leave then," my father growled, settling the periwig on his head. He stood, rocking back and forth on the balls of his feet. I could tell by the way he had looked at Antoni's shoes that tomorrow he would go to the cobbler and order himself a new pair.

"Perhaps I should," Antoni agreed with a malicious smile. "I've studied up on my Latin, Uncle. I intend to matriculate at Harderwijck in January."

"Harderwijck? *You?*"

Astonished, my father stared at his nephew. My cousin sniffed and proudly lifted his chin. He glanced quickly at me for support.

"And why not? Didn't your uncle De Mey, Maria? Didn't Cornelia Swalmius' brother? Why should I not go to the university?"

"What do you intend to study?" my father asked reluctantly.

"What else? Medicine."

"He'll *not* take precedence over me," my father muttered after my cousin had left. He circled the table eyeing the meat as if it were spoiled, the fruit as if it were rotten. His lack of education still smarted like an open sore. With all his newly won honours and his illustrious visitors, my father still had to give place at the Anatomy Chamber—not only to the burgomasters 'sGravesende and D'Aquet, but to all the other physicians as well. Leeuwenhoek, Fellow of the Royal Society—still forced to give precedence to men just as ignorant as boors of the invisible world, this great new book of nature of which he by now was as knowledgeable as anyone. But *not* within his own family. And never to a Molijn. Here, in his own house, he would never give way. Never.

Why could my father not understand that the same ambition that drove him also drove his godson? Antoni Molijn was going to study at Harderwijck because, having been to Paris, he found he could not settle in among the barber-surgeons. In fact, my cousin's ambition was more moderate than my father's. He wanted to take his place at the foot of the train of physicians, not head them up!

My father has never understood that it was Antoni Molijn's

admiration of him that encouraged the young man to train as a barber-surgeon, then to study medicine. My cousin Antoni too refuses to see his godfather's weakness, his fear.

That isn't quite fair. There was one occasion, that very winter of 1680, when Antoni did try to protect my father. Protect him from Cornelia Swalmius, my father's own wife. For, like cousin Antoni, Cornelia that year gave with one hand what she took away with the other.

Except with Cornelia it was much worse. My father could still strive to keep his superiority over Antoni. Cornelia threatened to supplant him completely.

How? By having a child without his assistance.

When Cornelia returned from Dort, where she had spent two months tending to her sister Elisabet who was ailing, she asked me to burn the string for her. As soon as I waved it under her nose, she turned pale and began to swoon. I helped her to the bed, where she rested until my father came home.

"You can't be," he said. "When you left, you were still bleeding. I observed the rags myself."

"Ask Maria," Cornelia said. "She burned the string. She held it under my nose."

"Foolish superstition," my father said with a snort.

"We'll see who's the fool, Antoni Leeuwenhoek," Cornelia said. "It might not take those animalcules. It might just take that nest of eggs Dr. de Graaf discovered."

"But certainly you'll not lie in bed nine months to prove the point, Cornelia."

"No," she said. "Of course not." But she pulled the coverlet to her chin and rested there a full fortnight, directing the activities of our servant Maartje.

I am not a superstitious woman, but I have sometimes wondered whether the magnificent comet that flared across our skies had something to do with this surprising turn of events.

"False pregnancy," assured 'sGravesende, the municipal anatomist, when my father at last went to discuss the matter with him. "Remember the Princess Mary."

"There's no way to hurry the event?" my father asked. "I don't want her to be so disappointed."

What he meant, Cornelia said, was that he didn't want to wait that long himself. But she would let no physician near her. It was bad luck, as every woman knew.

"Let nature take its course," the midwife said to my father when, in desperation, he sent for her.

It was February. Cornelia had never looked better. My father had never looked worse. His large eyes sank even deeper into their sockets. Cornelia flushed scarlet from her own heat even on the coldest days of winter. My father never removed his stockings, wore his fur-lined waistcoat to bed, and still he shivered.

"Nature!" he said to the midwife. "This isn't nature. This is some fiendish trick."

"I don't believe it, Sir," the midwife said. She was old and so crooked she came little above my father's waist. It was he who inclined to her.

"Are you sure?"

"She says it has already quickened. And I too believe I detected some movement. I don't believe it is the mole, Sir."

"Thank God for that," my father said, and meant it.

But he did want to blame his confusion on someone—or something.

There Antoni, my foolish cousin, saw his chance. Like my father, he believed in the animalcules, believed that without them generation could not take place. He made his suggestion believing it would ease my father's mind.

"How long was she in Dort, Uncle? With whom did she keep company? In France, where they ascribe such great power to the egg, even there, Uncle, if a Duchess comes to childbed eleven months after the death of her Duke, it doesn't increase his honor—or her reputation for chastity."

"Are you suggesting—" My father's face burned now with a flame as high as that which heated Cornelia.

"What other explanation can there be?"

"I don't know." My father groped on the floor for his penknife. He scratched his leg vigorously.

"Maria?"

"Don't ask me. I have enough to do preparing the basket. Let's just pray it thrives."

I excused myself and went off to assist Adriaen Beijeren in his shop. It was a relief to stand by the counter measuring out worsted, damask, silk, to sketch a pattern and send it to the weavers in Leyden, to accept the material two months later—or send it back again because it did not meet our specifications.

But could my father do that with this child—refuse to claim it as his own? Wasn't it all he'd ever wanted from his wife? Did it matter how it came into existence? Besides, I believed Cornelia. I know when she left for Dort she packed rags in her baggage. By March, there was no doubt life wriggled within her. These were the facts, and she was as baffled by them as my father. But she never tried to deny them.

To be honest, I didn't object to our new circumstances. Pregnancy improved Cornelia's humor.

"I don't care where it has come from, Maria. It is a miracle—and I praise the Lord for it. I only wish your father could join me in my rejoicing."

"A cock need tread a hen only once a month," my cousin Antoni suggested.

"But hens have no menses," my father said. "I have already considered that."

Spring came late and left early. The heat hastened Cornelia's delivery. It was a blessing in a way. I don't know how much longer my father could have tolerated the good wishes of Delft.

For Cornelia did not try to conceal her condition. She paraded it. She had me order forty ells of scarlet serge for the childbed. She lay, by April, half of each day in their bed. She busied herself with stitching clothes for the child, trimming each gown with lace. From there she greeted all who entered my father's study. No matter how much weight she gained, her chin remained sharp as a dart, but her little mouth blossomed. Her stomach was big as a kettle. She had no need now for an embroidery bolster.

"Isn't it time you considered joining your stepmother in the married state?" Adriaen Beijeren's mother asked me when she stopped by to visit Cornelia.

"I?" I blushed with confusion.

Who would dine with my father, then? Who would ease his pain? For one had only to look at the man to see he was suffering. His eyes were as clear as ever, but the skin around them was ashen. He was cold, even in May, in a way no fire could assuage. He couldn't settle in a place. He didn't seem able to settle in his clothes. He kept straightening his garters, rubbing his stockings. He had Maartje and I check him daily for lice. He rode his young mare for hours.

"I?" Cornelia mimicked me. "Why not, Maria? You're certainly old enough."

"Our cousin from 'sGravenhage has seen you and has expressed an interest," said Mevrouw Beijeren. "He has asked me to come and speak for him." Mevrouw Beijeren's eyes were gleaming, guileless. She smiled, straightened her black skirt.

"This isn't the time for it."

"Have you met him?" Cornelia asked. "Is that why you have no curiosity? Satisfy me, then, Mevrouw, for I know nothing. What is his name? His age? His trade? His fortune?"

"Cornelia," I begged. "Not today."

"When you're ready, Mejuffrouw, just let me know," Mevrouw Beijeren said. "My cousin is an honest man. Honorable. He is worth your consideration."

"What ails your Maria? You'll be twenty-five this September."

"Leave me be, Cornelia." Can't you see, I wanted to add, I am needed here.

Certainly it was me and not my father Cornelia called for in the dead of night the first week in June. It was I who went to his bed downstairs and drew the curtains to wake him and send him for the midwife. I who laid the fire in my stepmother's bedchamber to ward off all possible chill. I who bathed her forehead. I who muffled her cries. I who held her arms day and night as she writhed in the labor throes. What I remember now is the heat, the movement of the white sheets rising, falling, the smell of the unguents the midwife used to ease the child's passage. Honey. Turkey fat. On the second day, the midwife whispered there was little hope for either mother or child.

"She's too old for this," the midwife said. "Her body won't give way." Cornelia was forty-eight. "We should call in a physician."

"Not yet," I begged. I didn't want to set the seal on them, not yet.

I bathed Cornelia's face. I held her, writhing, in her bed. I kept the physicians away. I kept faith. But in the end it was my father's name she screamed, it was he who came and held her fast in the last great convulsion that propelled the small, blue-faced child into the midwife's gleaming hands. While I handed the midwife the warmed blanket, my father stayed with his face buried in the pillow, as still as Cornelia herself. His shirt was wet, wet as her face, wet as that of the mewling boy child.

It was as if the child did not exist for anyone but me—and the midwife.

"I did my best," she said. "But it was a bad business. I suggest you call a physician for Mevrouw Swalmius. I fear fever may set in. As for the child, all we can do is pray."

"He's alive," I said.

She nodded, tucked the blanket more securely about him. "He should be kept close."

I seated myself in the chair by the fire, the babe to my breast as if it were I who might feed him. I didn't understand she was trying to warn me.

"Maartje has the caudle warming," I said.

"I'll take none tonight, Mejuffrouw," she said, shaking her head. It's been a bad business. See that you send for a physician in the morning. Feed the mother small beer, cooling foods. She might recover."

Surely I heard her, surely I responded. But it was my brother's pale eyes I met, his health I had an overwhelming desire to preserve.

It seemed an hour before my father rose from the bed. He straightened the sheets around Cornelia's shoulders, he adjusted the pillows beneath her head. He walked round the bed drawing close all the curtains save those that looked out towards me, the sleeping babe, the small fire. Cornelia slept with her mouth open, her blonde hair ratted around her ears and across her throat. She breath was rasping.

My father stood beside her, his hands clasped behind his back. Dawn whitened the windows and blackened his figure. I couldn't see the expression on his face.

I rested the child on my lap, adjusting his green blanket. My apron was blotched, I could see now, with dark stains. Then I rose, holding the child close, and approached my father.

"The midwife failed to make the presentation. May I?"

I held the child out as I stepped forward, but my father suddenly reached into the bed and twitched the sheets up over Cornelia's bared arm. Then he leaned down and began to scratch furiously at his calf.

"It's a son," I said.

My father's bald spot gleamed like a coin. His hair straggled, thin and gray, over the thick nape of his neck.

"He *lives*. Won't you look at him?"

"Please, Antoni," Cornelia whispered.

"Ah," my father said, leaning into the bed again. "You're awake."

"At least hand him to me, Antoni." Her voice was low, almost a moan.

"You're in pain?" he asked. "I'll go now. I'll fetch Dieren, the surgeon."

"Father —"

"For God's sake, Antoni." Cornelia laid her hand on my father's sleeve.

He shook it off. He put his hand to the side of his face and raked it through his damp hair. The room was sweltering.

"I can't," he said. "Forgive me." He stepped away from the bed and stared out the window.

"Maria, give me Philips Antoniszoon."

My father wheeled around.

"I'll fetch D'Aquet."

He strode across the room without looking to his right or left. I laid the swaddled child in Cornelia's arms. But Cornelia looked beyond my shoulder. It was my father's step on the stair she listened for, not the child's cry.

"Convince him," she said to me. "Please. Why can't he believe Our Creator has given us proof of His favor?" She wet her lips, or tried. Her tongue was white with paste, clumsy as an ox's. Her forehead gleamed with sweat. Her arm did not grasp the bundled child.

"Let me open the window. Or lift off some of the bedclothes. You're too close." When l put my hand to her cheek, I could feel the fever raging. She opened her mouth to speak, and her breath sickened me. She had only begun her fast two weeks before, for the babe had come beforetimes. She should have fasted from her seventh month. I feared this failure would corrupt her milk as it had corrupted her breath.

My fear was pointless. With a gasp, Cornelia's head dropped back on her pillow. When I called her name she did not respond. Her eyes rolled back in her head, but her chest lifted and fell as monotonously as the sea. I gathered up the child and brought him back to the hearth. I dared not leave Cornelia. For the child's sake, I dared not remain.

I laid the babe in the basket and went to the window to see if I could see my father returning. I was surprised to see the steeple of the Nieuwe Kirke still black against the pink sky. I felt he'd been gone for hours. I could see the leaves of the limes rustle in the wind. I opened the window just a space to let the breeze in to relieve us. I could smell the canal. I heard Cornelia twisting in her sheets. I heard the child begin to cry, a sound so soft it sounded as if it came from within a gunny sack.

As soon as my father returned, l planned to go and find a nurse for the child. Until then, I would have to supply its hunger with what we had at hand. Honey. Wine.

I called for Maartje and had her bring the caudle to my own bedchamber. I left Maartje to sit with Cornelia while I carried my brother in his basket back to my room. It was there I discovered the terrible truth about him, a truth I can reveal only now that Cornelia herself has died. She never knew.

For two weeks, the fever raged through her, burning away the roots of her hair, her eyelashes, scorching her skin, stretching her heart. She tossed, raging, in her bed, indifferent to day and night—to my father, me, the babe himself. When she came to herself, the child had been dead twelve days, buried by nightfall the day of his death. Even so, my brother lived too long to preserve my father's innocence.

♕ ♕ ♕

I did what I could to protect my father. So did Maartje, and my cousin Antoni Molijn, for, horrified, I did confide my fears there. I should not have. Should he live, Antoni told me, the babe would have less wit than Willem Bolnes.

"How do you know?" I cried. "I'll ask Dr. 'sGravesende. I'll ask Dr. D'Aquet."

"You don't want to broadcast my uncle's shame, do you?"

"What makes you say these things?"

I paced the room. Maartje dipped the twisted linen cloth in the caudle we had prepared according to the midwife's recipe. We did not dare call in a wet nurse. Maartje crooned to the child as its mouth closed over the finger of cloth.

"They say God makes them this way to keep a woman companion to her grave," Maartje said.

"After that what happens to him?" I snapped.

"He has you. Failing that the weeshuis," Antoni said. "But I wouldn't worry, Cousin. He was born so beforetimes, I believe he'll not survive another day."

I looked at my cousin in his blonde periwig, his damask coat, and I hated him. For his foolish French clothes, his pretensions. What made him smile like that at the disaster that had fallen his uncle? What made him believe God wouldn't serve him so as well?

I believe now I probably wronged my cousin. Then I felt only fear, an icy anger. Even so, as I took the babe from Maartje, I could not prevent my yawn. I had not slept all night.

"How long can this go on?" Antoni asked. "How long can you keep the truth from him?"

"What truth? There are so many things that are not as they once seemed. What makes you so sure that my brother's extra finger is proof of idiocy? Why can't it signify an added capacity? What makes you so sure those eyes can't see, those ears can't hear?"

Antoni shrugged. Even Maartje shook her head. I felt the tears sting my eyes and was unable to keep them from falling. I kissed the baby's forehead.

"He weakens by the hour," I said.

"My uncle still refuses to acknowledge him?"

"Since he returned with Dr. D'Aquet four days ago, he hasn't left Cornelia's room. He won't let Maartje or me enter. We leave a tray outside the door. He's afraid, he says, of contagion. From childbed? It makes no sense. I am frightened, Antoni. When l wake at night, I feel as if the whole world has listed to one side. Nothing is clear to me."

"It will be over soon," he said. He hung his cape over his shoulder. "Even if Cornelia Swalmius does recover, I doubt she'll ever have another child. Certainly when she learns the truth, she will not aspire. It is her fault. An old womb provides insufficient nourishment. Next time there will be nothing come of it at all."

"That doesn't answer," I said.

But nothing did.

It was I who told my father two days later of my brother's death, who washed and dressed his tiny body for the casket, who went to Adriaen Beijeren's shop to purchase crepe streamers for my father's hat, and who openly wept when I learned from Predikant Grebius, newly come to our town from Leyden, that the child could not be buried in the church as he had not survived to baptism.

"Why did you not call me in immediately?" he asked. Petrus Grebius had a narrow bony nose, its nostrils like teardrops. His voice was high pitched and, because he forced it through those narrow passages, sniveling, wet.

Why indeed.

"It was my fault," I lied. "I was sure he'd survive. I refused to believe anything to the contrary. We hadn't even named him. My father is secreted with his wife. He has yet to make his son's acquaintance."

Predikant Grebius shook his head in short spasms of disapproval. My brother's brief appearance in this world would go unrecorded.

When I returned, I found Cornelia attended by Maartje. I heard my father then, moving in the room above where the child lay. Although I ran, I did not arrive early enough.

My father had at last come up to make the acquaintance of Cornelia's child. He had his hand cupped round my brother's small dark head. His other hand had drawn away the blanket that I had tucked so carefully over the tiny shoulders. My father gazed down at his open palm, at the child's lifeless hand which lay cupped there, smaller than a sparrow's egg, more frail.

"What have you done?" I asked.

"I wanted to cross his hands," he said. He slipped his hand from under the child's head. He stroked the small hand with the tips of his fingers. He studied his strange features.

"After all I've done," I cried, beside myself with anger. "Why could you not leave well enough alone?"

"It's not in my nature," he said. His little finger, flicking in his palm, lifted and riffled the infant's fingers as water riffles the reeds, wind riffles the leaves of the lime.

"Don't," I said. I spoke softly, but I wished to scream.

My father glanced at me, yawned widely as he dropped the child's arm. He rose to his feet.

"I'll not forgive this," he said. "It was a wicked deceit." I was not sure whether he meant the birth or the death or the reality of his son's deformity.

I ignored him. I knelt by the coffin and drew the blanket up over the body of my dear dead brother. The fourth of my fathers's sons who would have born his own father's name, Philips, assuring the continuity of generations.

"Wicked," my father, Antoni Philips' son, repeated from the doorway. "I never would have believed my own child would betray me so."

I wanted to accept his censure. Certainly it seemed easier than saying what I did.

"Yes," I said. "I tried my best to hide this from you. I tried to spare you. Blame me if you will."

"Spare me from the truth, child? From the *truth*?"

What made my father believe he did not need the comfort of ignorance—comfort he freely gave the dead child's mother, who believed until she died the child was born lifeless but perfect in limb and reason.

♕ ♕ ♕

It was my father who told Cornelia of the child's death when at last her fever abated. He praised his beauty. Then, for the first time since the birth, he called me into their chamber. Maartje as well. I was to assist Cornelia in changing her shift. Maartje was to change the bedsheets.

But Cornelia did not wish to relinquish my father. She held on to his hand with surprising force. The skin of his hand whitened with the pressure of her fingers.

"Antoni, it is you I grieve for. It was for you the boy was brought into the world."

"For both of us," my father said. He slipped his hand free "I'm off to the orchard. I'll bring you peaches. You must regain your strength."

"He continues his observations?" she asked as he climbed down the stairs.

"He's not left this chamber day or night," I said after I heard the front door close.

The tears tumbled down Cornelia's cheeks. "He said he was a beautiful child. Perfect."

"We did our best, Cornelia. Maartje and I fed him day and night. We—"

"Enough." Cornelia plucked at the sheets. "It is Our Creator's will, clearly." She tried to raise herself, but fell back.

"You're too weak," Maartje said, coming over and putting her arm under Cornelia's shoulders.

"We mustn't speculate," Cornelia protested. "Even your father. We must accept—"

"Yes," I said quickly. "Yes." But it was difficult.

Difficult for all of us.

When I changed Cornelia's shift, I was amazed to see how sickness had reduced her. She had the body of a young girl, and her demeanor too had become child-like. Much of the summer she languished. Save when my father came to her, carrying a bowl of apples, a plate of endive tossed with oil, a pot of tea—then she sat up in her bed, her cheeks flushed with pleasure.

Her body may have returned to its youthful state, but her face had aged, and her love for my father did not display a child's trust but something more abject.

"I am so glad you've come, Husband. Tell me about your day. Surely you'll stay, just for five minutes. Surely—"

My father kissed her cheek, shook his head, retreated.

My father treated her with a gentleness Cornelia found disturbing.

"It's true," Cornelia would sob. "I know it's true. Look at how he treats me, with such unfamiliar kindness. He knows I will not recover."

I shook my head. I busied myself straightening the chamber.

"Every day you grow stronger. Next week we'll carry you downstairs." I spoke brusquely.

I was sure, you see, that she'd not leave us. Daily her strength increased. It was my father who weakened.

He ate heavily, but to no purpose. He came to stool, five, six times a day. He could retain nothing over three or four hours.

His body could retain no food, the Golden Head could not retain his body.

"Where's your father?" Cornelia would ask, twisting in her bed to look out at the half open door.

Either he was sitting, groaning, in the outhouse, or he was walking the meadows around our city collecting materials for his observations. Materials! He was collecting cow dung, horse dung, the excrement of roosters, hens and pigeons. He was inspecting the contents of his own chamber pot. The ashy urine of his mare.

All summer, he did not share his observations with us. Rarely did he share them with the men, equally ingenious, who came from 'sGravenhage and Rotterdam to see him. My father was always busy. Too busy to sit still. To busy even to speak, to explain himself. Now I understand why he could not rest in one place, why he rushed from task to task.

If my father rested too long in one posture, one place, a terrible itching assailed him. It was worse than any thought. It was worse than the hairshirts worn by penitents. Clean linen could not relieve it. Neither could salves. My father did the best he could to conceal it. Even at the height of the summer, inspecting his garden, riding his mare, he went everywhere with his cloak, an overcoat, his periwig. But when he removed his clothes at night, the arms of his shirts were stained with blood where he had scratched at himself until he tore open the skin.

No wonder he insisted on sleeping apart from Cornelia. But why did he not come into their chamber even to converse with her in the evenings? Why did he not turn to her for sympathy? Worse, why did he let her believe it was her fault?

Quite simply, he couldn't stop long enough to talk! To me either, but it wasn't something I attended to. I had my hands full.

Fever was rife in our city that summer. Maartje, our serving girl, was taken with it early in August. When she recovered, she was as unfit as Cornelia. My cousins Molijn were also afflicted. I found myself assisting my cousin Antoni at my Uncle Jan's bedside. I emptied bowl after bowl of blood. Antoni bled all his sisters. His father. His new wife, Magdalena van Poelgeest.

In comparison, my father's affliction, even if I'd known of it, would have seemed much less dangerous. At this time what was important was that he could still walk. His skin wasn't parched with inner fire, but clammy with thought, with fear. Even then, he did not delude himself. He did not delude himself, but he held out hope. He had to. Hope was as necessary to him as tea—or asparagus.

"There will be another," he assured Cornelia. "There must be. But first you must regain your strength."

"You'll return then to my bed?"

"You think that necessary?" he asked. His voice was gruff. He rocked back and forth onto his toes.

I smiled and applied myself to gathering the skirt I was stitching for Cornelia.

"How can you ask?" Cornelia said. "I am sure you know better than I, Husband. I am sure you'll discover the reason behind all this. I am sure, if you are as devout as you are diligent, Our Creator will reveal to you His purpose. It is a test He must put you to."

My father leaned over and rubbed at his leg.

"Us?" my father asked, his voice barely audible. His hand rushed up and down his arm. "A test he has put *us* to?"

Everything, that summer and fall, was a test. Not just for my father. It was recovery, survival that tormented many. When my cousin van Berch, the brewer, returned from Utrecht, he came to my father in desperation. He brought with him a copy of the *Journal des Sçavans*. It was his last hope. He had burned the oriental moss, moxa, on his toes, his calves—to no purpose. Still the gout chalk drove itself through his heels, his elbows. His sores never closed. The pain, my father had already explained to him, came from the sharp needles of chalk in his blood. No matter what the brewer ate, milk, cheese, bread, tea, wine or brandy or small beer, nothing would soften those needles, everything would increase them. There would be, in short, no end to his suffering.

"I can't stand it," the brewer said. "I will take the blood of a madman. I will take the blood of a sheep."

For once my father sat still and listened.

My father's hands lay, firmly clasped together, on the table top. They did not scurry over his arm, scratch under his periwig, drum on his thigh.

"I would rather die," our cousin said mournfully, "than live this way another year. I know they don't practice the operation here in the United Provinces. I will go anywhere. Paris. London. Montpelier."

"I have not heard of its being done successfully," my father said. "De Graaf demonstrated the same to me in dogs. But he replaced the blood with milk. They are not the same."

"Perhaps he should have tried tea," I teased.

But my father ignored me.

"I will see what I can do," he said. "I will write the Royal Society and inquire of them."

Our wealthy cousin was profuse in his thanks. My father shrugged. It was the least he could do, he said. He understood the pain of gout defied description. He ushered my cousin out to the Hippolytusbuurt by the side path so he might not disturb Cornelia. I met him as he came back. Unable to restrain my amazement, I said, "You'll really write them again, Father?"

"Again?" he asked irritably. "When have I ever stopped?"

"Since last November," I said. "Since Cornelia discovered—"

"I don't know what you're talking about," he said. He leaned down and rubbed at his leg. "I've been making my observations regularly. I have simply not resolved things to my own satisfaction. Once I have, I will not hesitate to communicate my findings to that great society. "

"*What* things? What are you in doubt about?"

"Doubt?" my father asked in a voice so strange and cold I did not dare meet his eyes.

"Never mind," I said. "Never mind." I hurried inside. In this strange new humor, I did not care to be near him.

"It's not alkali in the blood that afflicts you," my father, weeks later, informed another visitor, a friend of Professor Craaven come all the way from Groningen. "I'm sure of it. I share a similar affliction."

"I myself am a healthy man—but I too endure a frequent and distressing itch. I am convinced it is not an affliction of the blood which is its cause, but the loss of hair which we, like other animals, shed each year."

"Certainly," the man said, "I have not a strand left." The visitor lifted his periwig and displayed a scalp white as any skull.

"The hairs, when they grow again, find their old holes closed. They must force their way out again. To do this they must slip between the scales of the skin. They set every nerve to jangling," my father explained.

"It is a terrible thing," agreed our visitor. "Sometimes I scratch myself until I bleed." He rubbed his sleeve as he spoke. He had a nose that listed a little to the left, a squint in his right eye. But he was a grand man for all that. He had pursued his studies at Hardewijk, he told us. Now he was one of the council in Groningen. He had his cabinet of curiosities. He had served his years as weesmaster, the head of the orphanage. He had corresponded with Thévenot, with scholars in the court of Cosimo de' Medici, and with those scholars Queen Christina left shivering in Sweden. But no one, he told my father, holding both my father's hands, shaking them out like handkerchiefs, had held out any promise of relief. Except for him—the distinguished Heer Antoni van Leeuwenhoek.

My father smiled and spoke earnestly. "Those worms the physicians in Aix-La-Chapelle claim to draw from the skin with honey and the heat from oak fires, they are not worms I have found, but fine hairs deprived of enough nourishment to grow, deprived of the strength to force their way to the surface. I've been thinking, however, that the same sweet friction that draws them through the skin might aid these new youthful hairs as well."

"Honey?" The visitor adjusted his hat. His eyes narrowed. He looked over my father's shoulder. "The doctors suggest the failure is in my blood itself. I must eat foods to soften the blood." He bowed to my father and quickly walked around the corner down the Nieuwe Straat. He had cousins living on the Oude Delft.

"Why won't he listen to me?" my father asked. He scratched the top of his hand, the top of his head. "I'm not a simpleton. I am a full member of the Royal Society. Why should my theories not be as well-regarded as those of—of—" He rubbed at his forearm with the palm of his hand.

"Bontekoe," I prompted. "Speaking of that great physician, Father. Would you care for some of his sovereign remedy?"

"His remedy?" my father said. "I have been drinking the decoction for years. I too have surmised its purpose. I spoke of this to him only the other day. Don't you remember, Maria? And why do you call him the very learned physician? When we talked of the various excretions through the skin, he did not even know the studies of Santori Santorious. He made the suggestion to measure them as if it were *new!*"

🐚 🐚 🐚

My father's mind was deeply uneasy about his work in these years I now talk of. He did not have the confidence to assert himself against those who came to visit, full of their own speculations. But he did not have enough doubt to abandon his work completely. He was like a man waist deep in a bog. Any movement mired him more deeply. But to rest there, immobile, was equally dangerous, equally insupportable to one of my father's temperament.

My father wrote only once to the Royal Society in '81, twice in the spring of '82. At that time, he was occupied with studying the fibres in flesh. He wrote of this to Mr. Hooke.

"The Royal Society," Hooke wrote my father in March, "encourages you to continue your observations. I am delighted you have directed your attention to the fibres in flesh. I am sure you will confirm my own observations, made so many years ago."

The sweat that poured from my father as he read that letter would have filled a tea pot. That spring, it was so cold frost laced the inside of the sills at midday. But my father sweated as if he laboured in the fields at the height of summer.

There was no help for it, unless my father wanted to print his observations in France. Unless he wanted to pursue his studies in complete secrecy. My father wanted to do neither. He wanted to do both.

"I have delayed writing," he wrote Mr. Hooke in April, "until I was absolutely sure of what I had seen. I did not observe once, or twice, but many many times." My father smiled grimly here. He would read this aloud to Christiaan Huygens, should that famous man honor him again with a visit. Hooke was like a hungry rat entering a full larder. He raced round and round the room nibbling on everything. He had set his teeth in everything. He had laid claim to all the Noble Mister Boyle's experiments upon the spring of air. To the famous Christiaan Huygens' pendulum. To the telescope. To the microscope—and every object ever perused by it.

"I have delayed answering," my father said, "until I was completely satisfied." He could have delayed a lifetime.

"Why bother?" he asked me as he blew on the ink to let it dry. But he had already answered himself.

When you consider the care with which Our Creator has constituted every part of our bodies, when you let your imagination consider how much more remarkable must be the sinews and arteries of the smallest animalcules, who cannot be amazed as we penetrate deeper and deeper into the mysteries.

Amazed, but never easy in our minds.

Those days my father was driven by a desperate hope. He was constrained by an equally desperate shame.

It was I, in the winter of '82, who gave a name to his affliction. I had to. I had to determine the extent of his claim upon me. I had to determine the extent of my own freedom.

You see, I had met a man who I believed wished to marry me as much as I wished to marry him. Oh yes, this time I was quite willing. Until that is, I came to understand the real nature of my father's ailment. Surely he himself had guessed when he wrote the learned gentlemen in London about blood transfusions for our cousin the brewer. There had never been any suggestion transfusions might cure the gout. But for the disease which afflicted my father, yes, there were days he would have exchanged his blood with anyone—even my gout-plagued cousin.

I am not making myself clear. For three years my father believed—and he did not believe—that the disease he suffered from was leprosy.

"I am a very healthy man," my father wrote the Royal Society in the fall of '81. "But I too suffer from a terrible itch." My father told them he ascribed it to the loss of hair he suffered every spring. It is true my father was a hairy man, a strong one. But he did not shed his fur every spring any more than did the cattle in our pastures. What my father shed, first only in the spring, then in summer, fall and winter, was his skin.

Our skin, he wrote later, is made of scales—like fishes. The scales of a man's skin are not overlaid like the lead tiles on our roofs, but placed edge to edge. They serve us like armor. They serve us like clothes, preserving our modesty. Imagine a world without them! It would be a world where pleasure was never known. Any pressure would be pain—as it is for the brewer in the throes of gout, as it is for the potter who has scorched his hand drawing the fired faience from the kiln.

So my father said. But he was more reckless than Prince William riding into battle—he shed his armor right and left, day and night. The more he shed, the more there was—and an itch fiercer and more fiery than any wound.

For over two years my father had white crusts upon his arms, his legs. He hid these under his clothes. But in the fall of '82, he also sported patches on his forehead. He hid them under his periwig, but I saw them myself. As Cornelia would have if ever they shared a bed. But he hadn't slept beside her since she had come to childbed.

I myself discovered the truth by accident one day when I interrupted him at his studies. He had removed his wig, for the fall day was unusually warm. He sat with his glass pressed to his forehead, his face lifted to the window. He put the glass down. He rested his head in his hands, then, shaking free of his palms like a cow shaking free of the water trough, he sat staring out the window. Suddenly he began to scratch at his forehead with his nails.

"What puzzles you?" I asked.

"*What?*" he yelled. "How dare you enter without warning."

"I thought you saw me—" I began, but stopped when I saw the fearful expression on my father's face.

"Father, what is it?" I exclaimed. "What have you discovered?" Even as I spoke, I couldn't imagine anything worse than what we'd seen already. Animalcules writhing in semen, in spit, in stool. Indeed, none of these, when looked at under the glass were horrifying at all. They were, instead, an endless source of amazement.

"Let me look," I said, coming up behind him and taking the glass. At first I thought I was seeing ore, but it wasn't, although its surface was rough and bright as a raw lump of silver.

"Is this some of Heer Bekker's transmuted sand from Sheviningen?" I teased.

"Fool's gold," he said. "This—"

My father picked at his forehead, presented me with a white scab on the tip of his finger.

It was then, as he sat staring straight into the light from the window that I *saw* my father's misery.

"You've scratched yourself raw," I said. "We must get you a salve. I'll go to the apothecary this afternoon on my way to Adriaen Beijeren's shop."

I thought by this to open up the subject I was fixed upon. My father proved more tenacious.

"Salve?" he scoffed. "There isn't one left that I haven't tried."

"Is it like that all over?" The patches on his forehead were red now with the blood he'd raised to the surface by his constant chafing.

"My arms," he said. "My shoulders. The backs of my legs."

"It spreads then?"

"Slowly."

"Like leprosy," I teased. I wanted to talk of other things. I didn't attend to what I'd said. I had no fear, you see. I had not brooded over the ailment alone for two years. I was sure it was a momentary thing, something he had touched wandering daily through his gardens, walking through the polders. I didn't know.

But I did as soon as the word slipped from my tongue. My father folded his hands in his lap. He closed his eyes. The tears ran down his face.

"I don't know," he said. "I don't know. I have read everything. Everything I can. Everything written in our Nether-Dutch. I have studied my own skin daily."

"It can't be," I said. "You're a chaste man."

"So I have all these years believed. But Our Creator may not see me so. He may not believe that I pursued my studies for the good of us all—not out of licentiousness, not—"

"But I do," I said. "I believe you."

My father's face, even when he spoke, was still as stone and his eyelids were white, as if he'd never once exposed them to the sun, as if he'd never spent a minute of the day with them down, lost in his own thoughts, never spent a minute blind to the world, blind to the mystery of God's Creation.

"Isn't there someone you could consult?" I asked. "Someone whose opinion you trust. Dr. 'sGravesende? The matron at the Lazarus House, the committee in Haarlem?"

"Forgive me, Maria. I don't want to know. I want to stay here," he said. "With you. With Cornelia."

"Father, surely it can't be—it must be something else. Isn't it better to know?"

"Never," he said, twisting his head away from the sun. "Perhaps Our Maker is just testing me. Perhaps there is still time to convince Him."

"And you want us to remain with you? Here, in the Golden Head?"

"What else can you do?"

I didn't know. To leave would seal my father's fate. To stay would seal my own.

"Don't you owe Cornelia an explanation?"

"Yes," he said. "And when I have it, I'll give it. But I can't as yet resolve the question to my own satisfaction."

"Yes," I said eagerly. "It may be nothing. It may disappear, like the crust newborn infants sometimes have on their scalp. And there must be some salve you haven't tried."

I was no better than my father. The entire fall I too continued to busy myself with hopes. I couldn't submit to God's judgement. Not yet.

"If you went to the Lazarus House," I told him. "If you asked to examine their sores, I'm sure you'd see a difference. Then, if ever you were called before the committee in Haarlem, you could prove your own innocence."

"Against the physicians?" my father asked. "Against the predikants?"

"You could consult Predikant Grebius."

"He has few more years than you, child. I must consult my own conscience."

Child? I looked down at my womanly figure. I held my coarse red hands up to the light. How could he delude himself so? Why would I?

TO EACH OUR OWN INFIRMITY

Leprosy is a terrifying disease. Here our sin becomes manifest. In this it is like the diseases that afflict men who lie with unclean women, giving dreadful proof of their lechery. But leprosy can afflict even those chaste in body. It can afflict anyone with an unclean conscience. And it can afflict all those who come in contact with him.

Once my father's illness was discovered, it would not be he alone who would be called to Haarlem to submit to examination by the Leper Board. No, Cornelia too. And me, Maria Antoni's daughter, for I was twenty-six and unmarried, still resident in the Golden Head. For years I had been unwilling to leave my father's house, and now, willing or unwilling, it was too late. I, like my father, would be given a Lazarus rattle, a license to beg, a bowl for alms and gruel. All because I had clung for years too many to the security of my father's house and his particular favor. I was guilty of both pride and disobedience. I wanted to share my father's highest fortune, but I did not want to join him in penury and exile.

I took charge of my father's clothes. I gathered full ruffles to hide the backs of his hands, cravats to hide his neck. I adjusted his periwig to hide the scabs on his temples. I bought five new pairs of undersocks. Adriaen Beijeren teased me for my many purchases.

"You'll ruin your chances," he said. "Such extravagance. I have made as many claims for your modesty as for your sagacity. You'll put me to shame, Maria."

I bit my lip. For wasn't shame already my constant companion?

I would rather have had another. I think the time has come to describe my own life. Describe the man Adriaen Beijeren alluded to with a meaningful smile. *Frans Corneliszoon*. He was a distant cousin of Adriaen Beijeren. He lived in 'sGravenhage and followed the same trade of draper.

He was the very same man Mevrouw Beijeren had mentioned to me before Cornelia had come to childbed. The one about whom I would hear nothing. A year later, I could not hear enough.

Frans Corneliszoon was younger than me. Two years before, he had opened his mercer's shop in 'sGravenhage, where he sold fine silks and Genoa velvet to the Prince's court. He sold fine silks, but he looked as if he'd be more comfortable in fustian. He wore no periwig, and he had the blunt face of a peasant. When I first saw him, I did not experience surprise, but recognition.

A mercer by trade, not a painter, when Frans Corneliszn. studied a person, it was not to mold them to his imagination but to enter into theirs.

"Have you ever thought of red silk?" he asked the pretty young Mevrouw Putmans.

"Red?"

"I have brought some with me today from 'sGravenhage. Mevrouw Bentinck just purchased enough for a gown. So did Mevrouw Huygens. For them," he whispered, winking, "it was a mistake. But you, Mevrouw! Maria, a mirror for the Bailiff's wife." When he held the swathe under her chin, the child was transformed. She glanced quickly over her shoulder, as if afraid her husband had seen. It was he, evidently, who wished to preserve the gulf of years and experience that separated them.

"I couldn't possibly," she said, caressing the silk.

I lowered the mirror, but she still gazed at the material falling across her hands and over her yellow skirt.

"Just think of it, Mevrouw," Frans said quietly.

"I can't." Her voice trembled. Her black hair tossed upon her lace collar. Her right eye began to twitch.

"Perhaps next year," Frans said. Although his voice was level, it entered both of us like a whisper.

I carried the mirror back to the wall.

Adriaen came across the room. Her purchases were wrapped up and tied. He handed them to the apprentice who carried them to the carriage. The servant, who had stood beside the door watching her mistress with a mother's fond attention, now approached the young woman.

"I'll send the bill to the Bailiff," Adriaen said. "You have chosen well."

"If you are ever in 'sGravenhage, come and see my shop," Frans said with a laugh as he folded up the silk. "It puts my cousin's to shame."

"She is my biggest customer, cousin. How could you?" Adriaen exclaimed as he turned from the door. The carriage rumbled across the cobblestones, drowning out most of Fran's reply.

"But he was right," I said. "About the scarlet silk. It became her enormously."

"And it would become you too, Mejuffrouw," he said. "Look, cousin. What do you say to Mejuffrouw van Leeuwenhoek dressed in red silk?"

"Impossible," I muttered. My face felt brilliant as the cloth, but when I looked in the mirror I was pale as bleached muslin.

"Frans, it is not seemly. Mejuffrouw van Leeuwenhoek is here at her father's request. She serves as my head apprentice."

With a nod at Adriaen, I went and sat down at the table and began to transcribe the previous day's transactions into the ledger. Mevrouw Boogaert had purchased a bonnet, and Heer Heinsius, our city's pensionary to the States of Holland had bought five ells of lace, a cravat and a black beaver hat. I had bought yellow taffeta ribbon for a bodice, a length of felt for Cornelia to gather into a winter petticoat. Mevrouw 'sGravesende had purchased ten ells of bombazine for mourning streamers. Kroonevelt, ten ells of kersey. Mevrouw Doublet, forty ells of green serge for bed hangings. Mevrouw van Ruyven, twenty ells of damask for the same.

Every time I closed my eyes, I saw Frans' face, those gray eyes so used to dealing with the trappings of honor, they had no vanity in them. When Adriaen Beijeren came over to check my progress, I looked up at his face in amazement. How could they be cousins? Adriaen's brown hair was pushed away from a forehead already creased with care. His fine eyebrows remained perpetually aslant, as if he were always puzzled. His nose was narrower, finer than his cousin's, but Adriaen always seemed to have to sight down it, as if it were too long for him to manage. His lips were thinner and his chin longer. And all these years I had thought Adriaen a handsome man, too handsome indeed for any of the young women he had considered taking to wife.

Even now, I would not say Frans was a handsome man, but just looking at him made me feel the world was brighter and more substantial than I had imagined. Looking at him made me aware of the white hip bearing up my bolstered skirt, the white breast beating inside my green bodice.

Frans, it was soon evident, returned my interest.

It could not be, of course. But for a month I returned Frans's glances, found myself smiling when, nearing the door to Adriaen Beijeren's shop, raising my hand to knock, I heard his laugh within. Frans often came to the door instead of his cousin, falling silent when he saw me, his eyes seeking mine, a slow smile spreading across his face as without a word he stepped aside gesturing to me to enter.

"Only Maria," Adriaen would say, immediately turning to some other task.

"Only," Frans would echo with a shrug of his shoulders, followed by a wink, and, once or twice his fingers touched my hand or my shoulder. Oh, the feeling ran like a light breeze across all my body.

I wept at night. I knew what I must do. But what was awakened by his laugh, his smile, the way he turned his head to watch me, did not feel like temptation, it felt like a completion of my nature. And when, alone in the shop with him one afternoon, he asked me if he could visit my father, I said what needed to be said.

"My duty lies elsewhere," I told him. I looked away from his face, but set my hand lightly over his. "I wish it were not so."

"Let me try to persuade him. I know you help him in his labors, but surely he does not wish you to renounce the richness of your womanhood. 'sGravenhage is not far. You could return often."

At that moment our maid Maartje came in search of me. Visitors had arrived. My father had immediate need of me. I quickly gathered my cloak.

"Mejuffrouw?" he asked.

I shook my head. I could not form the word.

"Mejuffrouw," Maartje said. "There are five of them."

Praise be my father's disease did not worsen. I would not have wished that. But I cared little that winter whether he should improve. Either way, my life seemed fixed as fast in his house on the Hippolytusbuurt as the bricks themselves were stuck fast in their foundations of cement. I went to Adriaen Beijeren's shop only when his mother requested. I went to assist her when Adriaen went to Leyden to consult the weavers, or to Utrecht to inspect and purchase some velvets. Frans' cousins continued to see him, but only when they visited 'sGravenhage. His name was never mentioned before me, but I dreamed of him constantly.

I dreamed wicked, licentious dreams. Dreams that if he had guessed them would have made him give me up willingly.

I dreamed we were in our wedding bed, that I welcomed him without false modesty, without any modesty at all. Suddenly, the bed curtains were torn apart. My father staggered toward us, his face redder than Uncle Jan's. His voice was low, harsh. His face was covered with sores. "Whore," he whispered, "It is all your fault." I covered Frans with my arms. I didn't want my father to touch him. But I couldn't protect him. Frans dwindled in my arms until he became a babe again. My hands were clasped around his head like a white cap. Cornelia came up behind my father. Her face too oozed horribly. There was a sore on her cheek, another on her forehead. She saw the child in my arms and shrieked angrily. "Give him to me. Give me my son."

I clutched the child more tightly. My hands were white with the force of my desire. I saw the tops of my hands begin to bloom, terribly, terribly. I wouldn't let go although I wanted to conceal my shame. "These are the wages," Cornelia said, pointing at my hands, the huge blown petals opening now onto fingertips and wrists.

"Of what?" I screamed. Wild with fear, I placed the heels of my hands over my burning eyes. Just as I did so, I felt her tug the babe free of me. I knew I had lost everything.

My breath when I woke was white as my linens, white as my father's disease, white as Frans' face when he heard me say, a second time, "No, there is no hope."

White, my father has taught me, is made by placing hundreds of nearly transparent layers one upon another. You can see the same in chalk, in muscovy glass, in the skin on his right arm. I have never asked him what makes the deepest black.

❦ ❦ ❦

Did dreams like these, I wonder, taint Frans' last sleep? I can't conceive it. Despair is a province of life, not of heaven or hell, and Frans, by the beginning of March, had escaped life forever.

"I've never seen fever take anyone more quickly," Mevrouw Beijeren said when she received the news from 'sGravenhage and came particularly to inform me.

"Never," I agreed.

"God's will be done."

Never.

"You must grieve," my father said, after the matter had been explained to him. "Our Creator's will is mysterious—"

I shuddered away from his hand.

"But we must trust his purposes. We must," Cornelia said. "It is the first sign of our calling. We must never doubt his mercy—or his favor."

It was my eyes made out their words, not my ears. There my own blood thundered, deafening as the sea.

"Never," I agreed.

My father's disease changed the relations between us completely. Between all of us—Cornelia as well.

For months I remained withdrawn as any leper. If I could have, I would have shunned my own company as well as that of all other men and women. There were nights I felt I had effected this. Looking at my reflection in the mirror, my features distorted by the wavering candle flame, I saw no resemblance to the girl Johannes had painted years before.

Again and again I went to the bed and drew back the curtains. I studied the painting. I returned to the mirror. I pulled the shoulders of my silk bodice lower on my shoulders. I adjusted the ringlets on my neck. Silk? Oh yes. It wasn't bombazine I purchased to mourn Frans—I purchased his own red silk, all that remained of it. When I put on the dress at night my skin raged more terribly than my father's. I stood in the middle of my room, my hands in fists, and let the flames lick my neck, my wrists, my breasts. I pressed my lips together. I would not cry out against the searing heat, the shame.

There were moments I wanted to open my window and scream out into the fresh spring air. It was spring, imagine. Lit by the moon, the leaves in our garden shimmered silver, like fish feeding in shoals in the deepest part of the ocean. I wanted to scream out into that warm, fragrant air the dreadful truth about my father. It was because of him I was here, alone in my chamber, barren as Cornelia, more deeply punished by Our Creator for my father's speculations than my father was himself.

My father lived daily with the fear that someone would discover the extent and incurable nature of his disease. He was afraid he'd be denounced by his neighbor, sent to Haarlem, his sores and scabs inspected, his sentence proclaimed. He would be removed, with his bed, his glasses, his grinding cup, his teapot and his tea to the Lazarus House outside town.

He was afraid! What about me? My seclusion in my chamber was as complete as any leper's. It was as necessary. It was more dreadful, for there was no one on earth who could console me. No one at all. The Lazarus House had more than one bed; the lepers who wandered the countryside to beg could troop together. But there was no one living who shared my disease.

My disease, it was clear to me those lengthening days of the spring, was my father.

The most terrible thing about my father is how nearly he clings to life. In January, recovering from fever, he wrote the Royal Society a full account of his speculations on the blood; he wrote down his further speculations on generation. In February, they responded, admiring the ingenuity of his thought, but doubting its truth. You might think my father would give up. He couldn't. Even when, shivering with mortification, he vowed to himself to abandon his studies, the world could entice him back in minutes.

Why does the green frog sit woozy and fearless on the edge of the road? Why does the male frog not join in union with the female? My father spent that spring, a glass in his pocket, an old beaver on his head, wandering along the edge of the polders gathering the frogs, squeezing their bellies to inspect their semen for the first sign of life, that terrible writhing.

It was as if nothing had changed for him. Imagine!

"Maria!" he continued to call coming into the house. "Come see what I have observed today."

"Maria! Maria!" Cornelia would second him. She was emboldened by his presence. When he was away, she kept to the fireside, her embroidery, her cups of tea with the cousins Molijn.

I didn't answer.

But this didn't stop my father. He carried his glasses into my chamber. He showed me the frog's semen, killed by the urine he had expressed as well in his harsh curiosity. He showed me the sickened frog whose blood seethed with transparent worms. It was a sight amused him greatly, the tails of the small animalcules flicking the globules of blood with their tails, like children tossing blown bladders.

"What do they feed on?" I asked him, staring out over the green leaves, the red roofs of our town. "Those worms wriggling through our veins? Do they feed on the globules? Do they, like the worms in the earth, feast on the flesh itself?"

"Daughter," he sighed. "I thought they were amusing. I thought they would make you laugh."

Cornelia stayed behind as my father climbed back down the stairs. Her face was full again, but white as the finest bread, made damp now by the least exertion. Cornelia's heart seemed to have weakened with her childbed fever. Now she hated to move without cause, she hated to move in haste. She never even raised her voice to scold, for anger, even her own, gave her qualms. But she had come, and here, obviously, she would stay until she had regained her composure. For all I cared, she could stay all day and night. It made no difference. I had no ears to hear her, no eyes to see. Certainly, I had no sympathy.

And she had none with me.

"What more can you ask of him? Hasn't he given you a roof, a private chamber, a store of goods, a trade? Every day he thinks of something else that might engage you. He was so pleased when he brought in those frogs—"

"Pleased at what? The terrible corruption in their blood?"

"Corruption? That was life he was laughing at."

"Life?" I said. "It was death. Can't you tell the difference any more?"

"It is not I who is confused." Cornelia sat down. She capped her hands over her left breast as if to slow the pounding. "You act as if your father had some hand in that mercer's death—as if it were he who refused you permission. But I have asked Adriaen Beijeren. I asked him before he too died of fever. It was you, Maria, who refused Frans Corneliszn. If anyone loosened his ties to this world, it was you. Your father can't account for your own coldness of heart."

"As he can for the weakness of yours?"

"He's not to blame," she said, panting now with anger. "I wanted the babe. I would have given my life for him. But Our Creator is the only one with the power of life and death."

"Then of what have you just accused me? If I had been informed of his illness, I would have rushed to 'sGravenhage. I would have taken him in my arms."

I put my hand to my mouth. I was sickened—with rage, and loss, and my own deceit. I *would* have touched him; I would have bound him to me more securely than my father had bound me to himself. I would have watched with pleasure as the Devil set his many bright seals to our wicked pact. If I had known, I would have done anything to keep him out of heaven.

"It's for your own good," Cornelia said. "Our Creator afflicts His chosen in this world to save us in the next."

"You tell my father this. He may have the patience to listen. I don't anymore. My heart is hardened to His words, His demonstrations."

"You mustn't depend on reason. It's faith that saves us."

"From what?"

"Loneliness," she said in a small voice crumpled as her handkerchief. The wind rippled through the new leaves. A dog barked. Across the canal, the fishmongers hawked their wares.

"You must pray, Maria. There is no worse sin than this one—doubt. He has His purpose for you and me and your father as He does for every living thing."

"I wish it were over. I wish I could see the shape of my fate— something square and solid as a coffin lid."

"Poor Maria," she sighed. "It is like the rim of his glasses. It has no end."

My fingers to my wrist, I felt the small eels wriggling through my veins. But my father wasn't there to prod me curiously with his foot. He wasn't there to laugh in foolish delight crying, Life! Life! On the chair beside the hearth, Cornelia, with hair like straw, a face like soiled linen, opened her mouth and panted with the heat of her own righteousness.

"You must believe," she said. "We *are* put here for a purpose." She panted more slowly, more harshly. She leaned over, her hands to her chest, pressing out the heated breath. "Help me, Maria," she gasped.

So I did.

I took a deep breath; I forced her mouth open with my fingers, I pressed my lips neatly upon her own. I filled her, like a bladder, with the same foul air that had sickened Frans, corrupted me.

But my breath did not kill, it brought color to Cornelia's face, steadiness to her heart.

♕ ♕ ♕

Cornelia learned of my father's disease in early July. I was not to blame. In the end, he informed her himself. It came about in this way.

In the first week in July a travelling fair came to our town. Since our own fair, the St. Odulphus, is held the second week in June, it wasn't an auspicious time for them to set up their tents by the Haguespoort. The curiosity of our townspeople was satisfied for another year. Indeed, no one would have gone at all if it had not been for the monstrous child they kept displayed upon a table.

When the rumor reached us, Cornelia insisted upon going, attended by the cousins Molijn. Even Antoni and his wife, home from the university at Hardewijk for the month, went with them. When they came back again, Cornelia leaned against my cousin's arm. They both reeled—but it was amazement not small beer made their gaits unsteady.

"Antoni! Antoni!" yelled Cornelia as she came in. "Make haste, Husband. We have something to tell you."

She turned to my cousins and beckoned them to be seated.

"I want to tell him first," she whispered. "For once. None of you breathe a word of it."

My cousin Antoni took a seat beside me. For the first time in weeks, I had taken advantage of my stepmother's absence to leave my chamber. He regarded me cautiously.

"How goes it with you, Cousin?"

I did not bother to answer. For me, it went today as it had yesterday. My cousin was changeable as the wind. Did he want me to shift with him? These days he dressed again in our sober blacks. His periwig had been trimmed. What had happened to the fine gentleman from France? I did not ask. I knew it was the influence of his wife.

"*Listen* to me, Husband," Cornelia burst out when at last my father appeared. "The child is turning into a fish before our very eyes."

"A bottom fish," said Antoni's wife, Magdalena, with a shudder. "Hideous."

"She's only ten years old—but she may as well be twenty."

"She may as well be dead." My cousin Geertruida's face was a pale green, like a peeled branch of willow.

"Certainly, she'll not entice sailors to theirs," Antoni said. "It is a strange disease."

"Disease," exclaimed Cornelia. "It is a marvel, Cousin. Our Creator's purposes are indeed difficult to fathom. Do you think, Husband, The Creator may have intended her for the sea?"

She smiled. Everyone did. It was a wicked question. My father has a great fear of the ocean.

"Don't be foolish," my father said. He gripped his right arm firmly with his left hand. He rubbed his calf secretly against the leg of his chair.

"Our Maker made man to walk the earth—"

"Or the ship's deck," said cousin Antoni.

"Not to wriggle in the waves. We're not eel. We're not made to fly in the air either," my father said.

"Or walk the cobbles like storks?" asked my cousin Geertruida.

"But if we saw a child covered with feather, Husband, wouldn't we consider it a sign?"

"Of what?" my father asked with a dangerous sweetness. "Our Creator's confusion?"

"*You mustn't,*" Cornelia gasped.

"I agree," my father said shortly. "It's *our* reason fails us, not His. It doesn't pay to speculate until everything is known—"

"Which is why, Uncle, you must see for yourself."

My father's broad mouth narrowed to a fine line. His fingers lifted and clamped regularly on his arm.

"Everyone is talking about it, Husband. The burgomasters and their wives. I saw the bailiff walking down the Oude Delft on his way to take it in. 'Has Heer van Leeuwenhoek seen the wonder yet?' he asked me. "I told them you would go today."

"You told them. *You* told them. What idiocy, woman. You make me out a fool, someone who believes people transform into fishes, worms are spawned from the air, eels from the wind. How dare you inform anyone of my intentions—"

He was standing now. His face was red—with rage, Cornelia would have said, but I could see how my father's eyes shuffled back and forth in their terror.

"I didn't mean—" Cornelia said with a sob. She bent her head. "I thought to please—"

"Come, Uncle," Antoni Molijn said, getting to his feet. "You can write an account for the *Philosophical Transactions.*"

I looked up at my cousin curiously. Did he know my father rarely wrote the ingenious company any more?

"We'll write one together for the *Journal des Sçavans,*" he said when my father hesitated. So perhaps he did know of my father's reluctance.

"I'll write my own observations, thank you," my father said quickly. "And I already have acquaintances in Paris should I choose to send my observations to that country as well."

"Yes," Cornelia said with a complacent nod. "The Pensionary Heinsius corresponds with your uncle."

"It would be better," I said with a laugh, "if Heinsius corresponded with the French King." Heinsius had been sent by our Prince William to negotiate with the French King, whom Heinsius detested.

With a sharp look at me, my father took up his hat.

"Maria?" he asked with a dangerous smile. "Would you like to see this marvel?"

"I'll take your word for it," I said. "Isn't that what I always do?"

When they returned from the fair, my cousin Antoni was flushed with triumph. My father hadn't a word to spare. He spurned his wife's company. He would have spurned mine as well should I have offered, but I had returned to the isolation of my own chamber.

It didn't last long.

Unlike me, my father must declare his discoveries.

My father, you see, had managed after much searching to secure a scale of the unfortunate child's skin that had fallen off into her shoe. He slipped it into his pocket without informing anyone. He had offended the master of the fair by asking to tear off one of the warts from the child's hands. But the man claimed this would make the child bleed. My father held his peace. He inspected the child from head to toe. Adjusting his spectacles, he peered fearlessly at the black, crusted skin.

"This isn't the least how a fish's scales are arranged," he announced aloud. Everyone paused in their talk and turned to my father gaping as broadly as they did at the child herself.

"And who are you to say?" asked the master. He was a fearsomely fat man, his legs thicker in girth than the child's chest.

"He?" my cousin Antoni had said. "Why he's Antoni van Leeuwenhoek, member of the famous Royal Society of London."

It was at this moment my father put the shoe down on the bench and slid the scale into his pocket. No one, he thought, had observed him.

"Come, come," he said. "My curiosity is satisfied."

But not for long.

My father soaked the stolen scale in water to loosen its parts. He observed it through his glass. He observed it again. It wasn't enough. He climbed the stairs to my chamber. I sat by the window sewing in the last blue light. Shamed by the look on his face, I looked down at my work. The needle was finer, more flexible than one of the worms he had shown me flicking their way through the frog's veins. It was lost in this gathering darkness—as I was lost in the enormous hollow in my father's voice.

"I must ask a favor of you, Daughter. l wish you to go in my stead to the traveling fair tomorrow. See if you can purchase me more of the child's scale. I need a larger specimen. As yet I have been unable to discover what distinguishes her disease from my own."

"If nothing else," I said, "the blackness of the scales."

"That is the fault of the unguent they smear over her, of that much I am convinced. When you soak the scale in water it comes apart into hundreds of the same, each as silver as one shed from my own skin, or those cut from a callus on the heel."

"She suffers, then, from abundance? Imagine that."

"I am asking your help, Daughter. I wish to resolve this to a certainty in my own mind."

"Why not go yourself?"

"My curiosity frightens them."

"What do they think, Father? You might expose them as frauds?"

"If I could discover more, I might cure her, Daughter. I might give her back her future. I could demonstrate before the physicians— "

"It's your own disease, not hers, they'll ask you to defend."

"I insist," he said.

"What makes you think they'll not suspect me?"

"The way you look," he said, turning on his heel. "These days there's not a soul in Delft doesn't take you for a perfect fool."

ᘜ ᘜ ᘜ

The next day when I returned from the fair, I found my father and Cornelia entertaining company out in the arbor.

My father's face was flushed with heat. Beads of sweat stood out on his face.

"Why not remove your coat, Husband. Roll back your sleeves. We are among friends." Cornelia touched his hand. My father twisted it palm up so the white scab on its back wouldn't show. He looked at his wife with sudden suspicion.

"Even when he works in the garden, inspecting the work of the laborers, he never removes his periwig, his coat."

"Nor does any other gentleman," my father said, coughing loudly. "Restrain yourself, woman."

But Cornelia's attention had already alighted on me.

"Maria, have Maartje bring out a chair for you. Let me pour you some wine. Where have you been?"

"Your order," I said loudly to my father, "will be ready tomorrow."

At this both Cornelia and my father blushed. What did they think me capable of? Cornelia looked anxiously at our wealthy friend from Zerikzee.

"Maria is of great assistance to both of us," she said loudly. "Especially since fever has weakened my heart."

While despair, it seemed, had firmed my own. Certainly, I was the only one at the sun dappled table who was not short of breath, whose temples did not throb with a hectic pulse. Those days I feared nothing.

Not even the monstrous child who sat, naked, unblinking, on the table in the dim close tent outside town. Like my father I had prodded her legs, her hands. I had tugged at the warts on her hands until her eyes closed in pain.

"What is your name?" I asked her. "Where do you come from?"

"She comes from France," the fat man said. "She understands nothing of our Nether-Dutch."

The girl's eyes belied him, but I nodded complacently.

"Does she shed these scales as a snake his skin? I have heard these scales may serve others as protections from the same disease. Will you sell me what comes off her in the natural course?"

"Certainly. But it will cost you five guilders. You must return tomorrow. We gather them each morning from her sheets."

"Why would anyone wish to be cured?" the girl asked in our own tongue as I left the tent. "How then would they earn their bread?"

"Tea?" Cornelia asked me when I returned home and joined them at the table in the courtyard.

"Have you seen the monstrous fish girl?" she asked our friend from Zerikzee.

"She should be secluded like the lepers," he proclaimed.

"It's like an enormous callus," my father said. "There is nothing that will spread. I have made observations."

"All these diseases of the skin are contagious. I am convinced of it. If they remain here after the week is through, I would report them to the officials in Haarlem." The man from Zerikzee spoke with authority.

My father moved his hand into the shade. He rubbed the back of it against the wood.

"*You* should, Antoni. You're a famous gentleman now. They'll consider whatever you say with gravity."

My father moved deeper into the green shadows. He smiled weakly.

♔ ♔ ♔

"Leprosy," Cornelia laughed. "You believe you have *leprosy?*"

She wasn't laughing, she was shrieking. She and my father were closeted in their chamber. Their voices winged through the chimney, fluttered out onto the roof, escaped over the town.

"Antoni. Antoni." She kept repeating his name as if that might change something, or make of this dreadful change something familiar.

"I must know," he groaned.

"What would you wish of me?" she asked.

"Silence," he gasped.

For a night and a day she gave him that. We both did.

But I wished she'd shown me the same generosity.

She was in my chamber at dawn.

"How long have you known?"

"Long enough to have lost all that's precious."

"Your father is not certain."

"That's not what I meant."

I climbed from my bed and went to the window. All winter we are so close in our houses, come spring and summer, I would breathe even the most dangerous mist rather than our own stale breaths. The bells rang the quarter hour. They drowned out Cornelia's voice. I leaned out my window. I ducked back inside, suddenly afraid. Where would we go? Our town was built too narrowly to allow us to rest forever within the Golden Head. We would have to seek refuge in the Lazarus House outside its walls—or beg our bread across the countryside.

"I would rather die—" I muttered.

"You shall, soon enough," Cornelia snapped. "We all will. But haven't you a thought for anyone but yourself?"

"To hear that from you!" I turned to her. She sat with her hands resting on the Bible in her lap.

"I married your father for better or worse, in sickness and in health."

"And in living death?"

"It is our natural state. There's no gain in this kingdom we take to the next. Not fame. Not fortune."

"We take our constitution," I said. "We take our fleshly shells. My father will take his."

"Cleansed and healed, yes, I believe he will. I take this as proof, Maria, of your father's salvation. Our Creator would not have sent him such a trial in this life otherwise. I have worried so long about the unusual favor he has found among the wealthy and learned gentlemen, here as well as in England. I saw his honors as temptations of the Devil. I saw your father giving in—"

"In sickness and health, you'll take him, then—but not in heaven or hell?"

"Careful , Maria, you tread too near—"

"It's not my desire," I said. "I wish to flee."

"You must have faith," she said. "Our Maker's purpose is so much larger than we can ever grasp. I am convinced now that He has chosen your father for grand designs. Just as He has chosen Prince William."

"Is that why the Princess is barren?" I asked cruelly.

"We must submit, Maria. We must not try to fathom these things."

My poor father! This was to be his succor until the end of his days. A woman who did not understand Our Creator had given us the Scripture not to recite but to decipher—just as he had given us the world.

"My father is not sure," I said. "He hasn't completed his investigations. This very evening I am to return to the fair and collect scale from the monstrous child."

"Yes, we must encourage him to go on. God has sent this disease to test his strength. It is the one unforgiveable sin—doubt. From that we must protect him."

"Should he resolve the matter to his own certainty, who will it be who will inform the committee in Haarlem? Will we wait until the whole world shudders at his face? Will you go, Cornelia, and condemn him yourself?"

"I will condemn us both."

"And what about me?"

"Have you no thought for anyone else?"

"Yes. That child—who is carried from town to town, stripped to exhibit her shame for burgers and potters, bakers and learned gentlemen, stripped and prodded in breast and buttock by the curious, cursed by the fearful, just to earn her father's daily bread."

"And her own," Cornelia said coldly. "You must not forget that. Her father could have cast her aside."

"He has done worse. "

"In your eyes," Cornelia said. "Only in yours, which are, compared to Our Creator's, blind, stone blind."

When I went back to the travelling fair I carried a purse heavy with guilders tucked in my bodice. It wasn't the child's skin I intended to purchase but her freedom.

But they would not admit me again to the tent. It was the child herself forbid it. She saw me at the door to the canvas room and crawled back to the edge of the bench, howling like an injured animal. Everyone in the tent turned to observe me.

The huge man made his way roughly through the throng. I awaited him, my hands knotted beneath my apron. The child's voice had fallen now, a persistent whimper. I could hear shoes creaking as everyone waited. I could hear their breaths quicken with curiosity. I could smell the stenching breath of the child's father, feel it wash hot and wet across my forehead.

"So you dare come back?"

"Dare?"

"You'll not have a piece of the child's skin. Not a scale. The girl says you threatened to put a curse on her yesterday."

"Curse?"

"She heard you. I may have heard you myself."

"You did, you did," the child cried. "While you busied yourself with your feet. You were trying to secure me for the fiend."

The oiled canvas was so dark and thick it was like a shroud. "You agreed yesterday," I said. "My purposes, I assure you, are honorable."

"Curses. I heard you. I heard you," cried the girl.

All I could see in the darkened tent were the gleaming eyes of the crowd, the spindly crusted limbs of the girl folded up into her body like a mantis's arms.

"What have we here?" a deep voice asked. A black sleeve brushed my arm, intruding between me and the huge belly of the master of the carnival. I stepped back, out of the tent.

"Is it not Maria Antoni's daughter?"

The man who emerged blinking into the sun was our new schepenen, Cornelis Vallensis. An advocate by training like the town pensionary, Heinsius, he was often seen in his company. He had never before spoken to me.

"Have you come to see the mermaid?"

"She's come to try and buy the child's soul."

"No," I said. I pulled my purse from my bodice. "I will give you all this," I said, shaking the bag until the coins rang, "if you let her go."

"Let her go?" the fat man exclaimed. "I see no chains by which she's bound."

"I'll take her as my own servant. I'll see she's treated with pity. "

"*Pity!*" screamed the child, emerging from behind her father.

She clung to his coat. In her black, scaling face, her pale eyes shone like pearls. "No one pities me. I am a marvel—I am one of God's mysteries. I'll not shift my allegiance to the Devil. It doesn't matter how much money rings in your purse. You'll not secure this attention for yourself—or for your wicked master."

"That's enough," barked Heer Vallensis. "Take the child inside. Heer van Leeuwenhoek's daughter is an honored member of our town. I'll not hear her defamed by you—you gypsies."

I put my hand to my cap, tucking back the loosened hair.

"They're simple people. You must pity their ignorance," he said to me.

"But the child. It's worse than slavery for her," I said.

"It's better than starving."

"Should she not be examined by the commissioners in Haarlem?" I asked slowly.

"She is no leper."

"How do you know?" I spoke so low I thought he would not hear me.

"She has no open sores. Her voice is clear, not rough and broken. But she does, I grant you, make us shudder."

Heer Vallensis pulled out a handkerchief and mopped his face. He was dressed as precisely as the Prince's old secretary, Constantijn Huygens, his black cloth coat relieved only by a lace collar. He did not wear a periwig and his brown hair clung damp and fine as silk thread to his forehead and cheeks. His eyes were so brown as to appear black.

"You'll allow my servant to escort you back into the town? I do not trust the temper of the crowd."

Without waiting for my reply, he waved his arm beckoning a young boy no taller than myself and so young his cheek gleamed in the heat, downy as a ripe peach. "Jan, escort Mejuffrouw van Leeuwenhoek to her door. She lives on the Hippolytusbuurt, opposite the Fish Hall."

"Thank you," I said, but he did not seem to hear. Already his attention was directed elsewhere. He waved at the three noble women come from 'sGravenhage whom he and Burgomaster Bleyswijck had escorted to the fair. He hurried to their side.

But as the boy and I passed by the tent, he turned and whispered, "I'll see what I can do about collecting a specimen for your father."

I walked away so quickly the servant boy had to trot at my heels. At our door, I dismissed him with a doit.

"You'll have to content yourself with what you secured by your own stealth, Father." I laughed. I repeated myself.

I called out loudly through the entire house, but neither my father nor Cornelia was there to hear—or so I thought until, climbing to my own chamber, I heard the sounds coming from Cornelia's sleeping chamber. I thought then it was fear drove them moaning back into each other's arms. Now I'm not so sure. They were spurred, certainly, but whether by God's wrath or his mercy I am unable to say. I have thought deeply upon it, but have been unable to determine the truth—to my own satisfaction. I can't let it go, or I won't. I won't submit to my own confusion. But it is not in this alone I am my father's daughter.

I cling just as certainly to my certainties, the truths my labor and attention have uncovered, and I, too, cherish my speculations. I believe it was my father's rollicking in his marriage bed that had something to do with his miraculous recovery that summer, not, as he would have it, the rapid and copious consumption of tea, hot milk, and other sudorifics. That is why, he wrote in December, we consider leprosy incurable. Its cure comes from within. Salves have no effectiveness.

Cornelia believed it was the sun, their ready laughter, the gospels and the psalms she read to him in the evening, but most she believed it was their submission, hers to the will of her husband, his to the inscrutable will of the Creator, that saved them. I too believe it was not sudorifics or sweat but his own unwonted humility and his wife's unwonted compassion that cured my father.

In May my father had written our Pensionary Heinsius who still rested in Paris, awaiting an audience with the great French King. Heinsius had been sent in January on an extraordinary mission by the States-General to treat with the King for the safety of the inhabitants of Prince William's principality of Orange. The French King disdained our ambassador's errand, but favored the man himself, particularly for Heinsius' public resistance to the war-like policies of our own Prince. Heinsius never forgave the King of France his favor. It was one thing to speak out in the States of Holland or in the Delft stadthuis against our Stadtholder's war-like ways; it was quite another to be asked to side with that foreign, civil, and rapacious king, Louis XIV. It was this loyalty in Pensionary Heinsius, this quiet but unassailable pride in his country and his countrymen that inspired my father to write to him. That and the great bafflement his disease had wrought.

These were the observations, my father wrote Heinsius in Paris, that he intended to communicate to the Learned Gentlemen in London: *Observations concerning the generation principally of frogs, and their male semen; also his opinion on the reason why many eggs are fertile when a cock treads a hen only once; also that generation is exclusively a matter of male semen, as exemplified in the case of rabbits; also the blood of frogs and numerous animalcules discovered in the mixed water and blood that came from the frog. The constitution of the frog's blood vessels; Also how the blood can be pushed through the wall of the lesser arteries (by a strong motion of the heart), which will cause red pustules, erysipelas and small-pox; Also the structure of the frog's flesh; Also how food is crushed in our stomach and intestines. Also about the excrement of a cod, and how its food is crushed; Also how the heart and pulse of a patient suffering from fever can beat quickly and strongly while yet the circulation is less than a healthy person with a slow pulse; Also why the heart of a patient suffering from fever will beat strongly and why the heart continually beating so strongly will become so tired that it cannot do its natural work and death must ensue.*

"And though," my father concluded, "the enumerated theses will turn out rather long, I will not neglect to send Your Excellency a copy, in case you desire to have one, immediately after forwarding them to England."

So my father wrote to our Pensionary in May, but it was two more months before he committed his observations to paper. No one reading the letter he completed in July would imagine the labor it cost him—the sweat. He had no need to drink tea; all he had to do was pick up his quill and his face beaded like a flower at daybreak. For two years my father had not dared defend himself. He had not dared draw the attention of the learned men. They would attend not only to his thought but to his scabrous face, his scabrous hand.

But neither had my father been able to relinquish his ideas. Now he wandered from his wife's arms to his garden, and then to his study, where he wrote and wrote and wrote. The scratching of the quill was like mice scuttling in the eaves, like his own nails rasping at his skin. My father wrote and wrote some more. The sweat poured down his face like purest rain water. "Bontekoe," he sniffed. *The gentleman did not acknowledge my thought concerning the supposed ferment in the blood. Neither did Oldenburg publish the speculations on digestion I wrote in 1675. I repeat them now. Hooke. Bontekoe. The world is prejudiced in favor of the ovary, but I insist—*

My father tirelessly preened and plucked his own feathers. This explains, he said of the contraction in the flesh fibre in frogs, why men sleep curled as they did in the womb, it explains why they can't stand still. This explains, he said of the thickening in the blood, why the heart is weakened in fever, how it is stretched until it can't contract again, like those people in The Indies who stretch themselves so far they can never walk nor stand upright again. All because they wished to be considered saints.

My father wrote and wrote, but in all those words there was no mention of his own disease, no mention of the real uncertainties under which he labored. This was an omission on my father's part, not a falsehood. It was a matter of time.

I intend, he wrote the learned gentlemen, *to inspect some lepers*—until then, he would content himself with describing the animalcules harbored in the mouths of men and women. He would describe how the skin was one huge pore. The same was true of the intestine. The nutritious saps oozed from the intestines into the finest veins and arteries, they oozed out again to feed the fibres of flesh, to feed the tender skin. The salty residue pooled on his skin even as he wrote.

The winter of '84 was even worse than the one which had preceded it. The ice froze in the canals. Our country was in uproar because of the actions of the French King—but also because of the actions of our own Prince William, who was determined against all reason to continue to contest King Louis' ambition. When the French entered the Spanish Netherlands in the fall, Prince William sent to Sweden for troops. Even when the ships were lost in the North Sea and the troops were drowned, Prince William was not defeated. He turned his wrath on his own countrymen. Angrily, the burgers in Amsterdam cracked the ice in their canals. It wasn't the greed of the French they feared, but the righteous indignation of their own Stadtholder.

My father ignored it all. His joy that fall and winter could have warmed and pacified an empire. What mattered was the curiosity of men— the magnificence of Our Creator's intentions. What mattered was his own salvation. When he entertained the beautiful but wicked Duchess of Bouillon, it mattered not a whit to my father that she had been accused of trying to poison her husband. What mattered was that he and his labors found favor in her eyes. In all the learned and magnificent houses in Italy and France and England, she had seen nothing, she murmured, that could compare with the marvels revealed in my father's own study. Oh, how my father smiled. How he preened himself. A learned woman, she spoke to my father in his own tongue. She listened to his speculations with deference.

Yes, yes, he said brusquely. He'd seen the girl people claimed was a fish-child. He hadn't wanted to go, but people had insisted. He waved his hands wildly; he tossed back his head and laughed. It was nothing but dirt. The girl had been unwashed from birth. Unwashed, then smeared with tar, and forbidden to move. There was no mystery there, he said. There was no disease. Her buttocks were clean, he observed, from so much sitting. A barrel of water, a scouring brush should effect her cure. If we too let the scale on our skin collect, we'd look no different. "I know," he said with a shrug, "for I once was afflicted with excessive scale—upon which I directed my attention."

Cornelia and I listened as submissively as the Duchess. The Schepenen Vallensis shared a small smile with the French Ambassador D'Avaux. I was indignant. What did they know? If they had followed the line of my father's thought as he himself that winter traced the fibres of the eye's lens, they would have been amazed at its intricacy and its order. Had they, like Cornelia and I, seen the trials Our Creator had imposed upon my father, they would not question the bluff conviction with which he now spoke. My father had humbled himself, as we all must, to fortune; he had no need to humble himself to men or women less eager than he to grasp and grapple with the truth.

It was here my father displayed his courage. He did not question his miraculous recovery. Cornelia and I were silenced by joy—and by a slight unease. How could his despair disappear without a trace save the slightly darkened disc of skin on his shin? What was it exactly, we wondered, convinced the Creator that my father was worthy not only to pursue his investigations into the great mysteries but also to communicate them without fear of ostracism to men like the Schepenen Vallensis, the Pensionary Heinsius twiddling his thumbs in Paris, and the learned gentlemen gathered together in London?

After his cure, my father was more trusting of the Lord, but he became both bolder and more calculating in his relations with men. "I intended to observe lepers," he wrote again in January to the Royal Society, "but my curiosity has been engaged by the lens."

My father built a model to demonstrate the structure of the lens to his visitors. He drove nails in a wood ball, then he wound these nails with string, glued the string, and removed the nails. This, he said, pointing to the coil, is how the fibres appear to be arranged. But they are not strings, these fibres. They are more like very fine scales set one inside another. The coiled string represents the rim of each scale.

The transparence of the lens comes with the perfection with which each scale is placed upon the one before, never obstructing the light. In this the scales in the eye differ from the scales on our skin, which are darker and placed more haphazardly. As we age, these scales become more numerous and less transparent. Compare the red skin of the newborn babe with the skin of its mother. As we age, we all have need of greater protection, for then our nerves have grown as numerous as our fears. As we age, we armor ourselves with white scale or dark. We renew our defenses continually from within, only to have them chafed away by the friction of our clothes, our families, the wind.

Save here in the eye. Here the scales are not arranged and disarranged by motion, chance. Here nothing distracts the light from its passage. It is here, in the center of the eye, Our Creator has crafted from the debris of the body a perfect window for the soul. *See?*

"*I will tell you what I have observed with my own eyes of that disease we call leprosy,*" my father wrote at last to the learned gentlemen in July of '84. Like our hair, like leaf or bark, the skin increases from within, he announced, so our cure should follow the same course, slipping through the thin and tender lining of our stomach, the even finer lining of our veins.

He explained all of this to the first beggar he inspected, a man who suffered intense scaling on his scalp. His head was crusty, but only because when it had itched he had scratched it until it bled. My father explained his cure again to the second beggar he inspected, a man with a healthy head but a body covered with white and red spots, the red spots marking where the scale had been chafed away. This man's disease, my father announced, differed in no way from what had once afflicted him save that the scales were more numerous. The beggar was thirty-six, a former soldier, who, when salves, purges: and bleeding had not cured him, had been forced to leave his company and appear before the commission in Haarlem. Now my father shared his own good fortune with the unfortunate man. My father provided him with a packet of tea, a pitcher of milk.

My father suggested the same cure to the woman he met in 'sGravenhage who complained, like the first man he'd inspected, solely of a crusting on her head. She offered to take off her kerchief and let him see for himself, but my father found it unnecessary. It was the situation stifled his curiosity. He was accompanied by the brothers Dieren, surgeon and advocate from our town. He was escorting them to the house of Christiaan Huygens to inspect Heer Huygens' new telescope. But with this woman too, my father shared his own story, he provided her with a packet of tea and wished her good health.

But my father's mercy did not extend to everyone. He turned quickly from the boy of twelve he met beyond our ramparts, whose face was blotted with blue warts, whose cheeks and forehead and hands were covered with oozing ulcers. For him my father felt only disgust. It was I filled his begging bowl. It was Cornelia who prayed for his soul.

By then my father's attention was directed elsewhere. The study of our skin and scale had led him to some new and wonderful discoveries. The first was that the scale of fishes differed from that which composed a man's skin. The scale of fishes is fixed, it remains year after year and there one can measure the animal's age, as one can the age of a tree, by the rings. He discovered that the slime that covered fishes, like the mucous in our intestines, serves as an extra skin. But my father learned something even more wonderful, something he believed would change the fortunes of the Jews. *He learned that eels have scales!*

Here in Holland we love our young *aal*. We love our big *paaling*. My father even more than some. It was for this reason he was ready to go to Amsterdam to announce his findings in the great synagogue. He explained it to the men and women in the market square, but they shook their heads.

"You'll not convince them."

"In Leviticus it only forbids them to eat of fish without scale. It does not specify the eel."

"You'll not prevail," the advocate Dieren said with a laugh. "Any more than if you showed the pig's hoof was carved not cloven. It's custom prevents them."

"Custom," my father exclaimed. He looked at the eels wriggling in his bucket. "I can't believe it. I can't believe custom would keep a man from feasting—on the truth." My father looked again into his bucket. He licked his lips.

"Obviously," Schepenen Cornelis Vallensis said with a laugh, "it has not prevented you."

I took the bucket from my father.

"And you, Mejuffrouw van Leeuwenhoek?" the schepenen asked.

"Do you find the *aal* as much to your taste as does your father?"

My father laughed at that.

"It's true she has not my craving," he explained. "But she does not leave them to waste as does my wife."

"But it's not custom restrains her," I said to Heer Vallensis. "She does not like their taste. It's my own consumption that's habitual. Since a child, I've followed my father's example."

"May you always do so," he said.

He bowed. I nodded but did not reply.

I looked across the canal to our house. The limed brick glared in the sun. As I walked home, the eels writhed in the bucket. They would writhe just as eagerly on the cobbles behind the house after I had severed their heads, laid the knife to rest, covered, like my hands, with their sharp, blinding blood.

In the end, my father wrote of his findings to the ingenious company in London. The Jews were men of learning, soon enough they should read the truth for themselves, they should embrace it more easily when sanctioned by print and the royal charter. Perhaps the news would filter as well to the learned men in France, find its way to Portugal, Spain. Van Leeuwenhoek, they would mutter in their incomprehensible tongue as they gripped the slimy black back of the *paaling*. Van Leeuwenhoek, they would say as they raised the knife. Van Leeuwenhoek, as they raised their bloody hands to wipe the sweat from their faces. Van Leeuwenhoek, they would shout as their eyes closed, stinging with a pain as blinding as it was new.

It wouldn't be reason they'd cry out for then, it would be relief. I knew for a certainty. I had seen it happen again and again. They would not always be answered. Even should an answer come, they would not always hear. But they would always call. At the age of twenty-eight, it was one of the few things I had resolved to my own satisfaction. But it was a truth I did not care to share with anyone. It was not just in this shortness of speech, experience soon proved, that I differed from my famous father.

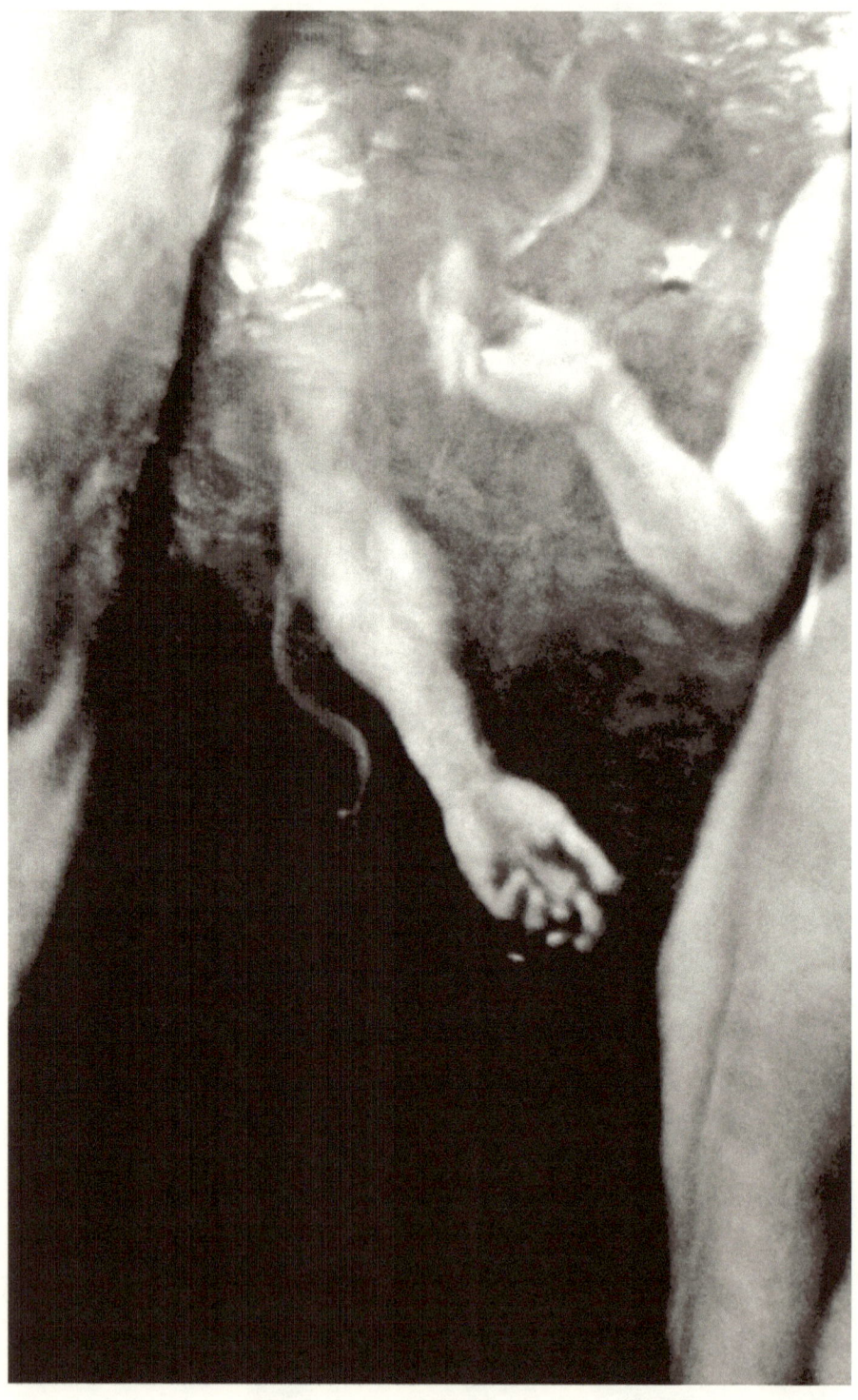

V
GENERATION
(1684-1693)

Although I am well aware that your Honors are better served by an accurate observation than with a whole volume of speculations, since these are nothing but brain-work, I have nevertheless again interspersed in this missive some of my reflections because it seems to me that, if I am qualified to judge at all, I am in a better position to draw conclusions from my observations than would be others who had never heard of such matter, let alone seen it.

Antoni van Leeuwenhoek

So that the species might be propagated, Nature decided that the connubial act should be linked with an enormously pleasurable sensation. If she had not implanted this sensation in men and women, the human species would surely have perished. . . . What woman would have rushed into a man's embrace unless her genital parts had been endowed with an itch for pleasure past belief? The nine months of gestation are laborious; the delivery of the fetus is beset with dreadfully excruciating pains and often fatal; the rearing of the delivered fetus is full of anxiety.

Regnier de Graaf

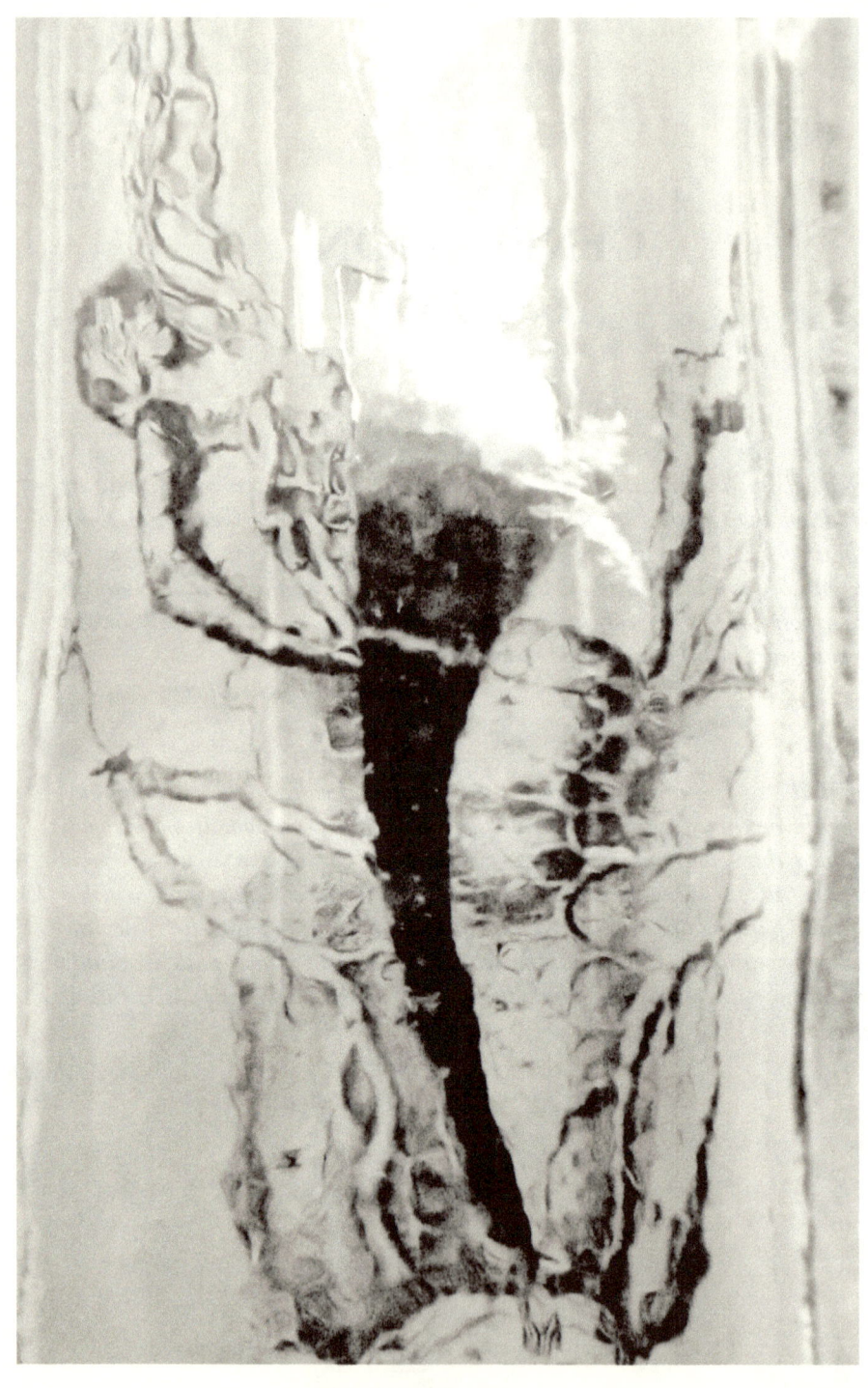

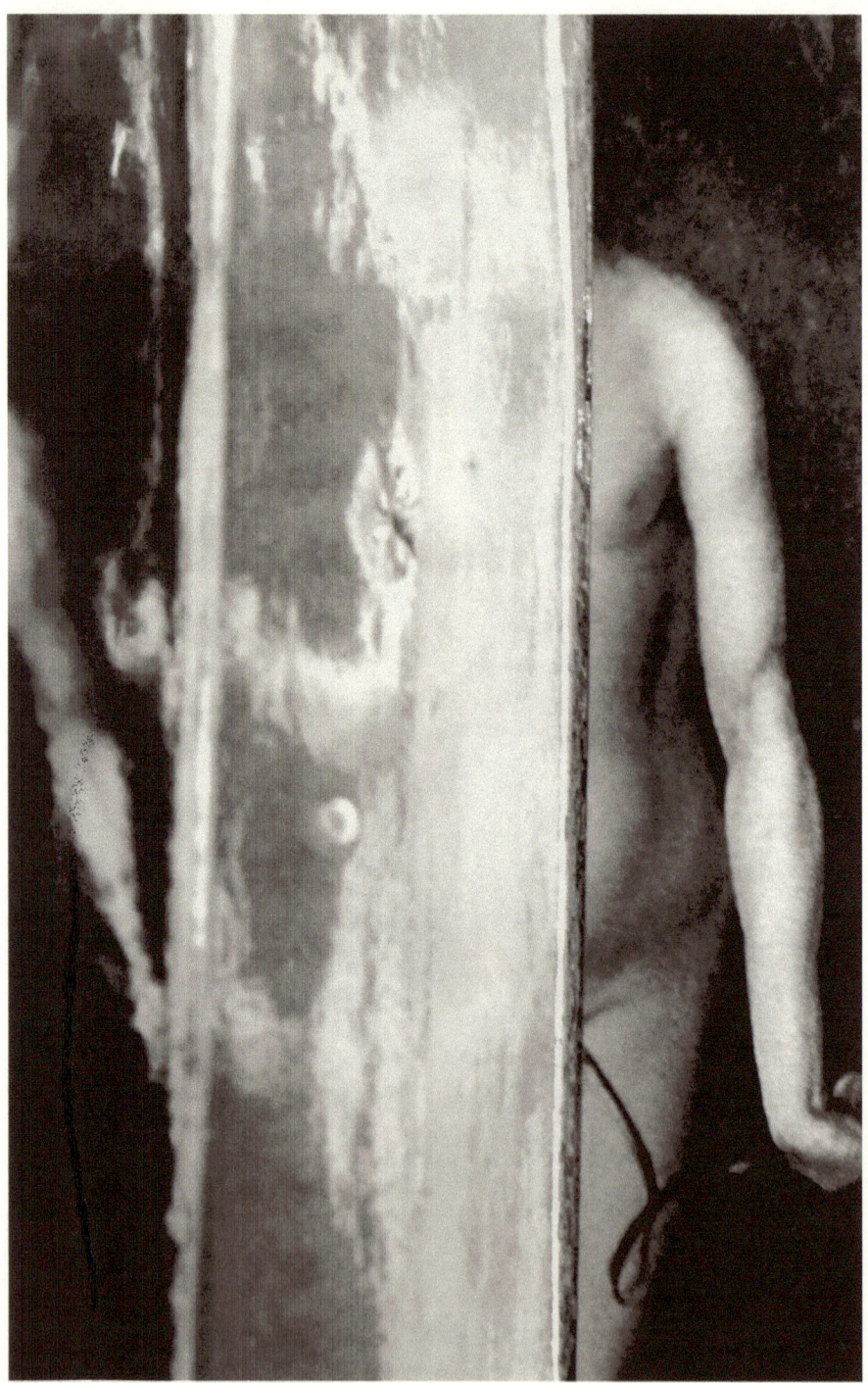

his Bo
ribus, co
nothing b
uch like ſpirit
a Contactum Vitalem.
ate Writer has reckoned up
ns, who have aſſerted the ſame
he *Ovarium*, yet I think they have been
As will appear by the following Tryals
beſpoke a *Bitch* of an ordinary ſize, to be d
e after ſhe had been once lined, which ha
3 oth of *December* laſt, upon the next day
he morning, the *Bitch* was lined
nd again at 2 a Clock in the aftr
her to be killed by running
inalis near the head.
legs to a Tabl
white ſubſt
cope, di
ich

❧➳❁〵 10 〳❀➳❧

AS EAGER AS ALL OF NATURE TO ADVANCE OURSELVES

"Come, come, Van Leeuwenhoek. It's useless, you yourself admit, to speculate," said Seigneur van Zuleichem.

"I never said that," my father protested. "I said we could not observe the subtle air. But there's much exists we can't observe."

"And much we can. Or *you* can, my worthy man. Surely you're not *tiring* of your observations?" Seigneur van Zuleichem turned his bright clear eyes on my father. His face was as deeply etched as oak bark.

"*Tire*," my father repeated. "Certainly I have not so much vigor as you."

"Few men do," his son said with a sigh. Heer Christiaan Huygens was fifty-six, his father near ninety.

Seigneur van Zuleichem looked around the room; he let his eyes rest on my father's grinding cup, the anvil by the fire, the large cabinet in which my father stored his glasses and his displays.

"You surpass me by far in your steady application to your art." My father blushed at the old man's praise. He blushed even deeper at his censure. "If you want to debate the learned men, Van Leeuwenhoek, don't do so over matters of speculation. You will gain nothing. It's your observations, man, will gain your fortune."

"Fortune!" scoffed Heer Huygens. "What fortune can be had from his endeavors?"

"None from the French King," Seigneur van Zuleichem cajoled his petulant son, "but we must not abandon hope of recognition by our own court—or our own assemblies."

"It's not the same," Heer Christiaan Huygens said. He adjusted his peruke. He continued to dress, as he had for his twenty years sojourn in Paris, in the noblest French style.

"Fame, my dear Archimedes, is as rich a diet as you'll find in any king's court," his father chided.

"It's the gut that ages," my father said with a smile. "But I have yet to sicken with surfeit. You as well, Meinheer?"

Christiaan Huygens looked down at his expanding belly, glanced at his father's meager frame. My own father's body, hidden behind his yellow robe, was as full as it had been for over twenty years. His tastes, like his appetites, had varied so little in all that time.

"What kind of recognition do you hope to gain from the Prince of Orange?" he asked curiously.

The old man stepped between his son and my father. He let his fingers rest on the table.

"So you've nothing further to show us today, Leeuwenhoek? We must be getting on then. We're to dine with the Doublets, then inspect D'Aquet's latest curiosities."

"I have intended to pursue further investigations into the question of generation, but the weather has hindered me."

"Surely you've proved the presence of the animalcules. No one could be doubting that."

"The animalcules, yes, everyone begins to see them. But they raise so many foolish objections I don't see how they will ever see the truth. They say they may rise from putrefaction, these animalcules. They say they have nothing to do with generation. Imagine! They say they may die upon touching a woman's flesh."

"De Graaf did observe the eggs travelling through the tubes, did he not?"

"Eggs!" My father's face was as red as if he'd choked on a piece of meat. He lurched over to the fire and poked at it furiously until he had regained his voice. "I have shown the animalcules live in the testicles. I will find them, I assure you, thriving in the womb as well."

The old Seigneur van Zuleichem straightened his thin frame. He bowed to my father.

"It's the sight will silence them, Van Leeuwenhoek, not your thoughts."

❧ ❧ ❧

My father stood watching at the door as Seigneur van Zuleichem and his famous son made their way over the bridge to the stadthuis where they would meet with their cousin, Heer Teding van Berkhout, councilor of our town.

"I don't understand," my father said, shaking his head. "What more could a learned man need to convince him than what I have already demonstrated?"

"A book," Cornelia said. "Preferably in Latin. Have you ever thought of getting your godson's assistance?"

"Phillip van Leeuwen knows no Latin," my father said shortly. Cornelia smiled and continued with her sewing. My father left the room and climbed the stairs with noisy haste. He returned in his cloak and his hat and left the house without explanation.

What explanation would have sufficed? Besides, it wasn't us he sought to persuade, but the learned gentlemen in 'sGravenhage, Amsterdam, Leyden, London, Paris, Antwerp. All those who told him to stick to his glasses and leave the speculations to the learned. Thus the only one my father satisfied completely in this matter was the municipal physician, Henricus D'Aquet, to whom he demonstrated on the following day the wonderful truth of his assertions.

I was the one my father sent to fetch the honorable councilor. His servant had me wait in the entrance room. I could hear voices, women's laughter. The councilor was still at table, entertaining those who visited from afar. Dr. D'Aquet was famous here in our city for his store of curiosities, as famous as Bleyswijck, Seigneur de Belois. At first the honorable councilor did not recognize me. Even inside, I did not care to remove my hood.

"My father," I whispered. "Antoni van Leeuwenhoek—"

"Yes, yes, What?" The good man's face was flushed with wine.

"If it is possible for you to come to the Golden Head? My father greatly desires your presence."

"What's this about? Can't it wait? A sickness in the house? Your father himself?" His voice softened. "Certainly I will come and consult upon it."

"No, Sir. It is nothing like that. My father wishes for you to come and see the living animalcules—"

"I have already seen them. In my own curious cockchafers, not to mention the testicles of rabbits and dogs, rams and bulls." In his exasperation, he almost shouted.

His wife appeared at the door, curious to see who had come. I lowered my voice. I kept my eyes fixed on the bows that fastened his shoes.

"My father has sacrificed a bitch," I said. "He has seen the animalcules moving in the womb itself. He wishes you to come and attest to this. The Royal Society, he says, will honor the word of our Municipal Physician."

"Why not Dr. 'sGravesende?" Dr. D'Aquet answered, but already he was crossing the room to collect his cape and hat.

"It is nothing," he assured his wife. "The worthy burger, Van Leeuwenhoek, has requested my assistance."

"What?"

"A matter of some delicacy. I am not at liberty—"

"A doit for his servant, Henricus," she hissed.

"That's his daughter." And it was here, out of pity for me, he tried to lower his own voice.

♛ ♛ ♛

When we arrived at the Golden Head my father had already cut the womb from the bitch and brought it into the house. The dog's blood steamed from its opened belly. Our breath steamed from our mouths. No one could see clearly.

"They assured me she'd mated several times three days past." My father spoke hurriedly as he ushered D'Aquet into his study. "She mated again this morning under my own scrutiny. You can see the animalcules everywhere. In the canal. In the womb. See for yourself."

My father handed D'Aquet the glass. The Municipal Physician handed my father his cape. My father handed it off impatiently, to me.

"Here, let me guide you. You'll never see them unless you happen upon the stream. The womb is an enormous place for such small creatures."

The two men leaned over the bright, fleshy purse.

"Aha!" D'Aquet cried at last. "Surely they're less vigorous here than they are in the testicle?"

"It's the air," my father said shortly. "The cold. They need the warmth of our blood and flesh. When first I caught sight of them, they could have been swarming in the tubules of the testicle, they were so nimble."

"And the eggs," D'Aquet asked. "Have you managed to observe them as well? De Graaf maintained it was the semen that released them from the female testicles."

"I did not seek them," my father said. "I don't think them necessary,"

"*You* don't think them necessary?" A smile twitched at the corners of the Municipal Physician's lips. "My good man, who are you to say—"

"You *will* attest to what you've seen?" my father asked him.

"Me? Certainly, Leeuwenhoek. It is not I who debate you. But the learned gentlemen in London and France will not abandon the words of Harvey and De Graaf that easily."

"If De Graaf had lived to make use of my glasses—"

"Next you'll be wishing the same of Vesalius, Galen, even Aristotle!"

"Yes," my father said simply. "Yes."

"I can't agree." Dr. D'Aquet shook his head. "These glasses will not change our entire lives. Surely God did not let us live from the Creation until now in complete ignorance."

"I did not say so," my father said with a shrug. "But it serves no purpose to discuss it further."

"Perhaps not." D'Aquet looked around for his cloak. "But be sure to show me the observations you send to the Royal Society. It is men like you, Van Leeuwenhoek—"

"Who support such fools as he," Cornelia said with a laugh when later my father went in to seek her sympathy. "No one who meets you can doubt your love for the truth, Husband. No burgomaster, no professor at the university has a greater passion for it."

"What will it take to convince them?" he asked again.

More than you would readily imagine.

♛ ♛ ♛

For three days my father carried in his pants pocket the womb of a second bitch wrapped in cloth. He put it beside him in his bed.

"You ask too much," Cornelia protested. But in the heart of winter, she needed my father's heat as much as the little animalcules wriggling in the reeking womb.

"No more, Father," I protested the fourth morning when he came to table. "The stench is too great. No one can rest in the same room with you."

It wasn't my objection convinced him, but his own observation. The animalcules had died. My father's heat could not sustain them.

"I'm sure they'd travel farther in the living womb. I'm sure they would swim to the horns of the uterus. They might even struggle up through the tubes, given enough time."

"I could follow De Graaf's practice and sacrifice rabbits each day or two—but the animalcules are so small the eyes would grow fatigued just seeking for them in that mighty expanse."

"Oh no, Antoni," Cornelia said, her handkerchief to her mouth. "It's worse than the Flesh Hall now."

It wasn't Cornelia's dismay persuaded him, but the weakness of his own stomach. My father has no taste for blood, the cumbersome anatomy of man or quadrupeds. Heart, lung, spleen, or human womb, these hold none of the attractions for my father of the shimmering animalcules swarming within the testicles of dog, hare, bull, man, or the despicable flea. This life that only a microscope can reveal.

♛ ♛ ♛

My father believed firmly that the truth revealed by his glasses was the larger truth. He could see its application everywhere.

The earth, he announced that summer, *is a giant womb, the foster-mother to all plants and trees. Nobody can deny this. We see again and again that throughout the world provident nature works in one and the same way.*

Stubbornly, my father transcribed his speculations and sent them to the gentlemen in London.

And although I have sometimes imagined, as I examined the animalcules in male seed of an animal, that I might be able to say, there lies the head, and there, again, lie the shoulders and there the hips, but not having been able to judge of this with the slightest degree of certainty, I shall not, therefore, affirm this as definite, rather hope that we may, at some time, have the good fortune to come across an animal whose male seeds will be so large that we can recognize in it the figure of the creature from which it has come. For we have had the good fortune to come across such a small seed as that produced by the ash-tree, in which seed such large leaves are contained, as said heretofore, which exceed in size all leaves in the seeds of trees which I have examined hitherto; and therefore it might well be that we came to dissect some small animal in whose male seed we should find large living animalcules.

But to demonstrate still further that provident Nature proceeds in practically the same way in all her workings, we must begin by contemplating and considering attentively, and regarding as quite similar, the animalcule from the male which is discharged into the womb, and the beginning of the plant that is made in the seed.

That spring, summer, and fall, and in the years to come, my father has studied the seeds of cotton, date, clove, nutmeg, gooseberry, black currant, lime trees, ash, oak, capre, Buparati, Kaukin, Adamboe, coconut, rye, barley, millet, buckwheat, canary seed, sorrel. Again and again he has pondered this great mystery, generation.

Since plants have no sex, each must play both male and female—so nearly every seed contains an embryo and flour to nourish it until it has rooted itself permanently in that larger womb, earth. This was not all my father surmised. The womb affects the development of the seed enormously. Drop seed on stony ground, on sand—you'll see what develops is not the same. This explains the yellow child who comes from the mating of a white man and a black woman—it's the mother's womb that has soiled the child's skin. As it is the nutrient in the ass's womb that provides the larger ear to the mule, its constriction that lessens the tail. My father reasoned from animals to plants as well. He believed that could one take an embryo from one seed and imbed it in another, imbed the walnut in the chestnut husk, some living thing as different from either walnut or chestnut as the mule is from horse or ass would come into being.

Although he saw nature working in one and the same way in animals and plants, my father could not accept that life came by chance, or that there could be an indiscriminate pairing between that which had life and that which did not. Maggots did not come from the dust, geese from barnacles, eels from the dew—or worms from the bark of trees. There had to be a seed, and its origin was its destiny. Man begat man and bee begat bee. At last, my father's fine glass and steady hand even revealed the animal seed laid within the oak gall.

But his glasses could not reveal everything.

What glass could ever reveal the vital spirit? *The minuteness from which man is produced from generation to generation is inconceivable,* he wrote. He paced his study, ground yet another glass. He returned to his paper and quill.

Unless we turn to trees! Here my father found answers to the questions that still troubled him. Here, in the ash, he could see the embryo he only imagined to exist in the male animalcule. Here, in the cherry or apple, he saw the years required for a tree to bear fruit. Why should not the same delay take place in man before the quickening of the animalcules?

My father now wrote upon generation with the same boldness he had shown when he contradicted the speculations of the great Des Cartes. As he said, "It is open to everyone of us to express his opinion, especially on matters the real truth of which is hidden from us." For my father, it was more than an opportunity, it was an obligation.

My father had—and knew it—as much right as any man to his own speculations. But what he was after was conviction, irrefutable truth. For this he must rely, as the old Seigneur van Zuleichem had said, on his eyes, and the keys of glass. There was no other way to convince his neighbor. If a man can't see beyond the end of his nose, what must you do? Why, bring the glass directly to his eye!

Obviously, my father needed evidence. It was for this purpose that, with Cornelia's assistance, he studied the silkworms. Silkworms interested the learned gentlemen in London. If my father could demonstrate there the truth of his own speculations, why, there would be no more argument, no more idle chatter. There would be instead the great laughter and applause for which he so intensely hungered.

My father desired to observe the silkworm egg for it was transparent, and he hoped to observe there what he so far had only observed in the seeds of plants, the growth from animalcule to embryo to the eager worm. He gathered eggs all summer, but when the autumn came and with it the cold winds, he could see no worms within the blue membrane.

In September he took a flat screwed top box and filled it with eggs. He put it into his pocket to warm it as before he had warmed the bitch's womb. This time, Cornelia joined him. She tucked into her bodice a second box. It was, I was sure, the promise of silk thread that lured her. I'd take no part in this. Even for my father, I would not have my breasts crawl with worms.

"They only feed on mulberry leaves," Cornelia assured me. "Besides,

Antoni intends to watch them through the shell—he'd not let them come to birth here." She patted her broad breast with a laugh. "Although I *am* honored," she whispered, "that he has again entrusted me."

Her face flushed with pride. Sweat beaded on her forehead, but she drew her morning coat around her neck. I don't resist the cold like Cornelia, and it was for this my father had chosen her, for the slight film of sweat that covered her breasts, her upper lip, and the inside of her palms upon the faintest exertion. When her skin was cooled by her dampened linen, she simply added more and more clothes every month until by January she looked as broad as she was high. She would have lain in bed under coverlets day as well as night if my father had allowed it. She and the worms if necessary. But my father did not persist in harboring the eggs the entire winter.

All September he opened one or two eggs each week but observed nothing. A month later he discovered a worm among Cornelia's eggs. But removed from the bigger womb of Cornelia's hot damp breasts, removed from the egg itself, the worm dried so much and so irregularly my father could not make head from tail. And in all the other eggs he inspected, the worms did not grow, and the eggs dried so they crinkled or became completely flat.

By the end of October, my father abandoned his observation. He relieved Cornelia's bosom and his own pocket of their burdens. He busied himself with more fruitful studies.

It was in May of the following year my father made his wonderful observation. The eggs he'd abandoned had begun to grow again. The worms he found in them had globules arranged on their sides, ready, he was convinced, to become limbs. Opening the eggs morning and night, he saw their bodies grow blackish with veins, he saw their heads and limbs threaded with an incomprehensible quantity of vessels, more vessels, he claimed, than he had seen arteries in the human body.

He saw these changes with his own eye. He shared them with Cornelia, with me, with Pensionary Heinsius, and with the pensionary's friends. But he could not share them with the learned gentlemen in London, for the moisture of the worm evaporated so quickly no draughtsman had time to record this wonderful network of vessels. My father was amazed as well by the structure of the egg, how tightly constructed it was to be able to keep these fragile worms moist for months. By the end of May, nothing seemed needed to complete the worms. Each had a head with all its parts, limbs, legs, a body covered all over with hairs. Finally my father cut open an egg and saw the silkworm within immediately stretch itself and crawl forth!

At this my father exclaimed with pleasure and amazement. He wrote again to the ingenious:

These observations made me reflect whether it might not be possible that, in the beginning of Creation, or when they were first made, something had been created inside them to cause the small movement, or living Soul of the Male Seed to lie enclosed in the Egg for more than six months without increasing in size, except insofar as was necessary to make, from the parts of the same, a beginning of the body, which would serve as protection and final nourishment of the little male animal, to wit, the aforesaid membrane; and that, if this were not so, the silkworms would all be dead within the year.

Nature pursues similar courses in all animals. For it was not just the silkworm eggs that developed in late spring. My father saw the same growth in the caterpillar eggs he had taken from their nests the autumn past, which he had thrown back into their box in disgust at their monstrous appearance— and at their stubborn stillness. By June these worms too had quickened and gnawed their way free of their eggs. They writhed in their box, ravenous for the green leaves unfolding on the elms.

This was not as I had expected, my father wrote the learned gentlemen, *for it had never entered my thoughts that a worm or caterpillar, having become fully grown in its egg in the late summer, and not crawling out of it, could nevertheless remain alive in its egg the whole winter.*

It was not as my father expected. He was torn, too, in his inclinations. My father loves the fruit of his garden as he does the fruit of his thought— and he for years had maintained that a warm autumn followed by a severe frost would destroy the caterpillars lured from the eggs by the unaccustomed heat, thus preserving the next year's crop.

My father's courage did not fail him. He praised the Creator's purpose, his generosity. The silkworm's cocoon, he would say later, is not made for man. And the eggs of each kind of animal serve only to preserve and foster its own kind. The world is no figment of man's mind, no garden or pasture for his sole delight. He is only one of God's many creations. God's mercy extends to the bream and the shrimp, the crane fly and the sheep. The Creator has made us all equally eager to advance ourselves.

♕ ♕ ♕

It was true. Ambition pumped through all our hearts that fall. In September of '88, while Prince William bought and bartered for supplies for his troops, and trained his cavalry on the Mookerheide, my father was proving his own worth to an equally general satisfaction. It was this autumn he discovered the circulation of the blood.

Discovered? My father? Certainly that is what he believed. Malpighi might have seen, once, small transparent vessels in the lungs. Harvey might have argued sixty years before that the blood in our bodies revolved, but no one had *seen* it so clearly, so indisputably as my father did in the tails and gills of the tadpole, in the tender tail of the aal. There is no man in Delft my father can't persuade of this truth. He just hands him a spyglass, a wide smile on his face.

"Don't take my word," he will say, taking the glass back, handing it on to the next visitor. "See for yourself."

Even then, eight years ago, when he first made and demonstrated his new discovery, he asked the learned gentlemen in London not to take his word alone, but to take that of our honored magistrates and city councilors, Heinsius, Vallensis, and 'sGravesende. All these men have seen what I recorded here, he claimed. Surely you'll trust them. My father showed the same to Kroonevelt, the printer, before he set my father's observations in type. That month my father shared his glasses, as he did his printed observations, with a general prodigality.

What delighted my father about the discovery of the circulation of the blood was, first, how it delighted everyone else! But my father cherished his discovery as well because of the years it had taken him to make it.

Most learned men simply shrugged at its mention. "I didn't think there was any debate. Years ago, Harvey—"

"But there was no *proof*," my father protested. "Now I, Van Leeuwenhoek—"

It was not an idea these men comprehended, jostling to look through my father's glass, it was a visible, irrefutable truth.

"What amazes me is the speed of their transit," said Heinsius.

"It increases with the magnification," warned my father.

"What worries me is their obstruction," said Vallensis.

"Like ice on the river Maas in November."

"You just need something to thaw the blockages," said 'sGravesende, the municipal anatomist. "Something hot."

"And softening," my father said eagerly, "like tea. Speaking of which, Maria—"

Passing the open door, I would nod and send in our servant Maartje. That year my father's sole companions were those burgomasters. They sought him as eagerly as he sought them.

"It was such a simple favor he wanted from us," Heer Vallensis explained to me later. "Everywhere else, enormous choices were being made. The French had invaded the Palatinate; 'sGravenhage teemed with soldiers and sailors readying for the English invasion. Your father only asked us to come and share his delight in that glittering, rapid transit."

Certainly that autumn we were all in need of such solace. To see our Prince William sail off to England to vanquish King James II, his own uncle and his wife's father, was unsettling even for the porters at the Schiespoort, not to mention our magistrates, or my father with his English honors. The prayers we offered for the Prince on the 27th of October were less comforting by far than meditating on yet another proof of the beautiful complexity of Our Creator's purpose, as seen through my father's glass. No wonder Vallensis, 'sGravesende, Heinsius, and Huygens spent hours in my father's study.

It wasn't just solace my father sought—or found. Nor was it merely proof of Harvey's argument. My father began to ponder the nature of pipes, the pipes we find in trees, in our teeth, in the tusks of elephants, as well as the pipes in our bodies we call arteries and veins. Might there not be even smaller ones designed to draw off each element for our nurture? Pipes for fat, for blood, for bile, for salt.

My father propounded his theses to Christiaan Huygens, who yawned, nodded his head, accepted another cup of tea. "I will mention the same to Thévènot," he said. "I will mention it to Leibnitz."

"You may send them my printed observations," my father said eagerly.

"We could slip a few into your brother's baggage when he sails for England," joked Heer Vallensis, for Christiaan Huygens' brother Constantijn had assumed upon his esteemed father's death the position of secretary to the Prince of Orange. He was soon to set off with the Prince to overthrow King James. The Pensionary Heinsius looked at his friend Vallensis with disapproval. Even though everyone knew of the Prince's departure, we merely filled our orders for woolens, leather, tea, harnesses and biscuits. We did not speculate openly. Certainly not in a simple burger's house.

"When do you intend to publish your next observations?" Heer Huygens asked my father, rising to take his leave.

"More?" my father asked, glancing fretfully at the volume on the table. He was both proud and frustrated by the book, which, like his letters published in the *Philosophical Transactions* of the *Journal des Sçavans*, recorded his discoveries in words he couldn't decipher or correct.

"As soon as you publish your treatise on light," laughed Heer Doublet, Heer Huygens brother-in-law, who had accompanied him from 'sGravenhage. "At least then you'll have the right to ask."

"The situation in England may prevent publication of the *Transactions*," warned Heinsius.

"And the situation in France is no better," agreed Huygens. "It is up to you, Van Leeuwenhoek."

"I have sent a printed copy of my observations to the Royal Society. You don't think they'll question my presumption?"

"In this age, a man must take the initiative," Heer Heinsius said kindly. "Everyone understands this."

"Have you seen my last work translated to Latin?" my father asked Heer Doublet.

"We can only hope you'll be luckier in your next dedication," Heer Vallensis said with a laugh. My father had dedicated his volume to King James.

"It is a confusing time," my father said, lifting his glass to his eye. "A man must follow his own conscience."

"Certainly," all the men agreed, but their eyes strayed to each other, then out the window toward the stadthuis, the market square teeming as it had for weeks with soldiers, peddlers, the curious populace of our town gathered to hear hour by hour the latest news from 'sGravenhage, Amsterdam, Paris, Brandenburg.

"What was that?" Heer Doublet asked, pointing to a man waving a pamphlet in the air with an indecipherable cry.

My father appeared not to notice their hurried departure. But he considered it as closely as all their behaviors. Those days my father's speculations concerned not only the circuit of the blood in our body, they concerned these very gentlemen, how they travelled with him through the same narrow channels, spun by the current of events as our globules are by the nutritious saps, as our good Prince's ships were by the wind-whipped sea off Den Briel.

"Save the wine," my father said to the maid, Maartje. "They will be back tomorrow—my worthy friends."

That is what my father called them. That is what he believed. But he was as confused in this as were all those who called the waxen globes in the anthills eggs, or those who believed eels grew from the dew.

That fall if I instead of Maartje carried into my father's study the tray of glasses, the pitcher of wine for the refreshment of the burgomasters, Heer Vallensis would always look up at my entrance. He would bow his head. He could tell, you see, the difference between me and Maartje. It is true that anyone with the slightest powers of observation could have noted the difference in our features, not to mention our dress, but to visit my father, these learned and able men had blinded themselves with condescension. To accept my father, they had to strip him of everything that distinguished him— distinguished him, I mean, from them: his house, his wife, his daughter. Only Heer Vallensis had the courage to see my father as he really was. Was this, I wonder, because my father, like most of Delft, never really saw *him*. They saw Burgomaster Dirck's younger son, they saw the grandson of Jacob, physician to the Princes of Orange. No wonder he nodded to me, Antoni's daughter, when silently I entered my father's study, or when, scorched with my own confusion, I departed.

Under his scrutiny I writhed like those animalcules my father demonstrated in his glass tubes. I had no idea how to behave.

Because Heer Vallensis is now dead, everything I say of him is shaped by this fact. I can't help that. Anymore than I could if he still lived on the Oude Delft and walked down the Nieuwe Straat daily to his duties at the stadthuis. The past is always distorted by the glass we observe it through. In time I will come to speak of the sands that scoured and shaped the glass that is my own memory.

But first I must try to describe the man as he appeared to me then, when I was a spinster of thirty-five and he a bachelor of forty-three. He was not a handsome man, but I took great satisfaction in his appearance. His hair was thin and fine, almost black; he wore no periwig although they had become much the fashion. He had a long straight nose, blue eyes widely spaced.

Unlike his friend Heinsius, his cheeks were lean, his natural expression intent but not stern. Like his friend Heinsius, he dressed more soberly than most men of his wealth and position. His collar and sleeves were of the simplest lace, his coats of sturdy serge.

What I remember best were his expressions, the way his eyes never left my face when I was speaking. The way, in great pain, his face didn't age but grew instead younger, softer, the still lips full and red as if they'd been bruised. Even though he showed me at times an almost boyish countenance, he was not foolish. Certainly, he was never indifferent to the opinions of all who surrounded him. He was never indifferent to mine.

It was not just within my father's house that Heer Vallensis acknowledged me. Even on the market square, when we stopped to purchase a news sheet, to learn that King James had escaped to France, or that the English had at last offered their crown to our able Prince of Orange and not just to his wife, the British Princess Mary, or that Heinsius had become Grand Pensionary of all the States of Holland, he would take a minute, not even separating himself from his friends, and, bowing say, "What think you of the news, Mejuffrouw van Leeuwenhoek?" When I would shrug, he would only smile and turn to my stepmother. "And you, Mevrouw van Leeuwenhoek?" Cornelia would burn with pride, I would freeze with shame.

"The Lord seems to have designed our Prince for great things," Cornelia said.

"And his princess," Heer Vallensis said. "It is her throne they share."

"And Heer Heinsius, your worthy friend," I added. "It is a great honor for our city.""

He looked saddened, which surprised me. "I know no abler man," he said. "But one wonders, sometimes, who will be left to guide us. We have given our Prince to the English, our Pensionary to the States . . ."

"How can you, one-time magistrate, now honored Trustee of our Orphan Chamber even *ask* this?" Cornelia said with a high laugh.

"How indeed?" he said with a lift of his shoulders. "And your father, Mejuffrouw van Leeuwenhoek, does he intend to leave us as well?"

"My father can't imagine life outside our city."

"There's nothing to compare with Delft. In that, at least, we agree. He still pursues his observations on circulation?"

"He attempts to. But his bat sickened and died—and he has yet to observe the circulation through the wattles of a cock or the ear of a rabbit.

Their skin is thicker than that of fishes. But he has just sent an account of all this, including his speculations on the fins of flying fishes, to the Royal Society."

"My husband has written," Cornelia said, "but he doubts again that he will receive acknowledgement. Perhaps Heer Heinsius, now that he is Grand Pensionary, could ask our Ambassador to enquire of the Royal Society about the fate of my husband's letters."

"Surely my father can speak for himself."

"As surely as can the Grand Pensionary," Heer Vallensis agreed. "Will you tell your father that Dr. 'sGravesende and I hope to wait upon him soon to educate ourselves further on the wonders of the True Circulation of the Blood."

He touched his hand to his hat, turned and hastened into the stadthuis.

"Why did he ask you to speak to Antoni?" Cornelia asked peevishly as we made our way toward the Hippolytusbuurt.

"Hurry," I said. "It is nearly noon. We will never be ready in time."

Cornelia gripped my arm with painful strength. "Do slow down. My heart fails me, Maria."

"I'll go on myself," I said, looking across the canal. Maartje was washing the front stoop. "You can follow at a more stately pace."

"Alone?" Cornelia moaned. I looked at her then and saw the blue shadow on her lips, the ashen circles under her eyes.

"No," I said, suddenly frightened. "I will wait on you."

But Cornelia shook her head. "Send Maartje back for me. You're impatient as your father. I will never catch my breath with you glaring at me like that."

If this was what my father felt, it was not impatience. It was dread. No wonder he left their chamber so quickly, muttering under his breath.

"Why you two can't pity me—" she said.

"Pity!" Now I was as eager to leave as my father. "If pity would force the blood through your arteries, surely I would pity you. It's strength of heart you're wanting, Cornelia. Not pity."

I left her then without looking back. Although I sent Maartje immediately to assist her, my stepmother returned a full hour later leaning on the arm of my cousin Antoni Molijn.

He gave her what she wanted—for a fee. It wasn't guilders he was after, but a glimpse of my father's latest observations. I protested.

"They are always asking me at the Guild," he said.

"It is no farther to the Golden Head than it is to your house, Antoni. They can come ask my father themselves," I chided him.

"So many *people*," Cornelia protested.

"My father communicates regularly with Dr. 'sGravesende. Surely he can answer any questions."

"Or we could ask you to come," my cousin said grimly. "Since you speak so ably for your father."

"Yes," Cornelia agreed sullenly. "You should have seen her on the market square this morning talking with Heer Vallensis."

"*Vallensis?* Cornelis Dirckszoon? What interest could he have in my uncle's occupations?"

"Ask him," I said angrily.

"*None!*" Cornelia giggled. "I believe he just uses Antoni as an excuse to talk with Maria herself."

"Vallensis?"

Cornelia pursed her mouth, rolled her eyes. My cousin Antoni slapped his knee. They both gasped with laughter. Even Maartje's face was slit from ear to ear.

"What's going on?" my father asked, closing the door behind him. "You can hear the commotion out on the street. Anyone would think we ran a tavern."

"They presume and presume falsely," I said. "They would be the first to admit it."

"Foolishly," Cornelia said, catching her breath. "What possible interest could a Trustee of the Orphan Chamber have in Maria?"

"It is your observations that interest him, Father," I agreed. "When he saw the blood struggling through the wing of the bat, no one could have been more amazed."

"Or touched by your solicitude," Cornelia added with a shudder. To keep the bat warm, my father had carried him in his pocket day and night. When he first caught the animal, Cornelia had screamed at the small fiendish face grinning at her from the covered wine glass my father had trapped it in.

"Devil," she had muttered while my father crooned over the poor shivering creature, feeding it bacon, milk, small beer, rice. Nothing could win her over. She still refused to ascend to the drying room and storage chamber where the animal had been found.

"Why *shouldn't* Heer Vallensis have an interest in my daughter?" my father continued stubbornly.

"*Maria?*" Cornelia looked at me, then looked equally stubbornly at her feet. Already she had begged my pardon. What use was that, I had wondered even as I gave it. Pardon wouldn't give us peace.

Her words were like new animalcules under the microscope. My father couldn't leave them until he had explored them to his own satisfaction.

"Yes, *Maria!*" my father exclaimed. "She is a modest woman. Able." He waved at my shop. "She carries on her own trade. What more could he want?"

"Youth," I said. "Learning. Wealth. Beauty." I rose to my feet. "You shame me, Father. Cornelia and Antoni spoke wildly. How can you not see the jest?"

"It is time you wed, Maria," my father said. "You can't live on here in the Golden Head forever."

"Wed?" Cornelia asked in amazement. "You still think of that for your daughter, Antoni?"

My father shook his head. "Still?" he asked. "I have just begun."

"She is older than Princess Mary."

"She would make a good wife," my father insisted. "She is the same age as you when we married."

"Stop," I said.

Only that day had I begun to understand that there might be the smallest grain of truth in what they said. There was interest there, but what Heer Vallensis wanted of me, the spinster daughter of Antoni van Leeuwenhoek, I could not presume to know—and refused to speculate upon. The distance between us, as the hilarity of my stepmother and cousin showed, was too great to contemplate. It pained me, more for him than for me, that my father could not see it so.

Certainly after his friend Heer Heinsius moved to 'sGravenhage to take up his new duties as Grand Pensionary for the States of Holland, the bachelor from the Oude Delft was a lonely man. But it wasn't a family he longed for. He lived with his widowed mother and his widowed sister, both of whom relied on him as they once did their husbands. His nieces and nephews, children of his older brother, Jacob, were often visiting from 'sGravenhage. You heard no children's laughter in our house, only the ting of Cornelia's mandolin, her high voice reciting psalms. There was the rasp of my father's grinding cup, the scratch of his quill, the rocking of his restless foot, and from my shop the mutter of serge, the hiss of silk, the rasp of my own quill recording accounts. I believe he found the quiet a relief.

I believe Cornelis Dirckszn. Vallensis visited us at the Golden Head because here he felt seen for himself. He did not have to meet his mother's pouched, calculating eyes or his sister's judicious, skeptical ones. He did not need to explain to us that at the age of forty-one he had no desire to take a wife. It is true my countrymen distrust bachelors, but none of them would have dared ask the question of our Grand Pensionary Heinsius that the whole city asked of Dirck's son: "When do you intend to join us in the married state?"

It was, certainly, neither lack of fortune nor excess of occupation that hindered Heer Vallensis' marriage. His duties at the stadthuis required no more time than my father's humbler ones of sheriff's chamberlain and wine-gauger. He wasn't given to debauchery like our once great Ambassador Beverningh. He lacked his friend Heinsius' ascetic temperament. He had been disappointed, most decided, when young.

Who was the girl who had incited such passion? No one knew. But more than one person remembered how violently opposed to one another Heer Vallensis and his father had been the entire year preceding Mayor Dirck Vallensis' death in 1673. The troubles of the Rampjaar may have had much to do with that—and much to do with their reconciliation. Certainly, Cornelis Dirckszn. wore mourning for two full years after his father's death. Even when he inherited his portion of his father's estate, even when the mourning bombazine was folded up and packed away, he approached no woman with remarkable assiduity, he sent no representative to discuss portions with an eager father.

It is true that he was not made a member of the Council of Forty until he was thirty-four, but even then, at evenings of cards at the Doublets, the Teding-Berkhouts, the Tromps, he showed no woman especial favor. How do I know all this? Poor Heer Vallensis! Even here in the humble Golden Head he occasioned talk. He had for years. He was no monk like Heinsius, no old woman set in her ways like, pardon me, the famous Christiaan Huygens.

The women who came, after the death of Adriaen Beijeren, to my shop to purchase their cloth often spoke of Heer Vallensis in my hearing. Sometimes they spoke directly to his mother, Agatha van Berestyn or his sister Corvina Maria Vallensis when they were inspecting my stores. More often they talked among themselves after his mother and sister had left. The sister of Bleyswijck spoke of him to his cousin Machtilde, who discussed him in turn with the pretty, shy wife of Putmans. Everyone, you see, had a cousin, either coming of age or languishing on the shelf. There was something about Heer Vallensis that did not put an end to all this speculation. Perhaps it was his ready laugh, or his slow smile and the gentle blinking of his eyes as you spoke that made you believe he gave you his complete attention, like a dear and obedient child—or a loyal dog!

"Cornelis Dirckszn. would be a good match," the men said, nodding at the probable marriage settlement, but shaking their heads at the thought of the man himself, as taciturn as his father had been voluble. It was the women who felt something close to rancor even as they tried to pair him off, for there was something about Cornelis Dirckszn. that made women long to win—and hoard—his favor.

Most women, but not his widowed sister Corvina. His unmarried state was a constant aggravation to her. How many plans of hers had he snarled hopelessly, like a kitten playfully raking through the threads of lacework? How many enemies had he made for her? The pretty widow Sarie Tromp, and the cousin of the cousin of the Doublets, whose name now escapes me.

"He even wears the same fashions he wore in '72. Forty-one and he dresses like a young man," Corvina Vallensis complained to her sister-in-law visiting from 'sGravenhage as they waited for me to draw forth another length of brocade for their inspection.

"It is not unusual to see him for weeks on end walking the streets without his periwig."

"Surely, it is not his duties that distract him."

"Nor his studies."

"Perhaps now with Heinsius at 'sGravenhage—" When in the same town, Heer Vallensis and Heer Heinsius were almost inseparable.

As I tied the women's packages of velvets and silks, I listened to the laughter floating down from my father's study.

"And you, Mejuffrouw van Leeuwenhoek," Corvina Vallensis asked me as she gestured to her maid to pick up the package, "have you had any more great visitors since last I came here? None greater, surely, than our Princess of Orange before she went to England?" Both women turned and peered down the hall toward the stairs. Corvina Vallensis, widowed by the age of twenty-three, had wealth enough to aspire to greater intimacy with the court. Her grandfather had served as physician to the Princes Maurice and William II, so there was also precedent.

"Unfortunately, we were unable to entertain the Princess. My father, to his great regret, was across the Maas that day."

"Entertain?" Corvina Vallensis said. "Surely the good woman would have come for instruction, not amusement." The women exchanged glances. "That wicked Duchess of Boileau left your house quite white—or so I heard. We hear that there are more than a few discoveries made here not fit for our ears."

"Your goods, Mevrouw."

The women smiled mischievously.

"Good day to you," said Heer Vallensis' sister-in-law, Maria Bleyswick. "I hope your own trade flourishes."

How could it fail? In those days we all succumbed to our dreams of advancement as readily as our devout Stadtholder William III and his devoted English wife, now proudly bearing the crowns of England.

WE MAKE OUR OWN FORTUNES

Prince William's aspirations enriched us all, soldier and arms-maker, money-lender, saddler, and baker. My own father's fame increased my trade as well. However, it was to neither the Prince nor my father that I owed the patronage of our Grand Pensionary, Heer Heinsius. When, in the spring, Heer Heinsius came to my shop to order new damask for his bed curtains, he came at the suggestion of his good friend Heer Vallensis.

"I have no more," I told him. "But you could order it yourself from Haarlem."

"Haarlem," he said with a smile. "We have King Louis to thank for this."

I kept my peace. It seemed unjust to benefit from the Sun King's savagery. But it was true, we Dutch no longer requested velvets from Genoa, tapestry from Aubusson. In their exile, the Huguenots had brought to us, along with their great sorrow, their knowledge of the makings of silk, leather, and paper, a treasure even greater than the goods they left behind. Our nation was the richer for it, which we well needed, for all the wealth of the country is still required to oppose the insatiable hungers of that man in Versailles.

But the Grand Pensionary had not come to talk to me about the French King's wickedness, or the revocation of the Edict of Nantes, Waldeck's next campaign in Flanders—or even damask.

"I saw the glass you gave Heer Vallensis." The tall man stood quietly, his knuckles resting so gently on the edge of the carpet covering the table that they did not even cause the threads to bend.

"The glass I gave Heer Vallensis is merely a curiosity. It is one my father gave me years ago."

"So Heer Vallensis explained. Made from a single grain of sand, I believe? At first I thought your father had so honored Heer Vallensis. I was, I admit, quite jealous of his favor. Your father, as so many men have learned to their cost, does not care to sell his glasses. Even to the Elector of Hesse."

I had given Heer Vallensis the glass in secret. I thought he had understood that in doing so I was challenging my father.

"Grietje," I called, suddenly frightened. "Grietje, come here and assist me." As I heard the child clattering down the hall, I began to breathe easier. I went on, "The glass I gave him was an early one given me years ago because my father had little use for it. I gave it as but a small return for the favor of recommending this child to me."

Grietje gripped my skirt like a small child. This austere man frightened her as much as he had me. I placed my hand on her thin shoulder. "Already she is able to assist me. She writes an elegant hand."

"How do you do?" the Grand Pensionary said to the child. "Heer Vallensis has told me much in your favor."

"Heer Vallensis?" Grietje stepped forward. "How come you to be acquainted with him?"

"Be still, child," I cautioned her.

Heer Heinsius drew himself up, startled by the child's boldness, which was, as it has continued to be, both my trial and my delight. Heer Vallensis, obviously, had not demonstrated as much confidence in his friend upon the matter of the orphan's character as he had in the matter of my father's glass. Heer Heinsius, as always the diplomat, was tactful.

"The magistrate and I have been acquainted since we were children. It was I first escorted him to Latin School."

"And I have followed you ever since," Heer Vallensis said coming up behind us. He startled us, having entered the shop so silently from the street. Grietje waved at him.

"You have made the acquaintance, I see, of the orphan. Isn't she a handsome child?" he asked his friend.

"And able," I added. "Remarkably so."

"You have no idea of her parentage?" Heinsius asked.

"Her foster parents, yes. Her foster mother was sister to my servant Peter," Heer Vallensis said. "She and her husband both died in last spring's fever. But she claims the child was left wailing under their window just hours after birth."

"And she wasn't sent then to the weeshuis?"

"My foster mother had just buried her last child, her sixth. She longed for a living one," Grietje answered pertly. "I was so vigorous, you see, she knew I would survive."

"Greedy," I corrected her when at last the gentlemen had excused themselves to go to my father's study. "Greedy for notice that does not belong rightfully to a girl, especially a servant girl."

"And greedy for sugar," scolded Maartje later in the day. "*Five* sugar sticks she received from the Grand Pensionary. Who would believe such indulgence from such a sober gentleman."

"How fares the child?" Heer Vallensis asked me when next he encountered me.

"She thrives," I said, shaking my head with wonder. "No help to our Grand Pensionary."

"He has a weakness—"

"Which she shares—"

We smiled at each other and fell silent. Grietje herself was our great weakness.

She was also, this frail beautiful girl of thirteen, the key to our freedom. The child, who had come to me six months earlier, accompanied me everywhere. She slept in my chamber until she was fourteen. With her in attendance, I could have conversed with the King of England himself without comment. All eyes turned naturally to her.

Everyone in the house took a hand in the making of Grietje. I taught her to keep accounts, to inspect bolts of serge for weak threads, to preserve my cloth from butterflies and worms. Cornelia supervised her sewing; Maartje insisted she scour, peel potatoes and apples, fetch water from the well. Brought by me twice a week to his house on the Oude Delft, Heer Vallensis challenged her penmanship and listened patiently to her stumbling recitations. Only my father left her in peace. As usual, he was absorbed by his latest discovery.

👑 👑 👑

There's no fortune to be found in all this labor! my father exclaimed more than once.

It was his refrain, indeed, every spring and summer since he had bought his second garden and planted his orchards of apples, peaches, cherries, his bushes of currants and gooseberries, his vines of grapes. Even if caterpillars did not tent the trees, black flies might hover and lay their small eggs on the blossoms, ants might seize the ripened fruit. Nothing was safe. Nature had provided each animal with its own private hunger. Calandars found the corn. Mites the cheese, the smoked meat.

My father could just as well have spoken of his own art. There was no fortune to be made there either, surely there was no fortune that could match his fame. It took my father twenty years to grasp what was understood immediately by predikants, burgomasters, even his wife Cornelia. Fame, like a shadow, can't be bought or sold. It can't be willed to your children.

It was a source of shame to my father that all the renown he had won through his own labors would not change my situation. He could give me less than my Aunt Maria De Mey had already bequeathed me nearly fifteen years before. Once he did recognize this, he busied himself feverishly with making more glasses, believing that after his death I might sell them at significant profit. He spoke with Heer Heinsius privately about the meaning of the Royal Society's silence. He arranged with Kroonevelt to publish more of his observations here in Delft. He no longer, even in the privacy of my chamber, referred to Heer Vallensis as anything but a benefactor. Like the magistrate himself, my father also concerned himself with the increase in my trade. He encouraged everyone to visit my shop. He had agreed without hesitation when I mentioned bringing home the child Grietje to assist me.

It was only then, when my father had begun to treat me like a son with his fortune yet to make that, to my own astonishment, I received my last marriage proposal. It was presented to me by Heer Vallensis himself on the first day of June as we walked along the Oude Delft. We had, I believed, met by happenstance. I had just delivered a package to the barge to Rotterdam. Heer Vallensis had been visiting Heer Bleyswijck in the East India House. I listened silently as he muttered his thought.

At first I could not take him seriously. Wasn't it I alone who had understood the past two years what he had sought in me? An ear as carefully attuned, a manner as taciturn as his friend Heer Heinsius. But surely he'd never made such a proposal to the Grand Pensionary!

"Even if it were a wife you're wanting—which I doubt—I would not make you a fit one." I spoke so quickly I could feel the foam gather on my lip. "I may be untutored, but I am no fool. If my father's observations have brought him as much censure as praise, this alliance can bring all of us nothing but blame."

"I will settle my wealth on you, such as it is." He said this with hesitation because in comparison to his older brother and his widowed sister, his own means were modest. But the differences between us could not be reconciled by wealth, certainly not his.

"What recompense is that for appearing more foolish than any jester in a travelling show? I do not aspire to be an object of mirth or of condescension." In my mind's eye I could see the looks of dismissal in the faces of his mother and sister. I could not live with these from morn to night.

"There is no one who has met you who does not admit your worth. Even Heinsius—"

"Who has observed me only under my father's protection. Observed me in my own sphere. I can't imagine leaving. The Golden Head fits me, or so it seems, more closely than my clothes. I can't—"

"Please consider it closely, Maria," he said softly. "I will not ask again."

When I returned home, I climbed quickly to my own chamber. I shooed Grietje out to play on the street, then closed and locked the door. Shivering, I slipped into my bed. I drew the curtains. On this June day, closed tight within that box of wood and cloth, the heat was stifling, but I was content to remain there forever. I heard Heer Vallensis' words ring in my head. I saw Cornelia's small mouth gaping in astonishment, my father's gleeful smile. I tossed my head wildly trying to free myself from the devil's grasp.

It was too much. I could not think upon it. I could not blot it out. The children playing by the canal, the carts rattling across the cobblestones, the fishmonger's cries, nothing was louder than the battering of my own heart. There was nothing softer than the voice of reason. Listening intently as I could, I could not make it out.

Grietje's screams brought me to my senses. I would have recognized them anywhere. I hurried down the stairs. As I descended I glimpsed my wayward ward through the open door. Nothing could approach the brightness of her hair, which now fell tousled to her shoulders. She and the boy she tangled with were ringed by children. Maartje stood on the stoop waving a broom; Cornelia, behind her, stood wringing her hands. The children paid them no attention. When Grietje threw herself again upon the ragged boy, I brushed Cornelia aside and hurried out into the street.

Maartje was batting at the children's hands and shoulders with the broom, but they shrugged off the rasping straw as if it were only wind. Nothing could draw their attention from Grietje's struggles.

I pushed my way between them to the center of the ring. With one hand, I grasped Grietje by the hair, with the other I gripped her shoulder. Fiercely, I tugged her to me. Equally fiercely she tugged her opponent to her chest; she drew him to his knees. His hair veiled his eyes; blood masked his chin. In desperation, I kicked and shoved at the wailing boy myself, trying to loosen Grietje's hold. Horrified I felt my fingers touch velvet, silk. Angrily, I turned back to Grietje. I cuffed her neck, slapped her hands. When at last I had mastered her, I clapped my hand over her mouth and drew her into the Golden Head.

"Hie!" Maartje screamed at the children. She waved the broom.

"She gnawed it," the boy moaned. "Like a leg of mutton."

"Home with you. Home with all of you!" screamed Maartje waving her broom.

"How *dare* you?" I screamed at Grietje. "Shameful. My own serving girl, a public spectacle."

"I have a right," Grietje screamed back. "I have a right to defend myself. I will not let anyone speak so of me. 'Whore's daughter' he called me. 'Devil's bride.'"

Her lips were blue with rage, her clenched hands white. Fine red lines raked her cheek. Her lip had swelled open like a rose.

I could not restrain myself. I began to laugh. Reaching for the back of the chair, I let myself down, weak.

"My poor child," I said, opening my arms. "My poor child. *Why?*"

"I'll not be talked to so," she said, still sobbing.

"How came he to seek you out?"

"We were fishing in the canal. Jan, Susannah and I, and he wished to fish as well. We gave him a string and a pin. He had no patience. He dipped it twice in the water, then threw it aside. He wanted to take Jan's fish, but we would not permit it—even for a guilder. 'Go to the Fish Market,' we told him. That's when he insisted I fetch him cider. 'I am no one's servant,' I told him."

"But my child," I protested, "you are."

"Apprentice. You said—"

"If you prove yourself worthy."

"It is obedience earns us honor in this world," Cornelia added gravely. The child's behavior shocked her completely. It also frightened my stepmother I realized as I saw her retreat quickly to the stairs when we heard the great commotion approaching over the bridge from the square.

"Wait for me in my chamber," I told Grietje, sending her up the stairs with a slap.

Outside I faced a crowd wild as the grauw, save it was made of brushed dogs, gentlemen in livery, a small man in an immense peruke who led Grietje's ragged and bleeding opponent by the hand. He was flanked on either side by our burgomasters Bleyswijck and Boogaert.

I clasped my hands over my apron, nodded my head.

"Mejuffrouw van Leeuwenhoek," Heer Bleyswijck said. "This is the Portuguese Ambassador and his godson. The boy has recounted a story I find difficult to believe. Your servant, he says, attacked him without provocation."

"I would not say that. From the girl's account."

"Girl?" asked Bleyswijck, blinking rapidly. "*Fille*," he repeated to the Portuguese Ambassador.

"No girl, surely, could do this," the Ambassador said, gagging on our Nether-Dutch. He pried the boy's lips apart and pointed to the large space in his upper jaw. He turned the boy's head to show the stained linen bandage over his torn ear.

"What's this? What's this? What do I hear of a savage attack on the Ambassador's son?"

"Godson," I said, turning aside to allow Heer Vallensis to join his acquaintances. But he stayed beside me, facing the red-faced Ambassador who kept gasping like a fish.

"You were responsible, I understand, for rescuing the poor boy, Mejuffrouw van Leeuwenhoek. That showed commendable courage."

"It was Mejuffrouw van Leeuwenhoek's servant, it appears, was responsible," Heer Bleyswijck said.

"Maartje?" Heer Vallensis' lip twisted in amazement.

"No," I said, meeting his eyes at last. "Grietje, our young orphan girl."

"Grietje," whispered Heer Vallensis, turning white then red. "I can't believe it."

"Indeed it is difficult to credit a girl with such viciousness," said Heer Boogaert.

"You must be mistaken," Heer Vallensis said boldly, "I recommended the child to Mejuffrouw van Leeuwenhoek myself. She is the niece of my servant Peter."

"Charges must be brought," said Heer Bleyswijck.

"I'll not hear of it—yet. There must be some explanation."

"But there is no excuse. No excuse at all," my father said loudly from the middle of the bridge. "I did not intend to keep my honorable guests waiting. Maria, escort them in."

The Portuguese Ambassador looked over in amazement at my father rocking happily on the top of the shady bridge.

"This town is filled with madmen. She-devils."

"That is the famous Antoni van Leeuwenhoek," corrected Heer Bleyswijck. "He is one of our city's most honored citizens. A member of the Royal Society of London, he has discovered through his glasses more remarkable sights than you could ever imagine. It is a great honor to be admitted."

"Let him show you," urged Heer Boogaert. "He has demonstrated his discoveries to the King of England, the Ambassadors of France, Spain and Sweden, the Landgrave of Hesse, the Elector of Brandenburg."

"And his little serving maid, has she served all their entourages so savagely?"

The Ambassador let go his grip on his godson's shoulder. He looked at the boy with an expression that mingled disgust with love.

"Come, come," my father said impatiently from the door. "The blood in the eel's tail thickens already."

"Do you have a taste for armor?" Heer Vallensis asked the Ambassador's godson as the men began to crowd through the door into the Golden Head. "I will be pleased to exhibit my collection to you before you leave this evening for 'sGravenhage."

"Are you a soldier?" the boy asked, looking dubiously at Heer Vallensis' soft hands.

"No," he said sadly. "But I am a student of history. My father, you see, would not give me permission when I was a young man to join our Prince's army. The only battles I've ever waged have been inside my head."

"My father is dead," the Ambassador's godson said complacently. "It is only my godfather's wishes I must attend to. Already he has had me painted in a full suit of armor. I hope they'll not declare a peace before I'm old enough to fight in Flanders."

He should not have feared. The last twenty years, our peaces have been as savage as our wars—and far less frequent.

Watching my father lead the gentlemen into the Golden Head, watching Heer Vallensis eagerly bringing up the rear, I did not think of wars, I even forgot the child sobbing furiously in my chamber. I entered behind them all beaming, convinced everything was possible.

When, leaving, Heer Vallensis touched his hand to his hat and bowed briefly. Without hesitation, amid that public swarm, I held out my hand to him. Thank goodness my gesture, and his own in grasping it, went unnoticed. It was no peace we signaled with these white fleshly flags. It was a wary truce. The truth of this became clear to me at the St. Odulphus Fair two weeks later.

♛ ♛ ♛

Our kermis, the St. Odulphus Fair, begins the Friday after St. Odulphus Day and ends the Saturday after next. Usually this is the third week in June. For a full week, the town echoes day and night with song and music. Tents are set up on all the streets. Merchants bring their goods out of their shops to take as much advantage of the passers-by as the peddlers. Traveling players set up their stages, draw across their curtains. Acrobats string up their ropes. Quacks take their seats under their bright umbrellas. All the guilds prepare themselves for the opening parade. The archers compete at the Doelen for the honor of choosing the prettiest girl in Delft.

And on the Thursday, all the men and women eager to change their solitary state file into the church and take their places. They will post banns the following Sunday, the streets still littered with sodden cakes and waffles, cobbles wet with beer and brandy, the air still charred by the fireworks and torches.

Thus we keep our word, our dearest fortune, untarnished. All bargains struck during kermis must be kept, no matter how deep a man and woman have sunk into their cups.

I explained all this to Grietje that first year she came to us. We stood at the highest window of the house. She leaned her body out, trying to see the acrobats on the far side of the stadthuis. It was here she had spent and would spend all the empty minutes of her day. There was no way we could permit her to leave the Golden Head. If kermis bargains were binding, how much more so those struck at the last stroke of noon out on the Hippolytusbuurt with Burgomasters Boogaert and Bleyswijck as witnesses.

"She shall be punished," Heer Vallensis and I insisted to the Portuguese Ambassador and his smirking blue-faced godson.

"For days on end."

"So long?" The girl had wept.

"Dry your eyes," Cornelia told her curtly. "You have gotten off lightly. If ever Heer van Leeuwenhoek heard of your shameful ways, you would not be allowed to rest here another day."

"I would go then to Heer Vallensis," she muttered so low only I could hear.

Would I have followed insisting on her return? In the six months since Grietje's arrival, I had come to depend on her presence—in my bedroom, sitting beside me in my shop, skipping ahead of me through the market square. It was not, I decided in the end, to Heer Vallensis we should look for succor, but to my Aunt Maria. More exactly, to the house she had bequeathed me. But only if all else failed—my father's inattention, the child's bewitching grace, the roaring torrent of her penitence.

♛ ♛ ♛

Even early in the morning on the days of the kermis, the whole town spins and lurches with life. One might as well be drunk. With the dizzying swirl of color, the confusion of sound, the fleet thoughts, raucous and bright as an entire flock of parrots—it's almost the same state.

Almost. But any bargains I struck that kermis I struck in all sobriety. Not so my father, buying dragonflies from the children, lice from the poor, live eels, our beloved paaling, from the fishermen. Not so Cornelia who put out her crossed palm for the fortune teller, the quack under his blue umbrella. Certainly not our servant Maartje, who was forced to sit, queasy and empty headed on the steps outside the church on Thursday morning unable to recall why she had reeled so far. Poor Maartje!

At the same hour, I was sober as the child Grietje who leaned dangerously from the attic of the Golden Head, but unlike our elderly serving maid, Maartje, I rested upon the ground without confusion. I knew what I had come for. Hands open in my apron, patiently I waited out the minutes in my father's garden.

To understand what I was about that Thursday morning in June, perhaps I should return to the beginning of our fair, to the events that had determined me. First off, my father had as little to do with the path I chose as I have ever had to do with the paths he's followed. No, I must make mention yet again of Vallensis' friend Heinsius, his mother Agatha and his sister Corvina, his cousin Machtilde, of my own cousins Antoni and Geertruida Molijn, my stepmother Cornelia. In the end, of course, I must bring myself to speak of the late Heer Vallensis.

At the opening of the kermis, I like so many other merchants, displayed my wares out on the street itself. I had linens from Haarlem, a few ells of velvet from Utrecht, Leyden wool. I had new silk ribbons woven by the Huguenots. I had five ells of damask. I had bright cottons from India, loved by our Princess as well as the poor. I set my table up close to the canal so I should be in the shade of the trees. It helped but little. Even the wind was dusty, close. I pushed my sleeves to my elbows. Leaving the table a moment under Maartje's unsteady supervision, I returned to the house and my own bed chamber where I rid myself of yet another petticoat. I brought out a pitcher of small beer to refresh us.

"Hie! Hie!" Grietje yelled from the attic. "I will come assist you next year dear Mejuffrouw Maria. I will come right now if you would forgive me."

I did not lift my head.

Maartje leaned dizzily against the trunk of the lime. Afraid she would topple into the canal, I dismissed her with a hearty shove onto the dry cobbles. I took up her conversation with the peddler.

He wanted my India cotton, my ribbons. Not for sale here in Delft, I made him promise. Winking furiously, he agreed. As I was winding the ribbon round a paper, Heer Heinsius, now the most powerful man in our country since King William resides in England, stopped before me. He accompanied the schout's wife and Heer Vallensis' mother, sister and cousin. Hurriedly, I weighed the peddler's florin against one of my own. With a shrug, he handed me another stuiver.

"Mind you keep your word," I warned him. "I will not sell to you again if I find you over by the Oost Poort or down by the Prinsenhof selling off my own goods."

"Trade is brisk, Mejuffrouw van Leeuwenhoek?" our Grand Pensionary asked me with a thin smile. Even for kermis, he was dressed soberly. Not so the women. Brilliant as our hyacinths and tulips, their silks blinded the eye to their dour faces, their foreheads furrowed more deeply than new plowed polders as they pondered the quality, price and origin of the goods I sold.

"This damask, Mejuffrouw, it comes from France?" Heer Vallensis' cousin Machtilde asked with a meaningful glance at the Grand Pensionary.

"I have carried no French goods since our Ambassador Witsen set his signature to the latest treaty in England," I said to her. "I order directly from the refugees in Haarlem. "

"There's little enough of it left," the schout's wife said, tumbling the damask out the length of the table.

"Enough for a bodice or a waistcoat. But perhaps it is not fine enough for you."

"It will do," she said. "How much do you ask for it?"

When I told her, her eyes gleamed, but the edges of her mouth remained anchored fast to her pendulous chin.

"So much?"

"There are peddlers here from all over South Holland. Everywhere in town tradesmen have set out their wares—" I began to fold up the damask, dismissing them all.

"Hie! Hie!" screamed Grietje from the attic window. "I will carry packages for you Mejuffrouw Maria, indeed I will."

"So that is the child Boogaert and Bleyswijck threatened with the spinhuis?" asked Vallensis' cousin Machtilde. She stood with her hands on her hips, squinting up at Grietje's pale face gleaming like the moon from the drying room window.

"The child your cousin recommended to Mejuffrouw van Leeuwenhoek," the Grand Pensionary chided her gently. "The one he himself tutors."

"I will take the damask," he said to me, equally quietly. When I had wrapped it, he presented the cloth to the schout's wife with a deep bow. The Grand Pensionary looked me up and down coolly.

"My servant will settle accounts with you."

Under the clatter of their heels, the music of a passing hurdy-gurdy, I muttered the cost to the servant. He measured the coin out onto the table, and I merely nodded, not bothering to count it aloud. I could trust my tongue as little as my watering eye, which doubled my money as it did my shame at the Grand Pensionary's obvious condescension.

It was Cornelia's high familiar voice brought me to myself.

"Grand Pensionary," she screamed up into that honorable man's closed face. "You will not find my husband home today. No, no, no." She leaned over, giggling, waggling her cheeks like a dog waking itself from its midday slumbers. "He's down in the carnival tents inspecting sights more terrible than any he keeps stored in his own study." My cousins Antoni and Geertruida both moaned with stifled laughter. "There's a cock with two you-know-whats and a hedgehog with one that's slit in half like a snake's tongue."

The Grand Pensionary, grasping the two burgomasters' wives, backed away from my reeling relatives. Looking behind me at the canal, wishing us all small and harmless as the eels that writhed between the reeds, I saw Heer Vallensis pause amid the peddlers on the bridge. He saw me too and immediately touched his hand to his broad hat.

It was then, I believe, I made my decision.

"Maria!" howled Cornelia, stumbling merrily toward me, arm and arm with an equally drunk Antoni Molijn.

"Heer Vallensis?" Grietje screamed from her window. "Have you come to save me?"

"From *yourself*, child? There's no one on earth powerful enough to do that. Certainly not me," he said shaking his head as he climbed down the bridge to join us.

"I can't even save my friend the Grand Pensionary from the lash of my cousin's tongue," he said more quietly. "Look at him now." He pointed over to the corner of the Nieuwe Straat where his cousin stood, her hands waving like the vanes of a windmill. Again and again she looked over her shoulder at my relatives, me. When she saw her own cousin, she waved wildly to him.

But already Heer Vallensis' attention was engaged—by my stepmother Cornelia who was recounting, amid wild laughter, the fortune-teller's warning.

"She-she-shee says it's not the lion will devour me, but the flea."

Heer Vallensis laughed with them. He ignored my stepmother's hiccups, my cousin Geertruida's loose grin, my cousin Antoni's weaving head.

I loved Heer Vallensis, this should be obvious. I loved him for his blindness. I loved him, equally, for his vision. It was the fearful twitch in Cornelia's eye he noticed, the grasping of her hands as if they would close up the truth again.

"Surely your husband's told you it's all superstition."

At that, emboldened, Cornelia threw her hands up. "My husband sees only what is in front of his nose. Only what fits within his little glasses."

"I don't know. He seems capable as any man in Delft of plumbing the depths of a wine barrel or an oil cask," said my cousin Antoni, blushing with envy.

"Come along with us, Maria," encouraged Geertruida. "Give the old woman a chance to read your hand."

"Not today," I said. "I would lose more than I would gain. My trade is brisk—but before the kermis is over, I assure you, I will know more than I do now about my future."

"Just when do you expect—" began Heer Vallensis.

"I will have sold all my goods, I believe, by Tuesday, Wednesday at the latest."

"Don't be so cold, Maria, "said Geertruida. "Once a year you can throw caution to the winds."

"When?" Heer Vallensis asked as he pretended to contemplate my last length of green serge.

"Thursday."

"The church?" he asked, glancing at me with a startled smile.

"My father's garden."

"Hie! Hie!" screamed Grietje. "I will throw myself at your feet. I can't stand it any more. Forgive me! I cannot wait."

"Excuse me," I said hurriedly. "I must go in and reprimand that wicked child."

"Hie!" sobbed Grietje. "I am a poor orphan, won't anyone pity me?"

Looking up at her, I shook my fist. She ducked her smiling face quickly inside the window.

Without asking, my cousin Geertruida slipped behind the table and assumed my place.

"It is difficult to contemplate serge in such heat, but I have never heard anyone complain of the quality of Maria's goods," she said to Heer Vallensis.

By the time I crossed the cobblestones to the house, Heer Vallensis had joined his friends.

"Dreadful!" I yelled at Grietje in the hot dim attic. "If you will not be still I will chain you in the cellar. I have lost all patience with you."

"And affection?" Grietje asked, truly frightened.

"There is no end to my shame." I buried my head in my hands. I wept wildly.

"So it seems," the child said, putting her arm gently around my shoulders. "So it seems."

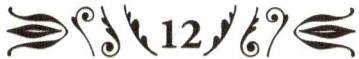

WHAT I CHOSE AND WHAT CHOSE ME

I did not submit to Heer Vallensis' will that third Thursday in June in the secrecy of my father's garden. It was he submitted to mine.

I did this to save us both. Surely you can understand. My father's fame would never change my standing with the burgomasters or their wives, mothers, cousins. To attempt to do so would only bring me shame. I was no more inclined than my father to endure blame or refutation. Indeed, I did not wish to change my condition. It suited better than damask and lace. As a spinster, as a draper by trade, and as my father Antoni's daughter and only child, I had a freedom greater than I would in marriage. I had only to think of the unconquerable melancholy that filled my Aunt de Mey when she married Peter the saddler to be assured in my decision. "There is nothing, not even my body, that belongs to me anymore," she told me.

But like my father, neither did I intend to blunt my own appetite for discovery. I wished to make my own observations on this vexing question of generation the real truth of which is hidden to all of us, men as well as women. I knew that to do so would assure that I could never again in good conscience consider a proposal of marriage. I liked that certainty. It was a cost I was most willing to pay.

Heer Vallensis was not a man of licentious habits. In our country, even young men are not encouraged in such vice. The French and the English call us cold, but they are confused. It is true our private honor is our source of deepest pleasure—we defend it, hotly! Indeed, I met with Heer Vallensis in such a secret fashion to preserve, I believed then and I believe now, my own honor. It was not the same for him. We shared all—and we shared nothing.

Until his death, Heer Vallensis always felt he had committed a great injustice to me that summer, not once but many times. An even greater injustice to God. Each man has a right to his own opinion. Each woman.

Especially concerning truths heretofore invisible. Heer Vallensis was never able to convince me of the sin in what we discovered together that summer. Nor could I convince him otherwise. Even on his deathbed, seeing his pain, I could not bring myself to agree with him. Even though I stood silent, weeping, by his bed, he knew I had not submitted to his judgment. I believe my independence of mind was both his anguish and his salvation. Nothing has ever convinced me we weren't those three months as bent on our Creator's business as we had been on all the days before—and have been on all the days that have followed.

After our first meeting during the kermis, there in the hot fragrant privacy of the summerhouse in my father's orchard, I met Heer Vallensis ten times over the summer, in deepest secrecy, both within and without our city. I cannot recall these meetings easily. In truth, I cannot recall them at all. When I try, my eyes burn as if I regarded a mirror flaming with the sun's own fire.

Awkward as I at first, Heer Vallensis took even greater pleasure in our growing mastery of the arts of love. "In your arms, I feel braver than any King leading a charge in Flanders."

"Or Ireland?" I laughed. At that moment, I could not conceive of what we were engaged in as war. I could not comprehend the idea at all. I comprehended only his fiery joy, I swallowed his soft cry of triumph.

It was not until late September, when I met Heer Vallensis on the beach at Sheviningen that I understood. Love is not war. But a woman, armed with nothing but her own opinion, can wound a man, wound him so dangerously that if the choice were his, he would not choose to live.

When I told Heer Vallensis that we must put an end to our uncommon intimacy, he said nothing at first. I was loathe to lose what had come into existence between us, but he had grown so fond, so eager for my company, he no longer feared discovery. Indeed, I believe he yearned for it so that he could make things right in the eyes of the world. He did not expect my words.

He put his hand to his chest, groping blindly for what had caused him such pain. But it was nothing he could put his hand to. It was nothing he could remove. It shouldn't have been, I still believe this, a wound at all. It should have been the brief pain of a torn maidenhead, the pain of waking suddenly into bright sunlight, the pain of the light behind my father's glasses, the pain of knowledge. I was protecting him as much as myself.

But Heer Vallensis shaded his eyes, he looked out at the sea.

"I would, even yet, take you for my wife."

"It wouldn't do. It never would. You haven't understood."

"That I have dishonored you? Can't you see, Maria? I must make amends."

I shook my head. Reached out and touched his hand. "I feel no penitence. Only gratitude. I wished for this intimacy. I wanted to know in myself what binds a man and a woman. I believed our intimacy would free us both. I know it has freed me. I know now exactly what I am choosing. The loss in it. The gain."

"What freedom? What gain?" he asked. "There is no going back. You gave me your virtue, I gave you my honor. Aren't we chained to each other now?"

"I would not name it so," I said, smiling in spite of myself. "Indeed, I have saved you from ties you would soon find onerous. You don't have to meet daily with the disdain of your friend Heinsius, the disappointment of your mother, the anger of your sister, the disgust of your cousin Machtilde. You have nothing to fear from me. This delicious secret will go with me to the grave."

"I never thought I could destroy so much. My standing in the town. The world to come—"

"Surely, you can't believe—"

But he never heard me. *Cornelis. My poor Cornelis.* He had turned by then and struggled with his head bent, his hair streaked across his wet face, against the endless wind. Slowly he made his way across the beach toward the long shady avenue to 'sGravenhage. At last I too turned—in the opposite direction. I struggled to the top of a dune and, shading my eyes with my hand, searched for Grietje playing along the water's edge.

I screamed for her as she leaped wildly through the foam, but she heard nothing but the crash of the waves. In the end, I had to make my way to the water.

Grietje ran eagerly to me.

"Have you sand in your eyes, Mejuffrouw? They are watering so."

Surprised, I reached down and gathered a handful of damp sand. I rubbed the sand between my hands, buying time.

"Did you know a man once thought he had discovered a way to turn all this into gold?" I spoke rapidly, drawing a breath even amidst a word. "Many representatives from the States General, even our own burgomaster

Heer Bleyswijck, all came down to observe him make the transmutation."

"Did he succeed?" Grietje asked with a glint in her eye.

"Not at all. To the burgomasters of Utrecht's great disappointment. They had made such plans."

"Silly men. We should no longer believe in the transmutation of the elements. Your father says—"

"They couldn't help themselves. They were desperate to believe. They had contracted enormous debts during the French invasion."

At last the lump of sand I had been chafing within my hands cut through the calluses and drew blood. I sighed with relief.

"They couldn't help themselves. They dreamed their salvation would take the same shape as their ruin. Gold!" I tipped my hand and let the damp sand, ruddied by my heart's blood, fall to the earth. Moving away from the sea, I leaned down and picked up another handful.

"Did you know, child, one of these grains is enough to make one of my father's marvelous glasses. One grain ground round could unlock some of the greatest mysteries. It could reveal," I swallowed deeply, "purposes more mysterious than any we can dream."

"While an ell of it left just as it is will blind us as well as any looking glass."

"Yes," I said. I put my hand on her shoulder to steady myself. I was dizzied by the light flaring from both the water and the sand, by the wind, by the smell of a bird washed dead and rotting high above the tide line. But I would not look away.

I was helpless as my dear love. I could not choose differently. But even then I could not believe it was any man or woman had wounded me. Even then I did not doubt my own recovery.

I did not doubt my own recovery.

In this I was more innocent than little Grietje. It was she who caught my arm again and again through the autumn when, dizzied, I lost my balance, paused, weak as an old woman, in the middle of my shop.

"Sit," she would hiss at me. "Sit down, Mejuffrouw Maria." Her face would thin with fear. Grietje, like my father, hates the very thought of sickness. That is why she lets it vanquish her so quickly."

"Shall I fetch the surgeon to come bleed you?"

"No," I said, trying to draw my thoughts together. My head still whirled, but I could speak clearly. "I will have you transfer the day's accounts to the journal for me."

"The journal, Mejuffrouw?" Grietje did not look pleased at the new honor. So far I had only allowed her to address parcels. "What if I make a mistake?"

"The heavens will crash, the earth will ring—" But I fell silent, unable to laugh, or to piece another word from the din inside my head.

It was not that I felt I had made a mistake in beginning, or concluding, my intimacy with Heer Vallensis. It was simply that until the fall I did not know what it was I had begun, what it was I had put an end to. It took time— and something more than time—to give meaning to what I had seen with my hands, felt with my tongue.

Death, I think I've said this, gives shape and meaning to man's life. A woman's too. Separation does the same, but differently. It was not longing I felt for Heer Vallensis that autumn. I knew all I would have had to do was look out the window at the hour he regularly made his way past our house to the stadthuis.

All I would have had to do was wave—and it would be as if I peered through my father's glasses in the middle of the night. It would be worse than blindness. Worse, certainly, than the dazzling confusion I had felt seeing our bodies move under our shifts and shirts, under our warm wet glittering hands.

I kept away from the window, for it was only in my dim shop, inspecting the new cloths from Haarlem and Leyden, from Spitalfields and Norwich, that I could see clearly. I could not watch his dear figure on the bridge without wanting to reach out again. I could not hear his voice behind me on the market square without shivering. But when I heard him speaking inside my mind in the privacy of my shop, I could laugh at his wit, I could weep for his pain, I could, in short, understand the man. And I could do so without giving in—giving way.

At that time, neither Heer Vallensis nor I had reason to fear exposure or public censure. I would not betray him and he would not betray me— and we both believed my father's assertions about the exclusive role of the male animalcule in generation. Heer Vallensis told me that Dr. de Graaf had expressed equal certainty about the role of the female egg, believing that it carried all the essential matter of our human history awaiting only a vital spirit found perhaps in the semen of men. A spirit that could well reside inside the animalcules my father discovered after the good doctor's death. Whichever theory were true, Mr. Vallensis revealed to me, he himself could not participate in the mystery of generation. His testes had not descended. This was a secret he had not shared with anyone. Our Creator had willed that in his testicles any animalcules, should there be any, would lie as motionless within their jelly as his father and grandfather lay motionless in the earth. He was, he believed, little more than a eunuch. He had, he said blushing, confirmed this through my father's glass.

Even should De Graaf's theory of the power of the female egg be true, he could not contribute that essential energy, that vital spirit, without which the egg lies inanimate as stone. For he also did not experience toward women the desire that he believed woke that animating spirit. He had, he confided, experienced his deepest pleasure in human company in his friendships with men like himself, bachelors devoted to the workings of our tumultuous world and to the life of the mind, like the men he studied with in Leyden, like his dear friend Heinsius. That is, he amended, until he discovered the pleasure of my company. I did not listen the way the other women of his acquaintance did—for proof of affections he was incapable of feeling. I listened for the line of his thought. I did not appear to hunger for motherhood.

His revelations did not cause me concern. Indeed, I believe he knew that his sterility would speak in his favor when he proposed marriage to me. Since my father had discovered the truth of generation, it had been obvious to me that, if life passes exclusively from father to son, my marriage could further his ambitions as little as the marriages of my cousins Phillip and Jan Leeuwen, or my cousin Antoni Molijn. It was not the fruit of my womb would enrich my father but the silk that washed over my arms, the florins that crossed my palm—and my fidelity to the truth of his observations. I had said as much to Heer Vallensis.

But it was for other reasons I made my own proposition. I felt this unaccustomed desire we felt toward each other had a purpose to it—one that brought us closer to Our Creator. I wanted to explore the full range of pleasure my body took in his proximity. I wanted to know this in a way that leapt beyond reason but remained allied with it. It was as if I was looking at all my life now through a different kind of lens. Suddenly I could understand what moved the people around me, those who had so often appeared to me as arbitrary in their actions as the pellucid animals in our water, tirelessly collapsing and expanding, but still so haplessly affixed.

It pains me now to repeat my old imaginings. Cornelis Dirckszn. and I were so sure that autumn, each of us, of our separate theses. More secure, surely, than my father still puzzling the question of the procreation of the eel, still asking Heer Christiaan Huygens why the Queen and the Royal Society would not acknowledge his packets.

Heer Vallensis ultimately believed our fornication was not just a fruitless passion but a sin so terrible it blotted out not only his own honor but that of his father and mine, that of the entire town—while I was as convinced that we had by our act preserved everything but my virginity. Certainly we had preserved my pride—and my independence of mind.

I am sure it must fatigue you to hear these thoughts as much as it does me to recall them. We were wrong, both of us.

It was winter before the truth pounced, shook me by the throat, tore me, greedily, apart. Two years later, the same truth sealed, gently as my own fingertips, Heer Vallensis' sightless eyes. But I get ahead of myself.

♛ ♛ ♛

In late December I was taken desperately ill. My cousin Antoni Molijn was called to bleed me. Dr. 'sGravesende, a day later, prescribed a relentless course of purges. But nothing could relieve the dreadful griping in my gut.

"Spleen," diagnosed Dr. D'Aquet.

"Abscessed liver," suggested Dieren the surgeon.

"Stone?" asked Antoni Molijn.

"Virgin's sickness?"

"Surfeit," my father said sternly as he came into my chamber carrying up a pot of tea and a single cup. "This autumn you have grown fatter than a maggot in an anthill. But I will not spend all my time fetching and carrying like the ant fathers."

Groaning, I turned my head into the pillow.

"And you too, Wife. You should not sit here waiting on her."

"Go out, Antoni," Cornelia said, closing her Bible with a slap. "There is nothing more to be done. All the doctors agree. There is no need to crowd her chamber."

"With your poor heart," he said, "I will not have you fetch and carry for her. A woman of thirty-five should know better than to gorge herself."

"Grietje," I gasped.

"Yes, yes," Cornelia said, gesturing the girl to leave her seat by the window and approach my bed. "The child will run errands for me, Husband. Surely I can pray with as little exertion here as in my own chamber. I believe it comforts Maria to have me here."

I felt the sweat break out on my back, the pain stabbing again deep into my belly.

"No," I screamed. "No more."

I heard my father slam the door. This was worse, I was sure, than any wound endured in battle. I was curled over like a babe in the womb. I shrieked like a hog at slaughter. Then I felt myself tumble into a dark well, softer and more silent than velvet.

The fever, they told me later, left my gut and travelled to my head. I slept a sleep deep as the dead's for a day and a night. I woke at dawn to Grietje's soft sobbing. But this time the fever erased no memories, disrupted no thoughts. I still recognized the grieving child although I could not make out her face in the dim light.

"You are suffering too?" I asked her. "When did it begin?"

"Oh my dear Mejuffrouw Maria," she sobbed. "You live. I could not feel your breath upon my hand. I never left your side. Not for a moment. Your father brought Predikant Grebius but he said it was no use. You could not see him, you could not speak."

"Where is my father now? Where is Cornelia?"

Grietje reached out and took my hand. A shiver ran down my entire arm. My teeth ached with the rattle in my head.

"Have they given me up so easily?"

"Don't say so, Mejuffrouw. You're not alone in your illness. Mevrouw Swalmius has contracted the same fever. Your father attends her now. Maartje too I fear begins to sicken."

I listened to the child carefully. I heard her words and understood them as well as I did the clatter of her teeth. I shifted away from her. I pushed against the coverlet.

"Come within, child. You're colder than the coals in the grate."

When she hesitated, I spoke again. "Touch my forehead. I am as cold as you. The fever has burned right through me."

So Grietje came and laid her head beside mine on the pillow. I could hear her breath, soon I could see it clouding the air above us, thick and white as my own. But her presence did not warm me. Nor her devotion. My body was numb as my heart.

"No one believed you would recover. Save me. I never left you."

"I wonder how Cornelia fares. I would not have believed anyone could endure such suffering."

"It appears milder with her. Now that Maartje is weakening, your father attends his own wife."

Nothing can convince me illness like this is something one can share. Nothing ever has. Even now, I cannot bear to remember the first month of the year '91. It is as if a stone has been rolled before it, sealing it away like a tomb. This I do know: The course of Cornelia and Maartje's fevers was much shorter than mine. Within a week they had recovered, while I, even in February, tottered on my feet.

My belly stayed swollen, as swollen as it is today. Neither bleeding or plaster have ever been able to reduce its size. I no longer try, for it dismays me no longer now that I have recovered my strength. In fact, I treasure it as a mother might a growing womb. It assures me that I serve the Creator's purposes as faithfully as any other creature, man or ewe, eagle or ant.

I have only one sorrow, but it is a great one. I was never able to convince Heer Vallensis of the same, neither when I saw him, once, shortly after my recovery, or, a full year later, as he turned in the quiet of his own chamber burned by a fever fiercer by far than my own.

☙ ☙ ☙

In January the King of England, our own Prince William, left his new country, England, in the Queen Mary's quavering hands and sailed through the fierce winter storms to return to us. Reckless as a boy, he jumped into an open boat when ice blocked the ship's way. Seventeen hours later, he arrived at Goeree, his new beard rimed with ice, his luxuriant black hair streaked silver by the frost. By February fifth when he made his triumphal entry into 'sGravenhage, he was shaved, perfumed, periwigged, a monarch of middle years, as wise as he was brave.

'sGravenhage had never looked so well. Every avenue was lined with torches, lined with people more loving and proud than the ones he had left behind more than two years before when he left Holland to fight then rule in England. This was the Prince whose hunger for war had made the Amsterdam burgomasters set hundreds to breaking the ice in their canals, more afraid of their Stadtholder's unruly passion for retribution than they were of the French King's methodical greed. This was the Prince who just the previous spring had been accused by the Amsterdamers of abandoning our little republic. You would never have known it from the smiling faces of the crowd. The whole country was bowing, singing his praises, blinking at his equipage, the numbers of his troops, the equally dazzling splendor of the heads of state who had come to meet our small determined Stadtholder, now also the English King.

All the members of the States-General and the representatives of the States of Holland were there to wave, to cheer, to jostle for the King's notice and his favor. But the King had eyes only for his own purposes. He sought out the Elector of Brandenburg, the Landgrave of Hesse, the Ambassador from the Spanish Netherlands, the Ambassador from Sweden. Everyone noticed, but without censure, the remarkable fixity of the King's purpose. We no longer felt abandoned. We no longer felt our liberty endangered. Our Prince, who crossed the North Sea and returned to us an English King, taught us the true shape of our allegiances. We were all, German Princes, English King, Dutch republicans, part of one vast animal whose only enemy was that ravening beast, the King of France.

I can speak this way now, but then, recovering from my illness, even the rumors, the cries in the street, the very idea of that noisy confusion of splendor and hope dazzled me completely. I did not, of course, travel to 'sGravenhage to see the King's grand entry. Neither did Cornelia. My father went with his nephew Molijn and Dieren the surgeon, but he need not have bothered.

Over the next month he saw most of the notable foreign visitors one by one here in his study in the Golden Head. It was only our own King William who had no interest in this hidden world. The only hidden world he wished to invade was the French King's reason, and that was a door no key would open. It must be forced. But the rest came: the Elector of Brandenburg, the Landgrave of Hesse, often escorted by Heer Vallensis, now our city's pensionary to the States of Holland.

Resting in my chamber, I heard accounts of all this from a breathless Grietje. I discussed it for hours with an equally breathless Cornelia. But it wasn't the honor dizzied my stepmother or turned her fair skin blue after only climbing a half flight of stairs.

"Your father says my heart is slack as my belly skin. It has been stretched too much by fever. But you know, child, I mind it much less than the pain in my back tooth. It feels a worm is gnawing there. I believe everything I swallow goes to feed it, for sure it tugs and twists more forcefully every day."

Cornelia set her hand to her soft, puffy cheek. She winced when Grietje clattered into the room waving her arms.

"Mevrouw, Mejuffrouw, your father suggests you might wish to come and see his magical demonstration."

Cornelia and I looked doubtfully at each other. Cornelia smoothed her apron over her green serge skirt. I tucked my hair securely under my cap.

"Please. He insists. Maartje has taken sick again. The study is filled with men. It sounds like the tower of Babel just before it toppled. Heer van Leeuwenhoek took me by the arm and ordered me to fetch you—both of you. Some ladies from the German court are at the door. He thinks it proper you assist him. 'We'll delay the magic show until you come,' Heer Vallensis said to me, and your father agreed. So hurry! I do want to see it."

"Heer Vallensis?" Cornelia asked with a sly glance at me.

But already I was getting slowly to my feet.

The magic my father demonstrated that day came from a mysterious stone given him by a high-born German gentleman. The stone's power is apparent only in the dark. Grietje and I assisted his demonstration by closing up the shutters to his study.

"I shall be faint," whispered a maid-in-waiting to the Electress.

The worm twitched angrily in Cornelia's tooth and she let out a moan. As I entered the room, she gripped my arm.

Only the fire gleamed in the hearth. Heer Vallensis had extinguished all the candles. My father, in the center of the room, shook a glass flask. His face appeared to us suddenly, green with the glow from the flask.

My father then dipped a quill into the glowing fire. He scratched his name upon a piece of paper. He held it up so everyone could read the glowing script.

"Another letter," laughed Heer Vallensis. "They've hardly had a chance to answer your last. You're too quick for the learned gentlemen, Heer van Leeuwenhoek."

I felt his fingers touch the back of my hand. I shook them off with a gasp. They were hotter than any flame.

With a cough my father went to the shutters and pushed them open. The visitors began to talk among themselves. Heer Vallensis had his back to me now. He was deep in conversation with the German maid-in-waiting.

"Untutored," he said, "but for all that immensely able."

"I am not finished yet," my father said. He raised his sheet of paper and showed its empty face to all of us. With a wink, he carried it over to the fire. Then he paused, glanced around.

"You," he said, gesturing in my direction. But when I stepped forward, he shook his head impatiently. "The child. The child."

Grietje without a glance to either side stepped forward eagerly. My father showed her how he wished her to hold the paper two hand spans from the edge of the fire.

"Aagh!" Grietje screamed when the letters of my father's name began to flame from the blank paper.

"Drop it, child," I cried over the clapping and laughter of my father's audience. "You will set yourself on fire." I started forward, but it was Heer Vallensis who reached her before me and struck the flaming paper from her hand.

With a mortified cry, Grietje fled the room. I turned to Heer Vallensis to apologize. But already, like all the other people in the room, he was occupied with my father's explanation.

"The High German Gentleman who gave this stone to me said it was distilled, by your leave ladies, from old piss. I can't see much purpose in it save idle entertainment." My father spoke quickly, with a haughty air, but the smile on his face betrayed his delight.

"Now," he said, "I will show you something more curious than any waterworks in Amsterdam." He raised his spyglass so everyone could see the eel's tail twitch as my father screwed it tight.

Quietly I made my way to the door. But this time, instead of returning to my chamber, I retreated to my shop. For the first time in months, I drew out my account book. I did not open it. I had nothing to add. I bent my head, dizzied, sick. I felt the weight inside me shift, wallow upright again.

I put my hand to my belly. I understood at last that the weight I carried was a face, a body. I felt his features flaring in the dark. Through flesh, skin, and cloth I felt the flames scorching the inside of my palm. For a moment I believed it was a monstrous face leering blindly through my body. But then, within my scorched palm, I believed I could make out the true impress of its features. He was beautiful, Heer Vallensis' son, small as a talisman, deaf and dumb as bone, stone, ore.

If I was his tomb, he was my secret fortune. My blood washed him, my flesh wrapped him closer than any papist relic. It was my breath, my steady gait secured him from all harm.

♕ ♕ ♕

When King William returned to England in March, King Louis had already taken Mons. King William returned to Flanders in the summer without pomp, soberly pursuing his endless business, war, as we pursued ours. Heer Vallensis came only rarely to Delft. He busied himself in 'sGravenhage with the affairs of the States of Holland. Like his friend the Grand Pensionary, he encouraged passage of yet more taxes to provision the troops and the fleet. But we gave all this little notice, here on our sleepy street in Delft.

I was busy again with my trade. Since Grietje daily demonstrated less aptitude for the occupation, Cornelia busied herself with training the girl to assist her around the house now that our servant Maartje had died in the last wave of fever. Now it was Grietje who answered the door, Grietje who followed her to market, Grietje who carried messages to Geertruida or Magdalena Molijn, Antoni's wife.

It wasn't until Heer Vallensis' death the following summer that I gave up all hope of raising Grietje to any occupation but the one she pursued so ably under Cornelia's direction. By then her limitations disappointed no one but me.

Even on his death bed Heer Vallensis could not stop talking of his imaginings, his aspirations: We were all blameless. No child inherited the weight of his father's sins, his mother's wickedness. We were all blameless at our birth. Thus he and he alone was guilty, he said, of dreadful iniquity. The sin he writhed under was of his own making. But I could save him even yet. He would settle his goods on me. We would marry. We would raise Grietje as our own child.

As he spoke, I looked fearfully at his serving man, Grietje's uncle Peter, but he busied himself preparing another draught. I had come at the request of Heer Vallensis' mother and sister to measure the house for funeral cloth. His servant had begged me when he saw me there to come and see Mr.

Vallensis in his chamber.

"Only you can ease his torment. He calls out to you constantly."

"Your master raves," I said. "You must not repeat to anyone what he says in his delusions." But I went with him anyway.

"I will not play the hypocrite a day longer," Heer Vallensis panted, reaching out and taking my hands as I approached his bed.

I pulled my hand from his with difficulty. "I must leave."

But then Heer Vallensis seemed to waken from his terrible dream. "Maria? Have you come to wish me good-bye? Wish me well."

"With all my heart."

"You must take this," he said, pointing to the package lying beside the bed. "It must not be found here when I die. It is no use to my heirs, no use to me where I am going."

I knew from its weight, its shape, what it was he wished me to take back to the Golden Head.

"You will yet recover," I said.

"I do not wish it. I go to my judgment eagerly."

"Our Father will lift you up," I said. "I am sure of it. He will grant you eternal peace. You are a good man. An honorable one. I know no one, *no one*, who speaks ill of you."

Heer Vallensis shook his head. His fever had burned away all tear, but his face twitched grotesquely with his grief.

"We know nothing, nothing at all of His Purpose."

"Except that it is as beautiful as it is awful."

"Please come with me," he cried out, reaching for my hands, but I pulled them tight around me, escaping as best I could his madness.

I learned of his death that same evening, when they sent his servant Pieter to me for the mourning bombazine and streamers. Poor man, he had hardly enough time to cover the mirrors and drape the house before he too was taken. Had he inclination, he had no time to betray his master.

A week later, Grietje shocked Cornelia with her wild, heartless laughter. We had dressed her in black to honor her benefactor, but I stopped my stepmother's scolding with a wave of my hand, a smile. I, like the child, grieved for no one. I took Heer Vallensis' death as an expression of Our

Maker's pity. Only there, safe in His Father's arms, would Cornelis's face assume the expression on the face of his own son hidden deep inside me here on earth, an awful joy. He could have left me no greater gift. He could have left me no greater burden.

I unwrapped the glass of my father's I had given him and with which he tested his thesis about his own sterility. I tested the glass's strength myself then alone in my room. I should have done so before. For it was nearly useless, little better than the naked eye. Under its surface, water was motionless. Even in pond water or pepper water, no animalcules frisked, writhed, fed, copulated. Under that glass, any man's semen would have seemed inanimate as our tears, whether it truly teemed with animalcules or no. He should have known better, shouldn't he, than to have trusted his future to this one lens alone? After all the different lenses my father had demonstrated to him, each with its own power. After all he himself had felt for me, shouldn't he have felt something quickening in him? Shouldn't he have doubted his own eyes, looked further?

He had, you see, no grasp of the art. His eye pledged blind allegiance to his mind. He saw what he believed. *Nothing.* I did not grieve for Heer Vallensis' death, I trust the designs of Our Creator, but for months I tossed in my bed at night, my skin scorched by a terrible pity for his anguish. You can see traces of it even now, not just in my face but on my hands, the flesh on my arms. Under its heat, the child I will never relinquish was transformed again and again, flesh to flame to ash to glass. An irrefutable answer *and* an irrefutable question. Somehow through the pleasure of our congress life began and life ended in me. Was I its origin?

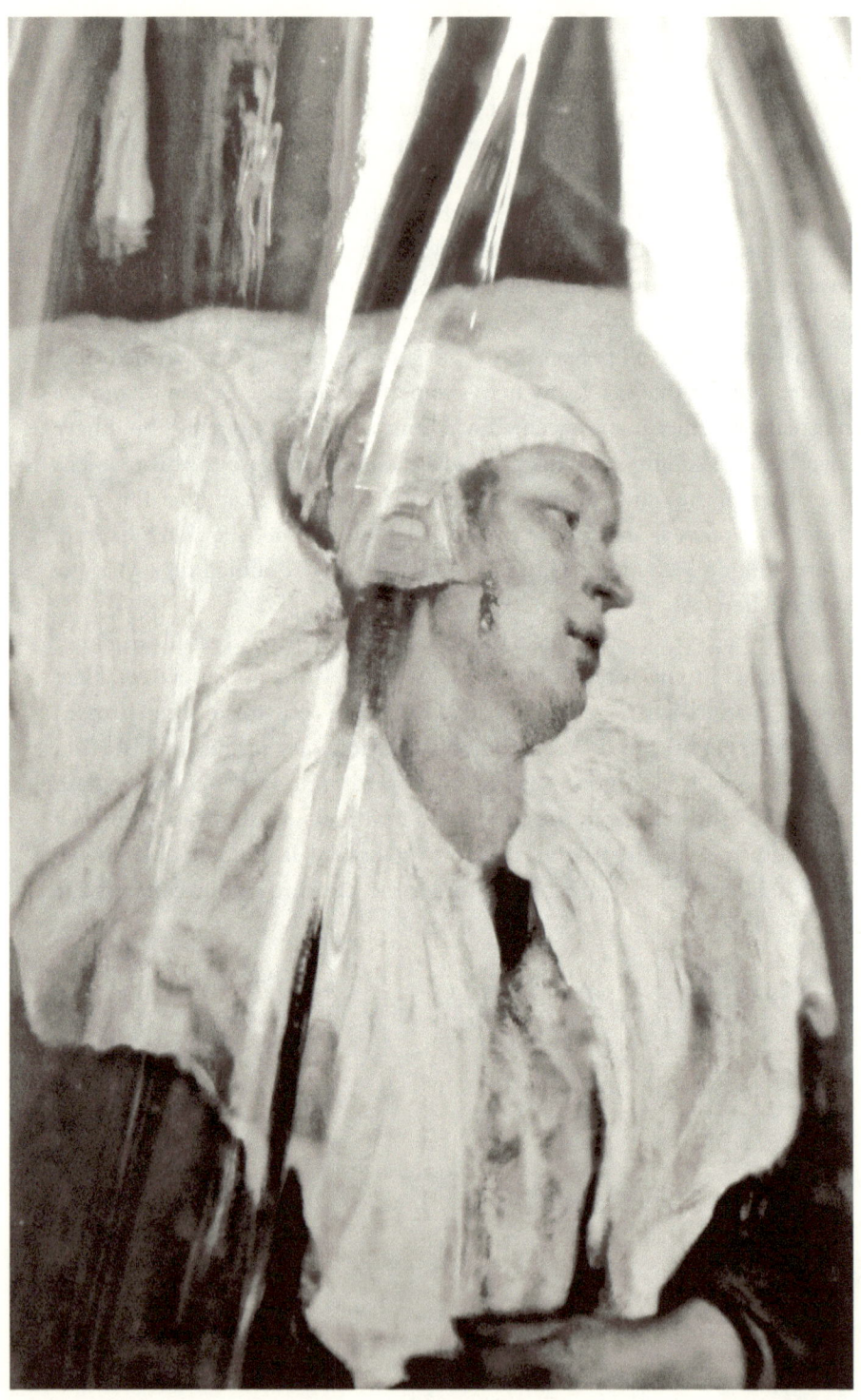

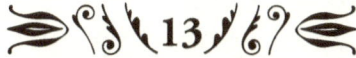

AS LONG AS THE LORD WILLS

"It is a great relief to me to discover at last the secret of the procreation of the eel," my father announced once the talk at the table had quieted. We no longer muttered about the defeat at Steenkerke, nor of the death of so many this entire summer through fever, nor of the earthquake in Middleburg that caused the streets to rise and fall like waves of water.

"You have proved by your own observation that they arise from dew?" teased Magdalena Molijn, my cousin Antoni's wife. Her eyes sank into her face as she laughed, her belly swelled.

"Surely it's none of our business," said Phillip van Leeuwen's wife. "If the Lord intended us to know such things he would have revealed the truth to us."

"Which He has. Which He has," my father said querulously. "If we would just use our eyes instead of our ears—not listen to the old stories but look for ourselves."

"Well, Husband, where do they come from, if not the dew? Do they spawn like bream or cod?"

"It took me more than two years to find the womb," my father said. "I filled every hollow with quicksilver, but I could not be sure. Finally I discovered two openings by its navel. And even more recently, Our Creator revealed this mystery to me. Pressing against the womb of the eel, I expressed from the orifice that I call the womb—"

"Oh, don't tell us, Uncle," cried Geertruida.

"*Living* young," my father exclaimed triumphantly. "They wriggled in the water just like their mother, they resembled her both head and tail."

"But so would a vinegar eel. All eels appear the same," I said.

But my father ignored me. "So many people have said, 'Van Leeuwenhoek believes everything comes through procreation. Let him prove to us, then, the procreation of the eel.'"

"You have done well, Husband." Cornelia helped herself to another piece of bread. Her heart may have weakened, but her stomach was strong as it had always been. She took a bite, swallowed it down with small beer. "That's not all he has discovered this summer," she hiccupped. "He has shown us there is no air in the blood."

"How did you do that, Uncle?" asked Phillip van Leeuwen, my father's godson.

"I have the machine yet in my cabinet. I will demonstrate."

"We're yet at table," protested my cousin Rickje van Leeuwen.

"I think I should get some recognition," my cousin Antoni said. "I sent my servant to uncle several times this summer with blood from my patients."

"So did the surgeon Dieren. When poor Heer Vallensis sickened, Dieren bled him daily and sent the blood over to me in an open pot," my father said.

"What?"

"Foolish of him. It was chilled by the time it arrived. It had been exposed to the open air, but even with that—" My father slapped the table in his excitement and continued, "Even with that I proved there was no air in the blood save the subtle air that is in all matter. I proved—" He paused, looked directly at my cousin Antoni, "that the surgeons and physicians who speak of ferments in the blood, who ascribe illness to a hidden flatulence, a pocket of stale air, are all of them mistaken."

My father glanced around the table. When he reached me, I saw his eyes drift quickly from my cap to my swollen lap and then, blinking, back to his nephew Molijn. "These surgeons and physicians would do better to talk of a constriction in the vein, a blocking of the blood."

"So you say, Uncle," my cousin Molijn spoke impatiently. "But many men would not agree with you. Any more than they agree with you about the purpose of the pipes in trees."

"I have as much right as the King of England to my own opinion," my father roared.

Phillip's young son Jan began to cry. My father looked around, blushing. He opened his arms to the boy, who ran instead to his mother's chair and buried his head in her lap.

"It is my principle to maintain my views until I become better informed," he went on speaking in almost a whisper, "or my own observations make me change my mind. I shall never be ashamed of changing my mind."

"Nor I," Rickje said with a laugh. "I think it is high time you left the table and demonstrated your miraculous instruments to your nephews."

Antoni Molijn, Phillip and Jan Leeuwen all rose to their feet. My father, with a quick toss of his head, rose too. Both Cornelia and Rickje nodded to him, accepting his silent apology.

"Have you read Kircherus?" asked Antoni Molijn as they left the room. "He insists that frogs come from slime, that eels come not from dew but from their own skins."

"Kircherus?"

"Everyone in Rotterdam speaks so highly of my Uncle Antoni, it is unbelievable to me," my cousin Rickje said.

"And here too," Cornelia agreed. "But for years the Royal Society has answered none of his letters. He gave up writing them completely. If it hadn't been for his many visitors, he might have abandoned his labors entirely."

"He corresponds again with the Royal Society, does he not?" Rickje asked. "Certainly Phillip says packets come to him from London almost as often as he sends goods out himself."

"It was the procreation of the eel that hindered him," I explained. "He felt he could not insist on their attention, those high-born learned gentlemen, if he could not unveil this mystery."

"It was the troubled times," Cornelia corrected me. "They hindered him most of all. His true occupations required most of his attention. He had his gauging. He had his garden. He had, like everyone, these taxes to pay. In an age so unsettled, it is amazing he has found any time at all to practice such an art."

I shook my head but said nothing. I cannot help but think it is this very uncertainty that permits my father's pursuits. The order he discovers with his glasses makes him as necessary to millers as to monarchs.

"*I say it of De Graaf. I say it of Swammerdam, and Des Cartes, and Harvey. I will say it of this man Kircherus too.*" My father's voice tumbled through the house like the frothing crest of a flood, "*If he had my glasses he would have written differently. He too would have seen the truth.*"

✤ ✤ ✤

Of course it was not as simple as that. Given glasses, Swammerdam, De Graaf, Kircherus and Harvey would have all made objections to my father's speculations. My father's whole life goes to prove this. If seeing is believing, many of us choose to blink rather than admit the rightness of another man's opinion. But as I have also said, there is something about our times that has made my father more welcome even than our Stadtholder-King William to many men.

In an age when adages are shown to be fables, when the boundaries of every country are unstable as our own seashore, when kings clamber up and down their thrones as often as a sick man mounts his chamber pot, when war plunders the entire world, when fevers consume us by the thousands, man, woman, and child, when our ships ply all the seas, North, Baltic, Mediterranean, Atlantic and Pacific as freely as they do the Zuider Zee, only in this age with its prosperity and power and dreadful confusion can an unlearned man from a small town in South Holland be made a Fellow of the Royal Society because of his steady eye, his patient hand, his stubborn application. What we need, all of us, learned and unlettered, is to trust ourselves—and our Creator. We need to believe it is Our Creator's grand purpose we were serving, even in our grief, our doubt, our desperate confusion, our relentless curiosity. We need the peace of that bright silent world secured behind my father's glasses.

Listen to this panegyric written by my father's learned friend Petrus Rabus, notary and preceptor of the Erasmus school in Rotterdam. All the summer of '93 he came to my father's house, his manner each time more eager and less presuming. He went home yawning with excitement, fear. But hear what he says for himself.

Dear Sir,

Did I not predict that I should be preoccupied with your magnifying glasses at Rotterdam? Believe me, during my return home my mind could do nothing but constantly recall the wonders and hidden mysteries of Nature I had seen at your house. Not only that, but in my sleep and during the night the images of the things seen, with all that was most desirable and diverting, were as clear to my eyes as if I were more or less in your study; and at the present moment my mind is finding great pleasure in all those ideas.

. . .

And now that I am departed from you, I still seem to let my eyes roam everywhere looking through the small circle of your magnifying glass, which magnified so perfectly the thousand thousandth of a grain of sand, and the smallest fibre of a shoot or plant, just as it was.

That's it. Now that I am separated from you I am the more astounded, the more surprised when I recall what I saw, and with amazement I realize what your genius (polished as precisely as the glass) has brought to light.

Whilst you, not holding fast to doctrines which you and I learned earlier, open up another path to wisdom, and allow no wordy talkers, no so-called scholars, or the blind and conceited to interfere with your observations.

Every little creature of Nature, however small it may be, endowed with its own special organs, chooses its mate and reproduces its like on land and sea. These indissoluble ties preserve the wide universe from harm.

Are we then to believe the Ancients—as if to invalidate the truth—that life at one time arose from putrefaction? That is language to beguile children with. This fog was bound to be blown away as soon as your eyes put it to the test.

O observer of hidden mysteries! Your observation has proved to us and given reasons how this old prejudice arose. It was that people did not sufficiently observe, that they relied too readily on what no one rightly proved.

But you, not content with empty words, undertook to examine every part of the body. You caused wombs to be opened up before us. Discovery was your comfort, not hearsay. O wonderful, devoted labor.

Pure love of truth, which seldom lies ready for man, inspired you, O famous man. As long as truth remains your companion, and you love her, you will see more than anyone else.

♛ ♛ ♛

"You see how poets gloat on it when they behold something beautiful," Rabus explained at the conclusion of his panegyric.

No more, surely, than my father gloated on this letter. He read it to each of us in turn, Cornelia, my cousin Antoni, Heer Christiaan Huygens, my cousins van Leeuwen when they visited from Rotterdam, even our young, yawning Grietje.

It was the fleas, Grietje insisted, were keeping her from her sleep again.

But we none of us paid her any mind. It was she who had brought the kitten into the Golden Head with its agile aggravating burden. Not, as Grietje claimed, to preserve herself from the mice in her chamber, but to assist her in her endless foolishness. Her laughter could be heard from dawn to dusk, it washed round the other sounds, the rasp of the cat's claws on my new damask bed curtains, the whisper as it tore the rush seats of the kitchen chairs and lapped the nap off our best velvet skirts.

As usual, my father put this happenstance to good use. One morning, when we all sat at the breakfast table scratching our ears, our forearms, our ankles, he had drawn from his pocket six glass flasks stopped with cork. He had handed them to the impenitent child.

"I want you to seek through all our sheets," he said. "Bring me only the fattest ones, the females."

The next day, Cornelia insisted we drown the kitten. Grietje's tears meant nothing to her.

"She just wishes to be cruel," sobbed Grietje.

Cornelia, resting in the bed, called me to her and tried to explain. "She is right. It is the child's own wild spirit I want to stifle. Her laughter rings in my head day and night. I can't sleep anymore. I look at her face, so smooth and foolish, and my heart batters like a bird trapped in a net. Her sorrow hurts me more than the terrible aching in my tooth your father finally cured with his little glass tubes of vitriol, but it hurts me less than her laughter. In that I hear my own death."

I think Our Creator sometimes teases us with the truth as we tease kittens with a dangling string, dipping and bobbing it in our hand. It wasn't her own death Cornelia feared, it was her life, rather the living death that was the loss of my father's esteem.

In September, you see, he had left her bed for good.

"I promise you I did not refuse to perform my conjugal obligation. I said nothing, Maria. He had no cause."

It was four in the afternoon. My stepmother had not risen all day. Even then, she lay under the coverlets, her hair in disarray. I stood on the far side of her chamber, my hands folded around my waist. I was impatient with her.

"When he came to me from his study, I knew that was what he desired. Even in this cool air, his red undershirt was dark with sweat. I made no objection. Even at our great age, the Lord might still allow—But your father, Maria. Now he permits nothing. As if it were my fault my heart quickened so terribly, sweat broke out on my chest and back until I was—"

"Stop. It is not fitting I should hear."

"Fitting," sobbed Cornelia. "Was it *fitting* I should listen to you in your last illness, *fitting* my dear servant Maartje should bless me with her last breath and I be left with this sly, unloving child?"

"Grietje?"

"Like a child," she went on, "he can't stand death. He can't stand the scent of it. I am not ready yet, Maria. Don't let me go—as he does, with a shrug of his shoulders, a brisk rubbing of his hands. *Don't let me die.*"

"He fears sickness." I spoke slowly, ignoring the arms she held out to me. "He always has. So many he has loved have been taken from him. My mother. All his sons."

"So he will relinquish me too, while I am still breathing." Cornelia was blue now, gasping. "Fetch Antoni," she muttered.

When I hesitated, she coughed angrily. "Fetch your cousin."

I don't understand why it is that what draws my cousin repels my father, but surely Antoni Molijn never refused my stepmother, while my father never again approached her more nearly than the foot of her bed. From there he read out to her those observations that so delighted Heer Rabus from Rotterdam.

"Oh Husband," she said twisting irritably in her bed, "it is the same old thing. From the egg comes the worm, from the worm the pupa, then the flea or fly or the moth, who drops eggs and starts it all over again—"

"Aha!" my father interrupted, "you have forgotten, we all have, the amazing conjunction that must take place."

"I have no patience—"

"Wait," my father begged.

"Oh Antoni," Cornelia said, spreading out her plump white hands.

My father started, stepped back. My cousin, entering hurriedly, brushed him aside. He took Cornelia's hand in both his.

"You have taken the draught I prescribed," he said, tenderly stroking her hand with his fingertips.

"Morning and evening. It does no use." Cornelia glanced over at my father, who furiously perused the observations he had drawn from Kroonevelt's press that afternoon.

"Help me," Cornelia whispered. "I am afraid."

"We live only as long as the Lord wills, but I have sworn to assist Him."

"Assist!" my father scoffed. "Humoring her in her weakness—you hasten her death. Every day she lies like that the blood collects in her heart and stretches it wider."

"Stick to your glass, Uncle," Antoni Molijn said angrily. "It is the louse's anatomy you have studied all these years, not your wife's, your serving girl's, or your daughter's."

"Off with you. I will have you out—"

"Don't shout so, Father. We have visitors from 'sGravenhage on the doorstep," I broke in at last.

With a furious coughing, my father turned and hastened down the stairs. Tenderly my cousin Antoni lifted Cornelia's milk white hand. Suddenly sickened, I too left the room.

It wasn't the thought of Cornelia's death gave me a turn, but my cousin's happiness. It gave him pleasure to treat with the sick. It still does. But those days with Cornelia, my cousin Anton fed as well on his godfather's envy. It infuriated my father to think my cousin's presence could effect what his own labors could not: his own wife's peace of heart.

When I came downstairs, my father was reading to the visiting gentlemen from his latest observations, the ones he intended to send on to the Royal Society on the next boat from Rotterdam.

In order that Your Honors may have a better notion of the copulation of fleas, I once again gave orders that all the fleas as might be caught should be enclosed in glass tubes . . .

On the 20th of September I was brought, in a glass tube, two Fleas which were Females, and in addition there lay a dead Flea in the tube, and the next day I was brought a second tube in which there was a Male Flea. After this Male had been enclosed in a separate tube for about 6 hours, I placed the Male with the two aforesaid living Females and the dead Female.

Now as soon as the Male was with the Females, it bent its abdomen even further upwards than it was, and at the same time thrust the Male Organ out of its body, wherever it happened to touch the body of the Female with its abdomen, even if it were at the head of the Female; and that with such alacrity, and continually moving about and seeking the Female Organ, that I was dumbfounded. And in this process it frequently got separated from the Female, and even if it happened to come across the dead Female, it hung on to it as tightly, trying to copulate with it, as if it had to do with a living Female. I then took great pains to get it away from the dead Female, and to move it aside, in which I succeeded after about fifteen minutes. After this time, the Male was trying to copulate now with one, now with the other female, and although the Male was not underneath the Female, but by its side, yet it bent its body so towards the abdomen of the Female, that I often thought it would copulate like that. While the Male was doing this, I could not see that the females were inclined to copulate, but in most cases they tried to get rid of the Male, but it was already holding too tightly to them.

The movements which the Male made for about half an hour at a stretch were so indefatigable and lustful as one might see in any beast whatsoever; nay, I believe that if a Stallion or a Dog, which are among the most hot-blooded animals, had to make such movements with their bodies during copulation, they would drop down dead before the end of half an hour.

At last the male got underneath the female, and it thrust its male organ, erecting it, into the female organ, without my being able to see whether the female made any copulating movement with its body, and thus they copulated and lay motionless as if they were dead.

My father waved the copperplate engraving he'd had made. The old man in the professor's gown reached for it with an avid air and laid it out upon the table. My father stabbed at it with his finger.

"Here it can clearly be seen that the body of the male has been made in such a way that the male must not climb on to the female when copulating, but the female must rather stand or straddle the male, and that in this way the copulation can be brought about most easily."

All the men bent over the table nodding gravely.

My father spoke again. "I put a male and female, while they were copulating, on a sheet of paper, assuming that they would thus not be capable of jumping away. But I found it to be contrary to what I thought, for no sooner were they on the paper than they jumped, though they were copulating, so high and far away that I was unable to find them, however much I searched for them."

My father's words were drowned out by his visitors loud laughter.

"He does tell the truth, Mejuffrouw Maria," Grietje whispered. "I helped him look. An entire hour I spent on my hands and knees cursing those creatures for their licentious ways."

Had she never, I wondered, cursed my father for his fumbling curiosity?

"I have already said," I heard him announce as I drew on my cape, "that fleas lay eggs—"

"And worms come from those eggs," Grietje whispered handing me my basket.

"And the worms in turn change into fleas," I added.

"As has been said many times before," my father went on.

Even out on the Hippolytusbuurt I could hear him from his half-open window. "One man assures us that fleas come forth from sand, someone else from peat-dust, another from the dung of pigeons. When we looked up Kircherus—"

"We?" my cousin Antoni muttered, pausing by my side and sniffing eagerly at the bright cool air as if it promised spring not winter. "Didn't I provide him with the reference? Didn't I translate it, he huffing and puffing objections all the while?"

"You presume—"

"I must say that, if Kircherus had spent a few days in studying Fleas with a good magnifying glass and keen observation, just as I have lost many days doing this, he would have spoken quite differently about the procreation of Fleas, even apart from the manifold fables about procreation and other fantasies which he put on paper and, as it were, scattered abroad," my father concluded.

My cousin's boots clattering along the Hippolytusbuurt nearly drowned out the applause of the visiting gentlemen.

As I started across the bridge to the Flesh Hall I heard my father tug his window closed.

👑 👑 👑

There was nothing, really, could seal us off securely from one another, any more than each of us could seal ourselves away from the truth.

Cornelia knew her days were numbered.

My father knew his observations were worth nothing to her.

My cousin Antoni knew at last he had my father securely in his debt.

Grietje knew my father's eyes followed her as curiously as any of those fleas.

I knew he was as baffled by his interest as he was by the mystery of the crane flies. I thought I knew which question he'd apply his mind to, which one he would ignore. I was wrong.

My father applied himself instead to observing the copulation of mites, an event even stranger than the copulation of the flea.

"It's the same old story," Cornelia gasped. Her breath made a frosty globe in the air. "Why can't he leave it in peace?"

"There are many yet who doubt him," Grietje said, beating out her pillow. "Or so he says." She shrugged, tucked the pillow neatly under her mistress' head. "I have seen enough to convince me. Ugh."

"Off with you," I said shortly.

"Tell me, Maria," Cornelia said softly, as soon as she heard Grietje's shoes on the stairs. "Does he console himself already?"

"Yes," I said. "But not with the child. Like you, he consoles himself contemplating the Creator's purpose. He's an old man, Cornelia. He's lived out his allotted sum."

"I too. I will not live to see the new year."

"Don't go on this way," I said. My hands were shaking.

"It is true," she said. "Don't deny it. You too are eager to see the last of me."

"If you would only fight to stay."

"Your father will suffer," she whispered. "He will suffer for his indifference. Only Antoni Molijn knows how deeply."

"If you are wise," I told my cousin Antoni that afternoon, "You will keep this to yourself." I spoke of his diagnosis. My stepmother's blood boiled with an unbearable heat. It was whipped back from her hands and feet by a terrible wind.

"I have done everything I could. I have consulted with 'sGravesende and the surgeon Dieren. It is God's will. There is nothing to be done but submit."

"Silence, Cousin."

By Christmas there was more silence than anyone could desire. Nothing dulled the sound of Cornelia's gasping, the parrot's obedient squawk, "God's will be done. God's will be done." Nothing dulled the sound of my father's wicked merriment alone in his icy study.

It was Grietje he called to listen to his latest thought. I sat by Cornelia's bed as I had each night for the past month. She could not bear, she said, to slip off without notice. My father would not even pass the open doorway to her chamber.

"Go on, go *on*, woman," he had roared at her only two days before, "Although what you will find there that is missing here I can't imagine."

"You don't care—"

"Care," he cried out with an angry gasp. "It's you that's determined. Determined to flout everything I've taught you. Everything." He bent his face to his hands, weeping.

"Oh, Husband," Cornelia said, struggling to sit in her bed, a gentle smile on her lips. "Even there you wanted to take precedence."

"It's only fitting," he said.

"You believe we'll meet there Antoni? No, no don't anger yourself. I have never doubted for a minute God will welcome you—and me. It is your first wife I am thinking of, all those lost children. It's the wife who might follow—"

"I'm an old man, Cornelia," my father said, shaking his head. "There will be no more. How can you entertain the notion?"

"How indeed," she asked with a smile. "I ask your pardon, Husband. Humbly."

"My time grows short," my father said, listening to the church bells. "I have yet to finish my observations."

Cornelia sank back in her bed without a sound. But it wasn't true. She never gave up fighting, fighting to be seen with the same attention my father gave to his glass, gave, occasionally, to Grietje's full young form, her warm breast heaving in amazement.

"He will suffer," she whispered. "He will suffer terribly when he learns."

Those last weeks Cornelia entertained many strange notions.

"Maria, you must promise to assist him. You must not let him be vanquished by his grief."

"I will do my best," I said, yawning.

"Listen to me." She gripped my hand so tightly her nails dug into my skin. "You must tell your cousin I was mistaken. He must never reveal my error to your father."

"You can ask him yourself. He arrives within the hour."

"Call your father—"

"He does not wish—"

"Insist—"

"First you must hear this," my father said with an imperious wave of his hand. Grietje sat owl-eyed, shivering, by the smoldering tower of peat.

"*I was not yet satisfied with these observations, but I resolved to continue watching, however tired my eyes might become—*"

"Husband, Cornelia called from the top of the stairs. Her voice was deep as a man's. "I implore you—"

"—*however tired*," my father repeated, "*my eyes might become, if not once, then many times, until I had seen the beginning of the copulation one or more times . . .* "

"I'll have no more of this," I interrupted. "Grietje, attend to your mistress. Now, Now!" I clapped my hands and gave the girl a slap on the cheek.

"What has gotten into you? What business—" My father stepped forward angrily waving his paper.

"Fool," I said to him. "It is your own salvation she is working for at this hour, not her own. It's assured."

"I never doubted Cornelia was meant to survive me." My father's eyes gleamed. "They were all meant to survive me, Daughter. My wives. My sons. We were not made to live alone."

He reached out and picked up a glass tube from the table. He held it before the candle, tapping the glass. "Even in this cold, these creatures increase. If you peer through my glasses you will see. No, don't leave. Just listen Maria . . ." He picked up his paper again.

"*While the Male thus tried to carry out copulation, the Female did not remain still, but quietly moved on, and the Male was, as it were, dragged along by the Female without the Male putting up the least resistance.*"

"She's dying, Father. Your wife is dying. Can't you just attend her?"

I backed away from him, sickened.

My father continued reading into the empty room. I heard him over Grietje's quiet sobbing on the stair.

"*Now, when the Male, with its male organ, had found the Female organ and brought it into the latter, I saw an incredibly rapid movement—*" His tongue stumbled over his words.

My father was, I understood, more helpless than his wife. It was life dragged him forward. It was death let her rest.

How many times must we prove a new truth?

How many times must we prove a new truth before we've proved it false? Even when my father watched the bearers, groaning, lift her casket onto their shoulders, he insisted it was not death we were all born to but life, eternal life.

VI
ORE
(1694-1696)

Briefly, as we try to penetrate deeper and deeper into the secrets of Nature, we become more and more aware that we shall not arrive at the great hidden mystery which is in it, though many people, when they look through a good magnifying glass, foolishly think that nothing can remain concealed from our view.

Antoni van Leeuwenhoek

. . . Since, because of the material at hand, Nature could not bring forth a man who was immortal, the Maker of the universe, so as to succor the frailty of the human race, contrived what he could in the way of immortality. He thought not to sustain a man for a few thousand years but rather to prolong his existence for eternity in the form of ever new offspring. With this as His end He constructed divers organs by which the work necessary might be performed and he did such a workmanlike job that with full justice we can proclaim that here if anywhere, Almighty God left a great testimony not only of His providence but also of his marvellous wisdom. Quite ridiculous therefore is the opinion of Chrysippus who thought that Nature fully equipped the male sex and added the female only as a sort of appendage like the peacock's tail. No less insultingly does Aristotle call the female an incomplete male, or, as the barbarian philosophers say, an animal which just happened. We ourselves think that Nature had her mind on the job when generating the female as well as when generating the male, for without females there would be no generation of any animal. And indeed being female is a kind of perfection of individual forms. So much for that. . . .

Regnier de Graaf

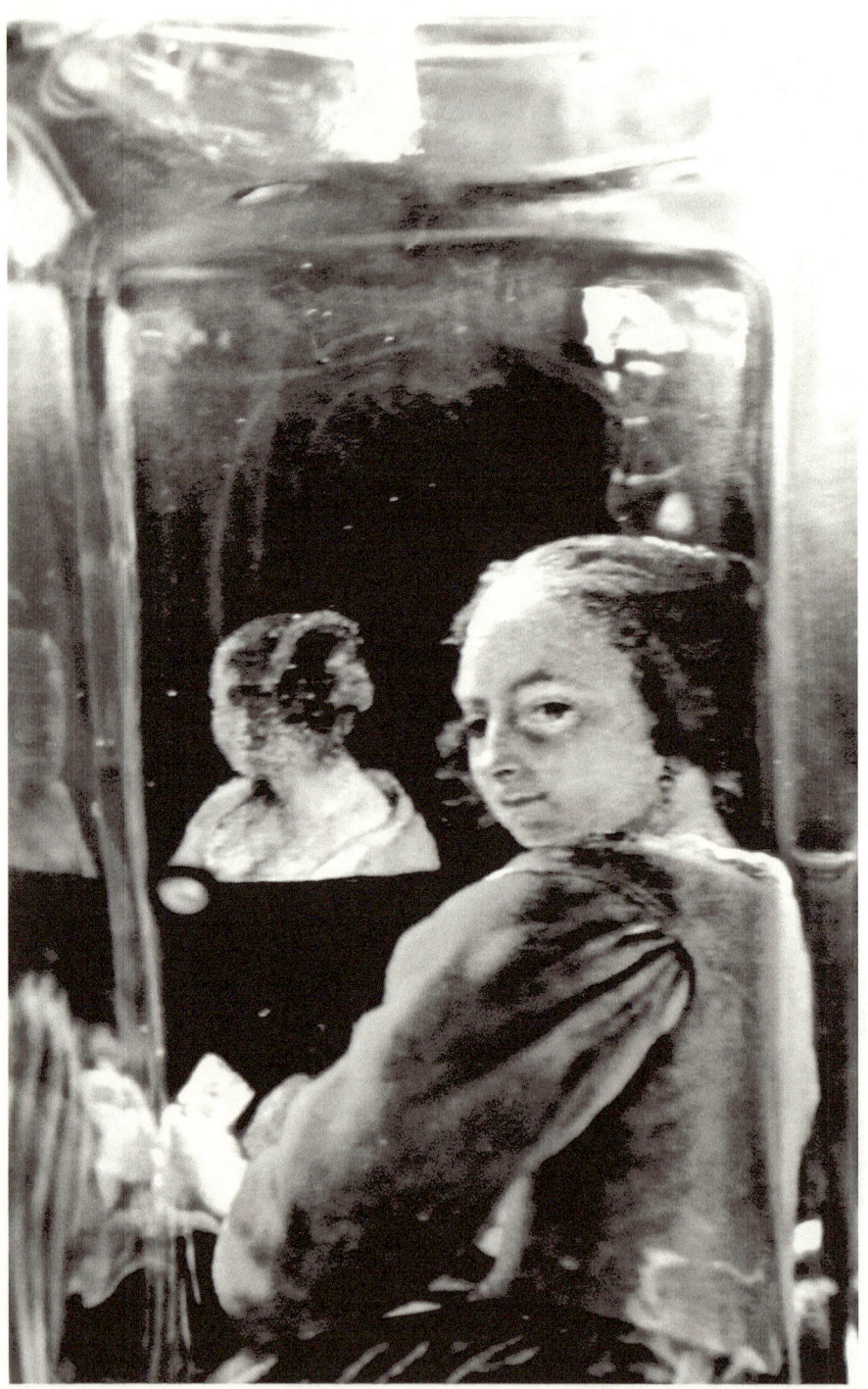

It resembles the Ornus or *Quicken Tree*; only the Draw
bears the *Flowers* and Fru... of the end, ... on the ... of
the Branch, Next the sun, the Frui... a dark...
...: and is about the bigness of ...
...ember, so much ...

...

of a Child ... Twenty fi...
this Belly, taken out of ... Journal de...
...being ... act of ... en from
2. Ju... the Author ... Journ... by M...
M...

...he said Author premises, that there ...ving
...many different Reports of this matter ... Mother
...took pains to give an exact account, a...ell of
...a...d ...at accidents befell the Mother during ...
... Taking also the Figure of the ...
...whole Town.
...Wife of *John Puget*, Shearman, ...
...received about the ... of the...
... such pains as... ...usu...
...abour. Her ...

...June this year 1678. She was opened the...
...a dead child ...found in her Bel y, out of
... joynt or fastened to it. The Head
... hanging toward the left side;
... ...ture the Figure ...

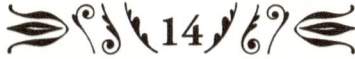

THE VEXING MYSTERY OF FRUIT LICE

"Powder of sympathy!" my father burst out before he had closed the door. There was no sympathy in his voice. He was in a rage. This was but a month ago. Indeed, the very day we first met, Aaltje.

"The St. Odulphus Fair doesn't begin until tomorrow and already they are invading the town, setting up their umbrellas, adjusting their fool's caps, their actors' robes," he complained.

It wasn't the actors disturbed my father but the quacks.

"And enriching the coffers of the physicians guild. The town reaps some benefit from their chicanery," I said.

"They encourage the common people in their old errors."

"Not just the poor," I teased. "You see the burgomaster's wife listening intently as the porter; the miller steps forward with the goldsmith. Even Cornelia, poor soul, bought more than one preparation."

"Powder of sympathy," my father exploded. "I saw this big tall German waving everyone closer. He spoke in a whisper as if he were sharing an enormous secret."

"What's that in your hand, Father?"

"Three stuivers it cost me, Daughter, and it's worth less than salt. That's all it is, that or sugar, I am willing to wager. Powder of sympathy! He claims it will cure the stone, gout, dropsy, fever, even small pox. It will ease the pangs of childbirth, it will nourish the orphaned newborn until the wet nurse comes. Hah! Soon they'll be showing that gleaming stone over there and claiming it too has curative power. The salts of a man's piss won't cure us of anything—"

"But boredom. Do you remember, three years ago, how you exposed the pedlar? He claimed his powder was more precious than gold or silver. Cousin Geertruida and Grietje came running back breathless with excitement to tell us about it. Even Cousin Antoni was taken in. But then you showed them it was the very same matter as the stone given you years before by that high-born German gentleman. What was his name? Leibnitz?"

"Hmm," my father said, breathing more easily now. The corners of his mouth twitched. "The pedlar packed up and left the same night. My godson should have done the same, gullible fool."

"That was the fair we spent all our time searching for a copy of your portrait to buy and send to the Royal Society to hang in their chamber in London."

"Which they have never acknowledged," my father grunted. "For all I know, this big bluff braggart of a German will soon be hanging there as well."

"You do them an injustice."

"Well, what have they done me?"

"A signal honor, Father!"

"I am famous all over the world, Maria. I correspond with the Grand Pensionary Heinsius, with the worthy Burgomaster Witsen in Amsterdam, with the noble Baron van Reede van Renswoude."

"Is there anything in particular you will seek for this St. Odulphus?" I asked.

My father missed his correspondence with the great English society more than he missed his wife. Indeed, the year after her death, he wrote them almost monthly. I have never seen him make or share so many observations. But they were greeted, nearly all of them, by a silence profound as the one Cornelia kept.

And that year, my poor father thought so much. He shared his investigations with Grietje and me as well as with the learned. We must restore ourselves daily, he said, three weeks after Cornelia's death. He waved the fogged flask in which he'd collected the moisture his hand had lost in just an hour.

"Imagine how much I would be depleted if I had relinquished myself to grief as have the two of you. Caudle," he insisted. "We must all sit and drink it together."

"Imagine the number of muscles in the human tongue," he said in February, March.

"Father, regard the hour," I protested. "The child and I have our own occupations."

"I prove my point," he said happily. "Did you feel your tongue tumbling in your mouth? More than one flesh fiber is required for every sound we utter. The heart's flesh is just as intricate."

"Please don't go on, Sir," Grietje begged. "I feel it twitching even now. There are things we are not meant to discover. I feel this as strongly as did my late mistress."

"Foolishness—"

"Insolence—"

But whatever word we used, her chatter effected what my pleas could not—silence, blessed silence.

🐚 🐚 🐚

And there was silence in our house that morning this past June after I asked my father just what it was he was seeking at the kermis this year. A silence just as sudden, just as brief. Broken as usual by Grietje.

"What is it I hear?" my father asked abruptly. "Surely my godson does not attend her again—"

"Grietje attends to us today. She has promised."

The eager clatter on the stairs proved me right.

"Mejuffrouw, Mejuffrouw! You can see the players setting up their tent on the market square. I can hardly wait—" She bobbed demurely to my father and escaped into the kitchen.

"So *that's* it," my father whispered to me. "You've bribed her."

"Not exactly. But as I could not cure her with that bitter powder, reason, I have lured her with a sweeter fragrance." I laughed. "As always, Father, it's simple hunger drives her."

"For what? What does she lack?"

"How can you ask?"

I clapped my hands loudly. When Grietje appeared in the doorway, I requested she not set my place at table.

"I am dining today with the matron of the Weeshuis." As I turned to leave, I saw both their mouths open in surprise.

The matron greeted me curiously as well.

"If you don't mind my asking, Mejuffrouw van Leeuwenhoek, why do you wish to part with Grietje?"

"Part?" I asked in surprise. "I have no mind to part with her. But I have not designed all these years that she should remain a servant to me and my father. Our needs are modest, her abilities many."

The matron observed me closely.

"Surely you agree with me?" Grietje was a great favorite of the matron. When she delivered a parcel, she often rested at the orphanage all the afternoon. It was she who assisted the young orphan girls in their sewing instruction.

The matron's fine mouth twitched. "You are a wise woman, Mejuffrouw van Leeuwenhoek. So many would try to mold her to their own purposes. But you know, since she's not resided here we can't provide a dower. I spoke with Heer Vallensis upon the subject six years ago. He promised he would take care of the matter himself, but I heard of no bequest when he died."

"I have arranged the dower myself. She will have her six-years wages, plus interest, and a chest of linens."

"And the man, Mejuffrouw van Leeuwenhoek?"

"I have yet to make my decision."

A bell rang in the outer room. Suddenly the hubbub of the schoolroom ceased, to be replaced by the amazing clatter of thirty pairs of wooden clogs knocking along the wooden floor toward the dining hall.

"I am pleased you have come to spend the afternoon. You will be able to observe them all at your leisure," the matron said as she led the way into the dining hall.

The children moved methodically as ants bearing their bowls from the steaming cauldron to their benches. They sat, heads bowed, hands clasped as the matron gave the blessing. Before the dinner was over, I had made my selection.

"But why that one, Mejuffrouw van Leeuwenhoek?" the matron asked me when I informed her. "I have nothing against the child, mind you. She does whatever is requested of her. But she has been here a month and no one has heard her speak. The woman who brought her claims she is not dumb. 'The voice of a lark,' she said. I don't know who to believe. The child behaves as if she had no tongue."

"She was orphaned recently?"

"Her mother died in childbed. Her father was a goldsmith, but he did not prosper. He died in April of smallpox, as did her younger sister."

"She is not marked."

"It was she brought the disease into the house, or so her neighbor said."

"Her age?"

"By appearance thirteen or fourteen. There is no baptismal record. I must say, Mejuffrouw van Leeuwenhoek, she's docile but not particularly able with the needle. We have other girls here who ply theirs nearly as swiftly as your Grietje. Gretchen Jansdr., for example, and her friend, Agatha."

"I'm not seeking a seamstress."

"What *do* you look for?"

"It defies words. It should be no matter to you. The judgement, for good or ill, is mine alone. I will never fault you. She will not be cast off or sent back. At worst, I will arrange her future as I am arranging Grietje's."

"At worst!" exclaimed the matron. "Grietje has already more than every girl here dreams of—"

"May I speak with the child? In private if you don't mind."

The matron nodded and went to the door. She called to her serving maid and asked her to fetch Aaltje Phillipsdr. Then the matron excused herself, and I waited, my hands folded over my best apron, relieved not to have to speak. I could not name what I sought, I still can't, but I thought I recognized it in your face, Aaltje.

When you came to me at last, I had risen from my seat and waited by the window. When I heard you enter, I did not turn around; instead I closed my eyes, letting them recover from the dazzle of the noonday sun. I still remember my very words.

"My name is Maria. Maria Antonisdr. van Leeuwenhoek. I live here in this city, on the Hippolytusbuurt, in a house called the Golden Head. I live with my father. Perhaps you have heard of him? He is famous for his microscopic observations. In the entire world, he is one of the foremost practitioners of this new art. Every day he reveals through his glasses more of the Creator's great purpose than ever we dreamed of knowing.

"I don't speak of my father because you'll be asked to assist him. You will assist me, and I ply a much simpler trade, that of draper. I don't even speak of my father because he owns the roof under which you will sleep, or because he has slaughtered the hogs, smoked the beef, and planted the orchards and gardens that will feed you. I speak of my father because once you enter the Golden Head you can't escape him or the truths he tells. You must know this. Without my help, you may never make your own peace with them either."

"I'll go." I still hear your voice, so low it was almost a whisper. But there was nothing hesitant in it. "I will go anywhere. I do not wish to rest here."

But I did not take you at your word. Remember.

"Not yet," I said. "I require even more of you. It is not just fear you must conquer. But indifference as well. You must feel a desire, a calling. Don't cry, Child. I am as certain you will hear it as I am that it has, as of yet, escaped you. When you hear it, it will ring louder than the bells in the Nieuwe Kirke. There will be no mistaking. It could happen today or next week or a year or two from now. When it does, go and tell the matron the time has come. I will send for you within the hour."

I can feel it yet, my palm closing over your shoulder, your cheek resting momentarily on the back of my hand. Your tear stung, sharper than sea water, as it slipped into the scratches. I drew away. I shook my hand in the air.

"You must leave that here, Child. There is no room for grief in the Golden Head."

There never has been. Surely, there was no room for grief, as I have said, the year after Cornelia's death. My father, in the many letters he wrote the Royal Society in the year '94 never mentioned his wife's death, even in the letter he wrote a fortnight after her burial. But he did not relinquish her quite so easily as it might have appeared. Take some of the subjects of his study. The flesh of the heart, the tongue. He wrote himself to the Royal Society of the wounds a heart might endure, the way its flesh fibers might falter, fail finally to move at all. This, he believed, was what physicians called an attack. But who or what offered the violence? Couldn't each flesh fiber just tire, like the spirits of an aging man and woman engaged in endless argument?

My father, whatever his inclination that year (and he yawned often, readied himself for bed as soon as the sun slid behind the Oude Kirke and the Prinsenhof), steadfastly resisted his own lethargy. Every month he wrote his letters to the Royal Society, whether or not they were acknowledged, for it was the strength of his hand and his mind, the agility of his own tongue he wanted to preserve.

Thus, he addressed himself for the first time in several years to answering some of the endless objections to his theory of Generation. In the end, of course, he convinced fewer than he wanted, but on this occasion he expressed his views as forcibly as any man could. He had no time, that year, for fine words. He had as little patience as ever for censure. But it is better for you to hear his thought as he himself expressed it. He was driven to do so by a letter from Dr. George Garden from Aberdeen, although he sent his response directly to the Royal Society.

Dear Sir, Dr. Garden had written my father, *Among all your eminent discoveries there is none more outstanding than that of the animalcules in the seed of Males (male seed) of every species, the truth of which I do not doubt. But nevertheless I cannot so easily be persuaded to think that the recently and lately made conjectures concerning the use of the Female 'balls,' which are called ovaries, are as unfounded and contrary to reason as you seem to consider in some of your letters . . . And since you do not seem to be convinced of the latter, I take the liberty to give you a summary of the reasons which seem to prove it indubitably . . .*

Firmly, my father refuted the ingenious Englishman:
As to the conjectures concerning the Female 'balls', or in other words Ovaries, I am still of opinion that these are mere figments, because in former days people have not been able to invent any better theses concerning generation. For when I began to speak for the first time about the Animalcules in the Male seed, and of their extreme smallness, among many people this could not find acceptance.

My father shared the reasonings of others who believed as he in the singular generative power of the animalcule in male seed. But my father did not content himself with the speculations of others. He addressed several of Dr. Garden's objections directly.

I have never heard that many foetuses have been found outside the Uterus. It does not follow from the fact that a foetus remained in a Woman's belly for 26 years, Philosophical Transactions No. 139, and that of the small foetus in the abdomen as related in No. 150, that the imagined ovary contributed to this. For how easily can an opening be formed in the womb by an ulceration, through which the foetus may be expelled from the uterus and remain there for some time, while this opening in the uterus may afterwards be healed again. Indeed, how many inconceivable events do not take place in accidents to which human beings are liable without our being able to imagine any cause for them?

My father provided much evidence for his views. He described the shortness of the horns of the uterus, how they could not reach the 'balls' of a woman to suck up the eggs, should such eggs exist—which he doubted.

My father did not deny that animalcules wandered the length and breadth of the uterus—he had seen them himself—but never did they struggle so far, he insisted, as to that useless female ball.

I might go further into this, but since I should have to repeat several things which I have already committed to writing or which I consider are of no use to the World, I will conclude now and tell you that I have said more than once that I do not intend to keep obstinately to my theses, but that as soon as plausible reasons are presented to me which I can understand, I will abandon my views and adopt another, the more so because my efforts always have no other purpose but to reveal the truth to the best of my ability, to espouse it, and to use the small Talent which I have received to draw the World away from its Ancient Pagan superstitions and make it adopt the truth and adhere to it.

♛ ♛ ♛

Before submitting his thoughts to the scrutiny of the Royal Society, my father sent a copy of his reply to Amsterdam to be considered by his very learned friend, Pastor Haan.

"Come, come, Daughter," my father said two weeks later, joyously waving the letter from Haan, "don't you think this should silence them? Pastor Haan provides me with several events here in Delft that support my speculations." Without waiting for me to seat myself, he began to read.

That a foetus can live and grow outside the Uterus can be confirmed by two events at Delft. The uterus of the second wife of _____ burst six weeks before her death (it was preserved by Doctor ____ in a liquor, burst and shrunk as it was). After her death the aforesaid Doctor, in the presence of myself, Doctor _____, and Conrector _____ , removed a big fully-grown foetus from the dissected belly.

I later saw a similar case during the dissection of the wife of ____.

Your theses of the opening of the uterus through an ulceration and its subsequent healing is completely confirmed by an event occurring to the mother-in-law of ____. This woman became pregnant: the foetus settled on one side of the belly and remained there for some years. Then she became pregnant, bore a Son (who is now 30 years of age), and about one year afterwards the hard protuberance began to disappear from the side and she entirely discharged all the bones of a fully-grown foetus along the ordinary passage, but mixed with much stinking phlegm. And this woman lived for some years in reasonable health.

My father looked at me for approbation.

I adjusted my apron. I tried to catch my breath. I rolled from one foot to the other trying to get my balance.

"I wish you would give it up, Father," I told him plainly. "I don't believe the Creator intended us to fathom His full purpose."

"You don't credit my argument? You! My own daughter! What do you know of the matter, woman? He's a man of God, Haan. But you, you know better than him?"

"I have not said that. I believe you have approached the truth more nearly than any other man, but as you often say, your glasses do not make everything clear, there are structures finer than any glass can fathom. There are truths—" I put my hand to my side where the pain took me.

"Daughter?" The anger washed out of my father's face as quickly as it had flooded in. "What ails you this time?"

"Nothing," I assured him quickly. "It is just a stitch. Perhaps I ate too much at dinner."

"You must learn to curb that unruly appetite. At your age, it is unseemly." He paused, listening with an expression of distaste, to Grietje's laughter drifting through the open door. "No more seemly," he continued, "than her behavior."

But Grietje's joy has proved as difficult to constrain as my own appetite, or my father's curiosity. We have all learned, however, to censure our expressions if not our thoughts. When Grietje dreams of crossing the sea, her face rests blank as an idiot's, her shoulders sag with sembled sorrow. My father in his deepest doubt seems stern, resolved. While I, in my ravening confusion, appear resigned.

My father did not content himself with refuting the ingenious Mr. Garden. All the remaining months of the year, my father wrote down his thoughts concerning the copulation, impregnation and reproduction of our women. When, in the winter, he decided against sharing his opinions with the world, he did so reluctantly, with much vacillation. He followed the recommendation of our Grand Pensionary, Heer Heinsius. Even the mask of Latin, that learned and imperturbable man suggested, was not secure enough.

"I would let the matter rest, Heer van Leeuwenhoek," he said. "You have convinced all those who matter."

So my father wrote to Heer Rabus, his new learned friend in Rotterdam, refusing his offer to translate the treatise into Latin. He listed his reasons for withholding such an important truth from the world. Although in his treatise he had, he announced, glorified us women above the females of quadrupeds—whereas others spoke with contumely about such happenings—still my father chose not to publish his thoughts because, "*on the one hand the treatises, which have been formulated by me in a straightforward way, in accordance with the nature of the matter, might appear indecent (although we merely investigate nature and the truth), and on the other hand fear that the World, evil and stupid as it is, might use the knowledge of Nature for its perdition and fall into even greater dissoluteness.*"

There was another reason my father censored his treatise on the reproduction of our women. It was not just fear of giving offense that restrained him, not just fear of assisting our licentious age in its perditious path. My father censored himself because he could not be absolutely certain of the truth of his speculations.

He had, we all agreed, as great a right as any man to reason upon the mysteries, the exhausting puzzles the Creator of the All has set up for us at the Creation of the World. But the summer of '94, six months after Cornelia died, my father made another observation, one that cast into question all that he had written so far upon this vexing question of generation. At first, it was this observation he wished to censor, not his treatise. Indeed, he held it from the learned world an entire year.

But in the end, it was his thoughts my father put aside, not the evidence of his eyes. And in the end, I too accepted the evidence of my senses. I took the aging and confused man, Antoni Philipszn. van Leeuwenhoek, not his dreams, his thoughts, his fame, but the man himself as the true object of my observations—and my loyalty. It was not easy for me. It required of me as difficult a divestment as his own.

What *was* this discovery of my father's?

Simply: the lice who swarm upon all our fruit trees, each to its kind, cherry and peach, currant and pear, all have this one thing in common: To reproduce they do not require the male animalcule. *There are no males.* These insects, unlike any other animal my father has observed, are all mothers. They give birth to live young by the score within a fortnight of their own birth. Nature has provided them with a terrible fecundity.

For three springs now my father has searched for sight of a male. He has found none. In the process he has discovered much about these little insects. For one, it is they who cause the shriveling of the leaves in the orchard which my father had earlier ascribed to ants. Indeed, the ants seem now less noxious to my father because of these smaller animals. The ants do perform some useful service to man, my father now admits; they don't just rob him of his sweet fruit. The ants also assist in the fruit's abundance, for it is they who devour these small fruit lice in the spring when the orchards are in flower and the fruit has not yet come into being. It is well that the ants do so, and that provident nature has provided these plant lice with other enemies as well, for they are more prolific even than the louse that feeds on our own blood.

It was in August of '94 my father revealed to me his latest discovery. He told me because he expected sympathy. Hadn't I listened to his treatise? Hadn't I nodded? Hadn't I agreed?

"I am sure that in time I will see here that the male animalcule is involved. It was the same at first when I could not discover their eggs—until I found they delivered their young live. For a moment I thought it would be as delicious as nuts for those people who still speak of spontaneous generation and feed their superstition. For a moment, Daughter, I felt quite lost. I felt at my wits end to fathom this new secret of generation. But when I opened them up to extract the eggs, for I could not discover them on the leaf, I discovered they were *all* mothers."

"This discovery does not make you lose faith in your own speculations?"

"They do not generate spontaneously. They are as like, mother and child, as two drops of water. Like comes from like. I am as convinced as ever that all that has received life originates from those things that were created in the Beginning."

"From Eve as well as Adam?"

"Leave me, Daughter. I have not fathomed the full mystery of these insects. They differ in their shape as well from ants and fleas and other segmented insects. That I can demonstrate now from one of their shed skins. I'm sure there is an answer to this other question. I am sure I will find it, as I have found the secret of the generation of the eel."

"Perhaps De Graaf was right. Cornelia too," I said cruelly.

My father flinched, but said firmly, "I am as convinced as ever of the truth of my thoughts on the reproduction of our women. This is a completely different matter."

"Then why don't you share it then with the learned gentlemen in London? I am sure they will be as curious as I."

"I will wait. Until I am certain. For they are, like Mr. Garden, prejudiced in favor of the ovary."

"It is not true, then, Father, that Nature works in one and the same way everywhere? You cannot study our own generation by comparison with trees and currant bushes?"

"Of course I can. Haven't I done so in more than one letter to the Royal Society? Your thinking is not clear, Daughter."

"You wish it was not." I was on my feet by then. I was stiff with anger. "Should you print your treatise Father, and withhold this—you are no loyal servant of the truth. You are as prejudiced as all the rest."

"I know the truth of my own observations. And the worth of my theses. I will not abandon them as easily as they would have me do. I have tried so hard, Daughter, to turn the world from its error. I need time. I need to be absolutely certain of the truth of this new observation for once they've heard it, Daughter, they'll not listen to my treatise. And my observations recorded there are those of an entire lifetime."

"*My* lifetime. Lies, all lies. Your own eyes have shown you so."

"No," he cried, knocking his glass from the table with a wide sweep of his arm, burying his face in his trembling hands. "Go," he cried.

And I did, but because *I* willed it, not because my father bade me. I had to think. What did this discovery of his, that mothers begot daughters begot mothers begot daughters mean for me? Did I—and Cornelia and my mother and Grietje—all carry the germs of Eve in an unbroken line from creation? Carry the germs of Adam too? For in my father's speculations it was his seed that gave life to me as well as those four sons. Was it true then that I could bear my mother's son? That those we grieved as Antoni's sons were really Barbara's? Should I not have been called Maria Barbara's daughter, nor Antoni's? My brothers, Barbara's sons, not Antoni's? Should any child conceived in me bear my name as well as Eve's?

❦ ❦ ❦

For months I could not hear a word he said. It was all his fault. I had trusted him. I had followed him unquestioning. And now not only was our world turned topsy turvy, but my father thought he could right it all again. I was not willing to give him the chance

Hadn't I, not he, paid out with my own life again and again, and in full each time, the cost for his speculations?

In the Oude Kirke, I visited the tombs of my mother, my Aunt De Mey, Cornelia. I stood even longer before the tomb of Cornelis Vallensis. I did not trust my thoughts among the living, whether the predikants, my cousins Molijn, or my cousins Van Leeuwen, but I could not relinquish them either to the dead.

"I will keep my own counsel," my father announced in November after having consulted an entire afternoon with the Grand Pensionary. "I will refuse the learned Rabus' offer to translate my treatise."

"Perhaps when you have satisfied yourself upon the mystery of these fruit lice, you will publish your observations in Rabus' *Boekzaal* instead of the *Transactions*." My father's face whitened with fury, but I went on. "That is if you fear the prejudice of the English. Here in Holland, you have said often enough, there are many learned men who are in accord with your thoughts. They would be as loathe as you to give much credence to these mother lice."

"Peace, Daughter. I can't pursue the matter until the spring. My attention now is taken with another question: the reproduction of our own lice. I intend to find an orphan boy to breed them on his leg so that I may judge whether it is indeed true they become great-grandfathers in just a day."

"An orphan boy? Why make him suffer, Father? It is you has this great appetite for truth. Shouldn't you feed it yourself?"

To my surprise my father agreed with me.

When, this past February, he at last set these observations down for the noble Frederick Adriaen van Renswoude, he said that he had first considered using an orphan boy, but decided against it because he would gain greater certainty doing it himself—and because he ought not to spare himself the itching and pain on one of his legs which most poor people were obliged to bear their whole life over their whole body.

My father studied lice because some ancient authors claimed they were hermaphrodite and my father was certain this was an error. Had he not discovered both male and female among them? Had he not discovered the male's organ? Eight times he bought lice from the poor and cut them in half to examine them behind his glasses. He called in Gerrit to record his observations.

My father studied the lice that fed on our own blood, not on the flesh of the fruits of his garden, because they reassured him. Didn't they reproduce in the natural way, the way my father had documented in the flea and the ant—save without metamorphosis? They came from eggs, not, as the ancients would have it, from pustules in our flesh—or from the wool of a sheep bitten by a wolf. Not, as Kircherus said, out of seminal spirits hidden in our food which, when carried up with the subtle emanations toward our pores lodge between flesh and skin where, if subtle, these food particles are transformed into fleas, if somewhat larger, into lice, larger still, into housebugs.

My father repeated all the old stories when he wrote at last to Baron van Reede van Renswoude. He added: "I could not help laughing about the old wives' tales on the various ways of the generation of lice which these people seem to have invented from their own brain, without any investigations. For if it were otherwise, they would have spoken of the louse's eggs, and thus each of them thought he made the best guess, whilst they all err."

Oh, yes, my father roared with laughter. He could well afford to. This time his observations accorded with his own desire. Lice did not, as the common people insisted, become great-grandfathers in just a few days. My father observed, to his own discomfort, there were near four weeks between the moment when an egg is laid and the moment when the louse has come from the egg and grown so big that it lays eggs in turn.

To demonstrate this, first my father placed nine lice in a box lined with black silk in which he placed a wool thread upon which the lice could affix their eggs. He put in one male and eight females, for he thought, like the hen, many eggs of the louse would be fertilized in one copulation. When the female lice were chary of laying their eggs, he put the box in a pocket in his belt to warm them. When, eighteen hours later, he saw their bodies were white with hunger, he placed them upon his hand. Seven of them fed eagerly. It was food, he decided the next day, increased their fertility.

My father went even farther in his tenderness. It was not enough to lay the box beside him on his bed, carry it all day beneath his fur-lined second vest. My father insisted on discovering how many eggs a louse would lay in warm, familiar surroundings—like the length of an old man's shin. To this purpose my father took off his white undersock. He chose a thin black stocking, and, making a flexible garter out of strips of its mate, he fastened it tightly upon his leg with two of the biggest female lice closed within. After six days, my father found that a single louse had laid above the calf a store of over fifty eggs. He was amazed that even in the dark she could lay up her treasure all together. He was even more amazed, opening up her body, to find more than fifty eggs remaining.

"And who knows," he said with a shudder, "how many eggs it had laid before I put it in my stocking, and also how many eggs were still sticking to the ovary, which escaped my sight."

My father, in the toe of his stocking, found another store of eggs laid by the second louse, but, more to his pleasure, he discovered a very small louse running round his ankle, which, he believed, had slipped into his stocking unnoticed. He replaced the stocking solely to see how great this louse would grow in another six to eight days. The eggs, he was sure, were infertile. Imagine his amazement, only four days later, to discover the little louse already half grown (it was a male), but to discover as well twenty-five young lice running round the ovary.

There proved to be a limit to my father's curiosity after all. The spectacle of all those young lice filled him with such aversion to the stocking that he threw it, along with all the lice, out the window.

I sent Grietje to fetch it off the cobbles and carry it around to the back of the house. My father sat by the fire rubbing his leg furiously to free it of all eggs and insects.

"Shall I bury it?" Grietje asked me, holding the sock at arm's length. "Or save it for the next time he sends me to buy some from the poor? His aversion will diminish, I am sure of it."

"We will burn it," I said. I had begun to pity my father.

I should not have bothered. By the time I returned to the front room, the stocking smoldering in the kitchen hearth, my father had welcomed Gerrit and set him down with a glass.

"Ah yes, Child. I want you to draw the male organ of the louse exactly as you see it fixed here upon this pin. You are sure you can make it out?"

My father returned to his calculations. "If we now see that, as said above, a louse lays as many as fifty eggs in six days, and that their body is then filled with even more eggs, we can understand quite well that a poor man, who has a hundred female lice on his body, and has no change of linen or garments and is too sluggish to kill the lice, can be devoured as it were by the lice within a few months."

"Horrible," Gerrit said with a shudder.

"Attend to your business," my father said, rubbing his leg vigorously again. "Grietje, fetch me another pair of stockings."

He rose to his feet and went over to inspect the boy's drawing. "Have you made sure to distinguish the small opening through which the Male seed is expelled? Ah yes I see it. Here. You're doing well. Very well."

"Next spring," he said, turning around the room briskly, "I will search every branch of my currant bushes for the currant lice. Remember how the crane fly puzzled me a whole summer when I could not find the male there either until one flew by chance through my window. I need discover only one, and then, save for the curiosity of such a small creature bearing live young, the secret of generation will again be clear."

"Should you not find him, Father, will you print off your observations all the same?"

"How could I fail?" he asked. He lifted his foot and set it upon his chair. He rubbed his leg again vigorously with a rag, He took his new stockings from Grietje. "The truth is everywhere evident, Daughter, if we have enough patience. Remember how many years I struggled with the question of circulation, how I despaired of understanding the procreation of the eel. But both of these have been revealed to me."

"I cannot fail," he repeated, tugging on his new stockings. "How are you faring, Boy?" He put his hand on Gerrit's shoulder. He poured over the drawing the boy had made. "The curve there, shouldn't it be sharper?"

"You told me to draw it as I myself saw it."

"Let me see." My father took the glass from him. "Move, move, Boy. Let me have the chair."

Gerrit stood in the center of the room, shifting unhappily from foot to foot.

"Is there anything more you want the boy to draw today?"

"I want him to draw the same, but to *my* scale. I want him to draw it as clearly as I myself can make it out."

"Another glass?" I asked. "One that magnifies that much more?"

"You could sketch it out yourself," Gerrit said. His voice was burred with remorse. "I could just refine what you saw for the engraving."

My father turned on the boy in a fury. "How dare you imply I would have you attest to anything but the truth. You will look again. You will sit there until you see it."

The boy looked wildly about the room for some refuge—from my father's work, my pity, Grietje's mirth.

"I hate these creatures, Sir," he whispered. "They're not like the young fen mussels."

"Can't you see God's hand in these as well?" my father asked. He clapped the boy on the back. "I never fail to be amazed at their perfection."

THE COSTS OF OUR SPECULATIONS

In the end, it was his awe at all Our Maker's Creation that preserved my father's honor. Although he searched unsuccessfully all spring and summer for the male of the fruit lice, he wrote finally to Baron Reede van Renswoude of these curious female creatures because here too he saw evidence of God's perfection, and he could not refrain from sharing his amazement any longer.

"*What appeared curious to me,*" he wrote, "*were the enormous number of young each creature carried live inside her belly.*" They were, it is true, less fecund than the human louse, but prodigious all the same. My father extracted forty young from one mother, forty-nine from another, and sixty from a third.

"*But what seemed extraordinary to me,*" he wrote boldly to the Baron, "*was that whenever I dissected animals of the normal size, I extracted young unborn animals from their bodies, and though I repeatedly selected the thinnest animals, imagining that if there were males among them it must be those with the thinnest bodies, it never happened that I came across any of these, or of the two preceding kinds of animals, which I considered to be male.*"

For the past few years, I have calculated the most private cost of my father's speculations to those around him, the enormity of his debt. I cannot stop myself. Every time I pass Cornelia's tomb, or Heer Vallensis', the calculations begin again—and I open my hands, shake my head, helpless to reduce the mounting interest. But my father like a careless spendthrift just charges ahead, oblivious, eager to make good on all the effort he has expended so far. To be honest, I rejoice when to his dismay he discovers in his garden yet another variety of these voracious *female* lice on the leaves of his medlars or his peaches.

What I have ignored—until this last month—is the cost of my own speculations. It is Grietje who, as usual, has tallied up my own accounts. I have been as reluctant to read what she has marked out for me as my father would be to see what I have marked out for him.

You are puzzled? Let me explain what has occurred in the Golden Head this past month. Perhaps then you will see as clearly as I do now the cost of living here, the cost of living with me as well as with my father.

🐚 🐚 🐚

"I believe I've seen enough," I said as I folded over the length of India cotton.

The young clerk shifted irritably in his chair. It was not to discuss his merchandise that we conferred now in my shop.

"I have seen enough of my servant to know what would suit her."

"I have no debts," he said. He pulled out a handkerchief and blew his nose. "I am moderate in all my habits."

Except dress, I thought, looking at his damask waistcoat, the red satin ribbons on his shoes.

"That is just the difficulty," I said. "The girl isn't."

"She seems to favor me—"

"I don't wish to disappoint you, but I believe she's drawn to those bright ribbons on your shoes, to the idea of the sea."

The clerk whitened at the memory of his eight months sea passage.

"Batavia is very far away," I said gently. "She might not survive the journey."

"I have requested of Heer Bleyswijck that they send me next time only so far as the Cape. He has promised they will consider my request."

"He may, but I have completed my own consideration, and I am afraid I have decided against the marriage."

He gripped his hands so tightly they whitened. "But why?"

Any explanation I would have given was drowned out by the noise on the street.

"Mejuffrouw Maria," Grietje shrieked. "The actors come at last! They are marching down the Nieuwe Straat. May I go watch them set up their stage?" She stopped, taking notice of my visitor.

"Excuse me, Mejuffrouw," she said, dropping her head. "I didn't mean to interrupt. But *please*," she said with a hiss, turning toward me with her hands outstretched.

"They will be here the entire week. We will go together."

She opened her mouth to object, but glanced over her shoulder at the clerk and restrained herself.

"Oh," she said, her underlip jutting out pink as a rose.

"Dinner," I reminded her. "My father will be home within the half hour." With a shrug she left the room.

"Sir." I rose, but I could not dismiss the clerk as easily as his proposal.

"I don't understand. What do you seek, Mejuffrouw van Leeuwenhoek? What better match have you fixed on? The girl is an orphan. She has no fortune."

"She has her youth. It is wealth enough. But it is not like coin or goods, it can't be loaned, returned with interest."

"With me, she would have a house. Servants of her own."

"Hie!" Grietje cried from the front door. "Throw it my way!"

With a whoop, the young boys along the canal turned on their heels and raced down the street. Grietje leaned over the latched door laughing wildly.

"I think I understand," the clerk said, blinking. "The girl, despite her appearance, is quite simple."

"Not a bit of it," I snapped, although I should have kept my peace. "But there is a wildness in her age won't tame. It makes her rail at all restraint."

"I can't believe it," he said, blinking quickly. He looked again at the Grietje's soft face, flushed with laughter, as she bent to her morning tasks.

"Simple!" Grietje protested as she readied the table after the clerk had departed and I had told her of my decision. "I may have no head for figures, but I am sure I write a clearer hand than he. But Batavia, Mejuffrouw! I would have considered it."

"He had a grasping heart. I don't think you would have left your house unless it was under his close supervision. He would hoard you closer than his wages."

"What makes you so sure, Mejuffrouw? He did not seem to scrimp on his clothes."

"But he scrimped on his ideas. Once he had one, he would not let it go, just because it was his own! It mattered not whether it was true or false."

"Batavia," Grietje said again. "I would not have minded."

"After more than half a year in a ship's cabin reeking of vomit and excrement, gnawing like a rat on hard biscuit, you would welcome anything— even your chamber here in the Golden Head."

"Even that?" Grietje laughed. "You will not go back on your word about the kermis, Mejuffrouw?" she asked me anxiously. She turned the serving platter so the smoked meat lay closest my father's plate.

"The fair?" I had thought she meant her dower. "No. But you must keep your own side of our bargain. You are not free to go until you have completed all your tasks."

"Which I have, Mejuffrouw. Just look." She waved her hands broadly, including the laid table, the swept floor, the polished windows. "You will come with me this afternoon to see the players set up their tent?"

"There are no performances until tomorrow."

"But I like to see it all begin," she said with a sigh. "I like to see it grow from nothing."

"Tomorrow."

"What am I to do with myself today?"

"Don't behave like a simpleton. You will assist Heer van Leeuwenhoek with preparing his costume. You will change the linen on the front bed so the Van Leeuwens, should they wish to rest here before they return to Rotterdam, may do so in comfort."

"Will the Molijns be coming for the grand dinner tomorrow?"

"That hasn't been determined," I said, glancing at her suspiciously.

"Surely Dr. Molijn will be pleased at my recovery."

"Surely."

"Where is that girl's mind at? She may as well go back to her sick bed for the little use she is to me." Fuming, my father mounted the stairs to my chamber. "Has she ironed my ruffles and cravat? Has she combed my wig? No? Not yet? It is five in the afternoon."

"It is longing drives her mind awry. She wants to slip to the other side of tomorrow."

"I have a good mind to set her on her way," my father said.

"You need do nothing to assist her. Her future comes apace."

"You have settled, then, on a match for her?"

"Not yet. I have decided against the clerk," I told him.

"What about Kroonevelt's journeyman?"

"Predikant Grebius' cousin comes from Leyden tomorrow."

"She'd make no predikant's wife," my father protested.

"He is, I believe, an advocate."

"You set your sights too high. She is a simple burger's serving girl and orphaned too," my father cautioned.

"You know, or should, that our talents do not derive from our position."

"You have twisted my thought, Daughter," my father said with a small smile.

"Your ability distinguishes you from other men. Why can't the same be true of Grietje?" I stopped. It would be easier to convince my father of this than it would be to convince myself.

The truth was I did not know what it was I sought for Grietje, I only knew I should recognize it if ever it happened before me. Until then, I gripped her to me as if with iron tongs.

👑 👑 👑

"Why not our journeyman?" asked Maria 'sGravelaar, the printer Kroonevelt's wife, when she came the following evening to share a cup of tea.

"Why not?" asked my cousin Rickje, who has become a frequent visitor and the person whose advice I am most ready to seek.

That night our house seemed full as the street outside. Fine gentlemen and ladies from 'sGravenhage stood gaping before my father's house as if it were a makeshift stage. Two more of the cousins Van Leeuwen from Rotterdam had arrived with their children, and their own serving girl, who sat now chattering with Grietje in the kitchen.

"This is not the time to speak of it," I said, putting down my cup with a clatter. "But your journeyman, Mevrouw Kroonvelt, intends to stay here in Delft does he not? There would be no rest for the girl. Everywhere she went, she would be recognized as a serving girl belonging once to the Golden Head."

"Is there any shame in that?"

"And he has, I believe, a weakness for gin," I said, thinking to dismiss the subject.

"I hear you rejected the clerk from Batavia because he lived too far away. And now you refuse the journeyman because he is too near. Is there no pleasing you?"

"You try me," I said sharply. "It isn't my judgement in question here."

"Of course not." Cousin Rickje bent with a smile to her knotting.

👑 👑 👑

But of course it was, although it was Grietje herself drove the question home two days later.

"What reason," she cried. "What reason lies behind your choice?"

I had forwarded the suit of Predikant Grebius's young cousin, the advocate. He would return to Groningen in July. He drove a difficult bargain, this young man, but in the end we had satisfied each other. I would increase Grietje's dower by half. He would post the banns come Sunday.

"I'll have none of it," she screamed. "I have not even set eyes upon him. Your father never served *you* so, Mejuffrouw."

"What right have you to make such comparisons?" I said angrily. "Your position here is completely opposed to mine. You're a fool if you can't see it."

Grietje came away from the window. She twisted her apron in her hands. "What would you say, Mejuffrouw, if I told you I had my heart fixed on another? Would you assist me? I'd give up my dower, everything, just—"

I sighed. I stood up. I looked over her head as I spoke. It wasn't that I feared to meet her eye, it simply tired me. "I have made what I believe is the right decision. It is a *fortunate* one as well. Why can't you grasp that, Child?"

"I have heard he has a limp, a cast in his eye."

"And a ready smile, an inquisitive air, an agile mind," I assured her.

"So has the one I have set my heart upon."

"Hush," I said. "I'll not hear of it."

But of course I did. I heard first not from Grietje's tongue but from that of my cousin Antoni.

"The child pines, Maria. Why not consider the match she wants?"

He had come out to where I sat in the small garden behind the house settling flowers in a pitcher before I brought them within.

"Yes, Maria," my Rickje said. "Why not listen?"

She sat at the table under the arbor, content to do nothing but heat herself with tea and the last sunlight.

"Would you?" I asked her. "If it were your servant girl?"

"I'd not marry her off at all—but then I'd not have reared her as my child either."

"Which I never did. I never did." For I had raised her, as I promised Heer Vallensis I would, as *our* ward. As if he still lived to share the burden and the delight.

"Will you look at that sky?" Rickje said. "Tomorrow the tents will droop, the streets will run with rain not small beer."

"Who is it?" I asked my cousin Antoni. "Who is it Grietje wishes to wed?"

He coughed once, twice, as if he'd caught a seed in his throat. "I don't know. She's not confided the particulars to me. A gentleman, she told me. A grand gentleman. He favors her, from what she says."

"To *wed*," Rickje exclaimed. "The simpleton."

"You mustn't speak so," Antoni scolded. "She is a virtuous lass. I can attest to it."

"You mean you've tested it?" Rickje smiled mischievously.

Antoni straightened himself, snorted. His pride threatened to burst his chest.

"If I'd not done my duty by her," he said coldly, "she'd be dead."

"Dead! Since when did longing kill a woman? Chastity is no disease, Antoni." Rickje smiled.

"Bah," Antoni said. "I have had enough."

"It's that new powder sympathy you're wanting, Cousin."

We waved him off.

"A gentleman," Rickje said thoughtfully. She put down her lacework. She is the same age as I, but marriage has given her a manner that imitates closely that of her mother, my dear Aunt Catharina. "Perhaps you should speak to your father, Maria. Perhaps he would agree."

"It's up to me," I said. "The decision has been left to me." I ran my hand through the flowers tumbling them loose from their array. Now they looked as if they'd come by chance and singly to my father's table, I preferred them so.

"Who is he?" Rickje insisted.

"I don't speculate. There is no limit to the girl's imagination."

Soon, there was no limit, either, to my own.

❧ ❧ ❧

"No and no and no and no," I said to Grietje when she came to my room the following evening. I was in my night dress, my hair loosed from my cap. Outside the streets were still light enough to see a pin by. Torches burned on every corner.

"Tomorrow's Thursday," she muttered. "During St. Odulphus, we can all choose our mates."

"You intend to beckon to this fine gentleman across the aisle of the church, is that it?" The mating custom felt as mad to me as beliefs about life coming from putrefaction. To ally for life with someone selected in a drunken, kermis stupor, what God would sanction this?

"There's no need," she said softly. "He attends me downstairs. I can hear him."

"*Here?* No *gentleman* waits upon my father at this hour, even during kermis."

I turned my head, but all I could hear were the voices of my father and my cousins Leeuwen and Molijn.

"You delude yourself, Grietje. There's no one here save our relations."

"Gentlemen, all of them."

"Oh Grietje! It is not my cousin Jan from Zerikzee you're eyeing. He's married as you well know. And even if he were not a close relation, he is my father's favorite. He'd not hear of it."

"If you talked with him, Mejuffrouw."

"You truly think for one minute my father would countenance adultery? Wicked!"

"The one I speak of is not married now. He said he'd talk to you, Mejuffrouw." The girl paced the room. She was still dressed in her new red cotton skirt, her India cotton underskirt and bodice. "A day and a night I've waited for you to admit to the conversation."

"You misunderstood—"

"He insisted he would speak on my behalf. I was not to worry, he said. I was to leave the matter to him."

I refused to believe what she implied.

"What dreams have you spun for yourself up there in your chamber, Grietje? Trust me." I spoke softly. "The advocate shall hear none of this.

Neither shall my cousin. My father neither. When you come from Groningen to visit, you'll be welcomed as a daughter."

"When I come from Groningen? I'd rather come from Surinam! I'd rather freeze in Stockholm!"

"I'll hear no more of it. Even if you refuse the advocate, I will still have to find you another place—in 'sGravenhage or Haarlem or Amsterdam."

"Won't you just ask him, Mejuffrouw?"

"Grietje! Why can't you grasp the truth before it grasps you? My father has worked too hard for his position in this town. I'll not let my own servant make him lose his standing."

"Why can't I raise my own? I am young. I am—"

"Incorrigible. I will hear no more. I warn you, I will not assist in my father's shame. Not for you. Not for anyone."

I rose from my table and began to pace. From now until I died, no one save me would ever be mistress here at the Golden Head, of that I would allow no doubt.

The torches caught the trees from beneath, the full moon from above. The leaves floated in the darkness, silver, a glimmering shoal of fish. Grietje too seemed to float ghost-like between the candle and the gleaming window.

"Think twice," she said. Her face looked unearthly old in the shadow. "You think it would not shame your father to hear the truth about Heer Vallensis?"

"Heer Vallensis?" I spoke slowly. My tongue seemed frozen. I had to bring all my attention upon it until I could twist it as I desired. "The mention of him *shame* my father? Heer Vallensis was an honored visitor here. My father's friend. My father remembers him with great affection."

"Would he do so if he knew—"

"What?"

"How often I accompanied you down the Oude Delft to the magistrate's house."

"Fool. I accompanied *you* to ensure your application to your lessons. Or we went together on my father's business—or my own. Just ask—"

"Who?" Grietje said with a smile I could almost hear, like ice breaking on the canal. "Who's left to vouch for you?"

"I need no one's testimonial."

"Oh no? What about that dreadful illness I nursed you through? What about that belly still swelled fatter than a blown bladder?"

"Age and surfeit, there's no mystery there."

"There are stories your father has told me. Twenty-six years a woman carried an unborn child."

"While I, my cousin says, carry a vat of wind or stinking humor. The virgin's penitence, he calls it."

"I'll not believe it."

"Nor I. "

"Nor your father."

"Certainly not," I agreed. "He's assured the weight I bear is fleshly surfeit."

"So many times you had me wait, Mejuffrouw. Not all of them, surely, were on your father's bidding. Even my Uncle Pieter began to mutter—"

"Look at me, Child." I spread my arms. "You suffer from a wild confusion. Some mad dream you wished for yourself. Heer Vallensis! It was he kept you out of the weeshuis. It was he who educated you. Why do you try and defile his memory?"

"Defile," Grietje scoffed. She slipped her finger under her cap, tucking back the loosened strands of hair. "It's not his memory I'm assailing."

"What have we here?" my father asked loudly, weaving in the doorway. "I'd thought you'd retired hours ago."

"And so we should have. Off with you, Grietje."

I waved the girl away. Grietje looked from my father's red face to my own white one. She smiled, bobbed her head.

"Until tomorrow, Mejuffrouw."

My father made way for her, but remained leaning in the doorway to my chamber.

"I hear she's refused the advocate."

"Not yet. You mustn't speak of it."

"I hear she has her eyes fixed on an unknown burgomaster."

"You never know," I said, laughing sharply. "It might be a noble—or our dour Grand Pensionary. It might be an apothecary. A gentleman is all she will say."

"The girl has great tenacity," my father teased. "Before you know, she'll grind your no into a yes."

I shook my head.

"She's met her match. I am Maria, Antoni's daughter. I have vast patience. This at least you have passed on to me."

"Don't grieve so," he said angrily. "The girl's a fool and better out of the house. Choose someone. Anyone. But don't delay."

"I'd be happier if I knew for certain I am choosing the right one."

"You presume to know the future, Daughter! Certainty is denied us, but every one of us has a right to his own thesis."

"Grietje too," I said slowly.

"In the end we make our own beds," my father said angrily. "We are forced to lie there."

"But we send our servants to bottle up the fleas that torment us. Oh, Father, it is as hard for you as it is for me to see her go."

"Hmm!" My father coughed, clapping his hand to his chest. "I am an old man. I will be gone before I have had a chance to relish the peace."

"You! Like the child, you feed on tumult."

"And you, Daughter," my father asked, turning unsteadily in the doorway. "What the devil nourishes you?"

"Your honor," I said quickly. "Your love."

"Hmm."

As I turned the lock in my door I heard him lumber through to his own chamber clumsy as a blindman. I sighed. I did not believe for a second I had taken him in.

I went to my own cabinet and opened it. From under the shifts I drew out another key which I used to open a small casket. I drew out the sheet of paper I'd stored therein. Sitting in my bed, I drew the candle dangerously close, but the testament Mister Vallensis had left me written in ink made from that magical stone was as invisible then as it had been years before when I unwrapped it, a month too late, from my father's glass. I studied it as eagerly as ever I had done. The only marks I could read there were inscribed by my own tears.

♕ ♕ ♕

"And what do you think of that?" I asked Grietje as we left the tent of the hermaphrodite.

"Monstrous," she said crossly. "Besides, he's shamming. I heard it from a boy who sneaked under his skirt this morning. It's just padding, and shaving, and clothing cut to delude the foolish."

I laughed. I could not help it. The girl was a perfect parrot. I could hear my cousin's stutter trip easily from her tongue.

"But *this* one, Mejuffrouw. I think he knows his business. He's come all the way from Brandenburg." She led me over to a stool and table set beneath an umbrella spread out to one side of the acrobats' stage. Here a tall man in a sober suit of brown wool, a collar cleaner than our predikant's, a wide beaver with a luxurious red feather, stood talking quietly with our townspeople.

Beside him, the acrobats in their bright ragged pantaloons, their bright shirts mottled with the heat of the day and their own exertions, scrambled upon each other's shoulders eager as kittens. They growled and squeaked, howled and laughed the while. The hurdy gurdy player marked a different measure, but it didn't matter. Nothing could be heard clearly above the din of the townspeople, greeting each other, directing the eyes of their friends and neighbors toward one booth, away from another.

"Have you seen the elephant by the Schiespoort?"

"I almost drowned when it decided to relieve itself."

"The dealer from 'sGravenhage is here with many engravings. He's set up on the corner of the market close to the Oude Langendijk."

"As far as can be from St. Lucas, you mean?"

"He has copies of the King's entry into England, his victory at the Boyne."

"And Namur? "

"The destruction of the French fleet at La Hogue?"

"The Queen's funeral?"

"Don't—"

"Shh. Listen to the man. Can you make out what he's saying? Push closer will you?"

Grietje gripped my hand as we were forced—like sap through the thinnest vein—out into the open.

"Come closer," the tall man whispered. He sported, contrary to our fashion, a fine black beard. His hands, white and soft as my father's, or any gentleman unused to hard labor, waved weakly, like grasses in a dying wind. We did as he bid us, and he smiled, showing small even teeth. His eyes were black, bright as beads, and wedged deep inside his face.

"What ails you, Mejuffrouw?"

I tapped Grietje's hand in warning, but she ignored me. She stepped forward, lifted her head high, not with pride, but to enable her to speak confidentially.

"Stone?" he repeated. He stood back and let his eyes run over her fine white neck, her tight red bodice, her white apron and colorful skirt of India cotton. "At your age, I can hardly credit it."

"Neither can my master, sir. But the physician insists—"

"Ah yes, ah yes." He looked to right and left, his eyes sweeping the crowd. "But you've come to me instead. My powder has amazed the learned men in Leyden. It has left them speechless. Here I have discovered a substance that can correct any imbalance in the blood. One draught and the acid is dulled, the alkali sharpened, salts are dissolved, vapors given substance. It even serves as a love potion, Mejuffrouw, although I can't imagine in your case it would be necessary." He looked directly into Grietje's eyes as he spoke, and this last insolence was uttered with a hissing intimacy.

I stepped between them.

"What are your degrees?" I asked angrily. "Have you studied medicine? Surgery? "

"These days it is unnecessary. Surely you should know."

"I?"

"Are you not the daughter of the wise Van Leeuwenhoek? Hasn't he discovered more in his house here in Delft than all the learned men in Leyden, Harderwijck, Montpelier, and Angiers?"

"He doesn't stand here on the market square deluding young children with false hopes, that much is certain."

"False? you speak more rashly than I imagine that great man ever would. I will give you gratis a bottle of my precious powder."

"What is it?" Grietje asked, putting out her hand and taking the bottle before I could stop her.

"Sympathy is what it is called. You might ask the illustrious Van Leeuwenhoek if he can distinguish with his glasses the source of its great power. I myself," he bent his head modestly, "can't explain. I can only attest to the fact."

"Doesn't matter," Grietje said, tugging the cork from the bottle and giving it a sniff. "As long as it heals as you suggest."

But the man had turned and was scratching something on a piece of paper with a narrow chalk. He handed this at last to Grietje.

"I have given you instructions. Don't lose them."

Grietje tucked them in her pocket along with the vial of powder that the charlatan called sympathy. She made no move to leave.

"We must not keep his expertise to ourselves," I said, giving her a little push. Others pressed us from all sides. We had to force ourselves away.

Upon their stage, the acrobats stood now in a single, high, wavering pile. A woman came and lifted up a young boy dressed in similar motley. He came only as far as the first man's shoulders. The crowd jeered. With an angry look, the boy scrambled from the woman's arms and ran to the side of the stage where a tall fat Moorish man stood with his foot on the edge of a wide plank balanced over a narrow barrel. The boy scrambled up onto the far side of the plank. He stood with his arms outstretched, wavering slightly as if he were sighting waves over the prow of a ship.

"Hie!" bellowed the great bare-chested Moor. He slammed his foot down on the board and the boy flew head over heels, heels over head, up and up. The crowd screamed as he rose, screamed even louder when he seemed ready to pass the fluttering outstretched arms of his older brother. But the boy's hands gripped the small child's heels. The men beneath grunted and turned red with concentration. The human tower bent like a tree in a high wind.

Then to hurrahs all round, the little boy steadied himself, raised his arms, stretched out his hands as if to clasp the sun, or failing that, the swooping sparrow. Then, with a wild hulloa, they all tumbled heads over heels safely to the ground.

"Sympathy," Grietje murmured. She had her back to the stage and was peering futilely through the crowd for another glimpse of the charlatan. "I hope it proves as powerful as he promised."

She pulled the bottle from her pocket. She held it to the sun, shook it questioningly. "There doesn't seem to be very much."

"You intend to take it then? Dissolved in one huge draught? More fool you, Child. More fool you."

"Not at all," she said, tucking it back into her pocket. "Besides, neither your father or the Doctor Molijn seem able to come to any agreement—why should not this learned man from Germany be equally certain?"

"Learned! why can't you see what's before your eyes?" I gestured toward the empty stage, the tents filled with terrible curiosities.

"Me?" she said. "I see clearly enough. Why can't you? All week I've been watching people walking with a lighter step, no stitch in their side, no pain in their head, all because of this wonderful powder of his. I'd be a fool not to taste it myself."

"Next I know you'll let someone dig the stone out of you."

"Never," Grietje said staunchly. "This will dissolve it, you heard him say so, from within. It is powerful, I'm sure, as your father's China tea."

"You'll not mention this in the same breath!" Without warning I was wildly angry. Above the crowd I saw the charlatan's broad brown hat, the red feather rippling like a flag. *This* was the man my father called a big blunt braggart, this handsome man whispering softly in Latin?

"It is easier to follow than the Doctor Molijn's prescription. I will show it to him for fun." Grietje waved the paper the charlatan had given her. "I will even show it to your father."

But Grietje did more than that. She tried to impose the medicine itself upon my father. That evening, she slipped some of the powder into his mug along with his beer. When I discovered her, she screamed with fear. I grabbed her by the nape of the neck.

"You'll drink that yourself, Child." I brought the glass to her lips. "If not I'll bring you before the schout, I promise you."

Grietje turned her head back and forth, wild with fright. "It would not harm him, Mejuffrouw. *I* would not harm him. It's not what I intended."

"My father is in perfect health. What could you have meant to cure him of?"

"Indifference," the girl sobbed. "His cold, cold heart."

She gagged as I forced the mug to her lips, but I insisted.

"If it works as the German suggested, changing its nature with the nature of the disease, it will serve as well to squelch your ardor as to incite my father's."

"Nothing," my father insisted. "It does nothing. Inspect it if you wish beneath my glass."

But Grietje, her white face green around the eyes, the edges of her lips, rushed again out of doors.

"Simple surfeit," my father said.

"You'll never convince her it is harmless as caudle."

When I led her to her bed, she leaned weakly against me.

"Tomorrow I will invite the Predikant and his cousin to the house. Sunday we'll hear the banns read out."

"Have pity, Mejuffrouw," Grietje protested, yawning wildly.

"I intend to increase your dower," I said, kissing her forehead. "If all goes well, I'll treat your firstborn as my heir."

"I'll not hear of it."

"It's *I* won't hear," I said.

In the morning I brought Grietje a package wrapped in brown paper.

"Open it," I said as I seated myself by her bed.

She tested it with her hands.

Her face sagged. "No gown?"

I laughed. "I will provide you with one on your wedding day. But this is worth more than ten ells of silk. Open it."

"What is this?" she asked, pulling the paper from the canvas.

She turned it to the light. "For a moment I thought it was the one you kept hidden in your own sleeping place."

"This is more valuable. It is not a single face."

"Yes, yes. I can see that. It is Mevrouw Swalmius who sits there with the lute on her lap is it not? And who is the serving girl? Why, is that you, Mejuffrouw?" She put her hand to her lips, tapping back the laughter as if it were a yawn.

I stared at the painting which I had kept hidden for years. My father had added it to those auctioned to settle Johannes Vermeer's estate. Cornelia had protested, but he was adamant. If he was selling off the others, he was selling this one too. He wanted no accusations of personal benefit from Catharina Bolnes or her mother. I had my Aunt de Mey secure it for me secretly. She did not need to ask me why. She knew how much I hated it. She found a third person to bid for her. We kept it at her house until shortly before her death, and then I secreted it among my own possessions. I refused to have the world see me so subservient. I refused to see myself so. But I had not been able to destroy it. I had no trouble giving it to Grietje as part of her dower. For her, the painting might hold another meaning. That maid clearly did not accept her place. Besides, in time there may be profit in it, for the prices his paintings commanded in May at an auction in Amsterdam were greater than what either Cornelia or my Aunt De Mey had paid.

"It was painted by a famous painter. Vermeer, his name was. Johannes Reynierszoon," I told Grietje. "You put that with your chest of linens."

"You look older then than you do now, Mejuffrouw," she said trying to humor me. "But Mevrouw Leeuwenhoek looks like a child."

"She was nearer forty when she posed for this. I can remember the day. It was the same time of year, just after kermis. She was telling us what the fortune teller read in her palm."

"She always forbade me to visit them."

"My father soon taught her their predictions were useless."

"He reserves his faith for dowsers." Grietje scrutinized the picture again. "This was not painted in this house, Mejuffrouw. You've never lined your walls with leather."

"Heer Vermeer ran a tavern, The Mechelen."

"A *tavern*, Mejuffrouw. And your father let you and his wife visit there?"

"The times were different, Grietje. He was a respectable man, Vermeer, headman of the St. Lucas Guild more than once."

"All the same, you've grown nicer with your father's fame."

"And why *not*? Haven't you grown nicer since coming to live with us?"

"For what purpose?" Grietje asked, smiling mischievously.

She had, she believed, driven her point neatly home.

"To marry a young advocate from Groningen. To be fruitful and multiply. What more could an orphan girl—what more could anyone want?" Again I was as angry as I had been the evening before coming upon her in the kitchen slipping that useless powder into my father's glass of beer. It was her simplicity enraged me. Her hope.

"I don't want to be unhappy, Mejuffrouw."

I started to laugh at the girl's foolery, but recalled myself.

"You'll be unhappier by far in the Spinhuis, Grietje. This energy you have in such excess will serve you ill if not restricted. Already you are misunderstood by those around you—your loose tongue used as proof of loose ways. To better your place in the world, you must change your circumstances, start afresh—but to keep it, my child, you must develop and practice probity. All this is possible with the advocate from Groningen. He'll not destroy your high spirits—but he will help you channel them. Why can't you see your good fortune?"

"Fortune?" the girl protested." I have earned my place here in the Golden Head. I have earned my right to choose my future."

"Grietje! What gave you that idea, Child? Who among us has that power? Did Mevrouw Swalmius choose her barrenness? Does my father even now *choose* the truth that his glasses will reveal?"

"You chose Heer Vallensis," she said. "I have thought back on it again and again in my mind, and I am certain there existed some understanding between the two of you."

"Understanding! Of course there was." I stood up and walked to the door, turned around. "We knew, both of us, that our town is not built on alliances of that sort."

"Pardon me, Mejuffrouw, but I must speak of it. I saw the way you regarded him. I saw the way he watched you enter a room. Surely I was not mistaken. All my days here I have dreamed, Mejuffrouw, of what might have happened should he have lived."

"You speak something worse than foolishness."

"You *taught* me," she said stubbornly. "You taught me to believe I'd find my place, my elevation, here." Grietje sat high in her bed, her gold hair falling in tangled strands below her shoulders. She closed her hands within each other.

"Here?" I asked aghast. "Here in the Golden Head? You were gravely mistaken. I have never intended that." Her shocking intimations of yesterday revived. Had I indeed understood her right? It could not, ever, be spoken of directly.

"In your *heart*. I felt you had taken me into your heart."

"And so I have. But I believe, like my father, we are born with our destiny intact within us. The only choice we have is to listen. Or to refuse to."

"Who are you to say I am not listening." She slipped out of bed with a sniff. She pulled her skirt on, and looked up at me as she buttoned her bodice. "Your father is a great man. No one in our whole city would deny it. But he is nothing by birth. Nothing but a servant to the burgomasters. What makes you think my birth is humbler? Or my fate?"

"My father is an extraordinary man. You cannot build a life upon his example."

"So you wish me to believe. But who is to say that God hasn't intended me, like your father, for great things? I could nurture a king's babe as well as an advocate's."

"Is *that* what you've learned from living among us?"

I looked at the picture Grietje had left lying upon her bed. For a minute I could not remember what had filled our hearts that afternoon at the Mechelen so many years ago. Then it all came back to me in a whirl. Cornelia's hope at the fortune teller's prediction, her sister's hard laughter. Catharina Bolnes' pleasure in my humiliation, Johannes unbearable patience with the brush. Where had any of that brought us?

"Maria!" my father cried from downstairs. "What hinders you? I need my tea." His voice was scratchy, even at this distance.

"Poor Heer van Leeuwenhoek," Grietje said with a laugh. She tucked her hair under her cap, tied on her apron. "He drank too deeply last night."

"So did you."

"But I relieved myself immediately. While he has let it stew all night, only to drive the distressing salts out this morning with the aid of his tea— through his veins, his flesh, his tender skin. See, Mejuffrouw," she flashed a smile as she gave her comforter a tug, "not everything has been lost on me."

"So I see," I said, but already she was racing down the stairs to do my father's bidding.

I followed more slowly, my hand to my hip, trying to slow the heavy, remorseless knocking in my side.

⮞⳯❨16❩⳯⮜

POWDER OF SYMPATHY

I was not home that afternoon when Predikant Grebius brought his cousin to the Golden Head. I had been called to the bedside of Gerrit, the engraver's apprentice. I have yet to piece out exactly what was said. I only know the results, glittering and bright as splintered glass.

Grietje was absent also when they arrived. She was bent on my business, she told my father. She left my father, against his wishes or his expectations, bent on hers.

"Why didn't you tell me," he reprimanded me when I returned.

"I informed you of everything, Father. It is my practice."

"Not that you'd meant to marry her off within the month."

"You weren't listening! I can feel my tongue shape the very words, Father."

"You did not tell me he was a simpleton."

"I would not tell you so this minute."

"I met him, Maria. A cast in his eye, a simpering mouth."

"Father, you did not forbid it?" I sat down, dizzied by the heat, the rush of air my father created with his endless pacing.

"He said the marriage might appear beneath him, save for the beauty and industry of the young woman, which he had observed himself, and the honor of her connection with the famous Heer van Leeuwenhoek. I told him, why should I not, that the fame would not rub off. He'd get exactly what he'd contracted for. A pretty girl in good health—a body broad enough for easy childbirth, should the Creator have so determined. It was dower enough, I said."

"Father, you have done harm. I promised him—"

"So I then heard." My father glared at me with his bright, stony blue eyes. "Half your own fortune," he said.

"Not exactly." I relaxed then, but only momentarily. "I give her her well-earned wages, which I have matched with earnings of my own. I give her the chest Aunt Maria de Mey prepared for me years ago. The linens are still good. It's not very much, Father." I shrugged. My breath was quick and shallow. The air today was thicker than our blood; it took all my strength to gulp it down. "It's not much at all after what she's done for us."

"He says you've promised to treat their first child as your heir—"

"Why not?"

"She's not kindred to me or mine. I'll not have my own hard labor squandered on another man's child."

"What I have earned, what I've inherited is mine to bequeath."

My father paced the room. He was in his shirt sleeves and his brown cloth vest. He had hung his periwig over the back of his chair. His baldpate shone with sweat, as did his gray furred chest, visible beneath his drooping cravat, as did his full cheeks, his sagging neck.

"I am not an elephant to be clambered upon. I am not to be asked to shift the whole burden myself," he shouted.

"You make no sense, Father. Are you ill?" I looked at his pale face, the beads standing out bright as diamonds across his chest, glittering on the tip of his nose. It was then I realized it was true, that my father himself wished with his whole heart to do what the advocate from Groningen considered reluctantly.

"He is not good enough for her," he said angrily.

"For that beggared *orphan*! Oh Father, no wonder we have turned that girl's head right around."

He passed his hand over his head, collecting the sweat from his naked crown as easily as raindrops from the gutter's rim. "It's that numbskull I protest at. Why should he be given such an opportunity?"

I opened my mouth to retort, but I could not. I burst into tears instead.

♛ ♛ ♛

I sobbed like a small child. But not for Grietje. Never for Grietje.

"What is it, Daughter?" My father stood above me, shaking my shoulder hard enough to make my head ache. "What makes you carry on so?"

"It's Gerrit," I said, wiping my face. "The draughtsman's apprentice.

Nothing our cousin could do could save him."

"Gerrit! Why only last month he was in the best of health, wasn't he? I'd several specimens all prepared. I was waiting until the end of kermis. What was it—fever?"

"He burned, surely. But it was a wasting disease. By today he was nothing but bone and skin. Oh, it was dreadful to contemplate."

"Why was I not informed?"

"It was my own presence was requested."

"Since when have you taken upon yourself to nurse the sick?"

"I don't nurse them, Father. I measure the still body, the coffin, for the shroud and underlining, provide the bombazine to drape the mirrors and the bed. It is my trade they ask for at the last, Father, not your art." I began to cough and could not stop.

"When did he begin to sicken? Why wasn't I told?"

"What purpose would that have served? They called in Cousin Antoni two weeks ago. He has purged and bled the boy each day with no result. The strife in his blood defied all human remedy."

"Strife! If they had shown me some of his blood, I'm sure I would have discovered a thickening, a blockage. They should have fed him, not drained away his little strength."

"I am no physician, Father. Do not argue with me. They tried everything. Even sympathy."

"Sympathy!" My father started up angrily. "My godson participates in that fraud does he?"

"Calm yourself. The draughtsman's wife prescribed it."

"To no purpose, evidently. It is a dreadful loss."

"We all feel it."

"I more than most, wouldn't you say?" asked Grietje from the door. Her cheeks were pink with the heat, giving her a guilty air.

"How dare you—" My father turned on her wild in his agitation. All said, he'd liked the boy, even with his wittling vision, his volatile sorrow.

"It's my marriage you've called off, isn't it? I heard you myself, Heer van Leeuwenhoek." Grietje forced her lips down but she couldn't remove the sparkle from her eye, or the easy drunken swagger from her hips. "Just when you'd so nearly brought me round, Mejuffrouw Maria! Your father spun me back to my original position. The cast in his eye, Mejuffrouw, was impossible. And the twist in his lips, even your father could not endure it. Imagine me!

Day after day, night after night."

I observed the girl's disheveled hair, her spotted skirt with disgust.

"It's Gerrit we speak of Grietje. The child died but an hour past."

"I heard he sickened apace," she said, suddenly sullen. "I saw his master's wife this very morning. She said no physician could save him."

"Which is why she turned to the pedlars, eh?" My father clapped his hat on. He was off, I was sure of it, to the meadows. At his age, the death of the young was almost impossible to contemplate. He behaved the same should he hear of the sickness of one of the Van Leeuwens or their children, even the brats of my cousin Antoni, and the children and grandchildren of his acquaintances and friends. This intolerance never ceased to amaze me, for he could calmly contemplate the number of dead at Steenkirke and Neerwinden, he could insist on the manifold deaths of the male animalcules that defied the imagination of so many. God's will, he said loudly as King Louis. *God's will.*

But let him have seen a single child draw breath, take a teat, a step. Let him observe, even, the loins it was delivered from or the loins it had originated in—and everything dissolved. His calculations flickered and died out like that magic fire. There was only this relentless agitation in his legs, an irresistible restlessness. He found it as difficult as the rest of us to accept that Nature favored us all with equal, cruel prodigality, fish and fowl, fruit louse and fen mussel, child of the burger, child of the King, people of Holland, people of Spain, women, men. The price of every life, however brief, is identical—and never forfeit.

☙ ☙ ☙

My father's walk through the town to the nearby meadow did nothing to relieve him. He returned more agitated than when he'd left.

"Can you imagine what I have just discovered," he said.

He raised a packet above his head.

"I won't even attempt it," I said.

"*This,*" my father cried, tearing off the paper. I found it at a pedlar's stall on the market square, just sitting upon the pots and pans. Right next to that braggart German quack. He stabbed at the painting I had given Grietje that morning. "My own dear wife. Who could do this?"

He didn't even see me in there. "It passed from us years ago," I said. "At your insistence, if I recall. God knows who has sought to garner profit now, but surely it is in their right. His paintings still rise in value.'

"*My* wife," he said again, clutching that ugly painting to his chest. "They said the person selling it looked like a serving maid. Five florins was all she asked. God knows from where she stole it. But it isn't fitting. Cornelia out there for all the world to see."

Yes, Cornelia, all those years ago. *Simpering.*

"What did they ask of you to retrieve it?"

My father paused, his face reddened. "Once he knew its value to me, he wouldn't part with it for less than fifty-five. He would have gone for forty but that German whispered in his ear."

"Let me help you hang it in your bed chamber," I said. "If Cornelia still breathed, she would be pleased to know it mattered so to you. I hope it serves to console you."

"Tell me again," I said to Grietje. "What was it drove you to this? A pedlar on the square. Why couldn't you have waited until you were in Groningen to sell it?"

"The sound of his voice, Mejuffrouw, that ugly advocate. Whish, whish. Like the sea it was. I'd not let it wash me away without a struggle. I had to escape it."

It was ten o'clock now but the full moon, the torches in the market square made candles unnecessary. In any case, it wasn't light we needed to make things clear.

"Wash you away? It's you threw yourself away. My father had decided to keep you with us, Grietje. But we can't keep you now. You must accept that. If he found out it was you who sold it, found out how cheaply you hold us—"

"Accept what? How cheaply you hold me, Mejuffrouw Maria! I set my own price, thank you. I will embrace my freedom more fully than ever you dared embrace your own."

"Freedom," I sighed. "Ah, Child, you really are lost to us if you believe that."

There is no freedom in this life, all my experience has served to convince me of this. There is something more—because there is something less.

Gerrit knew this. Grasping my hand, his forehead weighted with a glittering crown of sweat, he did his best to speak of it.

"I can't get it out of my head, Mejuffrouw. The little fen mussels turning and turning, merrily as tops, in all that blue water. Upside down and right side up, it made no difference, they each kept their own measure, their perfect distance within their sacs.

"Sometimes I see everything, Mejuffrouw, as if it were fixed behind such a lens. Not just the ones your father's made, Mejuffrouw, the ones the Creator fixed within us before our birth, at the very beginning of time, before man had time for wickedness. I think he meant them to be used as your father does the ones he's crafted—to turn the world round right.

"We have believed such lies, Mejuffrouw. It pains me to think on it. Then I think of those eyes of the crane fly your father showed me, and I must laugh. There are so many of us struggling to walk with our feet in the air, our heads on the ground. Upside down, Mejuffrouw," he said, smiling weakly. "You know what I mean."

"I do, Gerrit. But you must rest now, reserve your strength."

The boy shrugged. His face was little more than a skull save for the large eyes, as luminous and weak as Heer Vallensis' had once been. I wept. I wanted those eyes of his to last as long as my father's glasses. I wanted them to last forever. I knew better. The lens we call crystalline lasts little longer than our skin. Unlike our skin, it does not protect us. It lets everything in.

"Poor Gerrit," I said. I held his hand close between my own.

"One thing grieves me, Mejuffrouw. It's not that I mind leaving this world. It is God's will, I can feel it. But I take so many with me, Mejuffrouw. I can't help but regret that."

"What?" I looked over to my cousin Antoni, but he was busy talking to the boy's master and did not notice the child's quick slide into delirium.

"You go alone, Gerrit," I whispered. "The Creator will close you in his arms like a long lost son."

"Won't He ask me, Mejuffrouw, why I did not finish my appointed tasks? I can't deny it. I did not save the life of a single one." The boy's eyes were closed now. Tears ran down his face.

"The Creator will embrace you, Child. I am sure of it."

"I have felt them quicken within me, Mejuffrouw. Just like your father said. I have heard them plead for release. It would have pleased Him, wouldn't it, to know we each repeated His will in an unbroken line from Adam."

"My child," I said, "think nothing—"

"I harbor so many," he whispered. "Your father has proven that over and over. I can't understand why the Creator would sacrifice us so freely unless—"

"Unless He was lonely. Unless He longed for your company. In His arms every father becomes the son, every son the chosen one. Life never ends. It just completes itself."

"It is the truth, and I accept it, but I can't see it, Mejuffrouw, without grief. It's the same figure turned topsy turvy in every one of the dragonfly's eyes. It's the same black shroud masking the same corpse a hundred times over. It grieves me I wasn't wise or strong enough to secure for them a moment of this world's felicity."

"No man is," I said.

He began to cough, a sound weirdly low, soft as an infant's snore. And then he was no more.

🐚 🐚 🐚

"We are none of us to blame," I announced to my father the next morning. I pressed the paper out flat upon the mantel. It had been delivered minutes before. I had just climbed down from Grietje's chamber, my father had gone to the garden to search for her there. The boy who passed the letter to me through our opened door was one of those from whom we had once procured vermin. He waited hopefully.

"I have more," he said, scratching under his arm.

"Not today," I gestured him away briskly. "My father completed those observations. He's considered the matter to his satisfaction."

"Another time?" the child asked wistfully. His face was crusted with dirt, but his eyes glittered, clearer than my father's.

"Perhaps, perhaps," I said. I shook the paper. It was not just Grietje's handwriting I'd recognized, but the sheet itself, napped like velvet from its frequent handling. "Where did you get this child?"

"At the Haguespoort. A grand lady, Mejuffrouw. She repeated the name over and over again. *Van Leeuwenhoek*. I was to give it to Mejuffrouw Maria at the Golden Head. She was dressed in bright blue silk. She had a black cape with a hood. A grand lady."

"Her name?"

Under the grime, the boy's face pinkened. "I asked her, but she spoke to me quite sharply. It was none of my concern, she said. Besides, she intended to change it for a better as soon as possible."

"For your trouble," I said, dropping a doit in his filthy hand.

"But don't you come back," I yelled after him. "Don't you ever let me see your face again."

"If ever I catch a glimpse of him," my father said wrathfully, "I'll set upon him with my walking stick."

"It would serve no purpose. It would not return her to us. Nothing can do that."

"I don't want her back again. If she ever sets foot upon the ramparts, I'll have her clapped in the yoke. She's shamed me before everyone."

"How? It's her own life she's taken into her hands. Not ours."

"You don't believe that," my father said quickly, but he peered at me suspiciously. "Of all the people she might fancy, why him?"

"Can't you imagine?" I was amused for the first time. "Like you, he promised to open new worlds for her. He promised to lead her through them."

"That charlatan! What does he know of anything. He's as unfamiliar with the ancients as he is with the learned men of the day. He knows nothing. Nothing. As if a single powder could repair us all. *Sympathy!*"

I put my hands to my ears. It was not just within the house that my father's voice echoed; it rang on the quiet street, in the passages between our houses. The first Sunday after kermis, hours after dawn the town remained buried in a drunken stupor.

"Let me see the letter. What does she say again?"

"They intend to visit the Great Elector's court in Brandenburg, then they will go to Vienna, and on to Italy."

"To visit with the great Magliabechi?" my father sneered.

"No, with Cosimo III," I said, laughing in spite myself.

"Then to France to see if sympathy can stop the hole in the roof of the French King's mouth."

"They'd do better to stop his heart."

"Perhaps they will. You could recommend them to that pretty, wicked duchess, what was her name?"

"Mancini," my father said reluctantly. "Have you no modesty?"

"Modesty?" They could not, of course, be mentioned in the same breath, the duchess, the whore. I shook my head. I tucked the letter again into my pocket. My father did not notice. Already his thoughts were otherwise occupied.

"I carry the coffin for Gerrit," he said. "At my own request. Already I suffer the boy's absence. I don't know who I will find to replace him."

"Perhaps you'll find someone whose sight accords more easily with your own."

"Perhaps I won't," my father said, chewing on his lower lip. The very question distressed him more bitterly than either child's departure. With a grunt of exasperation, he left the room. He closed himself in his closet.

Mounting the stairs to my chamber, I felt giddy with relief. Securing the door, I drew out the paper the girl had sent me. Singing softly to myself, I went to the window and opened it wide. The church bells stirred the still air. I could see people making their way slowly down the Hippolytusbuurt towards the Oude Kirke. I could see them, loyal and staid as those making their way in the other direction, down the Nieuwe Straat, the Voldersgracht, toward the Nieuwe Kirke. My chest rattled with laughter.

I rubbed at the faint tracings with my finger. Of course the girl had not written to us as shamelessly as I pretended.

Forgive me, she pleaded. *I see no other way. He promises to marry me as soon as we settle somewhere long enough to post banns. Should I have a daughter, I will name her after you, Mejuffrouw. You need not serve as godmother, for I'll treat her here on earth with your own tenderness. It is all that matters.*

Forgive me. I could not leave without your glass. My little knowledge of your father's art is dower enough he says—but he'd not take me without it.

With a sigh I turned the paper over. I tried for the last time to make out the words Vallensis had scratched with that ink my father had made from the dissolution of his mysterious stone. At first I thought something indeed had become clear, but the dark misshapen spot travelled with me across the soft, stained sheet. For a moment I feared I had blinded myself, as the curious have, staring fearlessly into the sun. But it was only a fleck of dust blown in through the window. The tear it elicited washed it out and proved the truth to me.

There was nothing to be gained from preserving this paper worn softer than cloth with fruitless longing. All worth had always been, as Grietje herself saw, locked inside the brass case, inside my father's rough untutored handiwork.

I took another simple glass, the kind I use to examine the threads of silk and serge, and, standing by the window, I used it to concentrate the sun's own fire. I held it where I thought his pen might first have rested. Hope is insatiable, insatiable as the flame which did not leap as I had wished out of the invisible letters themselves. It tattered the edges of the paper like wind tatters a flag, like labor tatters the rags of the poor, like war tatters the fine uniforms of the soldiers, like water tatters the very flesh of fish and drowned men. Up there in my chamber, nothing was revealed to me. Everything was consumed, everything that mattered. Hope and doubt and, at last, that wrenching hunger.

The silence here in the Golden Head in the weeks before you arrived—Child, I shudder to think of it. The animals only made it worse. I kept King Louis covered a week. I woke at dawn and tossed seed among the fowl to keep the cock from crowing. Seriously! The laughter from the street tumbling in through our open door made my father and I both look up, dry eyed, breathless. We were old, Child. That is what my father and I realized. We had nothing to live for. Life had deserted us without a word.

But if anyone had dared to come, we would not have admitted him, even the King of England. Indeed, every time the barge was due to arrive from Rotterdam or 'sGravenhage, my father disappeared. It was his duties, he insisted, called him to the stadthuis. It was his duties drove him up and down the Oude Delft, the Wijn Straat, the Doelen Straat. His study was too hot, he said. He couldn't rest there. But it was his pride gave him fever, not the air, not the wind blowing continually from the sea up over Goeree, Brill, and the River Maas.

My father stalked the streets, but he sought no one. Well, yes, he did. He sought the utter stranger who had never heard of his tribulations, never heard of the inconvenient peach louse, or of Grietje, or Cornelia. I suggested he go to Rotterdam to see his godson Phillip van Leeuwen, but he refused, as he refused to go to Zeeland to see his nephew Jacob. He was bitterly ashamed.

He felt his theories had assisted Grietje in her wicked folly.

An entire fortnight each us twisting inside our misery like a worm in its cocoon. What do you think emerged? *More of the same!* At our ages, there's no place for transformation. What use have we with wings? What eggs have we to lay in obscure places? At our ages, cocoons! We were, I believe, more like the little peach lice, slipping out of one dry skin already wearing our next, identical one.

On the eleventh of July, my father picked up his pen again. He wrote to the famous burgomaster in Amsterdam, Nicolaes Witsen. He thanked him for the map of Muscovy—a great curiosity—and the knot of rock containing veins of silver and gold from a cave in Tartary. My father believes the precious vein was made by vapors forced from the heaving core of the earth like steam from a hearth pot, like sweat from the skin of a man dying of fever.

My father, after dinner, wrote Heer Witsen again. He wrote upon the model he had had constructed years before to demonstrate the truth of the earth's motion. Years ago he had given one to the late Heer Christiaan Huygens, who appeared delighted with the same. My father had more than enough to spare. Even now, six of the glass globes sit on the mantel in his closet waiting for my father to lift them down, swing them in the air like a child churns a whirligig.

Inside the glass globe, my father has strung a small lead ball. He has surrounded it by water and wax. When the lead ball turns, the wax pushes out through the water to the rim of the glass sphere. The lead ball spins free in the center. If the Universe, as the Papists insist, turned from East to West each day around the motionless earth, wax would coat our dead globe, clouds and water would rest on the earth, tight as the lid rests on the sleeping eye. But the universe, my father agrees with Heer Huygens, is like the glass sphere that rests motionless in my father's lap while his hands work the string. It is the earth's motion reveals the sun to us each morning, dims the moon, exposes the evening star. It is the earth's incessant revolution gives us room to breathe.

Motion delights my father. It is the unmistakable signal of the Creator's presence, here, on earth, among the animalcules, the insects, the beasts of the field, the fishes, the birds. The same power that drives the shoots out of the earth, the leaves from the tips of the branches, is present as well in the dizzying turn the Creator gave our whole world, this endless revolution that serves, like our own eagerness, to make everything clear.

Everything but my own thought!

Have patience, Child, and listen close. I feel what I am groping for eludes me as the mouse eludes the cat's paw, *of its own will*—not like the wax in the globe, driven off by the indifferent violence the lead offers to the water.

My thought returns to the fen mussels that so delighted my father, Gerrit, and me last fall. Each unborn fen mussel turned within its own sack like the lead ball turns within that globe of glass. As if suspended by a string, these unborn fen mussels kept continually a perfect distance from every point on the membrane.

"What a miracle!" my father cried.

"What a mystery," whispered Gerrit. He loved it best when the shell narrowed thin as a needle, then tipped over again, revealing its broad back. "It never tires."

The boy relinquished the glass at last with a guilty smile. I was just the same, Child. I could not take my eyes off the little creatures. Imagine, if you can, instead of smaller young within them, tiny pearls, turning in equally lucid sacks. Imagine little bits of sand ground finer than my father's glasses turning and turning until they are lenses, making everything clear. Inmost knowledge.

The fen mussels never tired, but my eyes began to burn. I handed the glass again to the boy. I can still see his smile. I can feel his head twist in the air between us. I can remember what my father said next.

"A learned gentleman just wrote me to say these animals come from the apple trees. From the exhalation of the fruit. That's not all. He says life comes not from like but from these exhalations. It comes, he declares like so many, from putrefaction. I can't fathom it. Life does not come from death. I am convinced of this. No child takes its life from the stench of a rotting corpse. How could we ever believe so?"

Life comes from life, I would never deny it. I believe my father has proved that the life that turns within us like the fen mussel turns within its watery sack is not our own. It was left there by the Omnipotent just as the fly fills the dead man with its own eggs. Like Gerrit, I believe that each death takes us back to the Creation and it takes us to the end of time. I believe it is the grief of the unborn within us that cause the terrible stench of death. We must not condemn ourselves. We are not alone. The same hand that filled my father's loins, the testicles of the cockchafer, the bull, the thunderpad just as, mysteriously, filled the belly of the peach louse, the beard of the oyster, the ovary of the eel, and, yes, you hear me say this, the ovaries of women.

Forgive me, Child. I can't go on. Let me sit a minute and catch my breath. Some days this weight I carry has a movement mimics mine. Sometimes it turns, I'd swear it, of itself. To what purpose? I may guess, but I will never know. It is a deeper secret than generation, I am convinced of it.

Each of us builds something that will never come to light. It amasses slowly from something as small and insignificant as needles of salt, a single globule of blood, an unsought surety or doubt. It builds more slowly than life itself. It is this, I think, draws us to each other like iron to the lodestone, the peeled hazel branch to the vein of ore. It is not God's will we're pursuing when we join so, it's our own, although we do not know it. But God's purpose quickens with our private desire.

I puzzle you? Surely you understand this much already. You would not have come to me otherwise. You smile. I treasure that, knowing as I do it hides a world of difference. It's that very difference draws me to you. It's not assurance you're looking for now, is it? For there's none to be had. Life leads in only one direction for us all: forward. But you knew that when you packed your basket at the orphanage. You knew that circling the graves of your father and sister. There's my girl. Even the swallowed tear contributes to that secret hoard. So does every unuttered word.

You have inspected your chamber thoroughly in the past few days? The portrait of me at your age in that red hat, and the chest of linens collected for Grietje are yours. I give them to you today. Should you leave tomorrow, they are yours to keep. I shall attest to that in writing. I should have done the same for Grietje, but it is too late.

But Child, when you leave us, in one year or eight, and you will leave because, for your own sake, I will not have you stay, you will leave with more. You will leave not just ravished by, but weighted with oft unsought, unwonted truth. The way we live here, our eyes fixed daily on the miraculous, there's no escaping it. This is no threat. Everything we see and feel and think, our own deathless secretions, unshared thoughts, dreams, tears, and gasps of pleasure, and our theories too, all transmute inside us in ways we have no hand in.

Sometimes I think that weight I carry bears a human face. I think it glares into the hot wet darkness. I think it grows like one of those stones my father received, distilled, some say, from our own piss. Miraculous!

You smile again. You think I jest? You think I sicken with a terrible madness? Even if I did, you'd not breathe a word of it to my father. You need not assure me. I trust you. But I am not mad, Child. No spirits dare intrude here in the Golden Head. My father's glasses have revealed to us a world larger, clearer and more awful than any the Devil can create. The Devil leaves us be, Child. He can't tolerate the light. While we, Child, like you, we blink less than the angels!

The learned gentlemen object to my father's theory of the male animalcules, you understand, because it proves Nature as cruel as she is prodigal. Nothing has been created in vain, they object. But my father counters them as roughly as his teeth encounter the prolific seeds in the sweet ruddy fruit of the fig he cultivates with such tender scrutiny in his own garden.

Do you remember what my father read out to us the first night you came to us before we climbed the stairs? He offered you a fig in greeting, but then he returned immediately to his letter. He couldn't let it rest. He never will.

If we now see that a common fig contains between four and five hundred seeds and each tree can annually produce many figs and from each seed an entire tree can grow, so . . . in one year we could plant not just a kingdom but the whole surface of the earth in fig trees—

"Sweet misery," I whispered, taking one from the bowl myself. "No asparagus!"

My father coughed. The seed had lodged in his throat, or so I thought.

We ought to lay our hand on our mouth and to think that the Omniscient has considered this necessary for the Procreation of all that has been endowed with motion and growth, so that we can only guess at the reason, which is incomprehensible to us.

♛ ♛ ♛

I've done, Child. Well, as nearly as the bells approach the hour! In a minute, I will leave you in peace. A minute! I see how your eyelids droop, how your smile devours the yawn. We ought, my father says, put our hands to our mouths. But is it to quench the yawn, tamp the fury, blunt the appetite?

You wonder why I brought you here? I intend to share with you my entire inheritance—not just my faithful youth or my increasing wealth but the ripe sweet fruits of my father's labors, his renown. I have given you the past, the present. When he hands you that brass plate, you take up the future. As you wish! I expect you to listen, to see, to learn, to question, to speculate, too, to your own satisfaction, not his, nor mine. Never forget, female as well as male, poor as well as rich, young as well as old, we are each of us called to witness and attest to inscrutable mysteries of Creation.

This work is not easy. Hearing what you have from me these days, you are free to leave. I have spoken more than I thought possible. I can do so again. Pity must not restrain you.

For whole days you've heard me contradict my father's teachings as surely as I embrace his life. They mean near naught to me now, the treasured fancies of an old man I hold dear. Except that their consequences were many and real, and I, because once I believed him, will live them to my grave. But his theories mean everything to him, they anchor him as securely on this whirling earth as mine now do me, so you must not ignore them. He believes his fame is what will live beyond him, not what is in those animalcules within him that connects him straight back to Adam, and through Adam to the glory of the Omniscient. If it were possible for me to preserve my father's place in that unbroken stream of life, I would have done so as willingly as any son. But according to his convictions, his life dies with me, a mere daughter, as impotent as she is beloved.

The truth is, I don't believe my father. I am as familiar as he with the grief—and joy—of life. I believe we have been put here to embrace it, in all its forms, with equal awe, equal anguish, wherever, and however we find it. I do not believe this call exclusive to male or female. I grant it may quicken at the sight of a woman's breast, her capable hip. Gerrit and my father both attest to this. But does it not quicken within a woman too and, as De Graaf suggested, *perfectly* so? Doesn't it take its permanence and its immortalizing meaning from our reciprocal desire for what lies hungering for completion in each of us and between us?

Isn't that why Cornelia died, as she believed, fat with life? Isn't that why when Grietje's body hoarded up splinters of salt she cried out in righteous wrath: This is not what I am intended for! Isn't that why I, too, thinking of Cornelis Vallensis, or of the poor dying boy Gerrit, clasp my hand to my waist, wincing as I feel the breathless child inside me tumble over and over?

I wish your presence here could reveal to my father how little it all meant, God's ecstatic transit through his loins. It's the man I've followed all this time. Patiently my father teases out God's purpose. I tease out his. I tell you this, Child: our appetite for truth is equally unruly. I can't say who's the wiser. I love my father with just such dear wonder as he loves the world. Soon you will too.

You hear him at the door?

Hurry child, employ yourself. He must not suspect we attend to him within the Golden Head with the same insatiable curiosity, the same independence of mind, that makes him attend so closely to all the rest of God's hungering and glorious offspring year upon year upon year.

CHARACTERS

Most of the characters in this novel were real individuals, including most of the incidental characters, but all are used here fictitiously.

MAJOR CHARACTERS

Maria Antonisdr. van Leeuwenhoek is the only child of Antoni van Leeuwenhoek who survives beyond infancy or early childhood. She does not marry and lives with her father until his death.

Antoni Philipszn. van Leeuwenhoek is a citizen of Delft, draper and civil servant, who becomes an extraordinary microscopist, member of the Royal Society of London.

Cornelia Swalmius van Leeuwenhoek is the second wife of Antoni van Leeuwenhoek.

Antoni Janszn. Molijn is Antoni van Leeuwenhoek's nephew and godson, a contemporary of Maria. He is a doctor in Delft. His mother is Leeuwenhoek's sister Gryetgen and his father is Jan Jacobsz. Molijn, a painter and art dealer and the son of Leeuwenhoek's mother's second husband. Leeuwenhoek's relationship with his nephew is contentious because of family history and professional jealousy.

Cornelis Dircksz. Vallensis is one of the elite of Delft, part of the Council of 40, who holds various civic positions such as magistrate, head of the orphanage, and Pensionary of Delft and becomes a close friend of Maria. Together they serve as informal wards of the orphan Grietje. He lives with his widowed mother and widowed sister.

Grietje is a young orphan who becomes the Leeuwenhoeks' maid and the informal ward of Maria van Leeuwenhoek and Cornelis Vallensis.

Gerrit is a young engraver who works for Leeuwenhoek.

Aaltje Phillipsdr. is a young orphan who takes Grietje's place.

SECONDARY CHARACTERS

FAMILY

Aunt *Maria de Mey* is Maria van Leeuwenhoek's maternal aunt and godmother, who helps care for Maria after Maria's mother dies.

Aunt *Catharina van Leeuwen* is Antoni van Leeuwenhoek's favorite younger sister. She lives with her husband and their many children in Rotterdam. They visit frequently and she is an advisor to her brother and her niece.

Catharina Swalmius is the unmarried sister of Cornelia Swalmius.

FRIENDS/NEIGHBORS

Maria Vermeer is Maria van Leeuwenhoek's friend.

Johannes Vermeer is an artist of Delft, father of Maria. Leeuwenhoek administers his estate after his wife declares bankruptcy after his death.

Catharina Bolnes is Vermeer's wife.

Adriaen Beijeren is a young draper who helps deliver Leeuwenhoek's letters to England and helps Maria develop her profession as a draper.

Frans Corneliszn. is Adriaen's cousin and Maria's first romantic interest.

LEARNED AND INFLUENTIAL MEN OF DELFT

These men have great influence on Leeuwenhoek at both a civic and a scientific level.

Regnier de Graaf is a young doctor and scientist of Delft who becomes friends with Antoni van Leeuwenhoek and encourages his scientific endeavours. He has written well-regarded books on the sexual anatomy of men and women and is a strong believer in the role of the ovary in sexual generation.

Cornelis 'sGravesende is the municipal anatomist of Delft. Leeuwenhoek often seeks his scientific approval and advice because of his status within the town and his higher level of education.

Henricus D'Aquet is the municipal physician of Delft, who is also a frequent visitor and advisor to Leeuwenhoek.

Hendrik van Bleyswick and *Adriaen Boogaert* are influential citizens of Delft, frequently elected as burgomasters and also involved with the East India Company. *Benedictus Haan, Henricus Cordes,* and *Alexander Petrie* and *Petrus Grebius* are pastors and predikants in Delft and the Hague who encourage Leeuwenhoek's work.

LEARNED AND INFLUENTIAL GENTLEMEN OF HOLLAND

These men are a source of encouragement throughout Leeuwenhoek's career, both because of the attention they give to him and their own positions of high social and political influence.

Constantijn Huygens is one of the most important men in Holland: a diplomat, secretary to two Princes of Orange, father of the highly accomplished brothers Constantijn and Christiaan Huygens, and Fellow of the Royal Society. He is instrumental in bringing many illustrious visitors to see Antoni van Leeuwenhoek's discoveries, as well as helping him join the Royal Society. Leeuwenhoek often turns to him for advice and encouragement.

Christiaan Huygens, son of Constantijn, the elder, is a famous mathematician and scientist. He and his brother Constantijn, the younger, built one of the largest telescopes in Europe, through which they discovered the rings of Saturn. Christiaan Huygens also developed a wave theory of light, invented the pendulum clock, and helped start the French *Académie des sciences.* He is supportive of Leeuwenhoek's investigations, especially after he returns to Holland from France.

Grand Pensionary Anthonie Heinsius is a citizen of Delft who goes on to lead Holland for decades once Prince William III of Orange becomes King William III of England. Even in times of great political upheaval, he has time to read Leeuwenhoek's observations and visit with him.

Other Dutch men with whom Leeuwenhoek corresponds about his microscopy, especially in later life, are *Pieter Rabus, Baron van Reede van Renswoude,* and *Nicolaes Witsen.*

Dutch scientists involved in the debate about generation, along with Regnier de Graaf, are *Jan Swammerdam, Jan van Horne* and *Nicolaas Hartsoeker.*

LEARNED MEN OF LONDON: THE ROYAL SOCIETY

Henry Oldenburg, Robert Hooke, Nehemiah Grew, and Hans Sloane are the first four secretaries of the Royal Society and editors of the *Philosophical Transactions.* They communicate with Leeuwenhoek, bring his observations up for discussion, question some of his findings, and encourage him to investigate various subjects of current scientific interest.

GENERAL TIMELINE: 1668-1696

The seventeenth century was a busy time politically, scientifically, and artistically—with endless wars and changes of rulers, new inventions like the telescope and microscope that vastly increased the scale of the knowable world, and myriad discoveries that followed upon their use. Antoni van Leeuwenhoek was also prolific in his investigations over a long lifetime. This timeline is designed only to give a loose outline and sequencing of some of these rapid changes that influenced the characters in this novel. The timeline is divided according to the sections in the novel. It does not list the imagined events in the novel.

LENS

1667

⅍ Treaty of Breda marks end of Second Anglo-Dutch war.

⅍ Louis XIV begins War of Devolution against Spanish Netherlands.

⅍ States of Holland adopts the "Eternal Edict" abolishing the stadtholdership, thus disinheriting Prince William III of Orange.

⅍ Regnier de Graaf comes to Delft to practice medicine.

⅍ The Danish scientist Steno publishes *Myologia* in which he concludes that the testicles in female mammals are analogous to ovaries in birds.

1668

⅍ Louis XIV invades the Spanish Netherlands.

⅍ Triple Alliance between England, Sweden and Holland to maintain peace between France and Spain.

⅍ Leeuwenhoek visits England.

⅍ De Graaf publishes his study of male genitalia: *De virorum Organis Gerationi Inservientibus, de Clysteribus et de Usu Siphonis in Anatomia*.

⅍ Francesco Redi publishes his book, *Esperienze intorno alla generazione degli insetti*, one of first to contest the widely held belief in spontaneous generation.

⅍ Jan van Horne publishes his book on the anatomy of the sexual organs, based on collaboration with Swammerdam: *Prodromus observationum circa partes genitale in utroque sexu.*

⟩ Leeuwenhoek begins to work with microscope.

1669

⟩ Leeuwenhoek passes exam and becomes a surveyor.

⟩ Maria de Mey makes Maria van Leeuwenhoek her heir.

1670

⟩ Secret Treaty of Dover created between Charles II of England and Louis XIV of France against Holland.

⟩ Vermeer becomes headman of the St. Lucas guild.

CIRCULATION

1671

⟩ Leeuwenhoek marries Cornelia Swalmius.

⟩ Mutual defense alliance between Spain and Holland in the event of French attack. Louis XIV makes treaties with the bishops of Munster and Cologne against Holland.

1672 to 1674 Third Anglo-Dutch War

1672

⟩ *Rampjaar*: In March, England declares war on Holland, followed by France, Munster and Cologne in April. In June, the French army crosses the Rhine and Utrecht falls, and an attempt is made on the life of Johan de Witt, the head of the Dutch government, by the supporters of the Prince of Orange. Prince William III of Orange is made Stadtholder in July and refuses the French terms of surrender. In August, the De Witt brothers are murdered and cannibalized by a mob. The French continue fighting under Luxembourg when Louis XIV returns to France and in December are able to cross the frozen water line into Holland but are forced to withdraw with the thaw. When they retreat towards Utrecht, they savagely, rape, murder and plunder the villages of Bodegraven and Zwammerdam.

⟩ De Graaf in March publishes his study of female genitalia, *De Muleirum Organis Generationi Inservientibus Tractatus Novus,* in which he identifies the follicle and experimentally demonstrates that eggs descend from the follicle in the ovary through the fallopian tube to the uterus.

⟩ Swammerdam in May publishes his own account of human generation, *Miraculum Naturae, sive Uteri Muliebris Fabrica,* and dedicates it to the Royal Society asking them to adjudicate who, De Graaf or he and Van

Horne, have priority in stating women have eggs. He sends a preserved uterus and other items of genital anatomy with a copy of his book.

≀ De Graaf marries Maria van Dijn.

≀ Leeuwenhoek sees "testicles of woman" at Delft Anatomy Chamber.

≀ Vermeer, debt-ridden, rents his inn, the Mechelen, for six years and moves with his family to his mother-in-law's house in Delft.

1673

≀ De Graaf introduces Leeuwenhoek to the Royal Society and Leeuwenhoek submits his first letter including observations on the louse and the eye of the bee.

≀ De Graaf publishes blistering attack on Swammerdam disputing scientific credit.

≀ De Graaf dies in August, weeks after the death of his son.

≀ Constantijn Huygens, secretary to the Princes of Orange, writes Royal Society to introduce Leeuwenhoek as well.

≀ November: The English Parliament refuses to provide Charles II more money for war.

≀ December: Prince William III forces French out of Netherlands.

1674

≀ Treaty of Westminster ends Holland's war with England.

≀ Leeuwenhoek is asked by Oldenberg, Secretary of the Royal Society, to investigate water and bodily fluids.

≀ Leeuwenhoek discovers protozoa and blood corpuscles.

≀ Catharina Swalmius, Cornelia's sister, dies.

≀ Maria de Mey marries at the age of 48 but separates within the year because of overwhelming melancholy and Leeuwenhoek becomes her guardian.

ANIMALCULES

1675

≀ Leeuwenhoek observes living creatures in rain water.

≀ Jan Swammerdam renounces science to follow Flemish mystic Antoinette Bourignon.

≀ Vermeer dies in December.

1676

≀ Leeuwenhoek discovers bacteria.

≀ In April, Vermeer's widow Catharina Bolnes, left with eleven minor children, declares bankruptcy and repudiates Vermeer's estate because of excessive debts.

⟩ In September, the court appoints Leeuwenhoek as executor for Vermeer's estate. He negotiates with a major creditor, who holds twenty-six paintings of Vermeer, and personally pays the debt himself, but requires that Vermeer's paintings, including one held by Vermeer's mother-in-law, then be auctioned off to resolve the estate—over the protests of Catharina Bolnes and her mother.

⟩ Maria de Mey dies and Maria inherits her house.

1677

⟩ Marriage of William III of Orange to his first cousin Princess Mary, daughter of James, Duke of York.

⟩ Henry Oldenburg, editor of the *Philosophical Transactions*, dies and is succeeded by Nehemiah Grew and Robert Hooke. Hooke's *Philosophical Collections* replaces the Phil. Trans. while Hooke is secretary of the Royal Society.

⟩ Auction of Vermeer's paintings at the St. Lucas Guild in Delft.

⟩ Leeuwenhoek writes on animalcules found in rain, well, sea, snow, and pepper water.

⟩ Johan Ham visits Leeuwenhoek with a glass phial of spontaneous ejaculate from a man who has lain with an unclean woman, in which they see animalcules.

⟩ Leeuwenhoek discovers animalcules in his own sperm.

⟩ Leeuwenhoek sends letter, translated into Latin for discretion, to Nehemiah Grew describing his findings.

⟩ Nehemiah Grew responds by asking Leeuwenhoek to explore this discovery in other animals as well.

⟩ Leeuwenhoek is made Wijkmeester General, district supervisor, another civil post.

SCURF

1678

⟩ Treaty of Nijmegan ends war with France.

⟩ Christiaan Huygens publishes first brief description of sperm in the *Journal des Sçavans* in Paris six months before Leeuwenhoek's letter is published by the Royal Society, noting this is an important finding for ideas of generation.

❧ Leeuwenhoek's findings on animalcules and on sperm are published by the Royal Society.

❧ Dr. Bontekoe writes his treatise on the medical benefits of tea, Leeuwenhoek's favorite drink.

❧ Robert Hooke publishes the *Philosophical Collections* in 1678-9, then not again until 1682-3.

1679

❧ Antoni Molijn, Leeuwenhoek's nephew, goes to Paris to study surgery and carries letters from his uncle to Christiaan Huygens.

❧ Leeuwenhoek becomes the official Wine Gauger of Delft.

❧ James, Duke of York visits Leeuwenhoek in Delft and sees sperm.

❧ Anthonie Heinsius becomes Pensionary of Delft.

❧ Nicolaas Hartsoeker visits Leeuwenhoek, questions his findings and asks to learn about Leeuwenhoek's methods of observation, but Leeuwenhoek tells him he only shares them with his wife and daughter.

❧ Joseph Williamson, President of the Royal Society, is imprisoned in the Tower of London, thus sowing confusion about how Leeuwenhoek should direct his correspondence.

1680

❧ Leeuwenhoek becomes a Fellow of the Royal Society.

❧ Leeuwenhoek continues to look at sperm in various animals, including rats and mussels, and studies the copulation of dragonflies.

❧ Leeuwenhoek corresponds with Hooke about his own investigations but also expands his correspondence, especially among Dutch learned gentlemen.

❧ Jan Swammerdam dies.

❧ Antoni Molijn returns to Delft from Paris.

1681

❧ 4-Way Treaty by Spain, Holland, England and Sweden to maintain the Nijmegan Treaty.

❧ Christiaan Huygens returns to Holland.

❧ Cornelis Vallensis becomes part of Council of 40, the elite of Delft.

❧ Leeuwenhoek included in Cornelis De Man's painting "Dr. 'sGravesende's Anatomy Lesson."

❧ Leeuwenhoek develops severe eczema.

1682

❧ Anthonie Heinsius sent to Paris by William III to negotiate with Louis XIV about the return of the principality of Orange.

❧ *Halley's Comet*

❧ Cornelis Vallensis appointed a schepenen, or magistrate, in Delft (1682-85).

1683

❧ Spain declares war with France over Spanish Netherlands.

❧ Leeuwenhoek corresponds with Delft Pensionary Anthonie Heinsius in Paris about his observations on generation.

❧ In his publication in the *Philosophical Transactions*, Leeuwenhoek questions whether ovaries really contain eggs, whether those eggs can travel down the narrow Fallopian tubes, and suggests that the animalcule itself within the womb creates a substance to seal itself, so appears encapsulated like an egg, and discusses the prodigality of sperm by comparing it to the prodigality of seeds not all of which come to fruition.

❧ Leeuwenhoek sees the lymphatic arteries and also the anastomoses between capillary, vein and artery. He learns that in 1661 the Italian scientist Marcello Malpighi in his book on the anatomical structure of the lung *De pulmonibus* has mentioned the connections between arteries and veins.

❧ Leeuwenhoek carries out various dissections of female animals after mating to track the presence of sperm in the uterus and fallopian tubes.

❧ Leeuwenhoek examines scales on the skin and in the mouth and intestines and sees the scaly child.

❧ Adriaen van Beijeren dies.

GENERATION

1684

❧ Leeuwenhoek writes about the scaly child, about the slime and the blood vessels in the gut and studies lepers.

❧ Leeuwenhoek visits Christiaan Huygens in his house at Hofwijck to see Huygens's telescope for himself because was not able to understand it by description.

1685

❧ James II, William the III's father-in-law, becomes King of England.

❧ Revocation of Edict of Nantes and large Huguenot emigration from France to Holland.

❧ Leeuwenhoek plants an apple orchard.

❧ Leeuwenhoek publishes observations on the scales of lepers and eels.

⟩ Leeuwenhoek describes his observations based on his dissections of female animals after mating and shares his thoughts about why this confirms the essential role of the male animalcule in generation.

⟩ Leeuwenhoek begins to publish his own letters.

1686

⟩ Alliance of Augsburg between Spain, Germany & Sweden.

⟩ Leeuwenhoek has his portrait painted by Jan Verkolje.

⟩ Leeuwenhoek buys animal wombs and incubates them on his own body. Cornelia helps him incubate silkworms.

⟩ Antoni Molijn gets medical degree from Harderwijk.

⟩ 1686-1693 *Philosophical Transactions* not published.

1687

⟩ Newton's *Philosophiae Naturalis Principia Mathematica* is published.

⟩ Constantijn Huygens the elder dies at age 90.

⟩ Anthonie Heinsius goes to Britain to negotiate for Prince William III.

⟩ Leeuwenhoek publishes his first book and dedicates it to King James II.

1688-1697 Nine Years War

1688

⟩ The Glorious Revolution: William III, with the permission of the States General, sails to England and successfully overthrows his uncle King James II, who flees to France. King Louis XIV declares war on Holland.

⟩ Catharina Bolnes, Vermeer's widow, dies.

⟩ Vallensis appointed weesmeester, master of orphanage.

1689-1697 War of English Succession

1689

⟩ William III and Mary II declared king and queen of England.

⟩ Great Alliance of Vienna (Emperor, Holland, Brandenburg & Spain) created to bar France from the Spanish Succession.

⟩ Anthonie Heinsius becomes the Grand Pensionary of the States of Holland (1689-1720).

⟩ Queen Mary visits Leeuwenhoek.

⟩ Leeuwenhoek sees the circulation of the blood in the tail of an eel and develops an eel spy-glass to share this observation.

⟩ Leeuwenhoek sends copies of his latest observations to Constantijn Huygens, the younger, Secretary to King William III, and to Queen Mary II, to whom he has dedicated his book. Christiaan Huygens writes his brother in London to make sure the observations have arrived.

1690

⟩ William III defeats James II in Ireland.

⟩ Christiaan Huygens publishes his *Traité de Lumière* on his wave theory of light.

1691

⟩ William III crosses to Holland to wage war against France.

⟩ Leeuwenhoek buys an adjoining garden to the one he has had since 1664.

⟩ Cornelis Vallensis appointed Delft Pensionary to the States, the position previously held by Anthonie Heinsius.

1692

⟩ Cornelis Vallensis dies.

1693

⟩ Hans Sloane becomes Secretary of the Royal Society and publication of the *Philosophical Transactions* begins again.

⟩ Leeuwenhoek writes on the copulation of the flea and the propagation of plants and animals.

ORE

1694

⟩ Cornelia Swalmius, Leeuwenhoek's wife, dies.

⟩ Queen Mary II of England dies.

⟩ The Dutch scientist Hartsoeker makes his first claim for priority on discovery of sperm—and includes pictures of a homunculus in his *Essai de Diapotrique.*

⟩ Leeuwenhoek strongly defends his theory of generation, particularly against the speculations of Dr. George Garden that both ovum and sperm may play a role. He comments on the feud between De Graaf and Swammerdam, asserting that if they had lived to see what he had discovered they would not persist in their ideas about the ovary.

⟩ Leeuwenhoek writes eight letters to the Royal Society from December 1693 to September 1694, and sends them six copies of his mezzotint portrait along with a copy of his book in Latin but receives no responses—so directs his correspondence and publications toward other learned gentlemen in Holland and continues to independently publish his findings.

⟩ Leeuwenhoek finishes his work on women's role in reproduction—and censors it upon the advice of various learned gentlemen.

1695

≀ Leeuwenhoek describes the false claims of a German quack who says he has a Sympathetic Powder that will cure all ills.

≀ Leeuwenhoek studies the fruit lice in his orchard, who give birth to live young, which in their own bellies also contain young—all of which demonstrates that life does not come from putrefaction but from life.

≀ Christiaan Huygens dies.

≀ Leeuwenhoek describes the wonderful spinning of the fen mussels.

≀ Leeuwenhoek dedicates his book *Arcana Naturae Detecta* to Antonio Magliabechi, librarian to Cosimo III de' Medici, with a personal library of over 40,000 books.

1696

≀ Leeuwenhoek publishes his fifth collection of letters.

≀ In May, 21 Vermeer paintings auctioned in Amsterdam.

≀ Leeuwenhoek explains to the Royal Society that not having had responses to his letters, he decided to share his findings with various learned gentlemen in Holland—Christiaan Huygens, Anthonie Heinsius, Pieter Rebus, Frederic van Reed van Renswoude, Hendrik van Bleyswick, and Nicolaes Witsen—and has published this correspondence.

≀ Leeuwenhoek writes that he is unable to find any males among the lice of currants, cherries, plums and roses that he is studying. They are all females that give birth to more females.

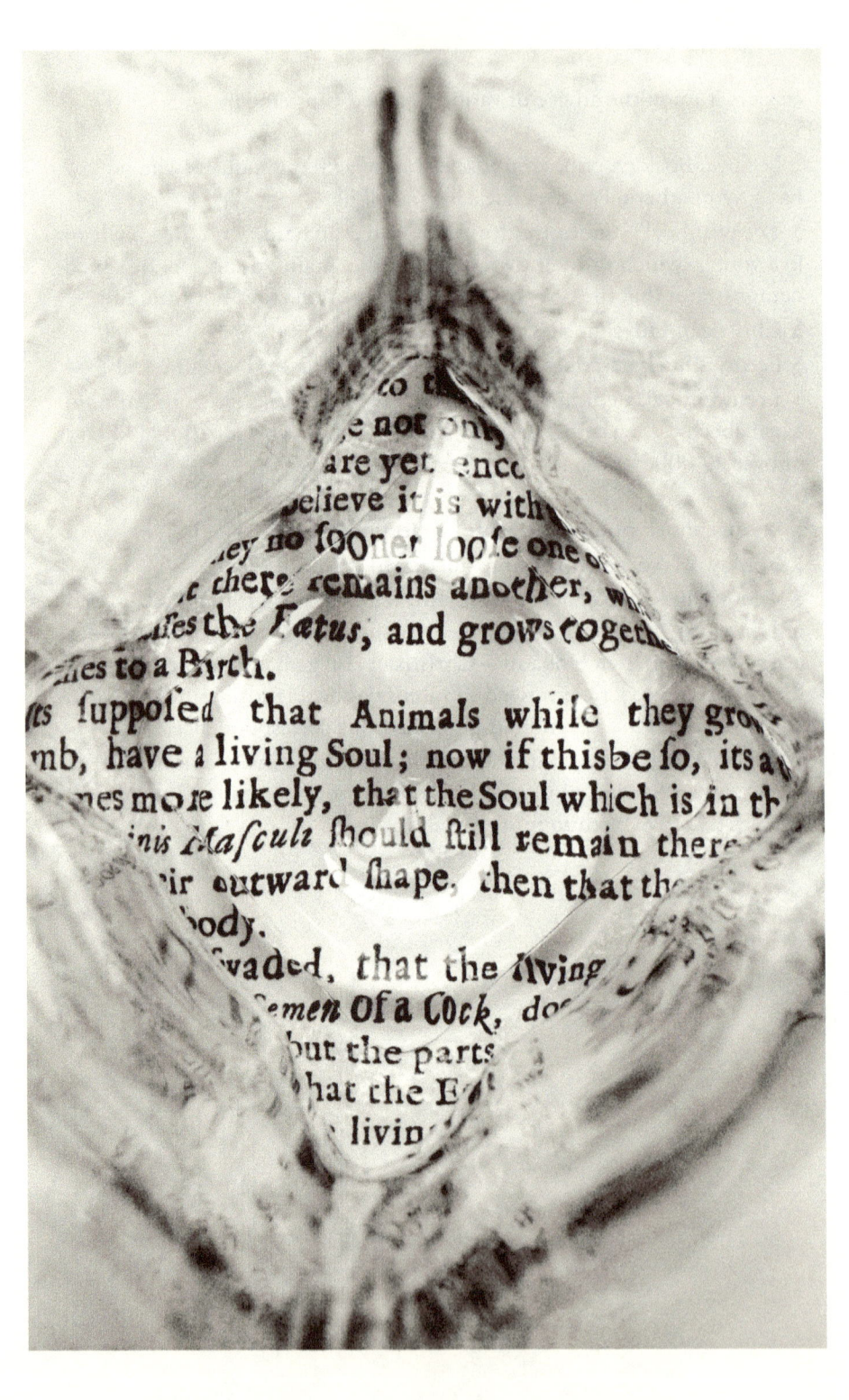

ACKNOWLEDGEMENTS

When researching and writing this book many years ago, I conducted extensive research on Leeuwenhoek himself, and on the science, art, history and culture of the seventeenth century, particularly in Holland. Most of the research was conducted before the internet, and I was very lucky that at that time I had access to the libraries at the University of California, Berkeley, in particular their splendid Bioscience library, with its many volumes of Leeuwenhoek's letters, and Bancroft library, with its rare books and history of science collections, both of which I used incessantly for several years. I focus here on the books that had the most profound impact on how this novel developed.

There are three books that provided the inspiration for this novel and without which it would not exist. The first was Clifford Dobell's biography, *Anthony Van Leeuwenhoek and His "Little Animals,"* which sparked my interest in Maria van Leeuwenhoek as well as her father. A footnote there led me to Francis Cole's *Early Theories of Generation,* which gave me a keen sense of what was at stake in these startling observations of sperm and eggs and the passionate debates they initiated about the roles of men and women in the generation and perpetuation of life, debates that were not resolved for another hundred and fifty years. This then led me to the marvelous *Collected Letters of Antoni Van Leeuwenhoek,* which was absolutely indispensable to this book. This series of bilingual volumes contains all of Leeuwenhoek's writings, scrupulously and lovingly annotated by a committee of Dutch scientists since 1939. I am especially indebted to the first eleven volumes, which cover the time span of this novel. They are the source of the direct quotes used in the story. L.C. Palm, editor-in-chief of later volumes in this series and editor of other books on Leeuwenhoek, kindly answered biographical questions at that time.

I found primary source materials, particularly contemporaneous letters, diaries, memoirs, and histories especially helpful for providing me with a feel for what it was like to live in a time of such rapid scientific discovery and constant social tumult. Works that were especially helpful were Christiaan Huygens's *Oeuvres Complètes* (volumes 7-9), especially his correspondence with his family (also the memoirs of his brother Constantijn and the London diary of his brother Lodewijk), the memoirs of the English diplomat William Temple from his time in Holland from 1672-1679 and the letters of Temple's wife Dorothy Osborne, letters of Princess Liselotte of Palatine, H.D. Jocelyn and B.P. Setchell's translation of Regnier de Graaf's treatises on male and female reproductive organs, the diaries of Robert Hooke, and the correspondence of Dr. Boerhaave. I also found contemporaneous travel memoirs and descriptions of the mores and customs of Holland helpful, including William Brereton's *Travels in Holland, the United Provinces, England, and Scotland,* and Roelof Murris's *La Hollande et les hollandais au XVIIe a XVIIIe siècles, vus par le français* and the anonymous *A Description of Holland: or, The Present State of the United Provinces.* Abraham Wicquefort's four volume *Histoire de Provinces Unis de Pais Bas* was valuable, also J.B.Christyn's *Histoire Generale des Pais Bas.*

When visiting the Bancroft Library, I was able to explore Renier Boitet's comprehensive description of Delft, *Beschryving der Stadt Delft,* a hefty and dusty book, centuries old, with satisfyingly thick and undulant pages that, because of my ignorance of Dutch, was as tantalizing to me as all those *Philosophical Transactions* written in English and Latin must have been for Leeuwenhoek himself. It helped me understand the changes of the guard among the Delft elite and, when translated, also provided descriptions of various customs in Delft. In the rare books room I could hold in my own hands the same volumes of the *Philosophical Transactions* that Leeuwenhoek received so eagerly from London. With their wildly various assortment of observations, they gave me a wonderful sense of what questions, what unexpected revelations, captured men's imaginations and where Leeuwenhoek's own studies fit in. I could imagine what it would have been like for Leeuwenhoek to receive these accounts, to feel himself invited to join into this wide-ranging conversation conducted by curious and learned gentlemen amateurs around the world. Invited *and* forever held apart because of language, culture, education, class. It was there I first read about babies residing twenty or more years in a woman's belly and began to wonder what it meant to these women to hold that knowledge silently but consciously until death.

Other histories, biographies, and cultural studies that were especially useful to me were Herbert Rowen's biography of John de Witt and Nesca Robb's of William of Orange, Abraham Schierbeek's biographies of Leeuwenhoek and of Jan Swammerdam, Paul Zumthor's *Daily Life in Holland*, Peter Geyl's *The Netherlands in the 17th Century*, John Michael Montias's socio-economic study, *Artists and Artisans in Delft*, Svetlana Alpers's *The Art of Describing*, and, more recently, Manon Van der Heijden's *Women and Crime in Early Modern Holland*. For the history of science, Frederick L.Nussbaum's *The Triumph of Science and Reason 1660-1685*, and the works by Dorothy Stimson and Harold Hartley on the history of the Royal Society provided context. Interesting and valuable books that did not influence my own but are worthy of note are Laura Snyder's recent book *Eye of the Beholder*, which also deals with the inter-relationships between Leeuwenhoek and Vermeer, and, of course Simon Schama's *The Embarassment of Riches*.

For information on Johannes Vermeer's life, particularly helpful books were Hans Koningsberger's *The World of Vermeer: 1632-1675*, and Harry Peeters's "Vermeer and His Work. A View" in *Dutch Society in the Age of Vermeer*. A recent book of broader interest is Ronnie Baer's *Class Distinctions: Dutch Painting in the Age of Rembrandt and Vermeer*.

Fact checking was simplified by the very thorough website on Leeuwenhoek developed by the passionate Leeuwenhoek aficionado Douglas Anderson, *Lens on Leeuwenhoek* (lensonleeuwenhoek.net). Brian J. Ford is an equally devoted admirer and popularizer of Leeuwenhoek (www.brianjford.com). *The Essential Vermeer* is similarly thorough concerning all things Vermeer (www.essentialvermeer.com).

Photographs

I have also, throughout this project and throughout my life, brooded over seventeenth century Dutch art in books and museums. These images *are* my Holland. Many of them have been drawn into this story, however in a way very different from what determined the rules of engagement for the story itself. The rules I developed as a younger woman were quite stringent: I could not ignore or contradict any historical fact I uncovered in my extensive research—but was free to imagine what could have happened—and why—in any interstices I found in the public record. This was, I believe, a freedom that Maria van Leeuwenhoek, as I have imagined her, would understand fully, both its price and its prize.

However, the rules of engagement for the photographs, developed much later in my creative life, are very different, intentionally and unapologetically so. Other than restricting myself to Dutch art of the seventeenth century (with one or two exceptions), I have given myself license to appropriate, distort, and illumine at will, loyal only to the living spirit of Maria's story—and to those so crucial dimensions of experience for which there are no words. I wanted to give both of us a little more breathing room.

Books consulted for this purpose include Michiel Kersten's *Delft Masters, Vermeer's Contemporaries,* Rolf Kultzen's *Michael Sweerts: Brussels 1618—Goa 1664,* Herwig Guratzsch's *Dutch and Flemish Painting,* Hans Koningsberger's *The World of Vermeer: 1632-1675,* Desmonde Shaw-Taylor's *Masters of the Everyday: Dutch Artists in the Age of Vermeer,* Marie Sman's *Dutch Society in the Age of Vermeer,* Peter Sutton's *Pieter de Hooch, 1629-1684,* Adriaan Waiboer's *Gabriel Metsu,* and the catalogues for *Cultuur en maatschappij van 1667 tot 1813* from the Stedelijk Museum Het Prinsenhof and *Pride of Place: Dutch Cityscapes of the Golden Age* from the National Gallery of Art.

Artists whose images I have mused on and transmuted freely through my own camera lens, many of which found their way into this book, are *Jacob Backer, Jan de Baen, Ludolph Bakhuizen, Job Berekhyde, Gerrit Dou, Jacob Duck, Jan van Compe, Pieter Janssens Elinga, Carel Fabritius, Janna van Fritjom, Jan Gossaert, Jan van Goyen, Regnier de Graaf, Jan van der Heyden, Gerard van Honthorst, Pieter de Hooch, Thomas de Keyser, Jan Lievens, Nicholaes Maes, Cornelis de Man, Gabriel Metsu, Willem van Mieris, Aert van der Neer, Caspar Netscher, Jacob Ochtervelt, Johannes Huibert Prins, Adam Pynacker, Jan Steen, Michiel Sweerts, Gerard Ter Borch, Esias van de Velde, Johan Verkolje, Johannes Vermeer, Hendrick van Vliet, Daniel Vosmaer, Hendrik Vroom. Emanuel de Witte.* The text in images comes from the *Philosophical Transactions.*

One person I would like to thank personally is the distinguished scientist Dr. Gerald Westheimer, who during the period I was working on this book was himself invited to become a Fellow of the Royal Society, a very significant honor for someone who, escaping from Nazi Germany, emigrated to Australia as a child, and began his lifetime focus on vision by working as an optician at a very early age. Through him, I came to understand vividly what inclusion and acknowledgement of this kind could mean to someone who had, like Leeuwenhoek, crossed so many visible and invisible boundaries of religion, class, language, culture and country in the service of his art.

At two very different points in my life, Charles Brockett and Michael Fendick each provided me with unconditional support on this project. My son as a boy patiently ate his meals for several years surrounded by elaborate timelines of events and discoveries of the seventeenth century. Fred Chappell, teacher and mentor, decades ago saw the value of this story when few others did and helped me hold it close. I can't thank them enough for their faith in me. I also thank my wise women, Kerry Langan, Kathleen Housley, and Michele Markarian, for reading this manuscript, encouraging me to continue with it, and helping see it into print and Maria into voice.

ABOUT THE AUTHOR

Heather Tosteson, the author of six books (poetry, novel, short stories, and non-fiction), developed a lasting interest in Antoni van Leeuwenhoek and, especially, his daughter Maria over thirty years ago when she was in her mid-thirties. A young mother, poet, and science writer, her interest wasn't historical, rather something more intuitive and visceral. Her fascination came from the understanding that, so many centuries ago, Maria and Antoni lived out her own most essential questions in ways as immediate, improvisational, and concrete as her own, and as enduring in their consequences: questions about the nature of faith and calling; the partiality of truth; the force of circumstance; the mystery of discovery and of our inner imperative to make coherent, individual sense of it, especially concerning the origin of life and the fate and purpose of women—and what any and all of this has to do with love. She wrote the novel because it was the only way she could hear Maria into speech—and she had need of her wisdom. Thirty years later, she still does. She hopes you may find value in it too.

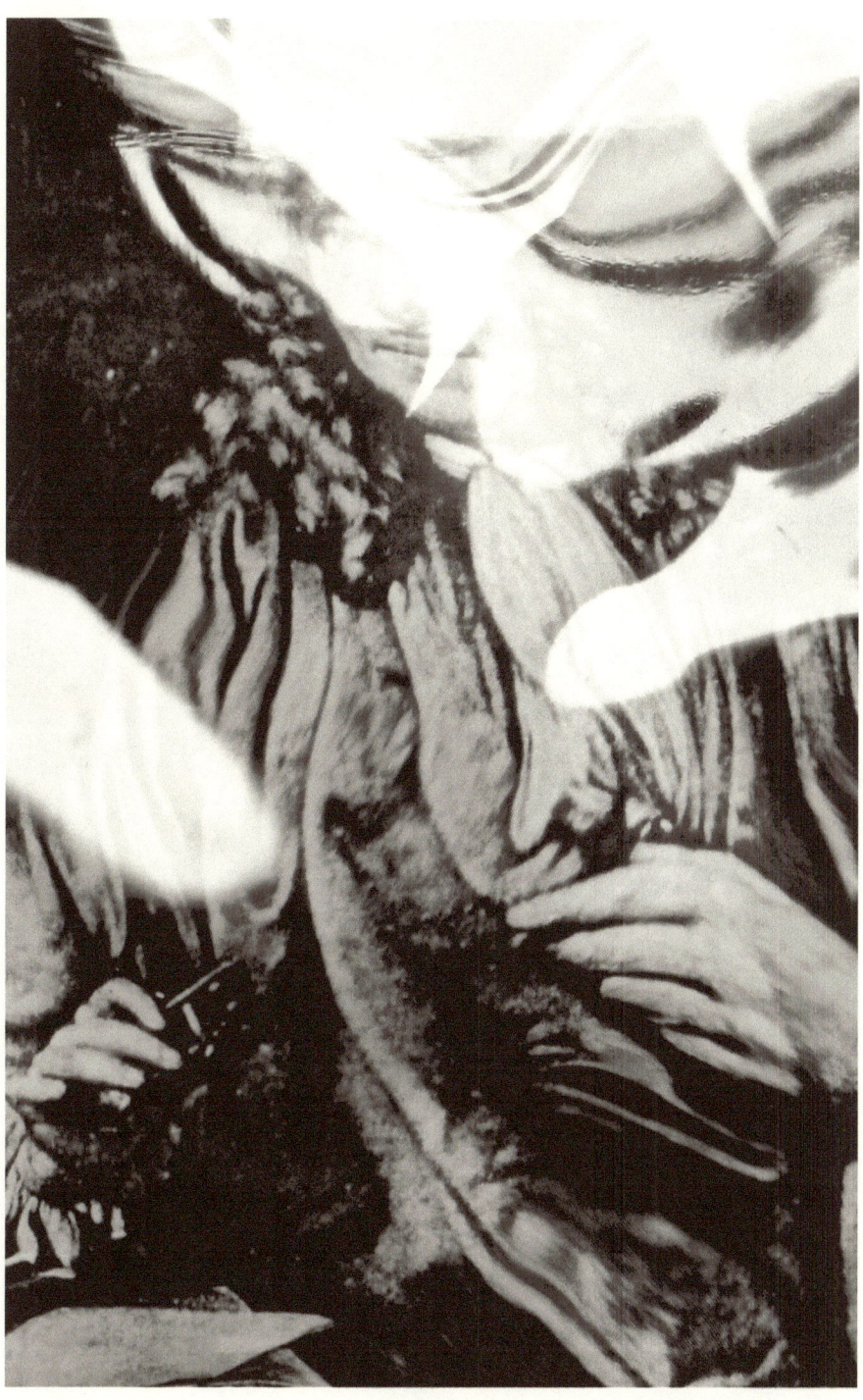